SANTA CRUZ CITY-COUNTY LIBRARY SYSTEM
0000112442405

D0342744

thine is the kingdom

thine is the kingdom

a novel by

abilio estévez

translated from the spanish by david frye

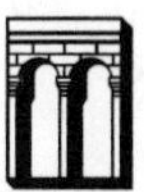

ARCADE PUBLISHING · NEW YORK

Thanks to Ramona and Luisa Pazó, Maydel Montesino, Alfredo Alonso, Bernardo Alonso, Gisela Gimeno, Ana Torrents, Beatriz de Moura, Ion de la Riva, Lorenzo Nadal, and Cristina Fernández Cubas

First English-language Edition

First published in Spain by Tusquets Editores under the title *Tuyo es el reino*

Library of Congress Cataloging-in-Publication Data

Estévez, Abilio, 1954–
[Tuyo es el reino. English]
Thine is the kingdom : a novel / by Abilio Estévez ; translated from the Spanish by David Frye.
p. cm.
ISBN 1-55970-451-9
I. Frye, David L. II. Title
PQ7390.E844T8913 1999
863—dc21 98-41958

Published in the United States by Arcade Publishing, Inc., New York
Distributed by Little, Brown and Company

10 9 8 7 6 5 4 3 2 1

Designed by API

BP

Printed in the United States of America

contents

For Elsa Nadal,
who has waited faithfully.
For Virgilio Piñera, *in memoriam,*
because the kingdom continues to be his.

Good Master, what good things shall I do,
that I may have eternal life?

—Matthew 19:16

I

One Night in the History of the World

So many stories have been told and are still told about the Island that if you decide to believe them all you'll end up going crazy, so says the Barefoot Countess, who is crazy, and she says it with a mocking smile, which isn't a bit surprising because she always wears a mocking smile, and as she says it she jingles her silver bracelets and perfumes the air with her sandalwood fan, on and on and on, sure that everyone is listening to her, and strolls through the gallery with her bare feet and her cane, on which she unnecessarily leans. She talks about the Island and with the Island. This is not an Island, she exclaims, but a tree-filled monstrosity. And then she laughs. And how she laughs. Listen, can't you hear it? the Island has voices, and indeed everyone believes they hear the voices because the Barefoot Countess's craziness is infectious. And the Island is a bounteous grove of pine trees, casuarinas, majaguas, yagrumas, palms, ceibas, and of mango and soursop trees that produce the biggest, the sweetest fruits. And there are also (surprisingly enough) poplars, willows, cypresses, olive trees, and even a splendid red sandalwood tree of Ceylon. And the Island grows a multitude of vines and rosebushes that Irene plants and tends. And it is crisscrossed by stone paths. And it has, in the center, a fountain of greenish water where Chavito has placed a clay statue of a pudgy little boy holding a goose in his arms. Forming a rectangle, houses arise, just barely managing to stem the advance of the trees. The trees nonetheless have strong roots and lift the paving stones of the galleries and the floors of the houses and cause the furniture to move, to wander as if they possessed souls. I tell you the day will come when the trees enter the houses, the Barefoot Countess insists in the tones of a prophetess. And though they feel afraid, Merengue, Irene, and Casta Diva laugh, they laugh at her, that crazy woman is full of surprises.

You get to the Island through the great door that lets out onto Linea Street, in a neighborhood of Marianao called (easy to see why) the Ovens. The entryway must have been sumptuous some years back. It has two severe columns supporting a pediment, and a solemn, well-rusted iron gate that is always closed. High in the gate, next to twisted iron letters that read THE ISLAND, sits a bell. If you want them to open for you, you have to shake the gate several times to make the bell ring, and then Helena will come out with the key and open the padlock. The times are very bad, Helena says to everyone who comes, by way of justification. The visitor has to recognize that, indeed, the times are very bad. And go into the courtyard. No matter that outside, there in the street, the heat might be unbearable. The courtyard has nothing to do with the street: it's cool and humid, and it feels good to stay here a while and let your sweat dry. In one corner you can see Merengue's cart, so white it's a treat to look at, with windows that gleam. There are also different varieties of malanga growing in flowerpots, and a coarse reproduction of the Victory of Samothrace. You still can't see the Island, though you can feel it; from the courtyard you can't make out the Island because a huge wooden screen blocks your vision. Before you get to the gallery, the walls are a tarnished yellow, and the ceiling, supposedly white, is as yellow as the walls. The lamps are of unadorned iron, and hardly a one of them has its glass intact. In the first corner, right next to Uncle Rolo's door, sit a dark metal spittoon and a wooden hat stand that has eroded away, unused. When you get to the end of the wooden screen and take a few steps forward along the left side of the gallery, you can declare that at last you have arrived in the Island.

And no one knows exactly when the Island was built, for the simple reason that it was not built at any one time, but at many times over the years, as a function of Godfather's advancing or declining fortunes. The only thing that's known for sure is that the main entrance was built when Menocal was in power and the "fat years" were in full swing. Everything else is speculation. Some think the first house was Consuelo's, erected around 1880, and they may be on to something if you notice that Consuelo's house is the most run-down. Rolo asserts, using facts he draws from who knows where, that a good part of the construction was already standing when the Treaty of Paris was signed. A fact that's hardly worth remembering if you bear in mind that Rolo is capable, for the sake of appearing to know something, of asserting the most ridiculous nonsense. Whatever the case, it is evident that this enormous rectangle of stonework that encloses one part of the Island (the part they call This Side) was not erected all at once, but rather was built up through a series of changing tastes and needs. And perhaps that's why it has the improvised air that so many attribute to it, the feel of a building that has never been finished. High and irregular time-blackened walls. Scant windows of frosted glass. Narrow double doors. Blue and mauve skylights. Why put a date on it? Professor Kingston explains, with irony, that the Island is like God, eternal and immutable.

And it is fortunate that the houses are in This Side, because The Beyond is practically impassable. A narrow little wooden door, built by Godfather many years ago and now almost in ruins, divides The Beyond from This Side. The Beyond is a wide strip of open terrain running down to the river where only one house stands, Professor Kingston's, and one shed, where in another time Vido's father kept his carpentry shop. The only path through that area that you can more or less see is the one the old professor has worn with his daily walk.

It happens that, taken altogether, the Island (This Side and The Beyond) is many islands, many patios, so many that sometimes even the people who have lived there for years get lost and don't know which way to turn. And Professor Kingston states that it depends on the hour, because for every hour and for every light there is an Island, a different Island; the Island at the siesta, for example, is nothing like the Island at dawn. Helena maintains that without statues it would be a different place. That's true, the statues. Who could imagine the Island without statues? The statues with which Chavito has filled the Island. They are beings, mute and motionless but as alive as everyone else, with as much consciousness and poverty as everyone else, as sad and as weak as everyone else. So says the crazy woman. And the others smile, shake their heads. Poor woman. Poor, crazy woman.

In one little corner that no one sees, between the Discus Thrower and the Diana, heading toward Consuelo's old house, the Virgin of La Caridad del Cobre stands in a case built of glass and stones (brought back from a quarry in the province of Oriente). The stones and the glass blend in with the foliage. You have to know where the Virgin is to find her. She's a tiny, humble image, no pomp, just like the original in the sanctuary of El Cobre. Everyone knows that this Virgin is the Patroness of Cuba; few know that there is no image more modest, more diminutive (barely ten inches tall), without any involuted splendors, as if it were purposely constructed to be hard to notice. The (eminent) artist who sculpted her mixed-race face is, of course, anonymous. Her (unadorned) dress was cut from coarse cloth of a nearly white shade of yellow. She has no crown; to be sincere, she needs none: her sloe-colored hair is crown enough. The child in her arms, mixed race as well, has a delightful expression on his little face. And where the anonymous artist proved his greatness was in the three young men at the Virgin's feet, who row desperately in their boat, trapped by the storm over there toward the bay of Nipe. Everyone knows that La Caridad appeared to these three young men who were about to die. She chose them to be saved. She chose to reveal herself to them. Since they are so small, you have to look very carefully at them to discover that the anonymous (and eminent) artist has endowed them with life, that is to say, with anguish. Two of them (who have not yet had the Vision) are sure they are going to die. The third, however, the most chosen of the three, has already discovered the radiance and is looking up above. The anonymous artist has been able to depict him right at the moment when the shock has not yet gone from his face but blessedness has already begun to cover it. It should also be recorded here that the wooden wave that is trying to swallow the three men is a display of virtuosity. Before this humble (because of its size, I mean) image, Helena has placed an unadorned vase that she always fills with yellow flowers. There are, besides, a few votive offerings. Don't lose sight of the glass case, of the Virgin, almost lost among her pagan companions (the Discus Thrower and the Diana). At some point she will be the protagonist of a singular deed that will mark the beginning of the catastrophe.

Did you know the sea was near? Yes, it is near and there are few people who know it. I couldn't say why so few know that, since in this Island, no matter where you get lost, the sea has to be near. On an island the sea is the only thing that's certain, because, on an island, the land is what's ephemeral, imperfect, accidental, while the sea, to the contrary, is persistent, ubiquitous, magnificent, partaking of all the attributes of eternity. For an islander the perpetual discord of man against God does not play out between earth and heaven, but between earth and sea. Who said that the gods live in the heavens? No, let me tell you once and for all: both the gods and the devils live in the sea.

I couldn't say why so few know that the sea is near, since after you walk past the narrow little wooden door that divides This Side from The Beyond, and you go beyond Professor Kingston's room, Chavito's studio, the old carpentry shop; after you cross the ditch that they ostentatiously call the River (what zeal for ennobling all that is small, poor, coarse!), you enter a grove of marabú bushes. They call this wilderness Mount Barreto. (Barreto was a kind of tropical Gilles de Rais.) In this grove, toward the right, a little path opens up. Perhaps, I know, it is euphemistic to call it a path. It is simply a narrow space where the marabú isn't so aggressive, where with a little bit of imagination you can walk without undue difficulty. Walking through there for half an hour you get first to the ruins of the house they say belonged to Barreto (where they buried him, where they say he still lives, despite the fact that he died more than a hundred years ago). Then the marabú starts thinning out, the earth begins turning to sand, and the marabú trees give way little by little to pine trees, rubber plants, sea grapes. Suddenly, when you least expect it, everything comes to an end, that is, a strip of sand emerges. And the sea appears.

I have decided that today should be Thursday, late October. It has gotten dark long before dusk because today was the first day of autumn (which is not autumn) in the Island. Even though the sun rose on a beautiful summer day, little by little, so slowly no one could notice, the wind began to pick up and the heavens covered over with dark clouds that sped on the night. Chacho, who had gotten back from Headquarters just past four in the afternoon, was the first to notice the coming storm, and he told Casta Diva to take in the laundry that was hanging outside, and he went out to the gallery. The woman saw him later, absolutely motionless, watching perhaps the tops of the trees. It's true, Casta Diva thought, it looks like the world's coming to an end, and she shut the windows not just because the wind was strong, it also blew in sand and filth and raised up swirls of dead leaves. And you could hear the windows slamming shut. Irene, who had left for the plaza of Marianao just after lunch, found upon her return a layer of dirt covering the floor and the furniture, and some poplar branches embedded in the grillwork over the main window. At the foot of her bed, smashed to bits, was her porcelain pitcher. Irene bent down to pick up the pieces into which it had broken. One of the sharp corners of porcelain opened a small wound in her finger. It was almost five o'clock. At approximately the same time it grew so dark you had to turn on the lights. And Helena lit an oil lamp in front of the little image of Saint Barbara she always kept with the family photos. She did not do it mechanically like at other times, but with a certain devotion, and mumbling something under her breath. Sebastián saw her illuminated by the slim flame and he felt that her habitual solemnity was leaving his mother's face. Sebastián had been home early; Miss Berta had cut short the geography class to tell them that, since rain was imminent, the afternoon lessons were over. That was more or less the same time that Tingo-I-Don't-Get-It went looking for Sebastián, and that Merengue decided he wasn't going to make any more sales that day, since very few people would slow down to buy a pastry with this kind of weather brewing, and he left his spot at the entrance to Workers' Maternity Hospital. In reality, the storm was a pretext: he had a tremendous need to hole up at home. Mercedes got back from City Hall at the same moment Merengue opened the iron gate to let his pastry cart into the courtyard. When Mercedes went into her house she saw her sister in the shadows, the tip of her chin fallen against her chest. She ran up to her, thinking she had suffered another relapse of her illness. Marta pushed her lightly away. Why are you sitting here in the dark? Mercedes asked. Her sister smiled: Why should I need light? Is it raining? Mercedes said no, and let herself collapse in the other rocking chair, and realized how tired she was. No, it isn't raining, but it won't be long before the downpour starts. And Melissa went out onto the terrace roof, holding Morales on one hand. She went out there smiling, happy at the inevitable arrival of the storm. From up high, from her privileged position, she spied Uncle Rolo in the gallery. It made her feel wicked to see that the foreboding storm did not make him happy as it had made her. And just as you might have expected, she laughed, laughed heartily, because that's how Melissa is and there's no understanding her. And Melissa was right: the afternoon had left Uncle Rolo feeling sad, or as he would say to excuse himself, it provoked "vague pains in his muscles and deep sorrows in his soul." Without closing the bookstore (was it really an oversight?) Uncle Rolo had gone out to observe the Island. At the exact instant Melissa saw him, he saw Lucio caressing the thighs of the Apollo Belvedere just behind the wooden screen in the courtyard.

Is it a lie to say the Island is like God, eternal and immutable? It had a beginning, it will have an end, and it has changed over the years. Is it also a lie that the main entrance was built when the fat years were in full swing, and that the first house was Consuelo's, and the nonsense that Uncle Rolo says about the Treaty of Paris? Lies. Fairy tales. False stories told to sow confusion. Legends. And as for the truth about the Island, who could say that they know it?

And if it is true that willows, cypresses, olive trees are not common in Cuba, why do they grow in the Island? Beautiful ones, every bit as good-looking as the yagrumas, majaguas, palm trees, and ceibas they grow next to. How do beeches, date palms, Canadian firs, and even a splendid red sandalwood tree of Ceylon grow there?

The lights are on in the galleries. For all the good that does. If today weren't today, Merengue would have taken a rocking chair out to the gallery as night began to fall, so he could smoke his H-Upmann and talk. Right away Chavito would have come out with his collapsible canvas stool and his shamefaced smile, and he would have sat down facing the black man, because there's no denying Chavito enjoys Merengue's conversation. Mercedes would arrive, bathed and dressed to the nines again, her neck and breast immaculate with all the Myrurgia talcum she poured on, and she'd lean against a column, sighing and saying with a smile that she comes there to forget for a few hours about City Hall and that damned Morúa. Casta Diva would arrive, with her hibiscus-print apron and her air of a diva, exclaiming, Please, don't tempt me, don't tempt me because I have so much to do. And Chacho would be following her, pretending to be upset, exclaiming with false anger, This woman! You just can't keep her in the house.

Irene would come too, with her palm leaf fan and her smile. If it were a truly special night even Miss Berta would appear, since she is at times capable of taking a break in her prayers to forget that she is an exiled daughter of Eve, as she says with the perfect diction of a doctor of pedagogy. It's highly likely that Uncle Rolo would also be sighted, since there are nights when Rolo begins to draw near, as if against his will, as if he were a victim of chance, and he would bring with him (otherwise it wouldn't be him) his melancholy, his defeated appearance, and a half-urgent, half-hopeful gaze, as if the people who got together in the Island were all superior creatures. And Merengue, who knows him well, would sit there watching him with sorrowful eyes and exclaim to himself, though making sure everyone could hear, poor man, poor man. Guffaws would break out. The conversation would begin. (None of this happens: we are now in a novel.)

Today the evening lights went out too soon. Lord, let me dream. Very early, Marta closed her eyes. Give me, at least, the possibility of having my visions, my own visions. Her eyes lived scarcely by the light of day. Since I can never know the real Brussels, the real Florence, let me walk through *my* Brussels, *my* Florence. And she went into the house without turning on any lights, why should poor Marta with her eyes closed need lights. I would love to see tall mountains bordering immense lakes with castles and swans. Marta goes to bed. Or doesn't go to bed. There is a strong wind and it seems like people are pushing on the doors and windows. Since You have condemned me to the rocking chair, to this constant, dark, nearly black redness, give me too the possibility of *seeing* a ship, a street, a deserted plaza, a bell tower, an apple tree. Please God, I want to dream. Dream. Since I cannot see what everyone else sees, let me have access at least to what no one sees. It's so simple.

The land of ice, and of fearful sounds where no living thing was to be seen, Professor Kingston recites, and he closes the windows with a stick. The windows are so tall this is the only way they can be closed. The world is coming to an end with this rainstorm, the world is coming to an end with this rainstorm and you won't even have a little laudanum to relieve the pain of staying up late. You've lived for years in The Beyond and you realize it doesn't matter whether you live on one side or the other. It doesn't matter, old man, it doesn't matter. Believe me. And you sit in the little rocker, Cira's little rocker, practically the only thing of Cira's you've kept. The little rocker and a few letters she wrote you during the months you spent alone in New York. Professor Kingston breathes with difficulty. He tries to cool himself with the cardboard fan they gave him this morning in the pharmacy. On one side the fan shows a color photograph of a cat. Professor Kingston turns the fan around. He prefers the ad for Veloso's Pharmacy on the back to the odious face of the cat. Now he runs his eyes around the room, looking for something to do. Today is Thursday, so he has no classes. Nothing waiting to be finished, either. The exams have been read, put in proper order, graded, placed on the table. The bed is clean and ready to receive him should sleep come. The kitchen, straightened up. With his eyes he reviews the room, which is spacious and cool since it has four windows that open onto The Beyond, and observes the grey walls, yellowish grey because it's been so long since they were painted, though the room is exquisitely tidy and smells of Creolina, as it is obvious that Helena has no equal anywhere in Havana. He observes the furnishings, the iron bedstead, the modest wardrobe with discolored mirrors, Cira's little rocker of excellent wood (majagua, perhaps), which is like the Platonic idea of a rocker, the rocker *itself,* and he observes the table, horrid imitation Renaissance, and notices the toy chest he has filled with books, and the nightstand with the lamp and the volume of Coleridge. That's fine. That's good enough. *That's OK.* Everything's fine so long as *he* doesn't show up, doesn't come near here. *I fear thee, ancient Mariner.* I don't want to see him, wouldn't want to see him for anything in the world, and in this I have to admit that I am no scholar. Professor Kingston tries out certain breathing exercises the doctor has taught him. He breathes in slowly, lifting his hands and counting to ten. Then he breathes out quickly through his mouth. Because *many things are lost in the labyrinth of the mind,* I can barely remember Cira's face, the tone of her voice; I can't remember the dress she was wearing. Sometimes I wonder if any of that was true. If I can say that she had an expression of joy when I found her, it's because I have repeated it and repeated it over all these years, so the phrase has become stuck, *expression of joy,* without my being truly certain that it was so. Even the cat, Kublai Khan, I see it lying there indifferently at the foot of her bed just because I know that cats are indifferent. Just words, not true memories. I mean, it's the rhetoric of memory that allows one, once the images disappear, to keep the illusion that one still remembers. Still and all, him I remember with absolute clarity. He remains intact in my memory, as if these twenty-three years had not passed. Yes, I should admit that I can't see Cira, that I can't see Kublai Khan, the way I can see him. The sharp uniform, the black, shining eyes, the skin evidently bronzed by the sun; the smile, the hands. And he halts his breathing exercises, sits motionless, listening. He has the impression that something has moved in the Island that is not the Island itself. Over these many years of living exiled in The Beyond, I have developed a sixth sense for listening and knowing the slightest intimacies of the Island. *Footsteps?* No, no, he thinks, he steels his nerve, not footsteps, must be fear, because the first thing fear does before taking shape is to draw near so that its steps can be heard, because fear is too much like that famous H. G. Wells character. Or perhaps it was just a palm frond, torn off by the wind that rose up today. Of course he knows that it is neither fear nor the knocking of a frond. And now he can be certain because he hears the footsteps again. There is a huge difference between this sound and that of the wind shaking the trees. These are footsteps, no doubt about it. The slow, heavy footsteps of someone who has difficulty walking. Professor Kingston stands up and steals to the door, presses his ear to it. Lowers his head and closes his eyes, as if by losing his sight he could concentrate better. The footsteps approach, stop, approach, stop. The old man thinks it must be someone limping with one leg. They come so close that he swears he can hear breathing. Then he feels that the door is moving as if they were pushing on it. For a few seconds there is just the language of the Island, wind, trees, swirling leaves. He thinks: better open. He thinks: better not open, turn off the lights, get into bed, cover up tight, because . . . What if it's him? Well, if it's him there's nothing I can do. Nothing. *Just open the door and let him in and allow him to say everything he has to say.* The footsteps begin again, receding from the door. Receding as if they are going to the carpentry shop. Slow, heavy footsteps, steps of someone who limps and has difficulty walking. They recede and recede until they cannot be heard. Again it is the Island, *like God Himself, the eternal and immutable Island.* He opens his eyes and realizes that at some point the fan has fallen from his hand. He goes to the wardrobe and puts on an old leather jacket from his New York days, and draws from a case the pistol that he won at the target shoot in a fair, a toy pistol that looks real. And of course it isn't loaded, since it is a toy it can't be loaded, it's just to frighten, and then he turns on the outdoor light and opens the door and cautiously sticks out his head. The light is weak, it disappears into the first branches of the aralias and marabú bushes. *Horrible weather.* The red sky, so low, a wonder it hasn't started raining yet. Windy, humid, smell of earth. Seems like there are thousands of people milling about but that's just an impression the Island often gives. He steps out onto the scant cement sidewalk in front of the door. I'm trying to listen because my hearing is more reliable than my sight, and I cannot discover, in the hubbub of the trees, any sound that should alarm me. I stand motionless for a few seconds. *That's all,* and he is about to turn back when he feels something make his shoe soles slip. On the sidewalk there is an intense red stain. He squats laboriously. Is it blood? He runs two fingers through the liquid, which is pleasantly warm, and brings them up close to his eyes. Blood, yes, blood. He stands laboriously. Holds up the pistol, squeezes the trigger, and listens to the metallic clack of the pistol mechanism. He turns back. Discovers that the door is also smeared with blood, and goes inside and closes the door well, with both locks, and his breathing becomes more and more difficult, and he walks to the center of the room, right beneath the light. If a man, he says, could walk in his dreams through hell and wet his fingers with blood as proof that his soul had been there, and if on awakening he found his fingers stained with blood . . . then what?

Eleusis is Uncle Rolo's bookstore. You can visit it by going out to the street and turning toward the south corner of the building. There, very near the stables, where Linea Street almost dead-ends at the train station, you will see the sign with hard-to-read gothic lettering and an arrow. Just a matter of turning a bit to the right and you'll see the bookstore, and you'll know it's a bookstore because it says so, otherwise anyone would just keep on walking, thinking that it's an outpost of Headquarters. Uncle has made the shop out of three walls and a wooden roof, and since it backs up to his own room, he has opened a door that communicates with the house, so that the house has become an extension of the shop. And since Uncle Rolo wasn't born yesterday and he knows that the bookstore doesn't look like one, he's seen to writing in black letters on all sides of it: ELEUSIS, THE BEST IN CULTURE FROM EVERY ERA, and he has opened a small shop window (there wasn't money for more) and has astutely placed several editions of the Bible. And he has lots of sales, because you can't deny that Uncle knew how to pick a good spot. Everybody comes here if they're on their way to Bauta, Caimito, Guanajay, Artemisa, and they want to buy themselves a paperback or magazine for the trip. And plenty of soldiers come here, too, officials from Headquarters going to and from Marianao to join in the monotony of the military camp, because what better way to kill time than with an Ellery Queen novel. And, of course, it isn't just the people passing through: Uncle has his regular clientele; professors and students at the Institute, the teachers from the Kindergarten and Home Economics normal schools, the English teachers from the night school (such as Professor Kingston), and the odd musician or intellectual now and then. Uncle does the selling: his business is not big enough to give himself the luxury of an employee. And Uncle Rolo doesn't complain, he feels good at his business and every single day (even on national holidays) he opens shop at eight A.M. on the dot and closes it at eight in the evening, with just a two-hour break at midday, because of course, however pleasant it would be to stay in the bookstore, lunchtime and siestas are sacred.

Several times he has thought that the rain was starting and he has come out to the Island to see it. It is always, however, the same image of a reddish sky, agitated trees, and everything dry, dry as a bone, as if it's been thousands of years since the last drop of water fell. You think you hear one thing and you hear something else and it's impossible to tell what you're really listening to. He lights an H-Upmann cigar (the only luxury he likes to allow himself) with the illusion that the smoke will scare away dark ideas. He lights the cigar well, turning it around and around, then he takes it from his lips, holds it a bit away, observes it. Good cigar, I swear. And there's nothing like smoking a good cigar after a long day's work. It's the only moment in the day you come close to Julio Lobo or that sonofabitch Sarrá. He listens to the rain falling. Deafening, ferocious, that rain. This time it can't be a mirage, because this time it's too obvious that it's raining at last, full force, to make up for all the rain that hasn't fallen all these months. He goes out to the Island to see the fury of the gods made manifest in this first October downpour. Ah, an illusion. The first drops are yet to fall.

And Merengue has brought out the rocking chair because he figures it's all the same whether it rains or not. He adjusts the cushion that Irene made to cover the broken cane, and he sits down to enjoy the cigar. It seems like it's raining and it's not raining: it'll be raining when it seems like it isn't. That's the way it is. He rocks. Softly. Last night he sat there, too, after everyone else went in to eat, to smoke his H-Upmann peacefully, in silence. And, of course, he recalls that last night he got home late, sales had gone better than expected. Chavito wasn't there. Nevertheless, that wasn't it. No, that wasn't it. He was actually hardly ever there when Merengue got back from his exhausting tour of Marianao, pushing his pastry cart. What had troubled Merengue last night was discovering that Chavito had apparently not been there all day, that the room had stayed just the way he (Merengue) had left it. His son couldn't hide it when he passed through a room. If there was anyone unruly in this world it was Chavito, a hurricane who could turn a house upside down, as if he had been raised without a mother. Merengue, who was always fighting about having to pick up the scattered shoes, the shirts tossed on the bed and the dirty underwear on the table, felt despondent because the room was all order and cleanliness, and you could see plain as day that his son had never been through there. As he rocked in the chair with the broken wickerwork, he thought that Chavito had become a different person. It wasn't (Merengue had given this idea a lot of thought) that he had become more serious, more responsible; not that he had become more of a man. No. True as that may be, to put it in so many words would be naive. Last night Merengue reached the conclusion that his son was keeping a secret. And he had reached this conclusion because Chavito seemed to have no secrets anymore, he would explain every one of his actions with exasperating prolixity. He had a ready, reasonable explanation for everything. Ah, but his eyes . . . What else could that evasive look mean? What did those silences mean, which could last for hours and in which Chavito would bang on the table and move his lips imperceptibly? Nevertheless, there was almost no way to describe what was surprising about Chavito's behavior. There could be no doubt that he had changed. Only, if someone forced Merengue to explain just what the transformation consisted in, the black man would open his mouth, not say a word, and make a perplexed gesture. The perplexed gesture he has now, sitting in the rocking chair, with his cigar between his fingers. He closes his eyes. You also closed them, Merengue, the last time you saw Chavito, and you fell asleep. And it was strange that you'd fall asleep looking at the picture of Nola with the fresh jasmines in the flowerpot on the wall, and when you were sleeping you kept on looking at the picture, the flowers, though it wasn't a picture and a flowerpot anymore but a woman, a smile, and a bouquet of jasmines. Knowing that it couldn't be Nola because Nola was dead. And you woke up because you felt a sound at the door. The key in the lock, the door opening. What time did the clock say? You don't know, you didn't see. Must have been near four in the morning, maybe earlier. In the shadows you can never know what time a clock says. Chavito, yes, Chavito didn't turn on the light, he thought you were sleeping, until you got up yourself and turned on the light so he'd see you weren't asleep. You stood there looking at him. And he stood there looking at me. He looked filthy, stinking of swamp, of royal palm seeds, several big tears in his shirt. I didn't ask him anything because a father shows his authority in silence. I looked at him for a long time so that he'd feel ashamed and talk without me having to ask him. Chavito is tough. Always was, really. Didn't say word one. Stood there as stiff as if Chavito had carved him. Merengue heated water in a bucket and plucked petals into it from the jasmines he had set out for Nola, poured in Eau de Cologne 1800 and scraped in powdered eggshell. He brought a clean towel and good Palmolive soap. He helped Chavito undress. He noticed the clumsiness in his son's movements, as if he were suffering from great exhaustion. He stood watching the whole time Chavito bathed, without saying a word, without the other taking the trouble, this time, to give one of his explanations that were too exhaustive to be true. When he finished, his young, black body was dotted with petals and powdered eggshell. Merengue helped him dry off, as he always did, careful to remove the traces of the bath dedicated to Saint Francis, Orula. Should I make your bed? No, old man, I have to go. Merengue raised his eyes to see, precisely, how his son's gaze avoided his own. I have to go. Tomorrow I'll explain. Tomorrow you'll explain, tomorrow you'll explain. He did not protest too much. He helped him dress, buttoned his pants, his shirt, tied his shoes and then buffed them with a shoe-shine cloth. He wiped his perfumed handkerchief across his son's neck. Be careful, he asked. Then, when Chavito was already in the doorway ready to leave, he called him and tossed a small wooden crucifix to him, a blessed crucifix that Merengue always carried. The boy caught it with a baseball catcher's gesture, smiled, and stuffed it in his pocket. Now, while he rocked in the chair, alone, smoking an excellent H-Upmann in the hopes that the smoke would dissipate his dark ideas, Merengue longs for someone to show up. Someone, anyone, Mercedes, Rolo, Irene, Miss Berta. He longs for someone to search him out for a conversation, for jokes, double entendres, bad words, anything. No one comes. Merengue stands up and stops the chair so that it won't rock by itself. He goes to the altar, stares at the glass eyes of the Saint Lazarus that he and Nola bought twenty years ago, when Chavito was born, in a little shop on Armonía Street. He looks at Saint Lazarus. Can't stop looking. Touches the wounds that the dogs lick. Old leper, you have to help me, dammit, you have to help me, he says, and he lights the candles.

Miss Berta's watch marks thirteen minutes past eleven while she is reading about Barabbas in *Figures from the Lord's Passion*. Sitting at the dining table, a small lamp shines a clear light on the book's yellow pages and large letters. Since her student days, Miss Berta has had the custom of drinking sips of cold linden tea while reading, for the first thing she does, very early, after bathing and before preparing for her classes, is to boil a great jar of linden tea that she later sets out to cool and puts in the refrigerator. The linden calms her, helps her to think clearly. And at night it helps her to sleep. Also, while she reads, she has the habit of marking the words with her lips. Something she does not permit her students but that she has never been able to eliminate. Also, she likes to pick her nose and take her feet out of her slippers and place her tired, calloused soles on the floor. These more or less are the habits of Miss Berta when she reads. She has others; they are not as persistent as these, acquired more than fifty years ago. Though perhaps one other custom should be added: getting up every now and then to observe the sleep of Doña Juana.

Stealthily, with the utmost care, Miss Berta enters the room and, without even turning on the light, stands in front of her mother's bed. She leans over not only to see but also to hear how the old woman is breathing. Doña Juana sleeps face up, hands crossed over her breast, holding the rosary, as if she wanted to anticipate death, as if this final position were the most natural one possible. At times Miss Berta even forgets about her pious reading and stays there in the room, and observes how her mother's great breast rises and falls, and studies as best she can in the darkness the expression covering the visage of Doña Juana, no different from the one she wears when she is awake. Miss Berta waits. She has been waiting a long time. Doctor Orozco told her one afternoon that Doña Juana had at most six months to live. Thirty years have passed since that prophecy, and twenty-five since Doctor Orozco was laid to rest in the Iberian Union Lodge section of Colón Cemetery. This year Doña Juana had her ninetieth birthday. Miss Berta has never called the doctor again. She waits. She studies, she prepares, and above all, she observes. There, in the darkness, she follows the not entirely steady rhythm of her mother's breathing. She watches at great length, and studies the vast body inch by inch. Some nights the linden tea does not work and Berta loses patience, looks for the little flashlight she keeps in the drawer of the nightstand and shines it on the old woman's body. Doña Juana, meanwhile, sleeps marvelously and never alters the rhythm of her breathing. Doña Juana gives herself over to sleep with the certainty of those who were born to be eternal.

She can't finish the page, can't read, doesn't understand what she's reading, and she returns again and again to the same words and it's no good, there's no way to understand what's happening to Barabbas in those vineyards he's getting into. Miss Berta lifts her eyes to the windows. She turns her head toward the room, turns it toward the kitchen. Nobody there, of course. Who would be there? The sensation nevertheless persists that someone, stationed in some corner, is following each and every one of her movements with insidious curiosity, with loutish obstinacy. She drops the book, turns off the lamp, approaches the window and opens the shutters in the conviction that there she will meet with the eyes that are annoying her so. There is no one in the gallery, it seems. She sees only a disordered darkness of wind, trees, and leaves. Air blows in through the windows, humid and smelling of earth, smelling of rain. She closes them again. Walks about the living-dining room saying to herself that she's a fool, she's crazy, that's enough stupidity for now, there's no one, absolutely no one, watching her. At the same time, however, she finds herself adopting attitudes: Is it that you are never yourself when you are in front of others, or that you are only yourself when you are in front of others? And where are those eyes? She doesn't know, she cannot know where the eyes are, the most terrible thing about it is that the eyes are everywhere. And Miss Berta lets herself collapse into the moiré easy chair and picks her nose. She recalls that a few months ago, around May or June (Pentecost Sunday), she first felt she was being observed. In the parish church. Very early. No one was there. The six o'clock mass had ended and it wasn't yet time for the next one, and no one had come in. She sat down in the first pew, and then she kneeled to pray and there, kneeling, she felt someone looking at her. The sensation she experienced was so vivid it startled her, she even stood up and looked behind her, searching among the columns, convinced someone had entered the church. No one was there, however. No one. Miss Berta returned to the pew, tried to pray, attempted to say the Credo, raised her eyes several times to the Christ on the main altar with the bloody wounds the color of sepia and the waxen skin, the sloe-colored hair, the sweetly closed eyes, and she could not say the Credo, the words escaped her mind, wiped out by the gaze that was stroking her body like a muddy hand. She thought she saw a flash of eyes in the confessional, and she said to herself probably it's Father Fuentes there awaiting her repentance, and she laughed inwardly. What a fool I am, it's not like it's the first time Father Fuentes was waiting for me in the confessional, and she walked over to the luxurious mahogany cabinet and fell on her knees at the prie-dieu and, as always, began her repentance with an exclamation: Father, I am so wretched, I have sinned again. She had the impression that the response from the other side was, as always, a throat-clearing and a movement of the head, nodding yes or shaking no (you could never tell), and a hand gesture that, rather than a priest's, looked like an orchestra director's. I have doubted again, Father, she exclaimed, and she lowered her eyes because she blushed to confess it, not so much for the enormity it implied as for having to repeat the same phrase every Sunday. She said she had blasphemed once more, that she had had impure thoughts about Our Lord, that she had called into question His magnanimous work, that she had referred to Him with obscene words. And she waited there for Father Fuentes to begin with his Well, let's see, his response and his penance. Instead, the only response was a little laugh. Miss Berta jumped to her feet, without even thinking about her arthritis, and felt so indignant she wanted to cry. Not stopping to weigh the consequences of her actions, she opened the door to the confessional and, though she had for one second the sensation that her eyes met another pair of inquisitive, mocking, overbearing eyes, she found the priest's seat empty and she backed away with the fear provoked by having nothing concrete to fear. She raised her eyes and discovered the eyes in the fresco. The Christ (blond this time), offering His hands in a generous sign of surrender, looked at her with an expression so sweet it could only be ironic. No matter that Miss Berta backed up all the way to the baptistery, the eyes followed her there, and then they went with her all down the nave, up to the high altar, and when Miss Berta couldn't stand it anymore and saw Father Fuentes come out and started to cry like a crazy woman, the eyes didn't have the benevolence to turn aside but stayed glued to her in an attitude of outright mockery. Of course, now, sitting in the moiré easy chair, while searching with her index finger through her nostril, she is positive that she had just been confused, that the eyes of the Christ on the church fresco weren't the ones that had been watching her, if that had been it, it would only have happened in the church, not in the plaza of Marianao nor in the Variety Store nor in the classroom nor in her own house as is happening right now. And she closed her eyes to escape that gaze. Except that closing them does no good and she keeps feeling the gaze that is a muddy hand on her body, all over her body, caressing her. And Miss Berta raises her eyes to heaven, which isn't heaven but the ceiling of the house, stained by dampness, and says, Lord, if it is You, listen to my plea, stop watching me, forget about me, don't go to such trouble for me, for this Your humble servant, do not illuminate me with Your eyes, let me remain in the darkness of Your ignorance, Lord, do not distinguish me with this insistence of Yours, divert Your divine curiosity from me, do not set me apart, do not give me an importance I don't deserve. So she cries out, and for all this she still knows she is being watched. And she repeats it several times because she discovers that when she talks, the insistence of the gaze lessens. And, as if God had decided to answer her, she hears a timid knocking at the door.

Pardon me if I'm bothering you, I know how late it is, I saw the light on and I dared to come visit you, and I know you'll pardon me, I hate to be a bother. It's Irene and she's sad. As if by magic, Miss Berta stops feeling that she's being observed. What weather we're having! says Irene. It just won't start raining. Delighted, content, Miss Berta lets her in. What strange weather, she sighs, trying not to make visible the pleasure she feels at her neighbor's arrival. Irene comes in; she stands in the middle of the living-dining room as if she doesn't know what to do or has forgotten why she came. Miss Berta asks if she wants a little linden tea, iced linden tea, it's very good, with just a squeeze of lemon, it helps you think, very calming, you know? Irene agrees. Miss Berta disappears into the kitchen and the refrigerator door makes opening and closing sounds, and then Miss Berta returns with a half-filled glass of the yellow-greenish concoction. Sit down, my dear. And it's all too obvious: Irene is sad, you can see it in her face, in the eyes she doesn't raise from the ground, in her body's attitude, as if she were bearing an excessive weight on her shoulders. Docile, Irene sits down in one of the chairs from the dining-room set. She does it in her own way, without completely taking up the seat; it gives the impression she is ready to rise at any moment, to take off running, to disappear into the Island, among the rosebushes and plants. Miss Berta, who has also brought a glass of linden tea for herself, sits down in another chair, facing Irene, and she is happy because the eyes have disappeared, and no one is observing her, no insidious gaze is following her; she has only Irene's eyes in front of her and those don't bother her. Irene takes a brief sip of the cold concoction and sighs. Miss Berta sits there watching Irene for a good long time, waiting to hear what she has to say, and, perhaps to break the silence, perhaps because it is a question she'd like to ask each and every inhabitant of the globe, she comes out, just like that, completely off the subject, with, And you, do you believe in God? Irene looks at her for an instant; takes another brief sip of the concoction and says, I went out this afternoon, down to the plaza, to look for chayotes for Lucio, Lucio just can't get enough chayote soup, and he likes the salad a lot too, and I went out early, walking you know, cutting through back here, past the Cinema Alpha, and what do you know but I met an old friend of mine from Bauta and she looked completely changed, the years had really taken a toll on her, she's a great old friend of mine, Adela, no, not Adela, Adela died of consumption a little after the hurricane of '44, her name is Carmita or Cachita, I'm not sure, and it doesn't matter, it was a really nice day when I left for the plaza, and while I was standing there buying the chayotes and other things like corn on the cob, the tender kind to make tamales with, the weather started to change, but really change, just like night had suddenly fallen, I remember they had to turn on the lights in the plaza so they could count the money, you couldn't see your hand in front of your face, and I came running back, I had left some laundry hanging on the line and I didn't want it to get wet, I came back in a taxicab with the nicest driver, Ramón something-or-other was his name, Ramón Yendía, that's it, and I got back in time to take in the laundry, though if I'd have known it wasn't going to rain I wouldn't have rushed so much, and what do you know but when I arrive I find a layer of dirt covering the floor and the furniture and some poplar branches embedded in the grillwork over the main window, and that's not the worst of it, Berta, it just took me a minute to sweep up the dirt and throw the branches back into the Island, because my mother always said, Everything that dies should go back to the earth, and the most terrible thing happened when I went into the bedroom, and I swear that when I saw what I saw there the sky came crashing down on me, with angels and devils, the whole heavens, on top of me, what did you ask, do I believe in God?

Irene had been praying to the little printed image of Christ that she keeps under glass on the nightstand. It actually isn't an image of Christ. That fact, however, will be clarified in its own due time.

If the reader has no objections, it can be five in the afternoon. The Island should be prematurely dark. Irene would be turning on the lights to sweep out the dirt and return to the Island the branches cut down by the wind and embedded in the grillwork over her main window. It's also likely she'd organize the chayotes and corn in the vegetable bin and take in the laundry from the clothesline. She should drink a cup of cold coffee, have a look at the almanac, and see again, fleetingly, the face of Carmita or Cachita, her friend from Bauta, the old face, so changed, and she would say that Carmita or Cachita must be her age more or less, so she would already be at least fifty (she wouldn't know exactly now). And she would reflect, The worst thing about time isn't what it adds but what it takes away. And if she should enter her room to change clothes, on the floor, between the bed and the wardrobe, in front of the nightstand, she would find the broken porcelain pitcher (tall, in the form of an amphora, with two gilded handles and a pink rococo landscape on the belly). If the reader has no objections, Irene would lean over to pick up the pieces.

You have to have a lot of courage not to believe, says Irene. You have to have a lot of courage not to believe, says Miss Berta.

What time is it? Drink the linden, it's good for you, it calms you down. What happened? I don't know. I don't know how to tell you. Excuse me one moment. Miss Berta disappears behind the bedroom door. Carefully she approaches Doña Juana, observes her, tries to listen to her breathing. And Doña Juana, as if she knew someone were monitoring her sleep, is the perfect image of the old woman sleeping in her white linen nightgown with tiny embroidered flowers and the rosary whose crucifix, they say, contains soil from the Holy Land and was consecrated by Pius XII. Miss Berta returns to the living-dining room and sits down again facing Irene and says, A pitcher breaks and memories appear. Irene shakes her head, no, no, let me explain, she straightens in her chair, closes her eyes.

The pitcher meant a lot to me; the real drama, Berta, is that I have forgotten why.

First she thought she had bought it for her mother in the little shop of the Jew who lived on the highway to Cayo La Rosa. A dark and humid shop, crammed with cheap pieces that did a fairly poor job of pretending to be originals from Frankenthal or Sèvres. She saw herself there picking out the pitcher with the rococo landscape. The Jew, an elderly man more than eighty years old, with a long yellowish beard and small, dark and impertinent eyes, leaned before her and explained the reasons why this pitcher was a true work of art, and why this selection therefore proved that she had exquisite taste. Irene held out her handkerchief with the money she had been able to squirrel away from what the match factory paid her for the little boxes. The old man in turn held out the pitcher with trembling hands. It must have no doubt been a May afternoon because she would have wanted the pitcher for Mother's Day, and there were still a few days to go and she would have to keep the pitcher at her cousin Milito's house. She vividly remembered the smell of wood and varnish in that dark shop, in front of which there opened a pasture full of beautiful horses. She knew, however, that the elderly man she saw in her memory drew a lot from the tailor in Santa Rosa who made Lucio's clothes. And on the other hand, hadn't Rita once laughed at her, saying that there was never any Jew with any shop on the highway to the Cayo? The only Jew who lived in Bauta, said Rita, was the Pole with the shoe store. Actually, Irene thought, I never bought that pitcher in any shop, my father gave it to me for my birthday. Yes, for my fifteenth. Her father got home one day from the textile factory with a large box and he said it was for her and she hugged him and gave him lots of kisses, and opened the box and was amazed by the pitcher, which she placed on the pedestal table in her bedroom, next to the bed. What pedestal table? That pitcher had never been in the house in Bauta and she had never had a pedestal table in her house. And she told herself that if she would just concentrate, as she had done other times, she would surely return to that house of her childhood and would find out if the pitcher had ever been there. She saw a long avenue lined with royal palms and at the end of it the wooden house, fairly large, painted blue and white, with a spacious wraparound porch that was a marvel. And she reached the garden planted with miniature palms and jasmines, country roses and plumbagos, and she climbed the four steps that divided it from the porch, and she could even hear her heels tapping on the polished floorboards. She entered the living room. She felt like an intruder, there was no way this could be the living room of her house. She realized the house she had actually reached was Uncle Rodrigo's in Baracoa beach. And she couldn't be certain of that, either, because it could easily be the house of her cousin Ernestina in Santa Fe, or any other house she might have invented. Then she tried to remember her own house, her childhood house, whether it was made of wood or of masonry, and she realized she had no way to pin down that detail. She felt certain that there had been a special smell in her house, a smell of charcoal from the little heaters her mother used to warm the irons, but that information didn't do one bit of good. She couldn't smell the charcoal or the irons or the hot starched cotton clothes; the only thing she smelled was rain in the Island on an October afternoon. She spent a long time entering other people's houses, strangers' houses, houses she had only entered in her thoughts, trying to find among them her own house, the house of her childhood, but she couldn't get her memories to return her to the one place she had been so happy she could die. And it was at that moment she thought she recalled that the pitcher had actually been a gift from Emilio on the day they had fixed their wedding date. Irene saw Emilio with his Prussian blue jacket and the timid air he always had about him until he realized he was dying. She saw him as he must have looked, entering the night in 1934 when they decided they would marry on the first of April the following year, with her pretty face illuminated by happiness and the pitcher wrapped in a golden taffeta cloth. She saw him enter several times. There was something false about the evocation, she didn't know what it could be, it became apparent that Emilio wasn't Emilio, she even thought the problem was his jacket. He never wore a jacket, but a handsome military outfit. By then, after Machado fell, he had been made a colonel's orderly at the Columbia military camp. And the jacket she was seeing couldn't be Emilio's, but rather Lucio's, and it had actually been not Emilio who gave her the pitcher but Lucio, and she thought she was going crazy.

Don't worry, these things happen, exclaims Miss Berta, actually thinking that these things do not happen. And she takes Irene's hand and caresses it because she thinks this is the best way of showing her support. Sometimes I forget my own name, Miss Berta lies, and she lies so badly that she notices how Irene looks at her with incredulity and briefly makes a face. Well, not that I forget . . . I mean, I forget. She falls silent. Stops caressing Irene's hand. You know, life is full of surprises . . . Irene nods. Yes, life is full of surprises . . . And she raises her head as if she were listening; no, it's not that, it's not that she's listening. And she puts up her hands. You need to sleep, Miss Berta says sweetly, sleep mends all things. Irene seems like she's about to leave, because she gets off the chair and stands up with a certain difficulty and approaches the door. She does not go, however. I still haven't told you the worst part.

A knock at the door. Irene opens. Mercedes leans forward, says her good evenings, explains, I couldn't sleep, this strange night is keeping me awake, just like Marta, I'm tossing and turning and I can't get to sleep and then to top it all off I saw a man at the window. Irene takes Mercedes by the arm and leads her inside. A man at the window? Mercedes nods. Miss Berta stands up, goes to the kitchen and comes back with a glass of cold linden tea for Mercedes. The three women sit down at the table. A man at the window?

Tall, thin, distinguished as an elderly exiled empress, you can see a mile off that the Barefoot Countess is, or was, a woman of class. All you have to do is see her coming down the galleries with her silver bracelets and sandalwood fan, leaning unnecessarily on a cane that is a serpent, proud in her bearing, sure in each of her gestures, talking to herself with precise and chosen words. She is not beautiful and apparently has never been able to boast of being beautiful. What does it matter? She has known how to appear beautiful. Her hair, now white, seems straight; actually, when you get close, you note that it has been painstakingly combed to seem straight. Black at times, her eyes turn green on some very bright mornings, and they have an intense gaze, mocking and wise (wiser still at those moments when she reaches the point of delirium). She has a surprisingly wide nose and thick lips that she hides by smiling, emphasizing the mockery in her eyes. Her skin, a handsome copper color, is always clean, untouched by the cruelty of the sun on the Island. And although she wears dresses from twenty or thirty years past, no one can call them anachronisms, much less laugh at her. The fact is that her elegance transfers to her clothes (not the other way around, as usually happens), and confers on them a mysterious modishness. They aren't dresses from any given era, Casta Diva states, perplexed. They are dresses for all times, Uncle Rolo observes, emphatic. And the most obvious thing is that despite her obvious mulatto background, there is something about her that does not belong to Cuba. No Cuban woman, Rolo tries to explain, is so dignified in her manners, nor walks with such majesty that, rather than moving through this burning Havana of ninety-plus in the shade, she seems to be strolling through the gothic corridors of a castle on the Rhine, and besides, in this era of confusion and shallowness what Cuban woman can cite Gessner's *Idylls* in perfect German? No; Cuban women, those sacred pearls of Eden, too busy with their *toilettes,* can at best recite the facile rhymes of José Angel Buesa, and they never hum Wagner, but the *Rico Mambo* by Dámaso Pérez Prado. Cuban women are too busy attending to their waistlines, says Rolo.

This is not an Island, exclaims the Barefoot Countess, but a tree-filled monstrosity. And she walks down the gallery jingling her silver bracelets and perfuming the air with her sandalwood fan. The cane on which she unnecessarily leans is a serpent carved from ácana wood. And her dress, tonight, is white linen in Richelieu embroidery. I tell you, there will be a day when the trees come into the houses, she insists in the tones of a prophetess. And she stands still next to the Apollo Belvedere right behind the wooden screen in the courtyard. She sighs. That all this should be destroyed! And the Island seems to respond. With this weather, with the gusty wind, with the rain that refuses to fall (it's as if it were falling), the Island seems to shout yes, it's true, everything's going to be destroyed, so much beauty ought to, has to, disappear. And the Barefoot Countess nods as if she has understood. And she continues walking toward Helena's house. She does not need to knock. Helena is there, standing in the shade, watching the Island with that expression of hers, of which you can only say that at times it is indecipherable. Good evening. Naturally Helena does not reply. She doesn't even look at the Barefoot Countess, at most it seems as if she has clenched her teeth even tighter. The Countess looks her over head to toe with her mocking face. And she stands still, looking at Helena, leaning on her cane, not moving the fan, smiling.

Countess, have you seen anyone in the Island? asks Helena. The Countess nods. I always see someone in the Island. A stranger, I mean. We are all strangers. Helena looks at her indignantly. I don't know why I talk with you. Don't talk, the Countess replies, with the sweetest mocking smile you could ever imagine.

She was sitting at the table going over the account book when she had the conviction that something important must be happening somewhere in the house or in the Island. She closed the book after carefully marking her place, got up and walked toward Sebastián's room. She opened the door without knocking, of course. Her son was sleeping with the lamp on. She approached, listened intently to the boy's breathing to be certain that he was truly asleep, turned out the lamp and withdrew, even more convinced that something must be happening somewhere in the house or in the Island. Sure, just as sure as could be, these forebodings never fooled her. And she went to the door and opened it and it happened, the thing Helena did not know whether to believe, the thing that left her perplexed. And it wasn't just that she saw a white figure walking through the Island, because that often happened and even Chavito's statues gave the impression of movement some nights, but that when she stepped out a bit to see whether it had been a hallucination, she found the Venus de Milo stained with blood.

* * *

Vague pains in the muscles and deep sorrows in the soul: it must be raining, and as usual Uncle Rolo cannot get to sleep. He has once again read chapter twelve of *Against the Grain,* the extraordinary chapter in which Des Esseintes travels to London without leaving Paris. You see him in a stagecoach leaving Paris for Calais to take the boat to London. It is a stormy night, it says, as he crosses the plains of Artois. Of course the landscape Rolo imagines is that of the Island with ceibas and royal palms, and the stagecoach isn't a stagecoach but a gig like the ones you see in Mialhe's engravings. It's Sandokán guiding the trotting horses. He opens his eyes. He realizes it'll be too difficult to let himself be overcome by sleep. He rises. He turns on the ceiling lamp and doesn't know what to do next. Almost without realizing it, just as if an unknown force were propelling him, he stands in front of the mirror on the wardrobe door. The mirror. He runs a hands across his forehead and observes the thinning hairline that foretells his baldness. Decidedly so, isn't it? Yes, Rolo, you're getting old, and the worst thing is: old age is bringing out a prodigious transformation in you; you're starting to look like the old men of the family. Your eyes are already almost as clouded over, your cheeks as flaccid, the wrinkles around your mouth, the bag under your chin. You have grey hairs in that fur on your chest, Rolo. Prominent stomach, thin thighs. It's true: you're forty. It wouldn't make any difference, if José María Heredia hadn't died younger. Forty years old. That means you've lived twenty-one years more than Juana Borrero, fifteen more than Carlos Pío Urbach, eleven more than René López, ten more than Arístides Fernández. Julián del Casal, the greatest of all, died at twenty-nine. Get dressed, Rolo, peel yourself away from the mirror and put on any old clothes, tonight I don't foresee sweet dreams for you.

It isn't raining. The Island lies. Uncle Rolo looks up at the reddish sky where low dark clouds are shifting, clouds that give the impression that the whole city is one enormous bonfire. On one side of the courtyard, in front of the screen and just to the left of the Apollo Belvedere, he has just caught sight of the unmistakable figure of Lucio. Tall, elegant, in a dark jacket that could be black or blue, it is Lucio scrutinizing the Island, looking in every direction as if he were afraid of being seen. Rolo hides. Closes the door a little and observes through the crack between the hinges. Lucio takes a few steps forward, looks back, raises an arm and lowers it with a certain brusqueness. Gives the impression he's about to do something. Stops. Stops before he does what? Now it seems he has decided to leave, only he suddenly returns with decision and caresses, with fear but with relish, the thighs of the Apollo Belvedere.

Many people have gotten lost in the Island, never to be seen again. At least that's what they say over here. Uncle Rolo (who is afraid and, by the same token, rather happy) has followed the stone path as far as the poor and anguished Laocoön being strangled with his sons by the two serpents of Pallas. It is a Laocoön without muscles, skinny, poorly sculpted, yet despite all that it is a startling sight on a night like this. There is no sign of Lucio anywhere. And Uncle Rolo continues up to the fountain, where today the frogs are not singing and the Boy with the Goose is not smiling, and he keeps on up to the bust of Greta Garbo (they know it is Greta Garbo because Chavito says so, otherwise you might think it's a bust of Miss Berta reciting the rosary), and it seems you can hear the voice of the Barefoot Countess: This is not an Island, but a tree-filled monstrosity, and she laughs, and how she laughs. Uncle draws back. The only thing he couldn't put up with at this hour is meeting that crazy woman with her air of a queen in exile. He doesn't take the stone path, instead he cuts through the thick vegetation that Irene tends, passes the Wrestlers (Chavito's inert Wrestlers), and reaches the Apollo Belvedere with those perfect thighs that Lucio caressed a moment before. Uncle Rolo searches, trying to discover some special movement in the vegetation that will tell him in which direction Lucio disappeared. The Island is awhirl with this October wind that threatens rain, and thousands of paths open up where Lucio could have disappeared. Paths that instantly reclose. Strange portals of branches. Uncle Rolo makes a gesture of discouragement, a brief sigh while lowering his head. Then he sees, at the feet of the majestic Apollo, an object shine. He bends over and picks it up, damp and mired with slime and dead leaves from somewhere. He takes his handkerchief out and cleans off the object and realizes it is a compass mounted in a seashell, mother-of-pearl. And the compass has its indecisive red and black needle. And on the other side of the seashell, a blurry photograph of the cathedral of Hagia Sophia. And you can hear, from the other side of the wooden screen, the sound of water and a voice singing low, a religious song in some other language or perhaps in terrible Spanish. And Uncle Rolo walks around and discovers the person he already knew he'd discover. Merengue is cleaning his vending cart, intoning religious songs under the unfurled wings of the Victory of Samothrace. Merengue turns his head when he senses footsteps; smiles lightly; interrupts neither the work nor the song. Uncle also smiles, with more zeal: seeing Merengue is always a relief. Merengue, he says. And the black man straightens up, tosses his damp rag in the soapy water, and smiles more broadly, showing the white, white teeth of a pure black. Bad night, says the black man. Every night's a bad night, replies Rolo, also smiling, as if meaning to imply that he feels happy to have met him here, in the courtyard. The black man, however, suddenly grows serious, looks nervously in every direction, crosses himself and says no, Rolo, tonight is a bad night. And Rolo is just about to say, No, old man, it's not so bad, I just had the luck of finding me a mother-of-pearl compass, the instrument that points out the way, the only thing that orients us, that keeps us from getting lost.

He opens the iron gate and goes out into Linea Street, which is deserted at this hour with the laurel bushes agitated by the gusting wind. Toward the left, toward the Columbia base, you can see the lights of the first watch houses. You can hear voices and knocking sounds. Uncle Rolo walks to the right, and it would seem he's heading toward the bookstore, though, of course, what would Uncle be doing in the bookstore at this hour? He goes by the horse pastures, and the place Rolo is really heading toward without realizing it (or realizing it) is the train station. A grey edifice (or a blue one turned grey by time), one of those built twenty or thirty years ago, grim, austere, with an imposing, poorly lit entryway that doesn't harmonize with its scant waiting room. An unpleasant edifice rising harshly in the midst of a landscape dominated by trees and poor houses with roofs of blackened tiles. Many nights, when he can't sleep, Uncle goes to the station and spends hours there, thinking about any old thing, and sometimes not even thinking, just watching the soldiers, or trying to talk with Homer Linesman, to get him to tell something about the tragedy of his life, though the linesman never yields one iota of his terseness, because if there's any man who doesn't say a word in this world it's that filthy and stooped old man who looks in every direction with the eyes of an animal lying in wait. At this hour there's hardly anyone at the ticket counter. At this hour no train is leaving. You can see a shadow pass between the rails that may be the linesman's. The four or five cheap wooden benches in the main hall are empty. However, there's a dirty duffel bag on a stool next to the Coca-Cola machine. Almost mechanically, Uncle straightens his hair, wets one index finger with his tongue, and rubs it across his thick eyebrows. He sits down on the best bench, the one that lets him see a good part of the hall, and adopts an attitude of unconcern. Then the door to the restroom labeled GENTLEMEN opens. A sailor appears, buttoning his fly. The sailor finishes buttoning the buttons of his fly, all the while watching Uncle with eyes that could be either mocking or reverent, and he runs his fingers over the fly as if to check that it is well closed. He walks over to the stool with sure steps (too sure to really be sure, thinks Uncle) and picks up the duffel bag. Uncle Rolo stands up. He tries to express indifference, tiredness, boredom, he raises his eyebrows, lets the lids fall. Doesn't smile. A smile is the first step toward complicity: you should never smile from the first moment. Can you tell me what time it is, says Uncle Rolo without looking at the sailor (so that it seems Uncle has addressed the question to no one in particular). Since, however, the sailor takes his time responding, Uncle observes him for a moment. The sailor is looking at Uncle with mute eyes and a face that doesn't tell him any more than any of Chavito's statues. And Uncle, who can't stand the intensity of those large, dark eyes, averts his own toward the rails, toward the countryside beyond the rails, which is a reddish stain agitated by the wind on this October night, and luckily at the same instant you can hear the whistle of an approaching train. He experiences the relief of having something to do. He goes toward the doorway leading to the tracks and feels the racket, a sound like the thunder that should have been falling tonight. A passing train, a swift light, enlivening for one moment the lifeless train station. A military train. He sees the soldiers pass, adolescents, smiling, waving good-bye, playing with each other, with the shield of the Republic flashing from their caps. Just one second for the train to pass, so little time, so quick, and then silence is restored, it's all too hard to believe it ever passed, and Uncle turns back and sees that the sailor is gone.

Although you'd say it's raining, Uncle Rolo says, No, it's just a trick, and he wants to sleep, and he closes his eyes, and he cannot sleep, and he turns on the lamp on the nightstand and begins to read, once more, chapter twelve of *Against the Grain,* the chapter in which Des Esseintes travels to London without leaving Paris.

You can't even read. Between you and Huysmans' words (which, as you like to say, aren't Huysmans' words, because they're translated into Spanish) floats the figure of the sailor. And you know that something about him troubled you, though you don't know what. And you can see him again now that you are lying in bed listening to the rain that isn't falling. You can see him again, tall, thin, with the slimness a sailor's uniform brings out so well, his dark, fresh, adolescent skin, and a mouth (the mouth really impressed you) that's almost thick, but not quite. The elegant motions of a dancer, not a sailor. Again you can see his eyes, shining, the color of honey. Since you were a child you've heard that the eyes are the mirrors of the soul; and if every man's soul is reflected in his eyes, what kind of soul does the sailor have? You thought from the first moment there was an insolent look in his eyes, but now you wouldn't be able to confirm it. Insolence? No. Perhaps the look of someone who knows everything or is able to imagine everything, perhaps the look of someone who doesn't see the other person's eyes but their insides. Large eyes, shining, honey-colored. And suddenly you know why he troubled you, you know that he troubled you because in his look, in his eyes, there wasn't a drop of pity.

And Uncle Rolo, who is a character in a novel, turns out the light. Tonight I won't get to sleep, he says, and he falls asleep in the way that a character in a novel usually sleeps (by disappearing).

Lucio turns on the light. It's easy to tell that Irene isn't home, he doesn't hear the stealth of her slippers, the footsteps pursuing him around the house, doesn't hear her too-maternal questions. He has reached his room without anyone showing him the time or asking him if he wants to eat or where he's been. No one has forced him to lie. And he undresses calmly, as if he had all the time in the world to undress. And when he is naked and turns off the light and lies down in bed and strokes his thighs and his chest, he feels dirty. He thinks about Miri's mouth running over his body, about Miri's little hands that touch him as if he were God, and he feels dirty. He also thinks, of course, about Manilla. He sees him, fat, lolling back in the easy chair with frayed upholstery, very serious, smoking a cigar almost down to the butt, with an expression of helplessness that can't be real, and he feels dirty.

And why did he go to Manilla's house? He has no answer to that question. Sometimes it's just a matter of getting dressed, in the firm belief that he's going to see Miriam, or perhaps thinking it's better to go to the movies because they're showing a James Dean picture, and suddenly, as if the devil were guiding his steps, he finds himself before Manilla's frayed easy chair, letting the money fall into Manilla's huge hand, and allowing the little girl's little hands to caress him as if he were God.

Nor had Lucio been thinking about going to Manilla's house today. He had spent the whole afternoon thinking he would go to the outdoor cafes on Prado to hear the bands, and that's what he had told Fortunato in the vinegar factory. It's even possible that he had invited him, and if Fortunato could have set aside that strange attitude he's had lately for a few hours, if he could have said yes, Lucio would certainly never have gone to Manilla's house. But the guy just looked at him with that intense look in his dark eyes, didn't smile, and said with a certain distaste, I'm not going anywhere. Lucio was so shocked at the aggressivity of the response that he lowered his head and didn't know what to do, he could only dissimulate by washing out the bottles. And the guy, who noticed, called him, Lucio . . . And Lucio paid no attention, and said under his breath, Son of a bitch, and the other heard it, or guessed it, stepped away without a word, and stayed away for a long time without going back to where Lucio stood, and if he did go back it was because Lucio, no longer angry, had called him. And Lucio thought now, if Fortunato had agreed to accompany him, he would have gone to hear the women's bands at the outdoor cafes and he would have saved himself from Manilla and Miri. That didn't happen. Fortunato yelled, I don't feel like it, and Lucio left the vinegar factory at six in the afternoon and went home, where Irene had a bath ready for him with hot water and essence of vetiver, and he bathed for a long time, because bathing was one of his few pleasures in life, and he stayed there for hours running the soapy sponge over his body and thinking about the things in life, not as they were but as he would have liked them to be, since the truth is that he never thinks of things as they are. He shaved. He came out into the room without drying off, with the big white towel tied around his waist. Naturally he didn't have to pick out the clothes he was going to wear; Irene, as if divining his intentions, already had his light-colored pants, his Prussian blue cashmere jacket, his white shirt laid out on the bed. Upset about the interference, however opportune as it was, upset because it gave the impression that his mother never made a mistake, he slammed the door shut and gave himself over to another of his great pleasures: lying down all wet on the towel spread over the bed, to let his body dry off by itself, while he thought about things, not as they actually were, of course, but as they ought to be. Then he dressed carefully, taking an interest in every detail of the clothes, with the agreeable sensation that his body would gratefully accept any piece of clothing, that everything fit it well, that he, as Rolo had once said without knowing he could hear, looked like a movie actor, and he went out into the living-dining room where the table was already set. He sat down in the hopes that Irene would not sit down facing him. As soon as Irene served him his water she sat down and said nothing for a long time, watched him eat with that sympathetic and admiring gaze that drove him to the edge of fury, and only when she began to clean up the plates did she say, Tonight the world is coming to an end with this rainstorm. Lucio replied with that brusqueness he always uses when he talks to his mother, For me, if the world's coming to an end I hope it catches me in the street, and he went outside and saw the Island was a reddish whirl of wind and leaves, and he went as far as the fountain and stood there thinking for a long time, without understanding very well what he was thinking, because he wasn't actually thinking but seeing images and repeating words, and he began to feel sad, feel a sorrow he knew all too well, one that made him long for a corner he could hide in, and for a higher force that would make him disappear. He stood this way for a long time until Sebastián arrived, and Lucio left the Island, and went out into Linea Street, and he didn't go to the outdoor cafes, instead he took off almost instinctively toward the Military Hospital, behind which, in a neighborhood nearly without streets, nearly without water, nearly without lights, practically in a country shack, lived Manilla with his daughter Miri.

As soon as the sun begins to hide, Melissa comes up naked onto the terrace roof with her parrot Morales on one hand. The reader should imagine her right now, in spite of the night, the wind, and the smell of rain, naked on the terrace. Anybody would say she feels like the queen of the world. Melissa repeats to Sebastián that the world is something Marta made up, that Venice doesn't exist, that Vienna doesn't exist, nor Brussels, nor Prague, nor Barcelona, nor Paris. She says the world is nothing but what we can see. She says this to Sebastián and you can see that she enjoys watching it disturb the boy, disturb Tingo-I-Don't-Get-It, and even Vido. The world is this terrace, the Island, and nothing else, Melissa exclaims, without smiling and apparently without trying to make fun of them, in the most serious manner you can imagine. Melissa seems to like walking about naked on the terrace roof while night falls, because then she is the whole world. She goes up there as if to meet someone, though you know she knows she isn't going to meet anyone other than herself. Sometimes she stretches out on the floor, caresses herself, closes her eyes. It's as if she had the impression she's nowhere; that is, that she doesn't exist. And she looks so happy! Melissa repeats, Happiness is being nowhere. On other occasions, the reader should imagine she limits herself to walking straight ahead, as if she were destined to be lost in the shadows, toward the dark end of the terrace, over there where the treetops come together to form a small and gloomy vault. She whispers with her parrot Morales. The bird moves its head, flutters its wings. Melissa smiles. Is she thinking about the implicit ingenuousness of believing the world exists, believing those strange and distant cities exist? There's nothing more than this, everything begins here and ends here, so why get your hopes up for no reason? People don't travel, they imagine they're traveling, they imagine they're dreaming. That's what her smile seems to say. The parrot moves its head nervously and flutters its wings. Melissa has told Sebastián not to kid himself, nothing truly exists for you except for what you can see, and therefore, since right now no one can see her, she only exists for herself.

And of course if Melissa thought that, if she really believed what she says, she would be mistaken. She does exist, because Vido has climbed a tree and is observing her walk naked on the terrace roof as if to meet someone who she believes is herself, but who's actually him, Vido. Melissa is talking with the parrot Morales. Vido doesn't listen to her, that doesn't matter, what matters is seeing how beautiful Melissa looks in the night on the roof.

At the beginning of this paragraph we should hear a bird hooting so that the three women will cross themselves. We should imagine them, seated at the table, with their glasses of cold linden tea served by Miss Berta. Sitting up very straight in her chair, Irene will have her eyes closed. A pitcher breaks, Miss Berta will say, and memories appear. Irene will shake her head no. Suddenly the two will be staring at Mercedes. A man in the window? Are you sure? Mercedes will sip her linden tea as slowly as she can, will wrinkle her brow as if puzzled by what she should reply.

I got home tired, with a kind of tiredness that I don't know if I should call it tiredness or sadness, I had just spent a horrible day at work, that old Morúa was in top form today, acting even more disagreeable than usual, he was wearing a white guayabera with black grime around the collar, trembling hands, dirty fingernails, the stench of cigar smoke suffocated me, he insisted on closing the windows, going on about the air, about his lungs, when the one who's going to die from her lungs is me, the spittoon must be overflowing, every time the old guy spit it made a splashing sound that turned my stomach, all I could do to keep from vomiting! and to top it all off, my work won't let me sit still for one second, thousands and thousands of files full of municipal nonsense, if it isn't the public park of who knows where, it's the funding for school breakfasts, or the accounts for who knows what monument to the anonymous heroes of the Volunteer

Fire Brigade, so! you spend your time wasting your time and while they're at it they make me waste mine for the few miserable pesos they pay me, today more than ever I was looking out the window with nostalgia, I always like to look out at the rooftops of Marianao, blackened from the dampness, the obelisk, the white-and-red tank of the Aqueduct, the trees of the Island that I don't know really are the trees of the Island but all I have to do is imagine that they are and I get a lump in my throat, whether they are or not, I look at the trees and manage to get myself out of the office for a few seconds, and today, when it was finally time for me to really go, I saw the open sky, and I don't know why I said open because it was really more closed than usual, it looked like the world was coming to an end, at City Hall they were saying, Hurry, hurry, the rain's almost here, I didn't hurry, what's more, it didn't even occur to me to take the bus, haven't I ever told you how much I love rainy days? Marta says I should have been born in London or Stockholm, does it rain a lot in Stockholm? where is Stockholm? there's no such city, in spite of my sadness, in spite of my tiredness, when I walked down the steps at the entrance to City Hall I felt something that I can't explain, pardon me, I'm so slow! something I'm incapable of explaining and it occurs to me, right now, to call it happiness, you understand? no, I know you don't, you don't understand, I don't mean I didn't feel tired or sad, but considering how tired or sad I was that afternoon with rain threatening, I felt happy, I often feel sad and happy at the same time, it's as if one thing were connected to the other and I can't explain it, the sky was about to fall to the ground, the strong wind, the smell of damp earth, a cloud was looming of dust, of dirt, of leaves, of papers, and all that increased my sadness, increased my new state of I don't know how to explain it and it occurs to me now to call it happiness, and I actually didn't know (I still don't know) what it was all about, I don't know if there really was a boy playing with a black rag, I was walking toward home, there wasn't anybody in the street except for the little boy that now I don't know if he existed, the houses were locked and bolted as if they were expecting a catastrophe, it had grown dark, it couldn't have been later than five in the afternoon, lots of times I come walking back and I like to see the houses from the high part of Medrano Street, I like to see the ladies, that's when they sit out on their porches and drink coffee or who-knows-what in elegant coffee cups, and they talk and they smile, when you live in a pretty house you have no reason not to smile, right? except today was different, first: there wasn't a single lady on a single porch; second: I felt tired, sad, and happy, I had the impression that neither the streets nor the houses were the streets or the houses they usually are, I was wandering around lost and wasn't coming back home but back who-knows-where, and the wind, as intense as it is right now, wouldn't let me walk, in one street (I don't know which one) I saw a wheel, no, no, it wasn't a wheel, a rim, some metal thing rolling downhill along the street, it slipped along a little ramp as if someone were guiding it, it went into the Apollo Park, the Apollo Park is the little park before you get to the ditch, pretty near the train station, and I call it that as my own joke, it has a statue of somebody, some patriot who won some battle, I call him Apollo because the ugliest old soldier in the War of Independence couldn't have looked half as ugly as that statue, not even if Chavito had made it, and the rim or the wheel, that metal thing rolling along like someone was guiding it, crashed into the base of the statue and made a musical sound, then I noticed someone was sleeping on a park bench, I approached, Irene, Berta, listen to this, a sailor, sleeping on the park bench, a sailor in full uniform and all, with his cap on his stomach and a duffel bag thrown on the ground, a sailor, listen, a young man, a boy, I'd say not more than twenty years old, thin, and he must be tall (he didn't fit on the bench), a lovely face, all well defined and a little Oriental-looking, Oriental as in the *Thousand and One Nights,* I mean, and his hands on his cap, smooth hands, hands that had never hoisted a sail (though there aren't sailing ships anymore, you can't help thinking of Salgari and the days of the pirates), I didn't see his eyes, like I said he was sleeping, but I did see his lips half open and, I swear, I had the impression that I had never seen such beautiful lips, and that made my tiredness or sadness more intense, my happiness vanished, I thought, There never was any happiness, that was just something I made up to keep from feeling so bad, I got back to the Island feeling like I was going into the cemetery to be buried alive, my sister Marta greeted me as she always does; that is, she didn't greet me, didn't respond to my kiss, didn't say a word,

I asked her how she felt and she answered glad to be blind so she doesn't have to see me, me and the rest of the world, because she thinks the rest of the world must be as stupid as I am, do you know what it is to spend your whole day under the nose of that old Morúa, writing and writing endless pages of municipal nonsense, just to come home and your sister, your own sister, your twin sister who shared your mother's belly with you, who shared the Cemetery and Typee with you, treats you like that? do you think that's right? I took a hot bath, a hot bath can't get rid of my tiredness, my sadness, but it does allow me to sleep as best I can, I didn't eat dinner, I drank the dreadful tamarind juice I had made myself yesterday, I lay down in bed, I must have fallen asleep right away, and I don't know what I dreamed or what I didn't, the wind was howling, like in the novels of Concha Espina or Fernán Caballero, which I've never read, probably I was dreaming I was Ida Lupino playing Emily Brontë, I would have loved to be a character in *Wuthering Heights,* to live in the pages of *Wuthering Heights,* at some point I heard a knock at the window, I woke up, in one of the frosted panes I saw, perfectly outlined, the face of a man, I let out a scream, the figure disappeared, I ran and even though I'm such a coward I opened the window, I just managed to see a white figure disappearing into The Beyond, I leaned against the window to be able to bend over and see better, and when I stood up again I discovered that the window and my nightgown were stained with blood.

Berta rises, goes to the window. It seems to be raining, she exclaims without conviction. There's no one out there but the strong wind that's trying to rip the trees out by their roots. I still haven't told the worst part, Irene says, opening her eyes. There is such hopelessness in Irene's gaze that the two women reach out their hands, as if by agreement, to hold Irene's hands and caress them. Mercedes begs, Don't get like this. Irene shakes her head and adds, How should I get if I saw my own son. What do you mean? A long silence. The two women keep caressing Irene's hands. Once more, in a quiet voice, almost a whisper, she explains that she couldn't remember who had given her the pitcher that the wind broke this October afternoon. She shows them the finger she cut on the broken porcelain, she wonders where that pitcher, which now resides in the trash can, could have come from. The most terrible part, what she hasn't told yet, took place when she wanted to remember Emilio, her husband of fifteen years, the only man in her life, but all she saw was Lucio, that really is serious, very serious, I must be going crazy. Explain it to us, woman, don't get hysterical. Irene talks as if it were someone else talking, there is a distance between what she says and her anguished face, the words slip from her lips with a strange coldness. She had lain in bed for a long while searching through her memories for the face of the man who had been so important for the fifteen best years of her life, and as much as she tried, all she kept seeing was Lucio in his blue jacket. She decided then to do what she had refused to do up until that moment, not out of an idle whim, no, but because she wanted to find Emilio's face on her own, without any help. But a point came when she couldn't take it anymore and she had to compromise, she went to the wardrobe and took out the box of photographs. I opened it as if my life depended on that banal act. First she found photos of Lucio as a baby, chubby, my son always looked older than he was because he was such a well-bred little boy; I found photos of me with him, of me alone, there in the Island, back before Chavito went into making statues; photos at the beach (what beach?) and a lovely tinted photo where you see me in a brown overcoat walking down Galiano Street, or San Rafael, or Belascoaín, how should I know, I look good in the photos, I wasn't always the disaster I am now. And at last I found a photo of Emilio. At last I could see my husband's face. In a field, shirtless, holding a stick for knocking down mangos. Lovely-looking, with that ingenuous smile he always had, wide eyebrows raised high over his big melancholy eyes; black, straight hair, stubbornly falling across his forehead. Athletic like Lucio, Lucio took after him, not a hair on his chest, better formed than any of Chavito's statues. I was in ecstasy looking at the photo of my husband and that was the only way I could remember him, see him in front of me, almost talking to me, I saw him (may God forgive me, there are things you don't say about the dead) the way he used to look when he wanted to touch me, I mean, caress me, kiss me, and he wouldn't do it brusquely, Emilio could be anything but brusque, he made his advances softly, the quieter and sweeter he seemed the more I knew he wanted me, I knew him better than anyone, by the way he would bring me a cup of coffee, or the way he wouldn't look at me, would avoid my gaze, when he was full of desire he seemed embarrassed to be looked in the eyes, and let me tell you, pardon me for speaking like this about someone who is dead, I know very well there are things you don't say about the dead, but timid as that man was, he could love with a passion that held not only his but mine as well, my passion was mixed into his even though my body wasn't, keen as I was to make me his, to surrender myself, to let myself be possessed, I'd get into bed, close my eyes, that's all I'd have to do, wait patiently, eyes closed, I would sense his footsteps around the bed, and the truth is I don't know how I could hear it, he would move around me so delicately that my heart seemed to beat louder than his footsteps, he would caress my head and I would stop being me, I would turn into anything, a defenseless animal, frightened, I never lost that fright, and I think that's what love is, a kind of fright, and when you lose that fright it means love is over, and the fear is logical, it's that when you're in love you're facing someone who is stronger than you are, someone you allow to be stronger, someone you give your courage to as a gift, someone who could do whatever he wanted to with you, turn you to dust if he wished, I liked the fright I felt when my body stopped being my own, and this afternoon I could recall it, I saw him just as he was in the photograph, smiling, his torso naked, and it was just as if the photo had come to life and he had dropped the mango stick to come closer, to tell me, without looking me straight in the eyes, that he loved me, pardon me, don't blame me if I tell you what I'm going to tell you, I got into bed, closed my eyes, I surrendered myself there in the bedroom where all you could hear was a rainfall that I knew wasn't rain but just wind on this strange, strange day, I surrendered myself, I mean, I waited for him, the fright gripped my stomach, I was going to be his again, not just going to be his but needed to be his, I had been waiting for so many years for the moment when he would lie down on me again, without talking, without letting me talk, without letting me say what couldn't fit into my fright at all, he always left me with the desire to tell him everything I felt, and now I shouldn't talk, out of respect, my husband was dead and I should respect him, and how brave I had to be to keep quiet, not to let any words betray me, and I spoke, I said everything I had ever wanted to tell him in all the years of silence, I said whatever I wanted to, and my hands gripped his back tight, I didn't open my eyes, I knew I wouldn't find anyone, and I didn't need to open them, I could see better at that instant with my eyes closed, I can't tell you the rest, I don't know what you are going to think of me, if you think I'm shameless, I still haven't told the worst part yet.

Berta stands up, goes back to the window. There's nobody there, she announces, and anyone could see she's saying it to hide her embarrassment. Mercedes is drinking from her long empty glass, she throws her head back, tilts up the glass so that the one drop of linden tea still in it will reach her lips. Though she is not crying, Irene dries her eyes, and you'd have to know her to understand this is a gesture she often repeats, drying her dry eyes. The worst part is that I stayed in bed with a happiness that I thought I had lost forever, I got up after a long time, with a strong smell of saliva on my neck, on my face, I looked at myself in the mirror, I had the marks of his lips on my neck, I thought my words (which I had spoken so desperately, as if I were expecting him to quiet me with his hand at any moment) were still echoing around the bedroom, they really weren't my words, of course, just the odious echo of that wind that's going to make idiots of us all. And when she went back to sit on the bed, she again picked up the photo of the shirtless man, the gorgeous man who was smiling and carrying a stick for knocking down mangos. She turned over the photo. There was the dedication: FOR MY MOTHER, A MEMENTO OF HER SON. Irene stands up, looks like she's about to run away. Don't you understand? It wasn't Emilio. It was Lucio.

The evening lights went out too soon. Still early, Marta closed her eyes. It didn't matter if she kept them open or closed: her eyes lived by the light of day. When night came it came once and for all, until the new sun rose, if there was going to be a new sun. She felt weary. The effort it took her body to make up for her eyes wore her out tremendously, and at the moment when the last light of the evening (and today the last light of the evening was a baneful little light at midday) shrouded the house, the garden, the Island, so absolutely, tiredness overcame her. A pointless tiredness because it didn't lead to sleep. And since today the evening lights went out too soon, Marta entered the house as if she were entering nowhere. Even the whirling wind went out when she entered the house, and it was emptiness, a supernatural absence; she felt afraid; maybe that was why she began touching the furniture, the walls, the decorations, searching for some link to the world so she wouldn't feel she was alone in a universe without people and without things. She lay down. She didn't lie down. She thought she was sleeping. Her dreams, of a reddish, almost black color, were no more than that, a color.

A deafening crash awakes her. She doesn't know it's a deafening crash from real life. (If only it isn't.) She gets up. She doesn't get up. She doesn't know if she's walking forward through the perpetual darkness with her hand raised to defend herself from the wickedness of the walls. She reaches the living room. She supposes it's the living room: she has bumped into a rocking chair, and the only rocking chair is in the living room. The door, where is the door? She feels along the walls, finds the switch, turns on the light, the darkness persists. Someone's outside the door. She hears a voice, a groan. At last she finds the latch. The door opens. Marta turns her head in every direction as if her eyes could possibly light up all of a sudden. The wind is so strong it obliges her to grip the doorjamb tight. It is raining, undoubtedly, a torrential downpour: the wind brings the sound and smell of a torrential downpour. The rafts. She recalls the beggars and the rafts. She recalls her mother. She has the impression that something has fallen at her feet. She touches the floor with her two hands. She feels that her hands are wet, a warm, thick liquid. If this is a dream, Lord, it is the most detailed, the most real dream, despite the reddish, almost black color. She is calling, Mercedes, Mercedes.

The light shines into the corners, the benches where at times you'd think there are figures sitting, figures that run from the galleries toward the Island. It's always like this, here you think you see things you don't see, things that aren't possible, so Helena wasn't so troubled when she saw, from the door of her house, a white figure walking through the trees, that often happens, even Chavito's statues give the impression of movement many nights. If it had just been the white figure, Helena would be calm, absorbed in the accounts. It so happens that what came next was indeed out of the ordinary and has to be cleared up as soon as possible. When Helena went out to make sure that the white figure was nothing more than a hallucination, she found the breasts of the Venus de Milo stained with blood. And that's not a matter of a game or a hallucination. Blood, real blood, fresh blood, a bloodstain in the form of a hand on the breasts of the Venus de Milo. She goes outside, shining the flashlight into the corners, into the dark spots left by the sorry ceiling lamps, shining it onto benches, flower beds, trees. She discovers nothing. It's extremely difficult with this October night, this lowering reddish sky, with this devil of a wind. And Helena reaches the Apollo Belvedere and inspects it carefully, as she also inspects the wooden screen, and she notices that there is someone on the other side, in the courtyard. Who's there? she asks with her usual severity. Without waiting for an answer, without fear, sure of herself, she goes around, reaches the courtyard. She discovers Merengue, who is cleaning his pastry cart. You? What are you doing up at this hour? The black man smiles, greets her, bows in comic reverence and doesn't answer her. What a night this is, the black man says, still smiling. Helena watches him for an instant. She doesn't answer his greeting, nor his smile. She shines her light on the Victory of Samothrace from top to bottom, and then shines it on the cart and on Merengue. There's someone in the Island. There's always someone in the Island, the black man replies. I mean, a stranger, a wounded man. Merengue lets his rag fall into the bucket of dirty water.

If Helena says there's a wounded man . . . Without a doubt Helena is the best manager the Island has ever had or could ever have. Helena knows it better than anyone. Helena knows better than anyone what has to be known about the Island. At any rate, everything about its *reality.* Because, as for all the rest . . . She boasts of knowing perfectly the path she's walking on. I always keep my eyes to the ground, she lies. Besides, she insists, to bother her brother Rolo a little, if you walk around with fantasies you'll bump into the trees.

Irene tells that when Helena first arrived in the Island one January morning, after her conversation with Godfather and after taking possession of her house (the first on the right, between the courtyard and Casta Diva's), Helena went out to reconnoiter the Island, both This Side and The Beyond, though at that time they weren't known by those names. Back then there were as many trees as there are now, and the cobblestone paths had been opened up, and the fountain hadn't dried up yet. The statues, however, weren't there (Chavito was just a little boy and still hadn't gone into making sculptures). For a long time people all over the area had been talking about the mysteries of the Island. It was said that many people had gotten lost in it, never to reappear. Irene tells that when she saw Helena ready for her first reconnaissance she felt obliged to call her and put her on guard, to let her know how many dangers lay in wait, *sotto voce,* of course. Godfather was alive, and that ill-tempered Spaniard couldn't stand to hear absurd attacks on the reputation of his property without boiling over in anger. In a very low voice, but very clearly, she told the story of Angelina, of Cirilo, the young flute player in the Military Band at the Columbia base who lived where Mercedes and Marta are today, and who composed the most despondent music in the world and played it with tears in his eyes and you never knew why. The poor flute player, dirty and sad, went deep into the Island one morning playing one of his most anguished melodies and he was never seen again. Irene explained to Helena that some afternoons, especially on rainy days, you can hear, though no one has ever been able to determine where it comes from, the heartrending music of Cirilo's flute. Irene also told her of a similar fate met by little Eduviges, a six-year-old girl with strange visions. The oddest little girl, if you only knew, she didn't seem meant for this world of ours, that is, for this Island where God and the devil have equal sway, the girl announced one morning that she was leaving because she wasn't ready to bear what would necessarily ensue, one way or another (what could she have been talking about?), the neighbors thought it was all a game, and little six-year-old Eduviges with the strange visions kissed her doll and got lost, over there, somewhere around the fountain that hadn't dried up yet in those years, and what do you think about Laria, that dark, ugly woman who was deemed a saint and who went from house to house touching the foreheads of everyone she could reach, to cleanse them of their sins, she said? well, that Laria was burned one night (what a night, heavens me, I remember it like it was yesterday!) at the stake and nobody knows who set it on fire, she cried out that the devil had tied her there, we couldn't do a thing, the bonfire was immense and for all the buckets of water and all our running back and forth, poor Laria was reduced to a little pile of dust that the wind swept away, just imagine, here the wind doesn't even respect the ashes of a saint like Laria, and we've written the Pope in vain, seeing about canonizing her, Saint Laria, virgin and martyr, because she was both, no discussion, with all the blessings she gave, poor thing, and the fact is that Laria still wanders around out there touching our foreheads, since there are days when you can hear her footsteps and feel an invisible hand (look, I'm getting goosebumps) on our foreheads, I swear, and I can tell you the story of Rascol Nico, the butcher who killed an old lady with an ax and purged his sins here, and I can tell you about Pinitos, he was seven years old and said the most outrageous things, for example, that he had seen a stranger who was crying because he had no shadow, it's true, he had seen it himself, in a clearing left in the trees, the man would stand in full sunlight and it was like there was no point in him standing there, nothing, not a shadow testified he was ever there, the man cried and he showed you a bag from which a sound of metal coins escaped, he also said that he had seen a young couple named Pablo and Francisca, beautiful and once in love, who were swept around by a gale of a wind that wouldn't leave them in peace and banged them into the trees of the Island, which as you know are large and many, the wind was full of howls, Pinitos would say this with eyes that looked like two stones and then he'd stand there with his mouth open, as if he couldn't believe such a story himself, and Francisca recounted amid sobs and tears that while they were reading together an irresistible force had emerged from their book that compelled them to kiss each other and to caress each other and to surrender themselves to each other, to sin, as she put it, swept around by the wind that wouldn't leave her in peace and that banged her against the tree trunks, the gale turns out to be their punishment for letting themselves be carried away by the force of a book so strong it had compelled them to kiss each other, one afternoon Pinitos came out of the Island more perplexed than usual, he told the story that a man named Abram had brought his son to The Beyond, near the river, and that the man named Abram had compelled his son to kneel down while he talked with his eyes turned upward; the youngster, hardly more than a little boy, laughed and said, My father, Abram, don't be afraid, for God is merciful, and then and there the man, who was enormous and had a dreadful face, had cut off his son's head, and the boy's head rolled to Pinitos's feet and he saw how the eyes of the bodiless head were still blinking and the lips were smiling and it still had something that seemed like a voice, though it didn't sound like other voices, a voice with no resonance, a voice that no one would call a voice, and it repeated two or three times God is merciful, until the mouth fell still with the smile frozen on it and the eyes no longer blinked, then the huge father, the man named Abram, cut off his own head saying God is a royal son of a bitch, and his head flew off like a baseball and landed who-knows-where, Pinitos had lots of stories that entertained you, though it's good to recognize that they scared us, one afternoon the mother of Pinitos came to talk with Godfather, the mother of Pinitos was the best lacemaker in Marianao, a woman so small that you'd talk with her without seeing her, it was like talking to a pair of shoes, she was so worried that she came to beg Godfather not to let Pinitos wander around the Island anymore, the boy had gotten home very late the night before saying that he had met two men who were not two men but a single man in two different ways, a certain Doctor Ecks and Mister Jay, that he had seen how a warmly dressed woman, in a hat and muff, had thrown herself in front of a train (something that is absolutely impossible in the Island, let it be said in passing, because, where are the tracks that a train can glide along here?), that he had seen a gondola go by full of women in heavy makeup, dressed up like for a carnival, who surrounded, kissed, and fondled a man with a white face and wig, and many other things that she couldn't remember and that had her deeply worried about the future of her good son, who aside from his bad habit of making up stories was proving to be an excellent child who could already multiply and read fluently, without mistakes, Dulce María Borrero's easy poems in his fourth-grade reader, and Godfather made a promise, and the pair of shoes that were the best lacemaker in Marianao, the mother of Pinitos, went away with her fears allayed, having fulfilled her motherly duties, except Pinitos kept on visiting the Island behind her back, we found this out later when it was already too late, I met him one morning with a bag, or rather a pillow slip, in which he was carrying, he showed me, several shirts, a canteen filled with water, a piece of chocolate, some olives wrapped in paper, six Maria cookies, a little hand mirror, and a book of the History of Cuba, he explained that he was going on a crusade to the Holy Land, I riposted that crusades were for men like Peter the Hermit and Richard the Lion-Hearted, but he smiled before clarifying for me that he was going precisely on a children's crusade, that there were already almost thirty thousand children ready to retake the lands usurped by the infidels for Christianity, that they would reach the sea and it would part to let them through by a miracle of God, because God protects those who love Him, he begged me to keep quiet because if his mother found out about his decision she would tie him to the foot of his bed, I can say without fear of being mistaken that I was the last person to see Pinitos, I saw him enter next to the Laocoön heading toward the Discus Thrower, it was an afternoon when a strange breeze was blowing through this land of dust and motionless trees, the Island swallowed him up, as his mother screamed afterward, so small it looked like a pair of shoes were screaming, and I can say the Island swallowed him because the plants closed up around him with a certain relish, a certain gluttony, I don't know how long ago that happened, not even his mother is still alive to clear up the date for us, Pinitos was crazy of course, all the stories he told were nothing but a pack of lies, and if it was all a lie, why did we never see him again?

These few stories are all that Irene told (among the many stories she could have told) before Helena went on her first reconnaissance of the Island. Helena did not so much as smile. Irene doesn't remember if she said thank you. She saw her enter into the thicket only to reappear an hour or two later with a ripe soursop fruit and an exact idea of what she would have to do with the woods to make them as hygienic and habitable as possible. You would have made an excellent captain of a Phoenician boat, Helena, said her brother Rolo.

Helena looks out of place in her pink satin robe, which, though old, still lends her a certain elegance. And the elegance must have to do with the wide sleeves encrusted with bunches of flowers, and the ample embroidered collar that looks like that of a queen, like the ones that appear in story book illustrations. She looks out of place, decked out like that, entering the Island through one of its stone paths, carrying a flashlight with a short beam of sickly yellow light that sickens Irene's trumpet vines and jasmines, murrayas, crotons, heliotropes, and creepers. The plants aren't the same in the nervous glare of the flashlight. They've lost the varied tones of green Irene boasts about. The plants look yellow, almost white, like fake plants, paper plants, when the sluggish glare of the flashlight passes clumsily across them. At times the light stops to make its way through some opening in the foliage. Other times it goes straight for one of the stones that form the path. For a few moments it climbs (and the light is all the poorer when it climbs) and runs across a tree trunk, tries to search among the branches where it seems the devil's dwelling tonight. Then it climbs back down and looks soft, slow, almost motionless, faraway as can be, and then it isn't light anymore but an imitation of light, a sort of mist that, instead of making things visible, erases them, hides them, or makes them more spectral. There are moments when Helena stands motionless next to the light, and closes her eyes, as if by closing her eyes she could hear better. Except that tonight, with all this wind, the Island is filled with a thousand different sounds. At times, footsteps, people fleeing, screams, shouts, songs. At times, something like a choppy river sweeping away stones. Helena knows that the thousand different sounds are of the Island: no need to worry about them. That is why she opens her eyes and keeps walking forward, sure of herself, along the stones on one of the paths of the Island. And when a light opens up between the Discus Thrower and the Laocoön, Helena isn't surprised because she knows without a doubt that it's Merengue's flashlight, and she can know that because the light moves the way Merengue himself moves, jerkily, falling to one side and then to the other, since Merengue always walks along pulling his cart, even when he doesn't have it with him. Helena looks into every corner with a meticulousness for which eyes are not enough. The devil is on the loose and is mixing everything up. Everything is familiar and unfamiliar. There's something here that isn't true, and Helena knows it.

★ ★ ★

My hearing is more reliable than my sight. He is sitting in the little rocker. Not rocking. Nor fanning himself. Trying to listen. After the footsteps receded and he found the bloody stain, silence ensued, that is, the beating of the gusty wind that is silence tonight. And he remained calm, and nodded off thinking that perhaps the blood was that of some wounded animal, a cat, a dog, one of those vagrant dogs that wander through the Island. And in fact he thought he heard barking, and then, later on, a kind of howling over there by the old carpentry shop. Only now, remembering the howl, he isn't sure what it was, it might have been someone crying for help. He smiles. How am I going to confuse a cry for help with a dog's howling? He shakes his head, still smiling. And what if the cry was no more than the wind among the branches? And how am I going to confuse a cry for help or a dog's howling with the beating of wind among the branches? He tries to listen. *My hearing is more reliable than my sight.* Nothing out of the ordinary occurs: the wind, the trees, nothing more. One night of wind shouldn't be anything out of the ordinary. A body falls near the house. Probably a dry frond from a palm tree. The blow is followed by a brief silence; then, again the sounds of footsteps. Immediately after, the sound of pieces of cloth flapping in the wind, which must not be pieces of cloth but the close-set branches of the poplars, the close-set branches of the laurels, someone is weeping, I'm sure: someone is weeping, a timid wail, a wail afraid to be heard, that is, a real wail, so silent it is scarcely a wail, there to the right, precisely on the opposite side of where the body or the palm frond fell, they say that bamboo weeps when wind blows through it, willows must weep too, they must call them weeping willows for some reason, there aren't any weeping willows in the Island, neither in The Beyond nor in This Side, the footsteps seem to circle the room, I'm trying to listen, *my hearing is more reliable than my sight,* they're the footsteps of someone with the strength of youth, no doubt about it, full of vigor, only extreme vigor and youth can induce such soft, swift, rapid, almost fleeting footsteps, whoever is walking around is doing it leaning against the wall of my room, the sound of their hand rubbing against the outer surface of the wall is almost imperceptible, my hearing is acute, from the height at which the hand is sliding along I can deduce that it's someone nearly six feet tall (man, woman, or devil), I know you're tall and young, *I know enough,* the racket of broken glass stops the sound of footsteps, I'm going to turn around to look toward the sideboard, a spasm in my back prevents me, for a few seconds only the wind seems to be alive in the Island, I stand up (with such difficulty, every day with greater difficulty) and stop the rocker: I don't like it to rock by itself, superstition, I don't know what to do and carefully place the fan on the bed, the odious face of the cat on the fan looks at me and smiles mockingly, I turn the fan over so you'll disappear, *miserable cat,* on top of the dresser all the glasses, jars, cups are intact, intact, nothing has broken inside the room, I decide to step out, confront whoever it is, I'm thinking I don't need the toy pistol anymore, at my age even fear should disappear, no? I look for the keys that I'm holding in my hands, and when I find them I'm upset because I was looking for the keys while holding them in my hands, I let them fall in my jacket pocket, the sound the keys make when they fall in my jacket pocket is similar to that of the glass that may have broken outside, so couldn't it have been the keys? it's pretty dark out there, there are just two lightbulbs, the one by the door and the one in back, weak lightbulbs, so I light an oil lamp, with that I'll see you, whoever you are, man, woman, or devil, or all three, because in the Island all sorts of freaks are possible, I am determined, I'm going to open the door, and if I'm so determined, why am I standing here motionless in the middle of the bedroom pretending to look for something I haven't lost, and what if it's the sailor? *the young sailor, what if it's him, dear God, what if?* he'll come whether I want him to or not, he'll come. Professor Kingston is in the middle of the bedroom with the oil lamp raised almost to the level of his eyes. At this moment the footsteps begin to be heard on the rooftop. And loud laughter. No, not loud laughter but the banging of some window that has come open. A window has come open and is banging and banging and it sounds like laughter. And it happens that the footsteps are breaking the tiles. Once again, the sound of pieces of cloth flapping in the wind. Loud laughter, or the sound of an open window slamming shut, approaches, recedes, approaches, recedes, and a sound of murmuring water, now, right now, like when the river crests on very rainy days, I even look down at the bottom of the door as if I expect to see water coming through there, something that only happened once, many years ago, during the hurricane of '44, a hooting bird passes several times above the house, I cross myself, voices, voices, a long whistle, I walk toward the door, the hooting returns, goes away again, I don't know if the whistling comes from the Island or my own ears, sometimes I hear the same whistling, it doesn't come from anywhere but from me myself, from within me, and the voices, what they say is *go, go, go,* or *no, no, no, I don't know,* and the whistling, fortunately, stops all at once, and a torrential downpour, like thousands, millions of stones hitting the roof, wipes out the sound of footsteps on the tiles, then there's the distant sound of bells tolling, and a song, a lovely voice rising above the hubbub of this night in the Island, and I reach the door, it's been difficult for me to reach the door, and I say I'm going to open it and I don't open it, and I open it, outside, The Beyond with the trees stirred by the wind, *'Tis the wind and nothing more,* it isn't raining, the river hasn't risen, no one is there, nor can I hear the bells tolling nor the lovely voice, what lovely voice was I going to hear? who would even think of singing on a night like this? I raise the oil lamp, only the pool of blood remains there, in front of my door.

She closes her eyes and thinks I'm tired I'm tired I'm tired, tries to imagine a landscape, a beach with coconut palms, translucid blue waters, a splendid, warm day, endless skies, not a cloud in it, or a few clouds far away, a sailing ship, no, not a sailing ship, but a lovely red transatlantic liner, or not that either, the horizon, just the horizon that doesn't seem unreachable, she's on the sand watching the horizon, she is naked, playing with the sand, building little piles of sand on her thighs, she has the sensation that her body exists, well, that's not exactly it, the sensation cannot be expressed very clearly, it might perhaps be better explained by saying that each and every part of her body has acquired life, she feels with every part of her body, or not that either, there's no way to say it, and she enters the water, the temperature is delicious. And all of a sudden it isn't a landscape, but rather a place she's never seen before or rather, yes, maybe she has seen it, a garden, an abundance of trees and of branches falling from up high though you can't say for sure what trees they're falling from, and the garden isn't a garden under the open sky, no, it's more like a spacious enclosure with a roof so distant it can't be seen, the sky has disappeared, in its place is a deep darkness from which blue and red lights escape diagonally, these aren't, shouldn't be, stars, in one corner there's a grave and a bouquet of irises sitting on it, and she doesn't approach it, all of a sudden, without her moving, she's standing by the grave and she discovers that the irises are made of paper, smelling of dust, rubbish, pieces of time-dampened cloth, the garden does not smell like a garden, she goes to the trees, that is, she goes nowhere, the trees appear there next to her, and they are pieces of cloth, enormous painted canvases, hardened, yellowed paintings, and when she touches the trees, in other words, the cloth, in other words, the trees painted on the canvases, a powerful light shines on her and she sees no more, her body, in this light, becomes transparent, silence gives way to music that is too loud, deafening, and nonetheless above the music she can hear applause, applause, applause. Casta Diva opens her eyes.

The dense darkness of the bedroom. She hears a laugh, must be Tatina. She also hears the wind of this October night. The window above the conjugal bed (the only window in the room) seems like it's being pushed in from outside, like it's going to open at any moment. Casta Diva sits up in bed. She can barely see her surroundings, yet she doesn't need to: she could walk around the room with her eyes closed. She knows, for example, that the mirror is in front of her. Large, rectangular, in a blackened mahogany frame, with beveled glass, occupying the bare brick wall that faces the door. There's the mirror, reproducing her with the clumsiness the lack of light lends it. She hates the mirror. Hates this and all mirrors. A mirror is a despicable thing, not so much because it inverts reality as because it multiplies it, as if reality weren't disagreeable enough without having to be multiplied. She doesn't see it. No matter: the mirror is there, in front of her. She sleeps on the left side of the bed, and what she has facing her is the large mirror. Many nights, when the moon is out and it is hot and the window may stay open, Casta Diva sleeps in front of the mirror, which is like sleeping in front of herself. She hates the mirror and she hates that image. (Within a few pages, this mirror will be the protagonist of a strange event.) She also hates the reproduction of Titian's *Last Supper,* stained by the dampness from the wall. She hates her bedroom set, so cheap, of poor wood, bought on installment at Orbay and Cerrato's, and she hates the easy chair, upholstered in gold damask turned black by years and years of sweat, and she hates Tatina's bed, which is a hospital cot with metallic rungs painted white. The only thing she loves in her room is the walnut secretary desk inlaid with marquetry. That's because the secretary is locked up with a key she guards jealously, and in it are her secrets, *her soul,* as she says, that which she truly is. She rises, puts on the house robe she had left draped over the little dressing table stool, and puts the satin slippers on her feet. She goes to Tatina's bed. The girl is a dark shadow among the white sheets. She laughs. Tatina laughs. Casta Diva hears the laughter, and also hates it, and she immediately reproaches herself, feels guilty. She lights the lamp on the nightstand (also metal, also hospital-like). She instinctively looks at her husband when the light turns the room into a real room. He sleeps, seemingly calm, nothing perturbs his blessed sleep. Then she looks at Tatina, who is looking at her and smiling. Her daughter's face is large, deformed, and has little in common with the skinniness of the rest of her body. Her chestnut hair spreads greasily over her pillow, sprouting from just above her eyebrows; Tatina scarcely has a forehead. Her eyes are small and restless, full of life. Tatina's eyes sometimes terrify Casta Diva; they are eyes with an intense gaze that seems to penetrate to the truth of things. Casta Diva trembles when she sees her daughter's eyes, which is the reason she rarely looks at them. Her nose is lovely, in that she took after her, the mother, a small and well-formed nose that in the end also bothers her, because that perfect little nose sits between two chubby jowls blackened by poorly treated acne, and above a gigantic mouth with powerful, widely spaced and dirty teeth and inflamed gums, a mouth disfigured by lack of words and excess of laughter. Her body barely exists. After the head, it's her poor chest, then the rest of her body, poorer still. Without looking at her daughter, Casta Diva lifts the sheet, feels the diaper. You wet yourself again, little bastard, she says, trying to make the phrase sound sweet, without total success. She completely uncovers her now and takes off the diaper. The dry, sickly darkness of her daughter's sex produces a repulsion in her that, rather than diminishing, increases with the years. She dries her off with a towel that always hangs from one of the bars of the nightstand, spreads cream between her thighs so the skin won't get irritated, and puts on a clean diaper. Now go to sleep, child, your poor suffering mother's not up to playing games. And she turns off the light. And goes to the bathroom. On the toilet (which she cleans and cleans and cleans, since her mother would always say that the cleanliness of a house begins with the toilet) there are a few yellow drops. Chacho is never careful, for all that I tell him, and tell him again, and shout at him a hundred times a day not to pee outside the toilet, fuck it, try and aim. She wipes up the drops with a bit of toilet paper. She lifts her house robe, lowers her panties, sits. She closes her eyes while she urinates, concentrating on the pleasure of urination, while again she sees a garden that isn't a garden, among the painted backdrops that smell of dust, of rubbish, of old, damp cloth. Once more the lights are on her; once more, applause. The music. *O rimembranza.* Applause, applause. Pursued by the light, she walks to the center of that place that gives the impression of having no limits. *A, perchè, perchè, la mia constanza.* Beyond, emptiness, dark zone, the abyss from which the ovation comes, crystal clear. She has opened her eyes, finished urinating, the last drops slip out slowly, and there is even, since she stands up without drying herself, a drop or two that roll down her thighs. *Son io.* She dries off, pulls up her panties. All of a sudden her gaze bumps into the medicine cabinet mirror. There you are again, damnation. Little as she wants to, she can't help looking at herself. I was a beautiful woman, my skin was like bisque, my black and abundant hair fell in natural waves across my shoulders, and my eyes were nothing like my daughter's, you could see my all in them, in my great, clear eyes, and my perfect nose (it still is perfect), and my short, precise lips that concealed or revealed (at my command) my teeth, which were pearls, *cojones,* they were pearls, no one should doubt it: I was a tall, elegant, beautiful woman, not a heavy-set woman (I am so glad), I kept (and still keep) my body at its ideal weight, and how gracefully I could (can) move, I was (am) made for success, *Deh! non volerli vittime del mio fatale errore,* and now . . . what kind of night is this, when it looks like the world is coming to an end with this rainstorm and it's nothing but a threat because the rainstorm doesn't get it over with and end the lousy miserable world? Casta Diva smiles at herself in the mirror and then sticks out her tongue. Listen, old lady, you've got nothing upstairs but cobwebs now, you're in worse shape than a whore during Lent. She leaves the bathroom, goes to the living room. Doesn't know why she's going to the living room. Coughs and tries to clear her throat. Drinks water from the faucet of the kitchen sink and then spits into the sink. *Sediziose voci, voci di guerra.* She raises slightly the curtain of the window that looks out on the Island and sees that in the Island the trees look like they're walking from all the wind, and she sees that the night is red, wine red, and she also sees lights in the Island, as if giant fireflies were wandering out there. Something terrible is going to happen, I just know it. And of course as soon as she gets this idea she thinks of Tingo and of course this frightens her, and she goes almost instinctively to Tingo's room, and she opens it without knocking, because she never knocks when she is going to enter Tingo's room (he's just a boy). She turns on the light. Her son's bed is rumpled but empty. Tingo, Tingo, boy, where have you gotten to? No one answers. Casta Diva returns to the bathroom, returns to the kitchen. Tingo isn't home. And at this time and in this weather, where could he be? Tingo, boy, come to your room. She shakes her husband by the shoulders. Chacho, Tingo isn't home and there's a stupendous downpour on the way. Chacho pretends he doesn't even hear. Casta Diva is furious, Fuck it, Chacho, you sleep and then you die. She turns, opens the door in the middle of the wardrobe and finds, in one of the drawers, her husband's flashlight. And, just as she is, in her house robe and satin slippers, without even putting a comb to her hair, no longer so black or so abundant, protected only by the flashlight, Casta Diva goes out into the Island.

From the Discus Thrower to the Diana, from the Diana to the David, nobody has come through here, otherwise it would be easy to discover them, real easy, because the impatiens and hibiscus wouldn't be standing, the mimosas would be stomped on, and the ferns wouldn't look the way they do, standing up straight, looks like the ferns aren't touched by the typhoon that's shaking the trees and the houses, that's shaking us all, I just think of Chavito and I get scared, I don't know why I'm thinking of Chavito now, I bump into a head made of plaster, heads, shoulders, arms, hands, torsos, feet appear at times, gigantic and deformed, if he wants to construct a figure out of all that it would be a sculpted monster, poor Chavito, poor boy, you're wasting your time, and I don't know why I feel sorry for you when we're all wasting our time, each in our own way, there's nothing here and nobody's come through, just me and my flashlight and, of course, this fear I have now of finding Chavito wounded, dead, I don't know, it's not even the first time it's occurred to me, on various occasions I'm selling pastries in the entrance to Worker's Maternity Hospital or in the building of the Anti-Blindness League, and it occurs to me that someone from the Island is going to appear to tell me that some misfortune has befallen my son, that he's wounded or dead, I don't know, now I'm really scared, a strange foreboding, the night's ugly, that's the truth, and I wish I could stop searching, just lock myself in my room, jump into bed, pull a sheet up over my head and forget about everything, start disappearing, like that, slowly, disappear so that when they come, when they force the bedroom door, they won't find a trace of me in the room, at most my clothes and the sheet, not me, because I disappeared, and that's all, I'd love to shout out that I'm scared, the light from this flashlight is yellowish, so everything I can see I see poorly and it seems unreal, could I be dreaming again? impossible, if I were dreaming things would seem real, that's the way it is, always, and besides, over there by the fountain I can see Helena's flashlight, and that proves that I'm awake, I'm not so crazy as to forget that she called me and said, There's a wounded man in the Island and we have to find him, let's go, Merengue, hurry up, grab your flashlight, that's what Helena told me, and I know nobody's been through here and fear is setting one of its traps for me: I say there's nobody wounded, it's Helena's imagination, and as soon as I say it I know I'm lying out of fear, if there's anything I'm sure of it's that if she says there's a wounded man in the Island, there's a wounded man in the Island, that woman, it's only right to recognize it, is infallible, now I have the David in front of me, and I dislike his tall, naked body (I come up to his knees), and that disproportionate hand holding a stone to kill I don't know who, I shine my light on it, I'm surprised (I'm always surprised) to see it still white, despite the rain and the night dew, could it be because that big sapodilla tree growing next to it protects it? it doesn't even have bird shit on it, the other statues are covered with shit, but this one isn't, and it's odd, besides, the Island is full of birds, once Chavito and I caught fourteen parakeets, fourteen, Chavito, I'm scared, no matter how much I talk and talk I'm scared and I don't like the looks of this arrogant giant, I'm thinking: maybe over by Miss Berta's classroom, over by the Martí memorial, I'll go find something, the light is going toward the door that opens onto The Beyond, a shadow, that's when I see a shadow, there, a figure approaching, stop, fuck, I shout at it, stop or I'll stab you to pieces, that's what I shout and it must be the fear: all I have is the flashlight, no knife to stab anyone to pieces.

He is stretched out on the ground. Intense pain pierces his arm. The bird flies over him and retreats, hooting in a way that sounds almost like loud laughter. You finally got what you wanted, he whispers. And wants to stand up, get to the house. The pain in his arm is so intense he stays there, still as can be, eyes closed.

It was the seventh night the bird had appeared. As if from out of nowhere. You'd think it was always there, hiding among the tree branches, waiting for him, allowing him a few minutes of ecstasy in the contemplation of Melissa's naked body, just to flap its wings and hoot, show itself, the big old buzzard, all pure lustrous white, with enormous eyes that threatened him as much as its beak and claws did. The seventh night it had come, as if it were looking just for him, and it would circle and land, threaten him again, fly, hoot, land, snort, close and open its enormous eyes. Tonight it attacked him with greater ferocity. Vido didn't try to defend himself, as he had the other nights, by rustling the branches of the evergreen oak, but instead he tore off a branch and brandished it furiously, get away, you shit of a bird, he said softly, he couldn't shout, Melissa might hear him and then it would all be ruined. Now he thinks it was one of those moments when the bird was still that he looked at the rooftop terrace and understood: Melissa wasn't there anymore, and he even remembers thinking then that anyone would have said that there was some complicity between Melissa and the bird, because as soon as its imposing figure appeared, spread-winged, she vanished into the darkness.

It was the eighth night he had climbed the tree. The first time he hadn't climbed up to look at Melissa, no, it was all because of the kite, by chance (by chance?). The kite was caught in the branches of the evergreen oak. Tingo-I-Don't-Get-It's kite, which Chacho had brought home from the Columbia base and which flew so well and looked so beautiful up there with its red, green, yellow brilliance, dissolving in the distance into some other color. The multicolored tail they had made from the bits of cloth that Casta Diva gave them transformed it into a small trembling black dot. The kite flew high, it climbed so well that at times they lost sight of it. In those days the afternoons were blue, the breezes transparent. The kite climbed higher when he, Vido, lifted it. Sebastián and Tingo didn't know how to. He showed them, from the superiority of his fifteen years. And he played out the string, and the kite stayed calm, as if set in a cloud. Later, when he passed the string to one of the others' hands, the kite began to tremble and lose altitude, became vulnerable to the wind, and finally fell. That afternoon it was Tingo's clumsiness that made it get entangled in the oak branches, and there it was stuck, in the crown of the tree. Tingo began to cry (typical of Tingo-I-Don't-Get-It). Sebastián stood there looking open-mouthed at the dead kite. Vido spat, as he always did when he didn't like something, and said bad words, the worst ones, which the other two heard reverently. *Cojones,* stop crying, he yelled at Tingo, don't be such a fag, and he started climbing the tree, the tall evergreen oak and its difficult trunk, with an agility that made him happy because he knew that down there they would be following him, eyes wide with admiration. He himself felt his every muscle tensed, his back vigorously straight, his hands and feet like four claws holding tight to the oak and dominating it. He climbed, climbed, climbed. The tree branches put up no opposition, rather they seemed to open up docilely. When he was at the top he looked around, enthused by the height. Seen from above, the Island was nothing like the Island. All the vegetation hid the stone paths, the galleries, the statues, and only the fountain with the Boy and the Goose could be glimpsed, as a dark stain that would have signified nothing to anyone who didn't know the Island.

There, on the ample rooftop terrace covered with dirt from the winds, in the formidable afternoon silence, you saw her naked for the first time. It was at the hour when the afternoon began to turn itself into the marvel that is the Island at the approach of nightfall. There was no one there but Melissa. You knew that the others were beginning to flee, to hide in their rooms, and that later they would come out again, that later they would converse, laugh, talk about the events of the day as if life were eternal. Now, at that moment, they would be hidden, feigning indifference, pretending not to care, seemingly preoccupied with putting the last touches on dinner, or skimming a page of the newspaper (the one that gave the details of the death of Pius XII), or seeing who would pitch for the Almendares, or simply closing their eyes so they could open them again when night was already an accomplished fact. The hour of dusk, and you were among the evergreen oak branches watching the only person unafraid of dusk, Melissa, naked, Melissa, standing on the terrace with the parrot on her hand, and that expression of hers that you can't tell if it's satisfaction or mocking or both at once. Protected by the oak, you could watch her all you wanted. You forgot about the kite. Forgot about the pair waiting for you down there, who at times yelled impatiently at you. You only had eyes, only had senses, for Melissa, naked.

The next afternoon, at the same hour, he climbed the oak again. She, naked, in the same exact place as the night before, had the parrot on her hand and the same ambiguous expression as always. You could almost have sworn that she hadn't moved from there, if it weren't for the detail of her hair, no longer loose as before but gathered and adorned with a flower. She was motionless, perhaps looking at the fleeting figures of a group of clouds that obscured the last sunlight. At times she seemed to move her lips imperceptibly, and she lifted the parrot to them as if she were directing to it the words that Vido couldn't tell if she had actually pronounced. Vido looked at her with a fixed gaze, trying not to miss any detail, so that his memory of it would be perfect in the comfort of the bathtub. And he realized the value Melissa had suddenly acquired.

The terrace grew dark. Vido couldn't tell whether Melissa had entered the house or whether she was lost behind the turn in the terrace, which, forming an angle, disappeared behind the casuarinas. The disappearance of Melissa had happened in a moment of distraction, in the one second he diverted his gaze because he felt a movement among the branches and a beating of wings, a strange snort. There was no one on the terrace, but the shadows were extending quickly, growing from the Island and propagating from there all over the world. Again the flapping of wings and the great white bird, as if from out of nowhere, the enormous eyes and the threatening beak and claws, flying bellicose above him.

From then on it reappeared whenever the shadows grew over the terrace, as soon as Melissa was no longer in sight, though Vido never could see where she had gone. Every night the bird returned, more aggressively. As soon as he saw it coming Vido would quickly climb back down the oak and run home, cutting through The Beyond, followed by the bird and its hooting, and when he came inside and went to his bath to think about Melissa, he would continue seeing the animal, the image of the animal interposed between him and the image of Melissa, and he would hear the hooting that would make Miss Berta, over in the living room, cross herself and cry *Ave Maria Purissima* and run to close the windows.

Now he is stretched out on the ground. He has been stretched out on the ground for a long time. He has seen night run through all the hues of darkness before reaching the shade of red it now has. Intense pain pierces his arm. The bird has flown away, or cannot be seen. In its place, its white shadow remains, like a ship's wake, the persistent sound of flapping, the echo of its hoots that sound like loud laughter. The bird has gone; the threat of it is still there. Vido stands up; not knowing how he can do it, with his good arm he holds and squeezes his other, aching arm, and walks toward the Island, crying.

On this page it is best to use the future tense, a generally inadvisable practice. It has already been written that Chacho had gotten back from Headquarters just past four in the afternoon, and that he was the first to notice the coming storm. It has been written, moreover, that Casta Diva, his wife, saw him later, absolutely motionless, watching the tops of the trees. The following day, after the events that will soon be narrated had taken place, Chacho will begin to talk less, and less, and less, until he decides to take to bed. No one will know what the problem is with Chacho (not even Chacho himself), whether an illness of the body or of the spirit (as a somewhat perplexed Doctor Pinto will suggest). Without fuss, without emphasis, without hope, he will refuse to return to Headquarters at the Columbia base (where, may it be said in passing, he has never had the talent to rise above the rank of radio operator in the Signal Corps, where his absence will not be noticed). Chacho will spend sixty-three days without talking. During that time, we will be able to see him obsessed with his rabbits and with Carlos Gardel. And, as it is best not to abuse this generally inadvisable tense, it is just and proper that we leave Chacho to his silence until such a time as he should reappear, as God wills it, in this narration.

A knock at the windowpane. A dry knock, like that of a pebble, followed by a short silence, only to knock again with greater force. The son of a bitch is going to break the window, Sebastián says. He recognizes the knock, so he leaves the book and the dictionary on the floor, goes to the window, and stealthily opens it, trying to make as little noise as possible. It is indeed Tingo. Sebastián doesn't ask, shows no curiosity, looks at the other with utter fearlessness because he knows that this attitude disconcerts Tingo. However, Tingo is far too disturbed to be disconcerted. He repeats a gesture with both hands, ordering him to come down urgently, it's a matter of real importance. I'm not up for silly games, Sebastián says without knowing whether Tingo has been able to hear him, he has said it with his lips, in barely a whisper, it's late and Helena might realize he's still awake. Without talking, the boy continues to perform his exaggerated gestures, and he displays something, a piece of paper, a letter, and points toward an inexact spot behind the building, down by the river perhaps. It's a motionless night of clouds that pass by almost touching the rooftops. Linea Street looks deserted, scarcely illuminated by the lights of the street lamps, lamps swinging half loose and at the mercy of the winds. The unsteady light makes the street meander, a sensation accentuated by the whirls of dust that the wind raises. The night, red and motionless, is enough to make you think no one will ever walk down Linea Street again. Sebastián stares at the dark, abandoned houses, and thinks they are mere façades, that nothing and no one could be behind them. At times you can hear shots fired, the sirens of police cars or ambulances. Nonetheless, who can be sure they are shots or sirens? At one point, the sound of footsteps. Tingo runs to hide around the building, at the corner of his house. He returns later, more nervous: there were footsteps, but no one passed by. The train station, dark as ever, has a special air of abandonment tonight: you'd swear no train would ever arrive there again. The pasture has also become a place that doesn't exist, though you can hear a horse galloping. And it's impossible to be sure it's a horse galloping, because Zambo doesn't let the horses run loose in the night air for anything in the world, much less on a night like this. What do you want? Tingo doesn't know what else to do but gesticulate and wave the paper, the letter, or whatever it is. Sebastián tries to make him understand that it's late, that if Helena realizes he's gone out . . . well, you know my mother. Tingo doesn't hear anddoesn't want to hear. So Sebastián moves away from the window, goes to the wardrobe and returns with a basket, onto one handle of which he has tied a rope. It's the basket they always use when they need to communicate after hours, for exceptional and secret cases. He tosses the basket to Tingo. The boy puts the paper, the letter, or whatever it is, inside. Sebastián pulls in the rope and retakes the basket. He goes back to his bed, to the light of his night lamp. He holds in his hands a crumpled, dirty postcard, with a few stains on it, that shows a half-naked young man with his body shot full of arrows; there is a foggy landscape behind him; above, angels rush to his aid. Behind, the printed letters read: SAINT SEBASTIAN, PEDRO ORRENTE, CATHEDRAL OF VALENCIA. Beneath, in careful calligraphy and black ink: *Lord, I'm coming, along a stream of arrows! Just one more and I shall fall asleep.*

Sebastián looks again at the black-and-white image of the martyr, and reads several times, attentively, the unsigned and undated sentence. The card gives off a strong smell of women's perfume. He decides to keep it in his desk drawer. From this he pulls paper and pencil, writes, Where did you find it? and throws the paper together with the pencil into the basket. He returns to the window. Tingo isn't there. From the street corner on the right, from the bookstore, the horse pasture, the train station, comes a sound of footsteps. This time someone's really there. A man appears on the corner, coming down Linea Street with slow but firm steps. Sebastián says to himself, Here's someone who's not in any rush, who's absolutely sure of the road he's taking. With great care Sebastián slowly closes the window. He leaves just a crack through which he can look out. The shadow of the approaching man sways together with the street lamps. It's a man dressed in white, or so it appears. He stops in front of the great iron gate. Looks into the courtyard. Sebastián can't calculate how long the man stands there looking into the courtyard. It seems to him that the man is carrying something on his back, some kind of duffel bag, which at some point he puts down. Searches in it. Takes out something that Sebastián can't make out and, then, holds it in his hand as if he were trying to weigh it. Shoulders the bag again. Starts to walk off, still looking at the courtyard. For a few seconds the man's pace slows down because of the fact that, for some mysterious reason, he can't take his eyes off the courtyard. At some point he seems to desist, he looks at his hand once more and at last lifts his eyes to the darkness that stretches before him: the road to Columbia is like the lion's mouth tonight. With his hand raised and the duffel bag across his back, he passes beneath Sebastián's window. He is a young and tall and proud sailor. There is something intimidating in his profile, something about his uniform or the way he walks or his whole figure, poorly illuminated by the bobbing street lamps, that makes you think he has come from far away, though he's obviously not in any rush but is absolutely certain that he's going down the only possible road.

On the same piece of paper Sebastián sent him, Tingo has written Please come down right away matter of life and death, in large and awkward letters. Sebastián goes to the bedroom door and opens it, taking precautions. All is dark, sunk in silence, my mother's gone to bed. He hastily takes off his pajamas and hastily puts on his overalls and the red checked shirt. Climbing down from the window is easy, less than a yard down an overhang in the old wall a piece of broken rock gives him a support from which he easily jumps to the grass. It better be something important, Sebastián says in the superior tone he always uses when he talks to Tingo. The boy brings his index finger to his lips in a gesture of desperation that Sebastián finds exaggerated, and takes him by the hand, forcefully, drawing him toward the corner of the building, where a walkway, torn up by the roots of so many trees, leads to The Beyond. Sebastián takes away his hand: the contact with Tingo's delicate hand makes him blush for reasons he cannot fathom. Tingo-I-Don't-Get-It goes in front, stepping stealthily, as if the gusting wind weren't enough to deaden the sound of their footsteps, as if the noise of the gusting wind weren't enough to eliminate any other sound, a whole battalion could march down this walkway tonight and not one person in the Island would ever notice.

In The Beyond, past the house of Professor Kingston, the dog cemetery, Chacho's banana trees, Merengue's pigpen, and the little grassy hill down which they sometimes sled on palm bark, almost at the riverbank, stands (or falls) the carpentry shop. They call it this out of habit, out of the custom of naming things for what they once were and not for what they are. Ah, the stubbornness of memory for fixing names! It's been years since the carpentry shop was a carpentry shop. Fourteen years at least. Or more. Since approximately forty-eight hours after Berardo, the father of Vido, was found on his carpenter's table with his mouth open, his eyes rolled back, and his pancreas torn up, as the coroner's report later revealed. It can be stated that from the moment they left him to rot under a hill of earth in his hometown of Alquízar, they had already forgotten not only the man who had caused so many disturbances lately, but everything that had ever in one way or another had to do with him (except for the boy, except for Vido, of course). It was easy to forget him: it proved necessary. To tell the truth, it had been quite a while since the carpentry shop had served as a carpentry shop, because Berardo, a courteous gentleman when he came to the Island, had lately left his wood, hammers, and saws for mulatta women, bottles of Bacardí and orgies that would end with an invariable and colossal brawl (the devil got into that man's body, no doubt about it). At his death, sudden and much desired (and may God forgive us), the carpentry shop was left unprotected, to the mercies of the Island's weather. And the Island's weather (this will be a secret for no one) is like the Island itself: deceptive, of phony gentleness. So it lifted the paint and cracked and rotted the walls, in the patient and merciless labor more proper to woodworms than to weather, but what is the Island's weather but a plague that gives the appearance of tropical paths, bright noondays, violet seas, coconut palms, and idyllic moonlit nights? There stands the carpentry shop (anybody can see it), old, vulnerable, still upright thanks to who-knows-what miracle, with a fragile roof and the absurd color of warped lumber.

Through the cracks in the beaten lumber escape lights that grow, weaken, flicker. Tingo and Sebastián come walking up the path that has mysteriously remained open through the Guinea grass. A little bit to the right, though in this darkness it can't be seen nor heard through this wind, runs the river. If tonight were a night like any other, you could even contemplate the wing of galleries that belong to Miss Berta, Irene, and Casta Diva, and the Hermes and the Venus could be seen, and perhaps even the bust of Greta Garbo, for the carpentry shop was built on a privileged spot. The night is an encircling wall. The Island isn't there, it has disappeared. At this moment only the carpentry shop exists, like a broken-down boat looming among the shadows. Tingo unknots the wire that holds the door closed. The door gives way with a creaking of wood and hinges paralyzed by rust.

We like it because it's scary, that's the truth, they say that here you can hear the music and the shouting from the parties, and many times you can see Berardo again, with his deformed face and a hammer in his hand, because Merengue told me that when you die you keep on being what you were in life, and we also like it because there's so much stuff. Look, old furniture, I mean really really old, clothes full of moths and years, and headless saints, childless madonnas, sad, looking despondently at the absence in their arms, and the stuffed peacock, remember? (it doesn't have any feathers in its tail now: we plucked them all when we were playing Indians and cowboys), and your papa's old gramophone, and the pieces of Godfather's ancient Ford, the army medals we found in a little wooden box inlaid with mother-of-pearl, and the blue silk kimono, and the slippers, remember the slippers? and the binoculars, and the doll with the needles stuck in its chest, and the Cuban flag that we laid across the carpenter's table, which is the only thing still in the carpentry shop (they've even stolen Berardo's nails from there), and the portraits of those people no one could identify, and I wonder, Did those people ever guess, when they were having their portraits taken, that years later they would be anonymous faces, incapable of extracting anything from another person, not a smile, not a memory, not a tear, nothing, nothing at all?

Two candles are lit. Each one stuck into a beer bottle for a candlestick. The candlelight leaves the walls sadly shaded. Shapes spread and vibrate in disorder. On the carpenter's table, wrapped in the Cuban flag, a man lies stretched out. Very young. Seems to be sleeping. His expression is calm; his breathing, regular. He's shoeless. His feet are large and covered with mud. Cracked, dry mud. He is wearing a cotton twill suit, dirty, and a shirt with no tie. The shirt is intensely red. Anyone could see that the red is on the shirt, not of the shirt (you can tell it's white and stained with blood). His hands, lying across the silk flag, are beautiful, delicate, despite the grime and the green stains on them. A few leaves of a tree of paradise are scattered over the flag. There is a wound on the boy's neck. Though it is small, a thin, unstoppable trickle of blood springs from the wound. His profile is not distorted by pain, rather you would think the contrary, this is the serene, content profile of a happy sleeper. You'd say he's smiling, even his very pallor seems strange given the great vitality that emanates from his body. On his forehead beads of sweat sparkle. His hair is dampened, slightly wavy, dark blond in color. Tingo takes one of the candles, holds it close to the boy's face and, with a handkerchief, cleans off the blood that flows from his neck wound. Timidly, Sebastián touches his hands and forehead. He has a fever. Since the flag is very large, they lift the silk that drags on the floor and wrap him up. The boy moves, says something impossible to understand. Then he really does smile, opens his eyes, and closes them again. He hugs the flag. This animation lasts for an instant. Then he returns to sleep, to motionlessness.

II

My Name Is Scheherazade

It's raining. Furiously. Since this tale is being written in Cuba, the rain is falling furiously. It would be another matter if this were being written anywhere else in the world. Here you won't find any scattered sprinkles (as an author might write in Spain), no endless Parisian drizzle. All you can describe here is a frenzied storm. In Cuba the Apocalypse comes as no surprise: it's always been an everyday occurrence. Which is why this chapter begins with a downpour that forebodes the end of time.

It's beautiful the way everything is disappearing, even the Island, turning into an impression, a mirage, I love the rain: it makes you feel outside of time and space, I love the rain, it takes me out of the monotony of one day after another, I'll close the bookstore, at this hour nobody will come to buy, much less with all this rain, a hard rain returns the true value to things, the house, for instance, it isn't the same when it rains, the downpour turns it into a place you want to stay, transforms it, makes it nicer, and I feel like reading or sleeping, or both things at once, yes, it would be great to be able to sleep while it's raining, and while it's raining and you're sleeping, to read, or not read, but have your dream be made of words, that kind of dream: the rain beats against the red shop window and the balcony railings where dense climbing vines dangle their flowery festoons beneath the poplar leaves trembling in the cool winds; you can hear the picaresque sparrows warbling in their chambers; I love this rain, same rain as ever, same rain as a hundred years ago, the rain Casal saw from the window of his house at Aguiar number 55, the same rain that comes back now to make you feel vague pains in your muscles and deep sorrows in your soul, the downpour awakens the smell of earth, the smell that, if it weren't for the downpour, you'd never notice, the persistent damp of it cools the house down, I love the way the downpour imprisons me, this is the only imprisonment, I suppose, that I could stand, I sit in the rocking chair with my feet up on the bed listening to the music of water on water and on the roof, I'm falling asleep, I think I can hear distant voices — let me close my eyes — rising from the infinite — I'm fading away and I know I'm not fading away — they're letting me in on strange delights, the Island transforms itself into rain, outside of this worrying world, it's raining, torrential, magnificent rain, I'll be in bliss as long as the downpour lasts.

I hate the rain, hate it because it closes me in, compels me to stay inside these four walls I abhor with all my heart, I suppose when I say "with all my heart" I mean I hate it more than I could hate anything else, the rain makes me feels imprisoned, forces me not to move, to wait here like a trapped rat, I feel cornered, I want the rain to stop, for me I wish the sun would always be roasting me, the sun, the fire, this Island is not an island, it's a blaze, a branch office of hell, the sun, yes, and every once in a while a few hours of darkness so as not to die from the glare, I don't even want to hear about rain, or about the smell of earth, of cemetery dirt, or the cool damp of it (which false poets ponder, the same guys who'd like to live in the mists of Scotland, the imbeciles that surround me), or the monotonous and terrifying sound of it, I'd rather be burning in the cauldrons of hell itself than in this Island, before I had to stand for this October rain that's going to end up bringing the roof down on me, the roof of the house is creaking, didn't I say it was going to creak! and now the leaks begin, the leaks, the leaks, one bucket here, one bucket there, the house fills up with buckets, and me here closed in, not even able to walk out into the Island, which is, you can't fool me, the Butthole of the World, I hate the rain as I hate myself, and if God thinks that's blasphemy let Him come, let Him come Himself with all His little angels and question me, not be afraid, just show up, I'm sure not going to let trumpets and fireworks frighten me, let Him come right now, appear this minute, He's going to learn a thing or two, I'm going to give Him a piece of my mind.

It's raining and I'm getting sad and that makes me happy, the rain is worth it if you're all alone, it's the best pretext for feeling nostalgic about something and for getting sad about not having it and for crying for no reason. And Lucio, who is lying naked on top of his bed, closes his eyes.

Lucio has closed his eyes. He sees a wooden house, on pillars, with a wide porch. The walls are white; not white (he can't see what color they are). The doors and windows are sealed with metallic cloth. Stairs rise to the porch. The floor is also wood. A rocking chair rocks by itself, perhaps an effect of the wind. Lucio enters the house. It's empty, there is hardly any furniture, just a few chairs and a table on which a lighted oil lamp sits. The rooms are also devoid of beds, dressers, mirrors. The only thing to see on the bedroom walls are photographs, austere men and women he supposes are dead because they are so austere, and because it is perfectly obvious that the photos are very old. In the last room, in one corner, a little girl, sitting on the floor, is crying. She is hiding her face in her hands. Lucio caresses her close-cropped head. He feels like crying, too, he doesn't know why, and since he feels like crying and doesn't know why, he goes to the window and opens it. The sea. Dawn begins to break. The sea is calm, grey. The sky, grey as well, is sketched with distant and motionless clouds. The girl stands up. Goes over to Lucio. When he feels her footsteps he turns and sees the girl with her head held down. Why are you crying? The girl doesn't reply. She stops next to him, looks too at the sea, takes Lucio's hand and caresses it. Why are you crying? He pinches her chin, lifts her little face to see her better. What's your name? Still crying, the little girl smiles, Lucio, she says, my name is Lucio.

Don't you think that the sound of a downpour is rare music? Three men in white tunics are playing instruments that sound like rain. It's a small bedroom painted red, with damask curtains and censers filled with burning incense. A smiling young woman, with ingenuous malice on her face, comes up and takes him by the hand. Lucio follows her, still hearing, very close by, the sound of the music that is the rain, that is the rain that is the music. A long corridor is full of natural plants: they have the odd virtue of seeming artificial. In a salon, various couples are kissing, caressing each other by order of an old woman in a wheelchair. She (the old woman) stares at Lucio. At last! she exclaims. The others separate, look at him. At last! they exclaim in chorus. Lucio approaches the old woman in the wheelchair. She (the old woman) touches his chest, his thighs, as if she were touching a handsome animal. You're hot, she says. The old woman is ugly, her dress is the same red color as the walls, she wears dark glasses. She does not smile. Lucio isn't ashamed to be naked, just strangely happy. With great ceremony they take him to another room where a cadaver is covered with a shroud. Who is it? Lucio asks. The sound persists of music that is rare rain. The young woman with the malicious face lifts the shroud and Lucio sees the cadaver, also naked, the very image of himself, identical. The live Lucio touches the hands of the dead Lucio and finds them rigid, cold. When did he die? When did I die? The old woman is wheeled in on her wheelchair by a strong, handsome black man. The old woman dries false tears. We're all alive, we're all dead, she exclaims in a choked voice. Does my mother know? Your mother died before you did. Lucio feels tremendous sorrow. He leans over the dead Lucio and kisses the closed, breathless lips. Could he be happy? He turns around, realizes no one is there, they have left him alone but he asks anyway, And why, if I'm dead, don't I know what death is? He is crying over the other one at the moment when they knock on the door. He hears the old woman's voice, Lucio, Lucio. They knock again. Irene shouts Lucio, Fortunato's here. Lucio opens his eyes in his own bedroom. Fuck his mother, how the hell could Fortunato get here in this deluge?

What are you doing here? Fortunato is soaking wet from head to foot. I have to talk with you. First you have to dry off, Irene says, and she hands him a towel. Dry off, Lucio orders him with the sense of superiority Fortunato always makes him feel. Dry off and change your clothes. Irene prudently closes the door so that Fortunato can change, I don't want you to catch a cold, young man. Fortunato is tawny, too tawny, practically mulatto despite his good hair and European features, and he is tall, cheerful, gentle, with an inexplicable look in his eyes, greenish with glints of yellow. His slightly thick, slightly livid lips are almost always smiling with a sweetness that contrasts with his body's strength. His hands are so large they seem timid. How did it ever occur to you to go out in this downpour? Fortunato keeps on smiling. No rain can stop me, he insists in a harsh voice that reveals, more than any other detail, that his father was black. I had to see you and I said to myself, No rain could ever beat me, and here I am. You're crazy, go ahead and change already. Look, even my underwear is sopping wet. Lucio hands him clean clothes without looking at him. Fortunato puts on Lucio's clothes, which are tight on him. Lucio takes off the robe he had put on to answer the door and falls back naked on the bed. What's this problem that's so important you had to leave your house in the rain? The other sits on the foot of the bed, not smiling now. Nothing, I wanted to see you. See me? just see me? Fortunato nods. Lucio breaks out laughing. Fuck, I think you must be a faggot.

Hear me, oh Lord, I'm lighting this candle before Your tortured image because I can hardly remember my own name, earlier, when it was raining, I lay down to remember things and of course I got sad and cried, and I shouted Stop raining, stop raining, I said I didn't want the memories, they disturb me, they just come to bother me, they're like a plate of cold unsalted farina, though I actually loved remembering things while it rained, lying in bed, before, when it rained, to keep from crying, I'd have to put a really loud and spicy Celia Cruz song on the record player, *Songo gave it to Borondongo, Borondongo gave it to Bernabé,* to keep the memories from harassing me, and I'd leave the bed and leave off crying and go to the kitchen to make up odd dishes, or I'd sew on the Singer that sounds like an oxcart, and talk with my son, shout, to keep the sound of falling water from getting into my head, and cook batches of sauce, wash the floor with perfume to cover up the smell of grass and damp earth, ah! today, oh Lord, look at me lighting this candle before Your tortured image to beg You to let a little ray of sunshine into my memories.

The rain today is for real, now it's really raining, full force, making good on the threat. And Merengue, who hasn't been able to go out with his cart and pastries, sits on the rocking chair with the broken wickerwork and smokes his cigar (there's nothing like smoking an H-Upmann on a rainy day like today). He would have liked to stay in bed, to sleep away the rainstorm, there's nothing like sleeping when it's raining, but he's not all that drowsy, and not used to spending so much time in bed. Besides, the rain, this rain, isn't a wonder to behold, far from it. Not an illusion, either. It's raining and it seems like it isn't, which is even worse. It would be a wonder if Chavito was lying on his cot and snoring like a saint, because Chavito did turn out to be a good sleeper, and I don't know who he took after to be so lazy, Nola and I never slept past six in the morning, either one of us. But Chavito now, he no more than puts his head down on the pillow . . . he'll close his eyes, really close them, with feeling, and he can stay there for eleven, twelve hours straight without moving, absent, and then open them with an expression on his face like he'd just lain down, he touches his belly and asks, Old man, isn't there anything to eat in here? And then in the afternoon he can still take a nap, no, this rain today is no wonder to behold. Last night Chavito didn't come home either. And was it last night that it started raining? Did they find the Wounded Boy in Berardo's carpentry shop last night? Well, time is an odd thing. You'd swear it's been months since Chavito came home; months since they found the poor boy almost bled to death and covered with the Cuban flag. And the wounded boy and the rain frighten Merengue. At times he feels the desperation of not knowing where his son might be in this deluge, he thinks about how many unused carpentry sheds there must be out there, how many flags, the possible number of wounded who must be in their death throes right now without any curious boys to discover them.

When it's raining it's better for Doña Juana to sleep. When it's raining is when Miss Berta most feels she is being observed, and there is no possible escape, no way to leave everything and run out into the street to forget that someone's gaze is obstructing her life. Now she is trying to see how the rain falls. It isn't easy: this rain (to repeat) is a torrential downpour, practically a hurricane, foreboding (to repeat) the Apocalypse. The Island has disappeared. There is no Island. She and the bedroom alone are left. Oh yes, and the hopelessness the gaze makes her feel. Even though it can't be seen, Miss Berta is trying to look through the window at how the rain makes the landscape disappear and imposes its presence. She doesn't even know what time it is nor does it really matter (in this book the time never really matters). She thinks she can see an old man with an umbrella walking with difficulty very near the Hermes of Praxiteles. That can't be, Miss Berta says to herself, and since she says, That can't be, the old man disappears.

Doña Juana is sleeping. The downpour makes her sleep better. Her white nightgown is whiter, the rosary and crucifix that belonged to Francisco Vicente Aguilera are more beneficent. By her side, a candlestick holds a lit candle. In the middle of the perfect sleep of her ninety years, Doña Juana wants to lift a hand and take the candlestick, perhaps to better illuminate the darker areas of her dream. (This is not yet known.) Miss Berta, who has entered to watch how her mother is sleeping, stops her hand and returns it to its place on her lap, to the position that seems to forebode how she will look when she sleeps her final sleep (if this isn't her final sleep already).

The Princess of Clèves. When it's raining, Mercedes transforms into the Princess of Clèves. She thinks her sister, right in front of her, is unaware that she's not sitting in the broken rocking chair, in the Island that is the Kingdom of Banality. No, she's not there. When it's raining (this is her secret) she gets to transport herself to the court of Henry II, and she stops being Mercedes (such a plain name) to become the Princess of Clèves (*née* Mademoiselle de Chartres). She is sitting at the foot of a window in the Pavilion of Coulommiers. It's raining outside. Not a violent, sweeping rain like this, but a drizzle that scarcely can veil (even throws into relief) the greenish yellows of the autumn landscape in the French countryside. For now, the Princess is finishing a task. When the rain lets up, she'll bundle up, put on her cape, and stroll through the garden where the Prince of Nemours lies in wait, madly in love, among the trees. God, what I wouldn't give to be a character in a novel!

She thinks I'm sleeping, she thinks I don't know her, I do know a thing or two, in short, what difference does it make whether she thinks she's the princess of wherever or Madame Bovary? I just want to dream, I also want to dream, and God hasn't conceded that privilege to me, when it started raining I had some slight hope, but I should go ahead and get rid of it now since it never turns out to be more than a hope, I thought: At last, it's happened before: a moment of vertigo, of nausea, as if instead of raining in the Island it were raining on the sea, when I was a little girl, when my eyes were still living, after the cemetery I lived by the sea, I'll never forget it, Mercedes was impressed by the water and the color of the waves and the foam and going in where gravity couldn't stop her, she said, I was never as impressed, for me the sea was always a sound more than anything else: an immense, deafening crash, could it be that I was already getting ready, without knowing it, for the blindness that came later? I enjoyed that deafening crash, it was nothing like any other sound I ever knew, an echo, a resonance that somehow held me, that I somehow participated in, nothing like that had ever happened to me (nor has it happened again), and when it rains, like today, I distantly recall that impression, and that must be why it makes me think of the sea, because on the high seas the sound of rain must be louder, I can't remember very well, it's been so many years since Uncle Leandro's house, no, it hasn't really been so many years, it's just that when you can't see . . . and today just as soon as I thought *high seas* I immediately imagined a ship, I think I can remember what ships are like, and I said Morocco, Sardinia, Cyprus, what difference does it make, rocky coastlines bathed by a sea the color of earth (so I imagine it), I'm in the prow, yes, just about to dream, the nausea is gone, it always goes away, I'm back in the usual darkness, this constant, dark, nearly black redness that I'm condemned to, there's one terrible punishment and it's being born on an island, there's a worse punishment, being blind on an island, and to top it all off, this lack of dreams! and if you have all these circumstances together there's no cure for it, you don't care whether it rains or clears up or whether it snows or whether railroad ties fall head on, whether it's spring or winter, you get sick of the senses of smell and feel and taste, you've gone blind on an island! as far as I'm concerned the sky can split itself open with rain, blind on an island, condemned to a rocking chair, which means that for me the rocking chair is the planet, it doesn't revolve around anything, though luckily it does move.

She has gone out naked onto the terrace. It's raining furiously. Melissa must feel like some force is compelling her to stretch out on the floor. And she does stretch out. From the expression on her face you could tell that she's experiencing a new sensuality. Wouldn't it be like thousands of hands caressing her? And when the sky opens up with lightning bolts, you'd say she was laughing and shouting with joy.

Don't play dumb, Vido, Melissa is out on the terrace and you know it. She doesn't care if it's pouring rain. She goes out like it's nothing: the rain obeys her. You know Melissa's out in the downpour, laughing, having so much fun, pleased that everyone else is hiding, hating, loving, dreaming, pretending not to dream, while she feels her body being caressed by thousands of hands. You, on the other hand, are all closed up in here. You can't go outside. The world is coming to an end with this rainstorm (whenever it rains they say the world is coming to an end) and they won't let you go outside, Aunt Berta insists you could catch pneumonia, don't go looking for headaches. I know (how could I help knowing) that you're thinking one case of pneumonia more or less won't make a bit of difference so long as you get to see her naked, her, Melissa, the only woman you've seen or desire to see naked. Melissa, with a body that cries out to be caressed. What do you care about the rain, Vido, what do you care! Listen to me, just take off your clothes and you go out too in the downpour. As bare as God brought you into this world. Just jump out the window like usual, nobody'll see you. There won't be any mud down there. There'll be lots of grass growing there, and linden and rosemary bushes and lots of other things to intervene between your feet and the earth. And the downpour will feel so good against your naked body! Don't you get how new it'll feel to sense the downpour on your skin? Your body will react in the best way; that is, as if you were already standing before her, with your mouth open, your eyes closed, and your prick standing straight out. Like that, naked, you'll walk past the Hermes of Praxiteles (which isn't a Praxiteles but a Chavito) and past the horrific bust of Greta Garbo. You'll also walk past the Venus de Milo (don't even look at it, it's made of clay). You'll round the building and get to the evergreen oak. Then you'll get a great surprise, because when you're about to climb it, you'll feel a hand reach out and stop you. The hand that lightly squeezes your shoulder, Vido, will be hers, it has to be hers, because nobody else (listen up: nobody else) could touch you like that. In your very best voice you'll say Melissa! She'll laugh even more. You'll turn around. It will really be her standing there, naked, the two of you naked in the pouring rain, saying nothing, just laughing. She will touch your chest and say something you won't understand, not even by reading her lips. Besides, what difference does it make. She'll come close, caress your back. Her breath will be delicious as the smell of rain. You'll lean over a little to kiss her on the lips. The little devil will move away, run off through all the trees, disappear, you'll search desperately for her, Melissa, fuck, don't leave me like this. And you'll find her leaning against the red sandalwood tree of Ceylon, laughing, waiting for you with her legs spread open. You'll stop in front of her without getting too close, to punish her, so the little whore will learn, you'll show her that big hard thing you have bursting triumphantly from your crotch, and you'll shout, scream, If you want it it's all yours. She'll reply, Yes, I want it, and she'll hold out her arms so you'll go to her at last. The downpour over the Island growing stronger as if it knew it would cover you both that way, and save you both. With marveling hands she'll place your prick in just the right spot. You'll enter, not knowing where but knowing you're entering happiness. You'll be as happy up in the oak as you'll be on the terrace as you'll be in your room, and when you open your eyes you'll see yourself embracing the bird that will flutter and fly away, and when you open your eyes you'll find yourself in your room, and there'll be nobody there, forgive me, Vido, when you open your eyes you'll realize it's all been a mean trick the author has played on your character, and you shouldn't blame me, because after all imagination is more magnificent than reality. And there, Vido, on the dressing table mirror, a white, thick, slow liquid, your cum.

The stage should be large, full of real trees, leaves, branches. Let's say it represents a forest of ancient Greece. A vestal maid appears. White tunic waving in the wind. The wind escapes from large fans between the curtains on the stage. The vestal approaches slowly. She had been nervous; no more. From the moment her bare foot feels the boards of the stage, her fear dissipates as if the prop wind had carried it off. Applause. The rain is made of applause. Since the rain doesn't stop, the applause doesn't stop. In any case, there is a great silence for her, a tremendous silence. She sees no one. The public doesn't exist. All that exists is the stage, the music, and she, dressed as a vestal in the midst of a forest of ancient Greece. She begins to sing a lovely aria by Gasparo Luigi Pacifico Spontini. She alone knows what she experiences when she is singing. A sensation like none other she can remember. Her voice is marvelous, she knows, she hears, she can do with it whatever she wishes. She cares about the public, that's true, and that is why its emotions reach her, the reverential, religious way it receives her song. She holds out her hands. The aria is really saying: My public, this voice is for you, I'm nothing without you, my voice and I were created to make you happy. The music stops. The purity of her voice is crowned with an ovation. Applause. The rain is made of applause. This one, today, so intense, can be called an ovation. Shouts of *brava!*

And if I were to remind you, Casta Diva, that rain is rain and nothing more, would that be cruelty on my part? And if I were to remind you that your fine husband has been lying in bed for days without addressing a word to you (to you or to anyone else)? If I were to remind you that Tatina has wet herself again, that Tingo is playing with a paper puppet, that there is no forest, real or fake, and you aren't dressed as a vestal? Look, look around you, one poor room. Listen, there's no applause, no ovations, no shouts of *brava*. Just an Island that's flooding, a husband who doesn't talk, a son who doesn't get it and just plays and plays, and an idiot daughter who wets herself every five minutes. Oh, and a mirror! Why don't you dedicate a glass of water to the spirit of Spontini? You're hoarse from shouting that the rain is making you hoarse, that you can't sing the way you and your public deserve. That's fine, Casta Diva, I don't want to be too wicked, I don't want to take too much pleasure in watching you suffer. Close your eyes, pay close attention, the stage should be large, full of real trees, leaves, branches. A forest in ancient Greece, and you come out dressed as a vestal. The rest of it, please, you can imagine for yourself.

Now's the time, Tingo. Take advantage while your mother's sitting on the easy chair hiding her face in her hands to imagine she's on stage, and leave the cardboard puppet, go out into the gallery, run to the courtyard, because Sebas is watching the rain pour down. What a great downpour! Besides, no classes. And did you see how it's raining? He sits down next to Sebastián, who says nothing, doesn't even stop watching the downpour, doesn't look like Sebastián, he's so serious! Tingo stays there a long time, silent, not knowing what to do. Then, when he's about to break out crying, Sebastián looks at him with his finest smile and asks, Do you know the story of my Uncle Noel?

Following this I will transcribe, without altering a single comma, the story that Sebastián told Tingo during the torrential downpour that fell on the Island.

Many years ago there was a rainstorm like today, and even worse, so the earth was flooded, there was more water in the Island than in all the seas around it, my mamá had an uncle named Noel who lived on a ranch called El Arca, between Caimito and Guanajay, Uncle Noel was a widower and he only had one daughter who died when she turned fifteen, what did she die of? nothing at all, when she turned fifteen instead of growing up and getting prettier like girls do when they turn fifteen, she got smaller and uglier, so small and so ugly that my uncle fed her milk from an eyedropper but first he would always cover his eyes with a bandage not to catch a fright, the girl was named Gardenia, one fine day, before the downpour I told you about had a chance to start, Gardenia shrank to a point and disappeared, then my uncle felt all alone, and he dedicated himself to his animals with more love than before on his little ranch, he had every kind of animal there you can imagine, Uncle Noel loved animals, he even had elephants (not like the elephants you see in the zoo that come from Africa and India, no, no way, he had Cuban elephants that don't exist anymore because a sadness epidemic killed them off), what were Cuban elephants like? small, red, with white ears, no tusks, or just one tusk, I'm not too sure, well as I was saying Uncle Noel had animals of every species when the downpour started, and it went on for a long, long time, so much water fell that the houses lifted up off their foundations, and houses from Baracoa landed in Guane, and houses from Guane ended up in Guantánamo, and folks would greet each other when they passed, and they kept on doing their chores up there on the uncontrollable river, unable to stop, my mother says they didn't get around on buses but on little boats, like in Venice, a city where it also rained a lot one time, Uncle Noel didn't want his house to drift away, he tied it up real tight with several ropes and he stuck the animals inside, waiting for the rain to stop, since he liked the animals and took good care of them, and while the rest of the animals on the island were drowning my uncle's were getting fat and looking better than ever, when the rain let up the earth looked like it had been swept clean with giant brooms, the houses were all in the farthest-off places, some had even ended up on Turquino Peak, and there weren't any animals, and the most terrible thing was: even though the rain had let up, people didn't believe it, because it had rained so much their ears had gotten used to the sound, and so even though not a drop was falling they kept on hearing the rainstorm, Uncle Noel, who was always an intelligent man, said to himself, Maybe this rain I'm hearing now isn't the real thing, but just what's left in my ears from the rain before, and to test it he sent a nanny goat named Chantal out to the fields, and the little goat came back a little later chewing grass, nice and dry, not even mud on her hooves, so that way my uncle learned it had stopped raining, even though my mother says that Uncle Noel kept on hearing the falling rain to the end of his days, when he died, because he died when a hundred years had accumulated in his heart, just a few minutes before he fell silent he said that he was drowning, that he was going in a rowboat along an enormous river and that the boat was foundering and he was going down with the boat, and he wasn't in any boat on any river, just in his own bed and it was a splendid day, my mother tells, what's for sure is that it's thanks to the animals that Uncle Noel saved in his house at El Arca that we have animals in Cuba today, otherwise we'd all be eating grass and flowers, since aside from my uncle's animals all the others drowned in that rainstorm many years ago, because it was a harder storm than today, and look how hard it's raining.

This rain is just like that other one, he remembers it, or rather, he believes he remembers it. It rained so furiously that Havana was disappearing, being erased, through the window you could only see mirages of walls and balconies. The empty street. Where did they live then? Maybe in the boarding house on Jovellar Street, the landlady was named Tangle (no, Tangle was the woman at the boarding house on Barcelona and Galiano; the one at Jovellar was named Japan, yes, Japan, a fat and jovial black woman, always laughing, and she was the only one who would accept Cira knowing the illness from which she suffered, she didn't mind, she said all I ask is that the other guests don't find out, and she left them and went away graciously, she must have died by now, she was already pushing sixty back then). Professor Kingston would give classes in people's houses. He prepared doctors and engineers who were going to Yale, Harvard, or Princeton, boys who paid him chicken shit, though it was enough to live on: they hardly spent a thing. At Japan's boarding house they lived for a breather, a time of peace, they weren't obliged to wander from one place to another, thanks to the generosity of the black woman who must be in God's heaven if there is a God and there is a heaven. It was several months (seven, eight, I don't know, *memory fails me*) that they lived in the small but clean and pleasant room on Jovellar Street. He has no doubts about the date, and not only because of what happened to Cira, but also (the whims of memory, why does one's memory at times like to make reference points of trivial facts or things irrelevant to one's personal history?) because that same year, that same month, the German cruiser the *Königsberg* went down, an earthquake completely destroyed the Italian city of Avezzano, two events that made Professor Kingston reflect that we civilizations should understand we are mortal. Mortal, yes, like Cira. And this rain is just like that one. And just as you can't hear anything but the sound of rain now, the monotonous knocking of water on water, the sound of solitude itself (if it were possible to hear solitude), so were they isolated in their room back then, enclosed for three, four days, while he was unable to go out to give classes nor to receive anything other than the visits of the black woman Japan, who would bring, along with her contagious smile, a bowl of her chicken vegetable soup, she knew this was all Cira felt like eating. And this rain today, eternal, impassive, makes him see his wife once more, sitting in her little rocker, her face hidden by her large black tulle veil, her hands gloved, and wearing her long dress, also in black. Again he sees her, beautiful in her thirty-three years (well, the part about her beauty is imagination, it had been quite a while since Cira had let anyone see her), rocking on her little chair, this very one, the little rocker he's sitting in today listening to the rain, or what signifies the same, remembering. How much time has passed? And Cira hasn't gone away yet, she'll never go away: what disappeared that day was everyone else's Cira. His Cira, though she's been slowly blurring, though she's lost her clarity, continues here in her rocker, hidden by veils and gloves. It was raining, yes, as if for all eternity, and above the permanent knocking sound of water he had heard a knocking at the door that sounded out of place, intrusive, there's no doubt that when it's raining you come to believe it's the only noise possible. Thinking it must be Japan, long as it was before the dinner hour, Professor Kingston had opened the door. And it wasn't Japan, no *(I fear thee, ancient Mariner),* and he doesn't know why he repeats *Ancient Mariner:* he saw before him a tall, handsome, slim young man with great eyes that held a certain sadness, and the most nicely defined lips anyone could imagine. He smiled. Professor Kingston didn't have time to ask him anything. He heard a creaking behind him, and when he turned to see, he found Cira on the floor. He hardly had to wait for the doctor to tell him what he already knew. The young sailor had disappeared. The rain continued for several days, uninterrupted.

This downpour is just the beginning, I know they won't believe me, they'll laugh at me, they'll say it again, poor crazy woman, poor Barefoot Countess as they contemptuously term me, the raving lunatic too, centuries ago they said the same of Cassandra, sad fate of she who comes to tell the truth, they're saddled with the stigma of insanity like the bells that lepers wore in the Middle Ages, I'm just here to tell what I know, to do my duty, if you don't want to pay attention too bad for you, sure, shut your windows when I pass, cover your ears, I know the knocking of my cane strikes terror into you but even so the prophecy won't fail to come true, know that this rainstorm is but the beginning, the end is near, soon, very soon, much sooner than even I can predict misfortune will befall the Island, the city, the planet, no one has an imagination strong enough to picture the atrocity that is to come and this downpour today is but a warning, pay attention, later when it lets up we'll begin to doze off, a paralyzing sleep will be the first symptom and your body, stretched out in bed, on the sofa, or in the hammock, won't realize how the light flees from it, and the fleeing light will be the love in each of your rooms, and love, which is the light, will vanish like smoke and leave your body in darkness, and we'll begin to live in the shadows, and from the shadows other evils will stem, no mother will remain who loves her son, no just king, no man who understands his fellow man, though we speak the same language we won't understand one another, no one will love, no one, the most passionate letters will be blank pages, the fieriest poems will read like tongue twisters, this will be the kingdom of hatred, and the kingdom of hatred is that of betrayal and lies and desolation and hypocrisy, masks will take the place of faces, your true face will vanish as well like smoke behind the mask, and we'll live with pistols and knives and razors beneath our pillows, we'll never sleep, waiting for a friend to fall, for an enemy pretending to be kind to fall, wives will turn in their husbands for the executioner to behead, husbands will dismember their wives to deny the executioners the pleasure of executing them, many will flee, thousands will flee, they'll take to the sea, swim and swim until they reach the mainland, they will gain nothing, they will profit nothing, a country is an illness for which there is no cure, they will leave, indeed, and something will not let them sleep, they'll cry for what they left behind though they leave nothing behind in reality, for never, hear me well, never can anyone completely escape the place they were born, a man who leaves his birthplace leaves half of himself and carries off only the other half, which is usually the sicklier half, and when he is far away, no matter where he be, he feels the missing arm or leg or lung and thinks: I'm a man suffering from nostalgia, and he's already dead, and this rainstorm is but the beginning, and much more, much much more, for after this rain the drought will last for decades, in the countryside, the lovely countryside of which poets and troubadours sing, trees will turn to ash beneath the relentless blazing sun, the sun itself will grow to punish us, the rivers will run dry, cattle will die, animals will fall victim to thirst and exhaustion, only the buzzards will be fruitful and multiply, and the fish of the sea will retreat from the scorched coastline, the phantom of plague will knock on open doors, blood will turn to pus, hunger will enter like a shadow in our bodies instead of love, and believe me, a man suffering from hunger will be the first candidate for betrayal, for betraying and for being betrayed, there you have two simple acts, like drinking spoiled water from spoiled wells, and on the footsteps of betrayal comes robbery, doors and windows will be barred in vain, robbery brought on by desperation can break through barbed wire, and the persecutions will begin, the same ones who rob will keep watch over us, we'll live beneath their persistent gazes, the eyes behind the windows, the eyes on the rooftops, the eyes in the ground, the eyes in desire and in sorrow, even the eyes in our hearts, and when the eyes penetrate fine as needles into our dreams, the buildings will begin to crumble, impelled by imaginary hurricanes, even the atmosphere will tire of all the atrocities, under the dust, under the ruins, we still won't find the peace of death, not even that peace is within our reach, for there will be judges beneath the earth to judge and pass sentence, everything we once said, the most innocent song, will come back to be used against us, to die a sweet death you must lead a decent life, and here we'll all fall into wretchedness like flies into flypaper, good-bye family, good-bye treasures we never knew, good-bye mercy, and good-bye tenderness, and there are things of which I will not speak, I don't know how to name them, I have seen them in dreams, and no matter how fierce dreams are they can't always be explained, what I say and enumerate here is the beginning of a much greater terror that I predict, of which this rainstorm is but the beginning, call me crazy, yes, crazy if you wish, it's all the same, crazy means you're still brave enough to tell the truth.

There's no autumn here. No winter. Much less spring. There would never have been a Vivaldi here. His sad imitation would have composed a requiem to lament the unending summer. There's a fixed sun here (eternal, like the Island) that doesn't let you live. A sun that opens windows and slips through them; a sun that pushes open doors; a sun that falls on rooftops like tons of lead; a sun that pursues you into the most hidden corner and takes over your body as fire takes over a roast, and enters your eyes for the sole purpose of leaving you blind, so that when night comes and with night a supposed calm, a supposed truce of a few lightless hours, you still see it, that impertinent and chronic ring, even with your eyes closed, even in your dreams; on an island like this, the worst and only nightmare is dreaming that you're naked under the sun. You search in vain for the redeeming shade of a palm leaf; in vain for the stream that will cool your burning temples or your dry throat or your ever feverish brow. In vain. You're born and you die with your body bathed in sweat. The monsters of light don't let you live, they lie in wait for you, waiting for the right moment to devour you. And you turn transparent from all this light. Of course there are some days when the sun clouds over before dusk. Those are the days of downpours, of sweeping rain that carries off trees and destroys the landscape, rain that's like another face of the sun, because it also pushes open windows, opens doors, knocks down roofs, destroys houses, annihilates you. The also chronic rain is like railroad ties falling head on. And there's nothing you can do about it but go to the seashore and try to dream about other lands that you aren't sure exist, other lands beyond the horizon, other lands where they say the sun doesn't punish you so intensely and the rain doesn't pillage, doesn't leave you so helpless. That's why, listen to me, this downpour today is holy. We're content. Are we deluded?

Listen, even though the downpour may be a blessing, even though it's here to interrupt the sun's outrages for a while, the truth is that this much rain can drive you to distraction. So I write, *The downpour stopped,* and of course the downpour stops. There's the Island, wet, intensely green, shining in its eternity.

Everything in the past was better, that's my motto, Irene declares while she softly, sweetly runs a damp cloth over the Wounded Boy's body. The Wounded Boy lies naked on a bed with clean sheets. She looks at him as if she were looking at Christ. Because you look like Christ, she says softly, whispers (fearing that Lucio, the others, might hear), at least you resemble the image my mother kept in her prayer book. (What mother? What prayer book?) She gets embarrassed, stands absorbed in thought for several seconds, she doesn't know if she remembers whether her mother kept an image in her prayer book, what nobody could ever take away from her is the memory of the image itself, the little print with its gilded frame. There's the image, under the glass of the nightstand. And it is time to reveal it: Irene doesn't know that the image she imagines to be Christ, the little print of the Son of God to which she dedicates flowers and candles and prayers, the one to which she prays on her knees for the return of her memory, for the welfare of Lucio, of the house, of the Island, of the world, is actually the famous self-portrait of Dante Gabriel Rossetti. She doesn't know (she has no way of knowing) how the photogravure came into her hands. What's for certain is that the picture is of the painter and poet: his face; his great eyes observing what he observes with a certain innocence, a certain apprehension, a certain surprise; his large, well-defined nose; his voluptuous lips; his long hair falling across the shoulders. So that, according to Irene (though she's unaware of it), the Wounded Boy looks not like Christ but like Dante Gabriel Rossetti.

Without knowing it, without realizing it, Irene is correct. If God is present in everything that has been created, you can worship God in anyone's image, since anyone could be the image of God.

Yes, it's true, everything in the past was better. Irene runs a damp cloth over the Wounded Boy's body. He no longer has a fever, his visage has taken on a delicate, serene expression, and as for his white and perfect body, it seems as if it had never been wounded. Everyone wonders how the wounds could have disappeared.

That night (it seems so long ago, actually it was just a few days back) when the boys found the Wounded Boy wrapped in a Cuban flag in Berardo's old carpentry shop, no one asked, no one doubted, they just brought him straight to Irene's house. Right away they made Doctor Pinto come, and he asked them to leave him alone with the boy. Doctor Pinto showed up drunk, as was to be expected, though everyone was pleased since Doctor Pinto is at his very best when he's drunk, because it's as if the rum opens up his brains, and he says, Yes, that's it, *rum* is short for *reason*. And when he came back out after an hour of keeping us there waiting impatiently, Doctor Pinto was smiling and exclaimed with his ethylic breath, He's out of trouble, you'll have to feed him and care for him but he's out of trouble, and above all, be very, very discreet, in this Island there are terrible times ahead. He paused to clear his throat, shook his head several times, and concluded, Well, in this Island when haven't terrible times been ahead? And he took Irene aside and told her about the wounds: They aren't bullet wounds, Irene, it's strange, this body was wounded by darts, arrows, understand? he'll get better if you tend him closely. Irene almost cried from emotion, from all the responsibility she had now, and she ran off to the self-portrait of Dante Gabriel Rossetti, and there she promised Christ that, yes, she would save him. And she asked the others (including Helena) to leave, Don't worry, I'll dedicate myself to him as if it were the body of my own son (may God forbid). And she didn't even serve Lucio his dinner. Let him work it out as best he can, there are more serious matters right now, and there went Irene to the boy's room, she took off his filthy dirt- and bloodstained cotton twill suit, cleaned his wounds with thimerosal and lots of hydrogen peroxide, rubbing the gauze over them brusquely, penetrating without mercy, as Doctor Pinto would recommend. The wounds were not from gunshots as they had originally believed, but arrows, arrows! and who would be so criminal as to treat a man in these times, however ominous they are, like he was some kind of early Christian? Irene saw the Wounded Boy's naked body, his beautiful face, the chestnut hair falling over his shoulders just like in the print of Christ (Dante Gabriel Rossetti) under the glass top of her nightstand, and she was overwhelmed by tenderness, by compassion. She poured alcohol on his wounds and was happy to see him move, utter a groan. Doctor Pinto had predicted it: When the alcohol hits the wounds he'll rise from the dead. The truth is, the doctor's ethylic breath doesn't matter a bit, nor do his trembling hands nor the flask from which he sometimes *gathers courage.* Yes, Irene, a sip of rum takes away my fear, and that helps me confront this horror of getting up every day, getting dressed every day, going outside and discovering that, contrary to every prognosis, a new day has dawned again. She counted the wounds. Twenty-seven bowshots. As if to annihilate him, how cruel! And the Wounded Boy was feverish, he looked shriveled, dark, lost among the white sheets. The violet hue of the wounds made Irene shudder and feel like crying. It was about four in the morning. Another October dawn was drawing near. It had started raining, or at least it seemed like it from the sound of the trees and the strong smell of earth. She left the lamp burning and sat down in front of him, ready to sit watch for what remained of the night and for the approaching day. He'll live, Lord, he'll live, You are magnanimous and You put him in my path so I would save him, here I am, doing my duty, and though I know You love him, don't take him yet, so young and so handsome, yes, Lord, so handsome that if it weren't a sacrilege I'd tell You he deserves to be sitting at Your right hand. The Wounded Boy moved slightly, smiled. He opened his eyes, which shone, which lost their dark color in favor of a limpid blue. The rings under his eyes disappeared. He said several words Irene couldn't understand. His lips recovered the lively, human color that lips need to be able to speak and kiss. His face acquired a gentle expression. His body began losing thinness and darkness, gaining harmony and bulk; the violet hue of the wounds disappeared and they became red, rosy; then the open slits in his skin swiftly diminished until they began to blur, until they began to disappear, until the body ended up looking as if it weren't the body of the Wounded Boy, as if it had never suffered, and of the wounds there remained only a scant memory in Irene's confusion.

Yes, child, my Wounded Boy, I saw the pitcher smashed to bits, and maybe it seems silly to you for me to place so much value on a broken pitcher, you don't have to say it, I know: a pitcher is just one thing among many, you should just give it the importance it really has, no more, I know, a pitcher, a dress, a fan, a table, a spot on the wall, things! but aren't things put in this world for a purpose? don't you think? yes, they must be, things add up to something, things on top of things form the whole world, and for that matter, what is man without things? thanks to things you know where you are and where you're going and where you came from, and I for that matter knew that the pitcher that broke was important to me, but at the same time I didn't know why, and I realized: If the things in the world begin to lose their value, the world begins to lose its value, and there's nothing you can do in it, the pitcher broke, I cried, I was aware it was important to me, but I had forgotten why, I wanted to remember Emilio, my husband, the result was: I found a photograph of Lucio, my son, and I took it to be a photograph of his father, and that confusion, do you know what it means? if the affair of the pitcher were just the affair of the pitcher, fine, what difference would it make, right, but what's terrible about this case is that when a pitcher breaks it doesn't break alone.

A few nights ago, Irene dreamed she was returning to the Old House, the one by La Laguna with the luxuriant chirimoya tree in its garden. Its porch had fallen down from age, and you could see cracks in the wood. That house must have been near a hundred years old. They all slept in a single room. Her father said, I can't sleep anymore, and he sat in a rocking chair with his head in his hands, Tomorrow, what will we do tomorrow? Her mother, striving to appear radiant, also got up and set herself to peeling the boniatos that would be their breakfast. She replied, God squeezes but He doesn't smother. Her father said I just make pennies for plowing the earth. Irene felt happy. They were hungry in her dream, they had no clothes to wear. They got out of their beds and sat on beer crates wrapped in bright paper to make matchboxes with pictures of models dressed up as rumba dancers. Irene raised her eyes and saw the starry sky through the crossbeams in the ceiling. Regardless, she felt happy. It was Christmas. The wooden walls had been whitewashed. At some point they sat at the table to eat ham and turron. She sang a carol (she doesn't remember which). Washed the glasses and plates. Her mother put out the tablecloth. A tablecloth of green dreams and sunflowers. And suddenly, as happens in dreams, the table was set. The family was sitting at it. Everyone but Irene, who was carrying a tray, without lifting her eyes, happily looking at the empty tray. She didn't set the tray in the center of the table, but the tray appeared in the center of the table and she saw she was sitting down. She didn't know why everything was so quiet. She lifted her eyes and looked at her sister, who had no face. Her sister's face was an eyeless, noseless, lipless blur. Her father's face, the same blur. Her mother's face, another blur. She started to cry. They laughed their lipless laughs. Irene ran outside. She was in a cemetery. She couldn't say how she knew she was in a cemetery. There were no graves, just a garbage dump. She entered the garbage dump. She was sinking into the garbage, into the mud, in that unbearable stench.

At the precise instant when memories are forgotten, at that precise instant, a female character whose name is Irene, after healing a wounded youth, goes outside to water the flowers. It is an October evening. There we will leave her. (For now.)

⋆ ⋆ ⋆

There's somebody out there, Sandokán declares. Rolo agrees. For quite a while he's been hearing bits of words, truncated phrases, above the howling wind. Rolo explains, The Island is like that. Sandokán says no more. He's lying on the bed, half covered by the malicious sheet. Again and again he sweeps his eyes around the room with an expression that could just as easily be ironic or ingenuous. At times Rolo looks sidelong at him, briefly raising his eyes from the book on Fra Angelico he's pretending to look at but isn't looking at, because what's before his eyes are the eyes Sandokán had less than an hour ago when he took him by the arms, squeezed him, and ordered him urgently and despotically and sweetly, Take off your clothes, let's go. Outwardly, he's looking at the gold foil of the halos, the wings, and the dress of the angel in *The Annunciation,* actually he sees Sandokán taking off his clothes for him, energetically undoing the buttons of the shirt that softly, discreetly fell to the floor. The Virgin crosses her hands over her breast with unwonted refinement, he sees before him, instead, the big virile hands of Sandokán caressing himself. Turning the page, he sees a detail of *The Annunciation:* Adam and Eve expelled from Paradise. In the dark blue of the sky he sees again the boy's white skin, clean to a fault, his perfectly proportioned body. The naked body shook him with anticipated pleasure. He stops at the plate of *The Coronation of the Virgin* and remembers how he leaned over to kiss his rosy nipples, his thick nipples, and he remembers how, at the same time, he squeezed his waist with both hands. The Virgin's profile is so finely sketched, he says, perhaps trying to justify the fact that at this instant he sees himself once more in bed with that raging man on top of him. Sandokán studies him with his half-picaresque, half-ingenuous eyes, in silence. Rolo settles back to get a look at him naked (the sheet is a euphemism). The fresco of *The Coronation of the Virgin,* in the monastery of San Marco, is painted in strikingly refined colors, nevertheless he is looking at Sandokán's thighs. The robes of Christ and the Virgin are marvelous, stunningly white, and Rolo is looking at the whiteness of his lover's skin. The fresco of *The Transfiguration* is imposing: he sees himself licking the triumphant virility of Sandokán. And he turns the page and reaches *The Crucifixion* right when the young man jumped on him and brutally penetrated him and Rolo complained but spread his legs, yielded to him, with resignation, with joy, both sweating, uniting his sweat with Sandokán's, enjoying it to the point of tears. He experienced something he hadn't felt in a long time, had the world stopped? This detail of *The Transfiguration* is marvelous, he observes in his connoisseur's voice, the truth is that Fra Angelico . . .

He pushes open the door to Eleusis. Helena has sent him in search of Uncle Rolo. A moment ago, after lighting the little oil lamp before her Saint Barbara, Helena turned to Sebastián and ordered him, Go to Rolo's house (she, of course, doesn't call him Uncle) and tell him to come, urgently, I have to talk to him. And Sebastián knows she is upset. Tell him to leave whatever he's doing, Helena insists, and come here right away. And no one has to tell Sebastián how obstinate Helena will be about this, because although her face is the same as ever, her voice is the same as ever, her expression is as serene as ever, there's something in it that betrays her and makes it all not the same as ever. This, of course, is something only Sebastián knows. And he hasn't told anyone (especially not Helena herself) that he has come to know her so well. Something very bad must be up, and Sebastián knows he's the bearer of bad news when he opens the door to Eleusis, the bookstore.

He's surprised by the bells on the door. If this were any other day, the ringing bells would make Uncle look out from among the mountains of books with his affable smile, his good morning or good afternoon (depending), a ceremonious nod of his head, and his mellifluous voice saying, How can I help you? Today the bells on the door ring but Uncle doesn't appear. Sebastián shakes the door several times to make the bells ring enough. Since Uncle still doesn't appear, he closes the door carefully, extremely carefully so the bells won't ring again, and latches it shut.

The small enclosure, somewhat smaller, Sebastián is thinking, than his bedroom, is crammed to the ceiling with books. It may be possible that it isn't small and that it's the profusion of books that makes the room look more scant than it actually is. Thousands and thousands of books squeeze into the small store, mountains of books, columns of books snaking sinuously and precariously upward, shelves sagging from all the weight, baskets overflowing, boxes so overstocked no god could lift them. There are a few narrow passages between the piles of books, through which you almost have to walk sideways. And you can't see the walls, it's impossible to tell what color the walls of this bookstore are, and sometimes you can tell there are some paintings hanging on them, and you can tell that because between one column and the next you can catch a corner of a picture frame, a bit of painted canvas, but the paintings themselves can't be seen, hidden as they are behind the books. In this disorder, Uncle often says, a superior order reigns, behind the apparent lack of logic lies the spirit of Aristotle. And though few understand what he means, it is well known that you can ask Uncle Rolo for any title, no matter how recherché, how extravagant, and without thinking twice he'll know whether he has it or not, and if he has it he'll go straight to it without the slightest hesitation, because books have voices, Rolo explains, and I'm the only one who can hear them.

At the entrance are the Cuban magazines, from *Bohemia* to *Vanidades,* not forgetting *Carteles,* and the collections of *Orígenes* and *Ciclón* that no one buys. Then come the French, American, English, Mexican, Argentine magazines (*Sur,* gentlemen, no more and no less than *Sur,* which is to say, the Platonic idea of a magazine). Magazines from all over the world meant for the most varied tastes, from those that show how to build a boat to those that speak of the private lives of the exiled (and by the same token, ennobled) nobility of Russia. Religious magazines, Catholic and non-Catholic, Japanese magazines revealing the wisdom of Zen (the fashion of Orientalism, listen up, comes to us from the feeble pages and exquisite taste of the brothers Goncourt), magazines of the occult (Schopenhauer too was, like Mallarmé, an Orientalist of culture and not of the occult), magazines for opera singers (yes, Casta Diva, for opera singers, where they say there never has been and never will be a Norma like Maria Callas, that she is to opera what Christ is to history, B.C. and A.D., you know?), magazines for gardening (Irene, for gardening) and for lawyers and delinquents (and now I won't mention names, if the shoe fits . . .). With utter disdain, like a Catholic priest speaking of the Delphic cults, Rolo has complained of having to sell magazines: You don't realize, he exclaims while rocking in his chair, that I'm turning into an accomplice of superficiality and mystification, you don't realize (he continues in his schoolmaster's pose) that magazines (begging the pardon of Victoria Ocampo) are an ocean of culture one inch deep, and he pauses to stress a gesture of impotence, My dears, you have to give in to the evidence, ours is a lost era, an era of frivolity, of insubstantiality, of fraud, the evil of our century isn't ennui (*hélas,* ennui is the sentiment of geniuses) but inanity, our century has run aground on a sandbar of magazines, magazines are the means that this era we live in has found for faking culture when in reality this era of ours is a barbaric and stupid one, when the idiot governs and philosopher shines shoes *(transition),* and what can I do about it, I don't guide the spiritual destiny of the twentieth century, I'm a humble bookseller, and as such all I can aspire to do is to make a little bit of money as honorably as I can, I'm just here to satisfy everyone else's tastes in reading material, and each person's life or stupidity is his own business, I'm not a policeman or a religious reformer, and besides *(brief pause; change of tone)* I think it's better for people to read magazines than not to read at all: you take what you can get.

Standing before all these magazines, Sebastián notices that, just to the right of where their disorderly and contentious presence comes to an end, there are whole shelves full of every comic book you could imagine, from *Prince Valiant* to *Little Lulu.* And then he sees the science fiction books (Ray Bradbury, Sebastián, never forget that name, Ray Bradbury), in a bookcase that leans against the wall of the main building; that is, against Uncle's room. Turning once more to the right, in front of the magazines and comics, against the wall that faces Linea Street, the detective novels are gathered (don't even glance at them, boy, no matter what the great Alfonso Reyes has to say) in super cheap editions, pirated editions from Bogotá and Buenos Aires. When Sebastián finishes inspecting this area, he finds the books on useful topics, cooking, clothes, makeup, furniture, decoration, books for farmers and gardeners, veterinarians and electricians. And farther on, the books that are useful in school: *Mathematics* by Baldor, *Chemistry* by Ledón, *Spanish Grammar* by Amado Alonso and Pedro Henríquez Ureña *(Uncle sighs in ecstasy), Literary Theory* by Gayol Fernández (more provincial than even we: he lives in Sagua la Grande), the volumes on English by Leonardo Zorzano Jorrín (don't waste your time with that, you don't have to read those big old tomes to learn how to bark). Then come the art books, the most famous art galleries in the world (in one hour you can visit the Louvre or the New York Metropolitan Museum), beautiful and solemn books with embossed plates and gothic lettering. And closing off the path, in front of what seems to be a sealed-off door, a sign with Uncle's unmistakable handwriting, SEVERAL CENTURIES OF KNOWLEDGE HERE, the encyclopedias, the books of criticism and essays. Smell of dust and old paper, a whiff of another era escapes from the austere bindings, most of them burgundy red, against which their illegible names stand out (the unjustly reviled Saint-Beuve, Taine the positivist, Lord Macaulay whom I read so often as a young man and who says nothing to me now). The smell dissipates when Sebastián moves a little to the right and discovers an enormous bookcase where the word *Theater* is repeated in thousands of forms and sizes, on cheerful many-colored bindings, and Sebastián remembers a gigantic chandelier, a large brown velvet stage curtain, and the vertiginous toast scene in the production of *La Traviata* that Casta Diva took them to see, Tingo and him, on a night when the poor woman couldn't stop crying. And the smell Sebastián senses before these books is the same smell he sensed that night in the theater, an undefinable smell, a perfume composed of many perfumes, smells of brocade and painted lumber, smells that he has never found again despite having searched for them in the most hidden corners of the Island. And he has to step around to avoid a large wooden base on top of which rests a bust of a fat, nearly bald man with enormous mustaches that end in points, and pupilless eyes. And it isn't easy to read the name written on the base (Flaubert, child, Flaubert, and if he hadn't been born what would have become of the modern novel?), and above, on an uncovered bit of wall, a mask, a death mask with closed eyes (on your knees now, this is Proust! the divine Marcel, read Proust and the rest can be fed to the bonfires). And when he crosses over it's as if he were in the middle of the Island on this night of gusting winds, because the smells at this moment carry the aroma of damp leaves and wood, and also the magnificent smell of earth when it's just starting to drizzle. The books on these shelves are large, robust, showy, but they don't have the fragile air of the ones that say *Theater;* to the contrary they seem like books put there to stay forever, books no one should touch. And Sebastián walks past the long bookshelf fastened by robust iron bars to floor and ceiling, touching the books, trying to read the impossible names of their authors, names that could never have belonged to people of flesh and blood. And he's about to take down a great big volume by some guy named Thackeray, when he discovers, in a reflection, the cash register.

Gilded, shining, sketched with scrolls that spiral and unspiral, wearing a little white plate like a crown, black numbers, keys worn out from use, sitting on a tall table covered in a dark cloth with poinsettias. Sebastián approaches, attracted perhaps by the reflections in the bronze of the light from the ceiling. And the light from the ceiling, which is scant, comes from a naked bulb hanging from a long wire coated with flies, and it is multiplied, intensified, in the polished surface of the cash register, so that it seems it is coming from there and is merely being reflected in the lightbulb. Sebastián now runs his hand over the bronze, not understanding what relation there could be between the books and this machine, because he has seen cash registers in groceries and variety stores, pharmacies and cleaners, but he had never thought there could be any relation between them and books. And Sebastián is about to touch the lever that juts out next to the black keys when the sound of voices stops him.

It's impossible to determine exactly where the voices come from. Most likely from Uncle's room, because the door that communicates between the room and the bookstore is right there, two steps away, at the end of the long shelf of large, robust, and showy books. And Sebastián doesn't have to think twice before he hides beneath the cash register table, aided by the dark cloth with poinsettias. The sound of voices suddenly stops and he hears the creak of a door opening. Now footsteps. Sebastián sees, first, a pair of well-polished two-tone shoes; then Uncle's clumsy orthopedics. The two-tone shoes stop and stand apart, very firm and rather bold. One of them, the one farthest from Sebastián, lifts up for a moment and reappears with a click of the heel. Uncle's orthopedics stand together, their toes turned ridiculously upward. Don't go, says Uncle, and the orthopedics move toward the others, which step back. The same two-tone shoe clicks its heel again. I'm begging you, don't go yet. The two-tone shoes turn around and come back. Uncle's orthopedics step back a pace. Wait a second, and Uncle's voice is so imploring it is nearly unrecognizable. Sebastián hears a laugh and it almost seems the two-tone shoes are laughing while they sketch a dance step. The four shoes remain motionless and the silence is the night wind. Then Uncle's orthopedics, with their ridiculously upturned toes, turn to face him. The sound of the cash register mechanism, and again the laugh and the dance step of the two-tone shoes, which dance nearer. The four shoes are, at this moment, very close together. Before they separate, there is the sound of a kiss, and the young, lovely voice of Sandokán: Ciao, old man, I'll see you tomorrow or the day after, or the day after that, one of these days, don't wait up for me, so long.

The bookstore is empty again. The orthopedic shoes said good-bye to the two-tone shoes and returned slowly, as if they didn't want to return, stood for a moment in front of the cash register, walked around among the books, stood here, there, indecisive or tired or sad, and then disappeared through the door that communicates between the bookstore and the house. He remains silently under the cash register and lets the time pass, a long calming pause, and when it's just the swirling wind outside again, he comes back out, holds his ear to Uncle's door and hears a distant cough. He thinks he should return, that his mother is waiting for him with her customary severity: Why did you take so long? it'd better not happen again, and he can hear his mother's voice as if she were standing there, he sees her white face approaching him, armed with that gaze no one could withstand. No, Sebastián doesn't leave. It's hard to resist the temptation to finish looking at the bookstore. The path, from here, becomes more intricate and promising. He has to walk around to continue the sinuous passageway that the books now find harder to leave open. He has to pass several wicker chests overflowing with volumes, face a sign that says GOD EXISTS: HE IS THE DEVIL, find another bust, of someone named Gertrudis Gómez de Avellaneda, before he gets to a small enclosure, a neat little living room where he discovers the most beautiful, the most orderly, the most elegant books. Here, the walls are whitewashed, the bookcases are polished, and there is, besides, incense and the portrait of a woman sitting languidly in a rocking chair, on a terrace, with the sea in the distance. The small living room smells of church. The floor is a blue carpet.

Strange joy. Inexplicable joy, stirring his breast and taking away his breath and forcing him to close his eyes. Joy without a cause. Perhaps an embarrassing suspicion. Perhaps as if a secret were about to be revealed from one moment to the next. Perhaps the contentment of discovering a new continent. Perhaps the awareness that a dream doesn't have to be a dream. Perhaps as if a lot of things had fallen into place though he can't say what. Perhaps a premonition of something big and surprising. Perhaps a light. Perhaps nothing. Perhaps. Or it may be much simpler: the best kind of happiness. Yes, the best, since it appears to have no object, form, reason, or end.

Eyes closed, he runs his hands over the rims of the books. Their bindings are leather and they allow themselves to be caressed. His hands stop at one volume, any one: there is nothing, to the feel, particular about it; his hands take it out gently and hide it in his pants, at the waist, behind his cowboy shirt. His hands are like two independent beings. He opens his eyes. He takes a few steps forward with the protection extended to him by the complicitous aid of the carpet.

The blue carpet cannot hide an unevenness in the floor. Sebastián kneels down, lifts the thick fabric. Underneath, a wooden door. In the floor: with no lock: a wooden door. He hesitates and dares: he lifts it. It barely weighs a thing. From the rectangle he just opened in the floor, stairs descend into a well of darkness. Sebastián begins to go down. It seems to him he should go down quickly: he's afraid of the fire that is sweeping the Island. He's under the impression that he can hear voices, he supposes he's really hearing them, except that at some point he realizes that his own thoughts have acquired real voice independent of his will. So, then . . . Stop! What fire is sweeping the Island?

Close, dangerously close, Uncle's baritone and affected voice. Vague pains in the muscles and deep sorrows in the soul, he says.

Since Rolo has given Sandokán a new pair of shoes, an expensive pair of two-tone shoes, Sandokán has left his cowboy boots at

Rolo's house. Rolo is smelling the boots. No one with the slightest sensitivity should doubt that the sweat of a beautiful man's feet is finer than the most expensive perfume in Paris. Rolo smells the boots and runs his tongue along the (yellow-stained) insides of the boots. If anyone were to discover him in this act, Rolo would explain, Don't be alarmed, I'm just like Emile Zola. Then he goes to the glass case with the Christ and the image of the Mater Dolorosa, and alongside them he deposits the boots, and he also places a vase full of flowers.

A deafening crash. Then another, louder. It was hard to say if it was just thunder. With the third crash the windowpanes jumped. With the fourth, a piece of the ceiling fell down, and the vase, in the center of the table, moved rapidly and smashed to bits on the floor.

Helena serves them each a glass of lemonade and sits down facing Rolo. Brother, have you ever been afraid? Rolo tries the lemonade, It's sweet, cool, exquisite, he fans himself with a palm frond, rocks on the little rocker. What do you think, sister? Helena smiles, embarrassed.

Then came gunshots, police sirens, gunshots. The paintings on the wall crashed to the floor. Helena thought first of Sebastián, though luckily he wasn't in his room. It seemed to her the ground was trembling and she herself was in danger of falling. The door to the living room began to burn from the bottom and at once was engulfed in flames.

I don't know, she says, sometimes I think . . . this fear . . . She falls silent. Helena is frightened. Rolo tries to break the silence with some witty phrase, something to make his sister laugh, except that nothing occurs to him other than to drink lemonade, fan himself, keep silent and get frightened in turn.

She ran through the flaming door as rapidly as possible and went out into the Island. She didn't go out into the Island. There was no Island. The trees, the ferns, the flowers had disappeared. The statues flew to pieces. She seemed to see Chavito crying in a corner with his arms around Buva and Pecu, only when she came closer she could see nothing but debris. The Island looked like a desert. Irene passed by shouting. Helena wanted to stop her and she vanished. Where is Sebastián, where is my son? She wanted to cry out and could not.

Do you think there should be a little more sugar in the lemonade? It's fine the way it is, I like it sour so you can taste the lemon, that's the only way to get your throat to cool off on this Island. These lemons have a special flavor. Observe: the smaller and yellower the lemons are, the better. That's because the big lemons are grafts, the small ones are natural. Do you mean to say that natural things are better than artificial? Don't start tripping me up in words, Rolo, I just mean that the small yellow lemons are better than the big green ones, that's all.

The fountain with the Boy and the Goose sank, turned into a well, above which Melissa floated, smiling, and shouted, This is the new world. Helena wanted to go out to Linea Street. She couldn't find the Apollo Belvedere, nor the courtyard, nor the iron gate, much less the street. In one direction and the other an immense wasteland stretched. She felt someone taking her by the arm. Not knowing how, she found herself in a long room full of cadavers shot through with arrows.

Can you imagine what would become of us, the scorched sons and daughters of this Island, without lemonade or palm fronds? And without hammocks and tamarind juice? And without porches and rocking chairs? And without sandals and cotton cloth? And without windows and beer? And without water, lots of water, water in abundance? And without deodorants and rainstorms? And without January and February? Can you imagine, Rolo, what will become of us if some day we lose these few sad gifts God has given to try and compensate us?

The cadavers still had the arrows in their bodies. She searched for her son. Her only obsession was to find her son. Sebastián, however, never appeared. Anyway, you couldn't see the faces of the cadavers. An old woman wearing a mask handed another mask to her and said, Take it, dear, this is the indispensable implement for living in the times that are coming.

A mask? Yes, a mask. Helena drinks down the remaining lemonade in her glass. Want some more? No, dear sister, what I want is for you to calm down, dreams are only dreams. You know, Rolo, sometimes I wonder, just what the fuck good are nightmares?

* * *

The mirror stands there, large, rectangular, in a blackened mahogany frame, with beveled glass, occupying the bare brick wall, facing the door. Until recently, when Casta Diva entered her bedroom she could believe that it covered a greater space, that she could keep on walking through the mirror into a vaster region beyond. Now she can't hold on to that impression. A few days ago she hung up a piece of black cloth and made a room that only measures ten feet by thirteen feet once again. It's better this way, she thinks. But anyhow she sometimes feels a desire to lift that cloth. She can repress herself and remain in bed, next to Chacho, listening to Tatina's breathing, waiting for she doesn't know what, or simply observing the confusion that reaches her from the Island. She entered the room some nights ago, tired out from a pointless stroll along the stone paths, among poorly carved statues, saying to herself, There's nothing more tiring than a pointless stroll, and she went straight to the mirror. She hated the mirror, hated seeing herself in it; perhaps for that very reason it filled her with fascination. The repulsion she experienced bewitched her. She abhorred the presages of old age that were starting to appear, the wrinkles that had, with a kind of subtlety up to now, begun to threaten her eyes and mouth. To ward off a paralyzing gravity she resorted, on nights like this, to makeup. She enjoyed smearing white foundation on her skin, outlining her eyes and eyebrows in black, painting her lips a scandalous red, accentuating, eliminating defects, creating other faces that inevitably referred to the one underneath. Then she'd sing. Sing, looking at herself. She actually didn't enjoy this, and after all, what does it mean to enjoy something? The night of the pointless stroll, Casta Diva looked at herself for one moment in the mirror before picking up the white cream, and she felt her image had taken its time in appearing. Later, when she began to daub herself with it, she again had the impression that the image delayed doing so, that it was resisting, and even when the reflection of herself that was projected on the other side of the mirror reproduced each of her movements exactly, she seemed to note a reluctance, or perhaps a distaste, and when she had finished and was made up to the point of exaggeration, and laughed with feigned cheer, the other face, the one in the mirror, stayed serious, you could even say seriously that it bordered all too closely on seeming intolerant.

The following day she didn't leave the house. She had a presentiment that something would happen but she had no idea what. She had started bustling about, and singing (in a low voice, feeling a little abashed). She expected a visit that never materialized, someone who would come and engage her in conversation or bring her some candy as a present. Nevertheless, other people had the habit of appearing when they weren't needed, never the reverse, and the wood of the door remained mute. It was from this awareness of inanity that she got the idea of looking at herself in the mirror. This time the mirror waited even longer to reflect her image, and when the other who was herself appeared, she had a sardonic look about her, or at least that was how Casta Diva wished to interpret her slight smile, her raised eyebrows, the intensity, the glare of her gaze, which was not only intelligent but sarcastic besides (if it is legitimate to establish a distinction between intelligence and sarcasm). What are you laughing at? she asked her image. She didn't even move her lips. Is there something about me that disgusts you? The one in the mirror stood immutable, until she decided to become serious, and lower her eyes, perhaps from embarrassment. She said, You're my image, it's your job to imitate whatever I do, imitate me till you're sick of it, that's your duty. The other blinked nervously, looked at her for a second, and then dragged over the replica of a chair that was in the room and sat on it with her face in her hands. (Need it be said that the real chair, the one in the room, remained in place?) Don't avoid me, she shouted, a bit exasperated, you have no right to avoid me. The image responded by sighing, standing up, and walking over to the window, which she opened onto the Island. Casta Diva could see how bright the day looked. (Need it be said that the real window stayed closed and that she, who considered herself the legitimate one, didn't leave her place?) She knocked on the glass of the mirror, shouted, You're unreal, abominable and unreal. Despite the fact that the image remained silent, she knew she had heard, something told her she had heard and was filled with fury. This supposition was later confirmed when the image took her change purse from the nightstand and went out into the Island. (Need it be said that the real change purse remained on the real nightstand? Would it be pointless to emphasize that the mirror was left empty?)

The image returned a few days later. You were lying in bed next to Chacho a little before dawn, sleepless of course, keeping an eye on Tatina, when you saw her walk up to the glass of the mirror, looking exhausted, older, with bags under her eyes, her clothing covered with dirt, a few leaves of grass in her hair, and an expression of such ferocity that it frightened you. You decided not to show it. Do you know what time it is? you asked, pretending not to care, pretending you felt like laughing, It's five hundred hours, time to be asleep, not standing there, mirrors also have a right to rest. While you were talking you noticed that she was holding the gold letter opener in her hand, and you instinctively looked for the real letter opener and couldn't find it, and you hid in a corner, and even though you couldn't see the mirror, you knew that she was looking for you, and your only relief was to think that she couldn't leave the mirror, that her place was irremediable, that she was condemned to being an image, and thanks to that certainty you were able to find the black cloth and throw it over the mirror.

A deafening crash awoke her. She turned on the light. She saw that the bedroom, like night in the Island, presented a sense of motionlessness, of abandonment. It was hard for her to understand (is it always so hard to understand?) that the crash had come from the mirror. She stealthily neared it, removed the cloth. On the other side the image was hurling furniture, vases, books, lamps, pictures against the wall. She did this with an economy of movement, at times barely moving at all. You could tell, however, that her fixity was a cover for a concentrated fury, the worst kind of rage, a rage that can premeditate. With the same violent parsimony she began to beat her head against the wall. Her fists were raised. She also kicked at the furniture strewn in disorder across the floor. She looked at the ceiling, impotent to reach it. She opened her mouth, trying perhaps to scream. Nonetheless, no sound escaped the mirror. Then the image stopped. It seemed she was looking at a photograph, yes, Casta Diva thought she recognized the photograph that had been taken of her as a girl, looking at a forested landscape, standing by a birdcage. She went to the desk drawer and looked for the photo. When she returned with it to the mirror, the image had fallen and was now on her knees, still holding the photograph. She saw how she squeezed it, crushed it, only to look at it again, at Casta Diva, singing, crying, the image crying, shaking her head, singing, crying, inconsolable, and Casta Diva heard her crying and above all her prodigious voice singing *Addio, del passato bei sogni ridenti* . . . and she saw how she stood up straight without ceasing to cry, to sing, and took the letter opener, and brandished it menacingly.

There stands the mirror, the hated mirror, large, rectangular, in a blackened mahogany frame, with beveled glass, occupying the bare brick wall that faces the door. Now it isn't a mirror: it is covered by a black cloth that keeps it from fulfilling its function. Sometimes Casta Diva gets out of bed (where Chacho plans to lie forever, it seems) intending to remove the cloth. Curiosity is stronger than fear, but fear is more tenacious. She returns to bed. She has thought of calling Mercedes, or Irene (they've both praised the mirror) to tell them, You can take it, I'm thinking of modernizing the room, any old excuse, in the end it doesn't make any difference to them, all they want is to take the mirror home with them. Only one detail stops her, and it isn't a small one or a simple one: they might notice that the image goes one way when she goes the other, that the image has lost it docility.

It's fairly late on a hot, sluggish night. The room is dark; not dark enough to hide the furniture, the pictures, the closed window, Tatina and Chacho, the cloth-covered mirror. She's not sleeping. She can't sleep. She has tried various prayers, but sometimes praying is as pointless as strolling around the Island. The silence amplifies the ticking of the clock. The ticking of the clock turns each second into an important event. She hears a sweet soprano voice, *Ah, con tal morbo ogni speranza è morta* . . . The black cloth on the mirror begins to rise. Casta Diva closes her eyes tight and hides her head under the pillow. If only it's a dream, she pleads, if only it's a dream.

Tall, elegant as a stylish singer. Mercedes. Beautiful, too. All the more beautiful if you compare her with Marta, her twin sister, terribly disfigured by the illness she has suffered from since childhood. Mercedes, on the other hand, is lovely and not ill. She wears costume jewelry necklaces, very high heels, pleated skirts puffed out with stiffly starched crinolines. Her long hair has a delicate, nearly blond color, while her eyes look dark, intense, alive (here again the comparison in inescapable: her sister's eyes look like glass). Mercedes's nose is more clearly defined than that on any of Chavito's statues. It could be that her mouth is not so pretty, perhaps her lower lip is a little too thick, but her smile doesn't hide her kindness. It's good to see Mercedes strolling around the Island, after she gets back from City Hall. Anyone would say: she's happy. She strolls among the trees, among Irene's flowers, as if there were no other place in the world like the Island, as if this were the perfect place. She sighs, smiles, and even sings a song, which is almost always *Those green eyes, that solemn gaze, in whose clear waters I saw myself one day,* a song no one knows why she prefers. As I described some pages ago, from the fifth floor of City Hall where she has her office she can see the blackened rooftops of Marianao, the Obelisk, the Military Hospital, the buildings of Columbia. I already said it, the only agreeable thing about the office is that you can look out the windows. Since she suffers six hours enclosed inside, she is content with knowing where her house, the Island, is. From her typist's chair she imagines life in the Island, Chavito's statues, the fountain, her sister Marta's rocking chair with its golden cushion, the trees, Irene's flowers, the river, The Beyond, This Side, Tatina's screams, Rolo's bookstore. I have to repeat it: that world, contemplated from afar through her eyes and from nearby through her imagination, lets her suffer less intensely the captivity of six hours of work, the torture of the typewriter. From the time she gets to work, she experiences a fatigue that consists of a premonition of the fatigue that will ensue later on. Besides, there's her boss, the grandnephew of Martín Morúa, implacably embittered, full of ambitions, whom she hates, or at least hate is what she likes to call the revulsion she feels when she sees, first, his long hands with more bones than are necessary, and second, his dirty teeth and his bad hair slicked over with green Vaseline, and when she smells the tobacco on his clothes and skin and his bad breath. That's why, when afternoon arrives and Mercedes returns to the Island, she feels as if she were arriving in Paradise. She walks through the bookstore, buys some books from Rolo (she loves gothic novels and biographies of famous people); she enters Helena's house for an instant, where Helena awaits her with a cup of coffee; she stops to converse with Merengue, who at this hour is already preparing the merchandise for tomorrow; she doesn't continue along the galleries but heads into the labyrinth of flower beds that is the Island to see whether Chavito has put up some new statue; at a window she greets Miss Berta, who has finished her classes and has now retired to a corner to recite the rosary; she gets to her house and kisses Marta on the forehead. Marta never responds to the kiss. Mercedes does all this with her kind smile, singing softly, *Those green eyes, that solemn gaze, in whose clear waters I saw myself one day*. And she seems happy. Irene, who sees her walk by many afternoons, says, Yes, she's happy, and Irene rejoices when she says, At least she is happy. And Mercedes enters the room that she and Marta share, the dark, poorly placed, scarcely ventilated room; she enters the gloomy damp of the room, knowing that if anyone were to arrive at that precise instant, no matter who it was, she would embrace that someone and would break down in tears.

How nice the Island looks after the rainstorm. It's dark green, shining, and the breeze that blows across it is so humid it's almost cool, with a smell of earth. Mercedes dresses in white. A linen dress with embroidered orange blossoms that go with her leather flats. She pulls her hair back into a well-formed bun that she fastens with tortoiseshell combs. She can't decide whether to wear the imitation pearl necklace or the silver chain with the medallion of Our Lady of Mercy. She tries each one on before the mirror; it's true, the chain looks better with her clean face, on which the makeup is imperceptible; on the other hand, it's already crazy enough to dress in white on such a bad afternoon, if it weren't that the Wounded Boy is young, so young, and that she feels like dressing in white (a color that goes well with her attractively pale skin). She looks at herself in the mirror for a few seconds, I'm pretty and besides that: I look distinguished, of good family, I know how to move, I know how to look. She smiles. She smiles ingenuously; she has one tooth that slightly overlaps another, that's attractive, I think. She puts perfume on her neck, the Bridal Bouquet she herself bought at Sears and then said it had been given to her by an admirer to whom she never paid attention, he never leaves me alone, he bothers me so much. She stands up from the dressing table, turns off the light. Marta is smiling in the rocking chair. Mercedes looks at her for one instant and feels despondent. She sighs, goes out to the gallery, it's true, the Island looks nice after a rainstorm, and her despondence gives way to a melancholy cheerfulness. At least this afternoon you can breathe, autumn has begun; in Cuba, this is autumn: cloudy, stifling days, rainy afternoons, a humid breeze at night, just for dawn to rise again on cloudy, stifling days, and so on until the first norther, which will be a poor grey bit of cold, a pretext for dressing better, a month of license for getting up your hopes of being able to wear a coat.

Nastasia Filipovna. Instead of Mercedes, she would have liked to be named Nastasia Filipovna. To have not only beauty but also Nastasia's force, her power to impose her will on others. She knows she came to a tragic end. She's been a long-suffering woman, too, but without the consolation of looking forward to a grand, unforgettable death of tragic dimensions, like Nastasia. It would be magnificent, she thinks, to awaken the love of men like Rogochin, and to awaken the tenderness of men like Prince Myshkin. To be tall and dark, with olive skin, slightly Oriental features, long, pure black hair, dark eyebrows well defined on either side of a proud nose, her red lips smiling, scornful. (I don't know if that's how she was described, I don't remember.) So she imagines her. That's better. Well dressed. Princess dresses. Long and murmuring, so that when she walks you can hear the swish-swish of it. God, how she would like to be a character in a novel! And to scoff at all the rest, yes, and not love any of them, or love only one. To be given a considerable amount of money and throw it into the fire in full view of them all, and they'll be fascinated, they won't be able to believe it, and to laugh, turn around with an elegant, graceful swoosh of her great skirt, to leave like a queen while the men who admire her, who worship her, remain there, almost dead, they don't know what to do without her. Nastasia Filipovna has knocked on Irene's door. When the latter opens, however, it isn't Nastasia Filipovna but Mercedes in a white dress who appears. Irene smiles calmly. To be honest, she wasn't expecting (couldn't have been expecting) Nastasia Filipovna. She wasn't expecting Mercedes either, but at least Mercedes belongs to her world and Irene isn't surprised to see her there, asking, How are you, my dear, explaining to her I've come to see how the

Wounded Boy is doing. And since Irene is happy to see her, she asks her to come in, Please come on in, make yourself at home. And at the very moment when Mercedes crosses the threshold, the little silver chain with the medallion of Our Lady of Mercy falls from her neck. She feels the chain slip from her neck, feels it fall down her breast. Sees it hit the floor. She must wonder, I suppose, how a necklace she had closed so well had fallen so easily. She doesn't know that this incident has nothing to do with how well she fastened or didn't fasten the necklace, but with my desire to interrupt her visit to Irene's house and to put off her meeting with the Wounded Boy. The two women are standing a pace away from the door, looking at the silver chain that has fallen to the floor. There we may leave them.

As you already know, or should know, Mercedes and Marta are twins. They were born in the middle of summer (Marta first). They grew up in the cemetery. City Hall had appointed the two girls' father to be the administrator of the Cemetery of La Lisa, giving him the right to live in the spacious and cool house that stood (and stands) inside the cemetery, between the mausoleum of the Veterans of the War of Independence and that of the Knights of the Lodge of Light. There they learned to walk, to run, to play. There they discovered one part of the world. They named the streets. They planted rosebushes. They painted images of saints on the walls. They played house and hide-and-seek in the vaults. They lay their dolls to sleep on top of the tombs. They took their dolls' names from the marble headstones (the same ones they learned to read from). In the shade of the poplar trees, reclining against the vaults, they sat down to eat mangos on stifling afternoons. There too they often slept the siesta. They devoted themselves to keeping the tombs swept clean and changing the water in the vases, which they filled with fresh flowers without drawing distinctions. That doesn't mean, of course, that they had no friends or predilections. Their friends were the ones with the nicest names on their headstones. Above all the rest, they had their favorite. Her name was Melania. She had been born in Santiago de Cuba and had died in Havana fifteen years later. They made up a history for her, invented a suicide for love on the very day she entered adulthood, the day of her grand debut. They didn't make her the daughter of an opulent family because the poor tomb in which she was buried (a rectangle of blue tiles with a jar for a vase and a plain wooden cross with her name and dates) did not leave room for many fantasies. They visited her every day. They dedicated the prettiest flowers to her. They brought her candies and caramels. For Epiphany gifts they would give her rag dolls and necklaces they made from sequins and beads that they bought for pennies in the Variety Store. One fine day they made her a crown of golden straw and decided to call her Queen of the Cemetery. They appointed themselves princesses. So when some funeral procession would enter, they would rejoice, jumping with happiness, and say that a king was coming for Melania. Then it was a matter of preparing for the betrothal, decorating the tomb with wreaths of miniature palms and fronds of royal palms, into which they wove a variety of flowers, bedspreads in festive colors that they took secretly from the house. The marriages, in any case, must have all come to bad ends: Melania would remarry every day: every day a new funeral procession would enter. Soon they realized that, if Melania reigned over the cemetery, the cemetery must have the rank of a kingdom. They gave it a name. Since La Lisa sounded too common, they called it Lalisia. They drew its coat of arms with two angels bearing trumpets, after an illustration they had seen in the missal, and they created a flag from some odd piece of green silk their mother gave them. On the other hand, any respectable kingdom must have, besides a queen and princesses, dukes, counts, marquises, and a cardinal . . . They sought out the finest tombs and created their nobility. Around that time (they would have just turned ten) they discovered the Common Grave. Toward the back, when La Lisa was about to turn to open countryside and you could already see the corrals and pastures and baseball fields, they found an enormous hole in the ground into which the gravediggers threw the bones of those who had no ossuary. As in every kingdom, there were both nobles and plebeians. As in every kingdom, the latter were more likable. Mercedes and Marta spent whole days among the confusion of bones, trying to put them back together, trying to return them to the bodies they had belonged to, as if they were caught up in a giant jigsaw puzzle. That was how they created the town. One afternoon, Mercedes found the bones of a hand the same size as her own. In this way they discovered that children also die. They wandered about sadly for several days, especially Marta (no one ever knew why, but she was the most deeply affected by the discovery). On another occasion when they were forming bodies with the scattered bones, Mercedes touched a skull and felt a chill breeze run through her body, and her skin reacted very strangely. She couldn't touch the skull; every time she tried, she would once more feel odd sensations in her skin. It was Marta who expressed what she, Mercedes, was thinking: This skull belongs to a man who has some connection with you. They kept the skull in a chest, which they secretly brought into the house. They baptized it, christened it Hylas. Mercedes imagined the young man to whom the skull must have belonged, she imagined him blond, golden-haired, and emerald-eyed, with a straight nose, not too large, and strongly defined lips, and she had an obscure intuition that a relationship was being established between herself and the skull that would last the rest of her life. Since the twins were getting big, they were allowed to go out at night. The cemetery at night was nothing like the cemetery in daylight. Night itself had almost nothing in common with day. At night you wouldn't sweat from the sun, a cooler breeze blew, the flowers were more intensely scented, shadows seemed more elegant, the most ordinary object acquired dignity, you could look up at the sky without fear of the glare and in the certainty that it would be more entertaining, for the sky at night would show you thousands and thousands of little lights called stars. There were other lights, of course. They came from the ground, especially from the direction of the Common Grave. Yellowish-greenish lights, lights that escaped from below, in no hurry, moving upward, perhaps aspiring to become stars. Will-o-the-wisps, Uncle Leandro said they were called. Their mother's brother, Uncle Leandro, would come on Sundays. He was taller than the average man and his athletic complexion contradicted his sweet ascetic face. He lived from the practice of law; his hobbies were swimming as well as asceticism. Though he was not yet thirty, he was spoken of as a confirmed bachelor. According to what they had heard (Mercedes and Marta had never gone), he lived in a bare little house on the beach at Jaimanitas, by the seashore, accompanied only by books. What was remarkable about Uncle Leandro, however, was the fact (especially important to Marta) that he had visited India. The Sundays that their uncle visited were charming in several ways. Their mother grew contented, professed admiration for her brother, and awaiting his arrival drew her out of the horror of her life. She went to great pains to get the house very tidy then and to prepare their lunch. During the week she was busy ordering the tender goat from which she would elaborate the dish of chilindrón her brother liked so much. Though he spoke little, Uncle Leandro enjoyed a rare charm that made you like him even in his silence. As a gift he always brought a box of candy from El Bilbao, an assortment of Little Crosses and Vanilla Temptations, Lemon Kisses, Heavenly Rolls, Chocolate Caresses, and Coconut Creams. After lunch, he went with his nieces for a walk around the cemetery. They would talk nonstop, telling him about the kingdom of Lalisia, Queen Melania, the counts, dukes, and marquises they lived with. He would listen to them, smiling, silent, pensive. Once Marta dared to ask him, Uncle, tell us about India, and you'd say his eyes shone with rays of gold and green, like the ones put out by the will-o-the-wisps. In those years disastrous events took place. One was that their parents, always belligerent toward each other, decided to stop hiding their disagreements. They argued at any time, over any triviality. Embittered, with a tragic air, their mother talked to herself, uttering curses. Irascible, like a caged beast, their father uttered curses and refused to talk. The situation became unbearable; the girls preferred to spend the day playing, wandering among the tombs. Another disastrous event was that a doctor attending the burial of a patient, as a casual or a causal guest (you can never tell), saw Marta's beautiful ruddy cheeks and approached her mother to tell her he was almost certain the girl was or would become diabetic. Her mother got angry and pelted the poor doctor with insults without respecting either mourners or funeral (it must be recorded that, like many people, the mother believed in anathema as a form of exorcism). Whether their mother liked it or not, the fact is that after that day it was possible to understand the fainting spells Marta suffered when she played, as well as the desperate thirst that assailed her at every turn. One night when it was pouring rain, their father and mother had a very loud argument over money. Their father grew enraged and got dressed to go out. Go on! their mother yelled, you're a bad father, a bad husband, go on out and I hope lightning strikes you! Although the curse did not come about exactly, half an hour after leaving the house their father was run over by a truck that had left the road when it skidded on the wet pavement. Despite the fact that his death brought the relief of a few days of silence to the house, happy days when their mother limited herself to moaning quietly in the corners (disoriented perhaps from having no one to attack), despite the fact that their father's death took who knows how much weight off their shoulders, they were soon to mourn the loss of the house. In effect, when the administrator disappeared, there was no more reason for them to stay there. The new functionary assigned by City Hall demanded his space. That meant saying good-bye to Queen Melania and the kingdom of Lalisia, good-bye to the nobles and plebeians and, despite the fact that they weren't mature enough yet to notice this (transcendent) part of it, good-bye to childhood. Mercedes and Marta turned eleven a few days before they gave up the cemetery, to which they would only return when they had reached a different and perhaps superior stature. Uncle Leandro came in his ramshackle Ford to pick them up one morning when the sun was carrying out its patient and habitual labor of turning the city into an immense lake of shimmering water. He moved them, with their few suitcases of clothes, into his house on the beach at Jaimanitas. It was an old wood-frame house that stood, the worse for wear, alone among casuarinas and sea grapes, shortly before Soldiers' Circle. To get there you had to take the sandy, hidden little road, half covered by weeds, that led down to the sea. When you thought you were already at the seashore, you found the house, raised on pilings, painted green-blue in some remote era (which is why it was lost against the sea, appearing to form part of it). The back terrace had a wooden floor, nearly in ruins, and a clumsy staircase that almost entered the water. The sea there had an emerald hue, and the white sand gave the union of the two a kind of deceptive, postcard feel. Inside the house there was little furniture and many books, an infinity of books, overwhelming quantities of books that filled up every corner. There's no denying that the books inside the house, together with the incredible sea that was visible through the ever open windows, created an odd contrast, symbolic of some mysterious wisdom. For Mercedes and Marta, after eleven years enclosed in the cemetery, arriving at Uncle Leandro's house was like discovering the world, or rather like arriving at another world, another island; the one-hour journey from the cemetery to the beach at Jaimanitas became a long journey of several days through marvelous oceans inhabited by deities. For this reason, they always knew Uncle Leandro's house as Typee. As for their uncle, you could call him a man worthy of living in Typee. Every morning, just before dawn, you could see him swimming; then he had a few fruits for breakfast, put on his collar and tie, took his ramshackle neolithic Ford and went to work in the law firm of Doctor Chili, facing the plaza of Marianao; he returned around midday, as contented as he had left; he stripped himself once more of the bothersome clothes, swam for another hour, ate more fruits, sat on the ground (he would later say, This is called the lotus position) with his legs crossed and hands turned upward, index fingers and thumbs together. Uncle Leandro practiced Buddhism. He spoke little, was never seen upset, always smiled. Mercedes began to notice that she liked being with him, that she felt protected in his presence. When, in the afternoon, between meditation and more meditation, her uncle took the trouble to teach them how to swim, Mercedes found herself flooded by a new enchantment. It had nothing to do with anything physical, concrete; it was a state of inexplicable happiness (isn't happiness always inexplicable?), rather as if a god had taken her under his wing. So that at the beginning, life was even happier in Taipi than in the cemetery. And it would have been much more so if one fine day the beggars had not appeared.

Between the Discus Thrower and the fountain with the Boy and the Goose, the afternoon following upon the downpour has caught Vido by surprise. He lies down beneath a white ateje tree, almost hidden among the aralia and hibiscus flowers. For the moment, no one could be sufficiently discerning to explain why he has lain there. Even the most ingenuous, even the simplest sorts of people realize that not every human action can be explained. At least not with the clumsy faculties we've been given. That is, it would be proper to write: Vido has *felt free* to sit under the ateje tree. This is even what he thinks himself. It turns out, however, that the ground and the grass are damp and agreeably cool. In this case, what is agreeable is not merely the coolness Vido discovers, but the way the damp makes Vido discover his own body, stretched out on the grass, experiencing the dampness. Likewise, right when he lies down, the breeze (a cool breeze, unusual for the Island, that has picked up following the rainstorm) begins to sway the branches of so many trees. Raindrops left behind by the downpour fall from the branches. From where he lies Vido sees them fall, and sees the afternoon sun shining in each one of them. It is a drizzle. At last, a drizzle, more discreet. More luminous, too. These don't look like drops of water but drops of light, if that's possible. Vido begins to hear the white ateje branches moving. Then he distinguishes the sound the breeze produces when it enters the casuarinas. The voluptuous whistling of the casuarinas is different from that of the serious white ateje. The guava tree moves with the sound of a silk curtain, while the royal palms send out a stern warning. The likable dragon tree laughs. The rubber plant laughs even more uninhibitedly. The bamboos, on the other hand, complain. The frond of a coconut palm falls to deafening applause. Vido puts his hands to his ears. He stops listening. He listens. He stops listening. He listens. Yes, I hear you all! he shouts.

My mother gave me this chain days before her disappearance, Mercedes says as she leans over to pick the chain up. Irene fastens the chain around Mercedes's neck. It's pretty, she says. How is the Wounded Boy? Better, much better, he doesn't have a fever anymore and he's breathing easily, sometimes he utters words I don't understand. And you, how are you? Irene collapses in an easy chair, dries her eyes, which are already dry, tries to smile. I don't know, I don't know, I still can't remember, I spend hours thinking about Emilio, about my mother, about the little house in Bauta, the day flees past while I try to find a memory, and here you see me with my head empty. Mercedes feels compassion for Irene, caresses her head. Forget about losing your memory, dear, you'll drive yourself crazy, look at the Island, it's so beautiful, so happy to have gotten that downpour. The other woman listens to her without seeming to listen, and shrugs. Do you want to see him? Mercedes nods. Irene stands up, content to be able to do something.

There lies the Wounded Boy. Irene has given him the best room with the best bed, the master bedroom, and for herself has prepared a chaise longue at the boy's feet. Irene cares for him as if he were a son, as if he were Lucio (may God forbid). Two nights ago, when the children found him and came running to tell about it and raised a commotion among everyone, when Merengue and Lucio carried him, with the help of Rolo and Vido and followed by all the rest, after they decided that calling the hospital or the police would mean giving him up into the hands of his murderers, no one doubted, no one had to ask, they just brought him straight over to Irene's house, fully aware that she would pay closer attention to him than anyone else, that she would attend to him better than anyone else. Not even Helena herself said a word. And when they called Doctor Pinto, he didn't have to ask. As soon as they opened the great iron gate that faces Linea Street to let him in, he went to Irene's house and asked her in the cracked voice of a rum drinker: Where do you have him?

There lies the Wounded Boy. Irene feels his forehead and smiles with relief, whispers, No, he doesn't have a fever. Mercedes looks at him, closes her eyes and looks at him again. She instinctively arranges her hair. It isn't possible! She feels a very odd sensation, something inexplicable suddenly paralyzes her, leaves her motionless, without gestures, without words, in the middle of the room. She tries to remember the moment when the rumor spread that Sebastián and Tingo had found someone wounded in The Beyond, in the carpentry shop of Vido's father, and they had been walking around like crazy from one end to the other, illuminated by Merengue's and Helena's flashlights, trying to find out who all the blood had spilled from that appeared in every corner of the Island. Mercedes remembers she was getting lost around the watering hole, around the bamboo, near Carmela's Elegguá, when Tingo came running, shouting, A wounded guy, a wounded guy. Wounded, where? someone asked, perhaps Helena, who is always the first to react. And Merengue — Merengue? no, Lucio, yes, it was Lucio who yelled, In the carpentry shop! And they set off running through the weeds toward the shop as best they could, since it's true The Beyond is impassable. And although that happened merely two nights ago, it seems to Mercedes that years have gone by since the moment they arrived in the old warped wooden shack and saw the boy there, covered with blood, on the carpenter's table, wrapped in the Cuban flag. She was struck then by his handsome tanned skin, his curly jet-black hair, his strange Bedouin profile, the dark mole at the corner of his mouth. Drying her dry eyes, Irene approaches her, Is anything wrong? Mercedes smiles, No, I'm fine. Yes, there lies the Wounded Boy. He is white, very white, with a sweet, gentle profile, and straight blond hair, and young, young . . . No mole darkens the corners of his mouth. When his eyes open at times, you can see two striking blue beads. Mercedes comes up to the edge of the bed and stands there observing him. Young man . . . who could have wounded him like that? Irene (sometimes you could swear she could read your thoughts) caresses Mercedes's shoulder and lets another whisper escape, It must have been the devil to wound an angel like this, only a devil, and lowering her voice yet more, making the whisper even more of a whisper, she adds, Listen, Doctor Pinto says they aren't bullet wounds. No, don't look at me like that, they aren't bullet wounds, Doctor Pinto explained to me confidentially this morning, listen up: confidentially, no one is supposed to know this, hear this, they aren't bullet wounds, no, they wounded him with darts, with arrows.

One fine day the beggars appeared, yes, they were seen arriving around sunset, there were two of them, a man and a woman, ragged, dirty, we couldn't get near them, only Uncle Leandro, who was getting close to sainthood, was brave enough to bring them each a bowl of soup, to be friendly, even to exchange a few words with them, after eating they went wandering around the beach for a while, a moment came when they disappeared and we didn't notice, and when they reappeared the next day we didn't notice that either, the next day four of them came, no, I'm wrong, five, yes, five, they came with a little girl who was even dirtier and more ragged than they were, Uncle Leandro fed them again, my mother went and helped too, I remember, my mother didn't talk, she stood there watching them like when she used to go into the Chapel of Christ Washing the Feet, the one in Corrales Street next to the fire station, and see the image of Our Lady of Sorrows there, they have an impressive image of the Mater Dolorosa there, all dressed in black, with black lace, real tears, or they look real, holding a handkerchief in her hand, the Dolorosa they have there always deeply impressed my mother, and you can still see her if you go there today, and they (the beggars) went into the water after dinner, they didn't take off their clothes, just went into the water, and they stayed in the sea until late at night, followed by my mother's watchful gaze, she'd sit down to sew, but she wasn't really sewing, that was just a pretext, just watching them, and my uncle would shut himself inside to meditate, haven't I told you yet that around that time Marta started losing her eyesight? to read she had to stick her eyes right up against the pages of the book, when she woke up in the morning she went to the window and asked, What's that out there, and that out there was a ship, she also bumped into the furniture and mixed up the medicines and barely could write, I was the one who noticed that Marta was starting to lose her eyesight, my uncle was such a saint he only worried about swimming, meditating, reading enormous old tomes, you know, saints don't have time for anybody else, and as for my mother, she spent hours sitting in the rocking chair facing the window, watching the sea with a strange, cheerful expression, like someone who's just about to become happy, an expression we never could figure out, never did figure out, my mother only stood up when the beggars arrived, more of them every day, greater numbers every day, one day six came, the next day ten, the next fourteen, until there were more than twenty, and every day they stayed longer, wandering around the house, swimming in the sea, shouting, singing, laughing, they seemed like the happiest beings on the planet, though Marta and I were terrified of them, we only dared contemplate them from afar, while my mother (my uncle, busier all the time with his own sainthood, no longer bothered with them) brought them food and conversed and laughed with them, one night we even heard her singing in the center of a large circle they had formed by the seashore while they applauded each verse of the song, a Spanish song that went something like *I'm the woman from Lagartera and I bring Lagartera lace,* I remember: I got closer, hiding behind the sea grape bushes, and saw how she sang, restless hands, fiery eyes, trembling voice, while the land breeze stirred her hair and made her voice vibrate ephemerally yet nevertheless lent her an image of timelessness, the image of a woman who had sung forever and who would sing forever a song with no beginning and no end.

The downpour left Professor Kingston feeling cold. He still feels cold. He is sitting in his little rocker and looking in horror at the cardboard fan on the bed. Also in horror he looks at the notebook on the table with his English class notes prepared. Professor Kingston hasn't been able to get up from the little rocker. Every time he tries, a sharp pain in the area of his hips, and farther within, in his sacrum, and farther within, much farther, a pain so strong and so profound that it no longer seems like a pain in my body but a pain in my soul, a pain in the world . . . the fact of the matter is that the pain keeps me from standing up, I've been sitting here for I don't know how long, sitting here for an infinity, I can't stand up, I give it a better effort each time, I tell myself I have to be brave, and I call on more strength than I have and I can't get to my feet, my legs won't obey me, *I must be brave.* Professor Kingston is thinking that if the sailor were to show up now, he would have to sit still before him. There's nothing else he could do. What bothers him most is his hearing, which up to a few hours ago had always been more reliable than his sight, and right now he seems to have lost it. It's as if the Island had disappeared and only he has remained, sitting forever in the little rocker. No sound reaches him from outside. The trees can't be heard. Could it be that no breeze is blowing? Impossible, outside there should be a different song coming from each tree, it's me, it's that I'm deaf, deaf and motionless, *What to do?* I remember when I would sit in the countryside and listen to the particular way each tree had for responding to the breeze, there were irate trees and happy trees and hapless and sad and euphoric and elated and timid trees, there were trees like human beings, but not now, there's no one, no one, and to top it all off I can't move, and I'm also cold.

★ ★ ★

It is necessary to have Irene go shopping to find the right justification for letting Helena stay by herself, taking care of the Wounded Boy. We have decided that this should be an enjoyable task for Helena, we have decided that she should enjoy watching the youth with his long, straight chestnut hair, the eagle profile of his face, his thin, pallid lips. We have decided that, as for almost every inhabitant of the Island, for Helena, too, this should be like having access to a saint. No one knows why this occurs to them. No one can explain their veneration for someone they don't know, with whom they haven't even spoken, for someone lying speechless, motionless, sick in bed. Like human beings (on whom they draw, after all), these characters are unaware of an infinite number of things about themselves. And the author, for all he would like to appear like the Creator, is also unaware of many things.

Every time Irene goes to the marketplace, it is Helena who stays to take care of the Wounded Boy. For her this is an enjoyable task. She likes to watch the youth, with his black hair, curly and short, and his soft profile. From the moment she learned he had been shot with arrows, Helena has looked at him with unction. Suffering always leads to devotion and respect. When, as now, she is alone with him, Helena talks to him as if he could hear her, and perhaps aid her. Like other human beings, the characters in this tale feel helpless and in need of a higher being.

Sometimes I feel afraid, boy, no, that's a lie, it isn't sometimes that I feel afraid, it's always, I'm always afraid, boy, remember that I am, they say, the best manager the Island has ever had or could ever have, and I carry on my shoulders the responsibility of saving it, that's why I go outside when everyone else is sleeping and scour the Island with my flashlight, I shine the light into every corner to see if every corner is still in one piece, I go looking for the spittoon, the hat stand that has eroded away unused, the wooden screen, the Victory of Samothrace, each one of the monstrous statues, the rocking chair, the Virgin of La Caridad in her modest glass case, I go looking to see that no tree has been damaged, no flower has been cut, I track, I follow every odor that doesn't come from the Island, I look for traces, I know every sound, every corner, and I love these trees and these horrible statues, and I love the infernal heat, and I love the houses that make up the

Island, these houses with their yellow-black walls, and I love the downpours that forebode the end, and the droughts that also forebode the end, and I love the way time stops in the Island, its handless clocks, the confusion, the labyrinths, the mirages, these stories that are told about it and if you come to believe them all you'll end up going crazy, I love the senselessness of our lives, the hopelessness, the exhaustion we all feel when dawn comes, tell me, why should you want a new dawn in this Island? I love Merengue's white pastry cart, I love Merengue and I love Merengue's lost son, I love Chavito who's off wandering I don't know where, I love Casta Diva, and Chacho, and Tingo, and Tatina, and Irene, and Lucio, I love Fortunato, and Rolo, and Sandokán, I love Miss Berta, I love Marta and Mercedes, I love my son, Sebastián, who . . . my son, my son Sebastián, tell me something, Wounded Boy, are you here for Sebastián? I want to know what will come of everything I love, if you could let me glance ahead to the end, the epilogue, if at least I knew my efforts did some good, if I only knew that this Island was able to stay on the map of the world, that I'm not taking my flashlight and scouring the Island in vain, if I only knew that the cracks I see opening up every day will close up again some other day, if I only knew that the red sandalwood tree of Ceylon would always be a red sandalwood tree of Ceylon, if I only knew, if you could reassure me that . . .

He has closed himself up in his room with the book he stole from the bookstore. It's a book with red covers. On one of the covers you can read: JULIAN DEL CASAL (a beautiful name, isn't it, Sebastián?). The sepia-colored pages, the large, round, decorated letters. His room, like Noemí's, is illuminated by a lamp. Sebastián opens the book at random (what he thinks is at random) and reads.

Noemí is sinful. Noemí is pallid and sinful. Pallid (applied to persons whose faces lack the normal rosy color of the healthy). Sinful (against the law of God). Noemí has red hair and green eyes, she is lying back on cushions, which are satin (a silk fabric), which are lilac-colored. Since she has nothing else to do, she is pulling the petals off an orange blossom. At her feet is an oven that heats her room. The piano, its lid raised, stands nearby. There is also a folding screen of

Chinese silk in the room. Folding screen (device formed of several frames, united by hinges, so that it can be folded up or extended). Silk (fabric made with special fibers). The folding screen of Chinese silk shows cranes (long-legged bird, ash-gray in color) flying in a cross formation. On a night table stands a lamp. The white fan, the blue parasol, the kid gloves recline on the settee (referring to a seat or couch, with or without arms, on which one may sit or lie). At the same time, the green spirit of tea steams up from a porcelain cup. What is Noemí thinking about? That the prince no longer loves her? That her anemia is wearing her down? That in her Bohemian vases (Bohemia: region of Europe famous for crystalware) she would like to trap a moonbeam? That she perhaps desires something even more impossible: to caress the feathers of Leda's swan (Zeus in disguise)? No, poor Noemí has been counseled that in order to relieve the tedium (weariness, boredom) that is sowing a fatal quietude in her soul, she should drink, from a cup of carved onyx (agate, chalcedony), the red blood of a royal tiger, a king tiger, a tiger king.

It's been days since Chavito came, it's been days since I've heard from Chavito, explains Merengue. Helena listens to him, trying not to express anything, trying to keep her serenity, her strong woman's air. Your son is at the disappearing age, it's only proper. And she stands up, aware that nothing she could say would calm the black man, and the only thing that occurs to her is to go to the kitchen and come back with a bowl of custard and a fake little laugh, Come on, Merengue, you can't hold on to a son, you know that. Chavito is all I have. For now, but the time will come when he'll give you grandkids and great-grandkids and greatgreatgreatgrandkids, since you, being a black man after all, will live to be two hundred. Merengue laughs sadly, without feeling like laughing, and eats, also without feeling like it, the custard, which has a strong flavor of cinnamon. Nobody can make custard like you. That's what Rolo says, I learned it from my mother, she could make it better. And they sit in silence, in the humid light of Helena's living room. Merengue finishes his custard and leaves it on the table in the middle of the room. The times are bad, and the phrase is enough for Helena to understand that he actually meant to say something else.

Yes, bad, terrible, would you be so kind as to tell me when they've ever been good? this Island! You're right: this Island! Whoever thought of discovering it? The Spaniards, it's all their fault — the spirit of adventure, the urge for nobility, the ingenuous sense of honor! — if this little bit of land hadn't been discovered, you'd be running around the Ivory Coast in a loincloth, and I'd be cleaning the floors of a convent in Santander. Now Merengue does laugh with feeling. And I wouldn't be selling candy? Helena shakes her head: You'd be going around with your cart selling elephant tusks.

Today he didn't go to El Bilbao and didn't take out his pastry cart. He dressed up in his best linen guayabera and brought down the straw hat his wife had given him as a wedding gift, in the days of El Chino Zayas. He stood for a long time in the courtyard, at the foot of the outspread wings of the Victory of Samothrace, crossing himself and praying to her, Little Virgin, if my son reappears I'll buy you the finest glass case you've ever seen. Then he left without knowing for sure where he was going. A rowdy bunch of soldiers entered Rolo's bookstore. Anyone who sees them would think there's nothing the matter, that Cuba is Eden, Merengue said to himself, continuing toward the train station, which was full at the time, since the train to Artemisa would soon arrive. In one corner Merengue discovered a black man sprawled on the floor, facedown. He ran over to him. With fear and with hope. Ran over and turned him face up. It's a drunk, said a woman who sat on a bench, knitting. Yes, a drunk, and also a young black man lying with his mouth open, sleeping off an excess of rum. Merengue tried to wake him, Come on, young man, they must be waiting for you at home. The black man opened his eyes, tried to smile, said something Merengue couldn't understand, and fell asleep again. Merengue tried to insist, but just then the train arrived. The train whistle, the movement in the station, and the sleepy face of the drunk reminded him that Sirocco had been one of the first people he had thought of. The association was not inappropriate, since Sirocco never took a bus to return home when he came to visit Chavito, but always waited for the train from Artemisa, and since he was a friend of the railway workers (and of everyone else) they would have the train slow down when it passed through Zamora so Sirocco could jump off, almost right in front of his own house. Of course Merengue couldn't do any such thing at his age, so he went out and walked down Calvario Street, with the rapid pace of a man accustomed to pushing a heavy cart loaded with pastries. After passing the park where a bronze bongo drum stood on a pedestal as an attempted homage to Chano Pozo, Calvario Street began turning more and more squalid, narrower, darker, until it became a tangle of wood-and-tin huts, tree stumps, and Coca-Cola ads, in front of which naked kids ran with swollen bellies, and inside of which men sat to play dice, with naked sweaty torsos, their hair uncombed, their faces unshaven, but making, on the other hand, a great show of their heavy gold chains. Drying their hands on their aprons, the women came to their doors to watch the old black man pass by in his dignified guayabera and straw hat, looking as if he had stepped out of another era. Sirocco's room, built like its neighbors from materials found here and there, built from any old thing, stood almost on top of the railroad tracks. Merengue noted that as he approached the room, on whose lumber he read, "I'm an adventurer and what do I care about the world," the doors and windows of the neighbor's rooms closed discreetly. Merengue knew that, even if he rang, no one would answer at Sirocco's house. He also knew that no one would answer at the other houses, either, that no one would give him the tiniest clue of where he might find Sirocco. Only an old man who came walking along the railroad tracks, using a tree branch as a cane, his eyes hidden behind a fog of old age, shouted in a trembling voice, No, sir, I don't know anything about Sirocco, and don't bother asking, they'll all say nobody has heard from him, don't be surprised, sir, in this country everybody wants to know everything and nobody wants to know anything, this I-washed-my-hand-of-it attitude is going to sink this Island.

Gunshots were heard when Merengue flagged down a bus next to the Military Hospital. He was set to go all the way to the house of La Rusa, who lived in the district of Regla, on the other side of the bay, in a tall house, on top of a hill from which you could look down on the sea and on Havana. Merengue had gone there once with Chavito, on a September 7, the feast day of the Black Virgin, eve of the feast of La Caridad del Cobre. From that occasion Merengue recalled with emotion the Cuban flag, so large that, draped from the top of the church, it even filled a small part of the arch over the main entrance. (He recalled that when they were returning the Virgin to her place at the altar after the procession, her crown became entangled in the flag, which fell on top of her. The procession continued into the nave of the church with a Virgin of Regla hidden under a Cuban flag, and a silent public trying to divine the precise significance of that omen.) The gunshots could still be heard when Merengue climbed on to the bus. The driver said something he couldn't understand. There weren't many people on board: a nun with a package in her hands, two girls in uniform, a gentleman with a suit and briefcase, a policeman. Around the Anti-Blindness League a blind man with a pair of maracas climbed on, stood before the driver, and began to sing, *On the trunk of a tree a girl, carved her name swollen with pride* . . . His voice had a dull timbre and always seemed about to die out; hearing him sing made you feel sorry, and perhaps that was his intention: as soon as he stopped he went by each passenger saying, A contribution for the Cuban artist, and collecting their few coins in a can. Afterward he sat down next to Merengue. Can you tell me the time? Merengue saw that his watch had stopped. He turned to the policeman, What time is it, please? The policeman looked at the watch on his wrist and apologized, Pardon me, it looks like mine has wound down. The policeman turned to the nun, Sister, do you know what time it is? The nun looked at her watch and said with surprise, My watch isn't working. The conductor, in turn, took the pocket watch that he carried in his pants pocket out of its case and saw that it had stopped. The gunshots were coming closer and closer. And the police sirens. Past the Almendares Bridge, a woman got on to the bus holding a child in her arms. The child wouldn't stop crying. The woman made every effort to quiet him, explaining to him that crying was his worst option; the child, for his part, made every effort to ignore her. The blind man started singing again, *With your meaningful name of Cecilia, supreme in the musical world* . . . At 23rd and 12th an old woman dressed in red, and a dirty, bearded man wearing a tunic made of sackcloth and carrying an image of Saint Lazarus, got on board. The man was barefoot and Merengue saw his feet were covered with sores. I'm a leper, the man explained as he begged with his outstretched hand. At the corner of 23rd and Paseo, the bus braked sharply and the nun's package flew out of her hands, broke open, and spilled out a skull, a tibia, a femur, and several other bones. The nun exclaimed, Dear God! while the leper fell to his knees and the blind man sang, *Listen to the story I was told one day by the old gravedigger for the county.* The girls in uniforms screamed. The policeman stood up and grabbed his pistol, but the old woman in red, quick as a flash, took a knife from her purse, pounced, and stabbed him.

After his swim in the river, Vido lies down naked on the bank, under the sun, which is hot (as it always is). Vido feels the sun's heat caressing his body, and a moment arrives when he doesn't know if the heat is coming from the sun or escaping from his body. It's as if his body were shining and burning like a star, my body is a star, my body is the sun, I'm shining, warming everything around me, I have my own light, my bones are so hot they've turned incandescent and glaring bright, the sun is inside me, I am the sun.

I'm so cold, *I'm ashamed to say it,* with all this heat I'm ashamed to admit I'm cold. The pain in his legs has diminished a little and Professor Kingston has put on his jacket and scarf and gone out to get some sun. Despite his jacket and scarf, he's trembling. It's a cold that resembles the pain, that comes from within. It's as if my bones had turned to blocks of ice, as if the sun had no power to melt the ice that is my bones, I could stand for hours beneath the sun of the Island, *the relentless sun of the Island,* my body wouldn't even notice, my body ignores the sun and the sun ignores my body, and between the two ignorances I'm dying of cold.

When Vido sees Professor Kingston coming, he jumps into the water. He thinks he hears the water crackle when it receives his body, hot as the sun. The professor greets him with a faint smile. It so hot! Vido shouts in too loud a voice, in a voice whose vigor and whose cheer he can't control. Yes, indeed, it's hot, the professor says, shivering, arms crossed over his chest, adjusting the scarf around his neck.

The scarf doesn't adjust properly and falls to the grass. The professor tries to lean over and pick it up. The pain in his hips, in his waist, in his body, in his soul, in the world, stops him. Vido runs out from the river and in no time flat picks up the scarf. Professor Kingston looks at the naked boy, the new skin refulgent with water and sun. Boy, he asks, did you know you were eternal?

Captain Alonso talks with Casta Diva for a long while. The captain looks worried: it's been more than a week since Chacho last reported to the base. The woman with reddened eyes tells him, Chacho only gets out of bed to do the necessities, he doesn't eat, he doesn't talk, he doesn't bathe, he doesn't look at Tatina or at Tingo much less at me, my husband has stopped living *(sob)*. Captain Alonso seems tired, looks restless. As you know, Casta Diva, the times are very bad. The woman blinks, coughs, moves impatiently. Captain Alonso takes out a handkerchief and wipes the sweat from his brow. His military jacket is soaking. Yes, the times are very bad, Columbia is a hotbed of unrest, all this is going down. She moves a few steps away; it is obvious that she prefers to watch the trees, or perhaps the Venus the Milo that can be half-glimpsed through the foliage. Don't speak to me of bad times, she says at last. We're on the verge of catastrophe, the captain explains, trying to smile. Casta Diva stands motionless, like one more statue. Catastrophe? what does that word signify for you, what does *on the verge* mean? on the verge of what? It signifies that a time of horror awaits us, and the captain points toward the trees as if the horror were out there. She remains standing motionless for several seconds and then shakes her head no, lifts her arms to the heavens, theatrically (and by the same token truthfully), There is a God up there, a magnanimous God, Captain, whatever takes place must be necessary, don't you agree? The captain takes a few steps, his boots are heard echoing in the gallery. This time God will abandon us, irremediably, we are on the verge of disaster, he says. The woman lets her arms fall. In this country we've always been on the verge of disaster. Until the day, adds the captain, until the day that we stop being *on the verge* and at last we meet our downfall, downfall, downfall (the man emphasizes the word in a way that proves difficult to reproduce here), pay attention to that word, how the transition from the first syllable to the second, from the *ow* to the *a,* gives the sensation of going over the precipice. And who says, Captain, that we haven't fallen already? who says that this Island hasn't always lived in tragedy, as you say? Ma'am, you are more pessimistic than I am. No, don't call it pessimism, I know all about dreams that don't come true, doors that slam shut, paths that get lost, precipices that open up, hurricanes that level, a sea that overflows, a sky that splits in two, the fatalism of destiny, the inevitability of fatalism, I am the Republic, Captain, I wanted to do something I didn't do, wanted to be somewhere I'm not, I aspired to something I can't aspire to, I gave birth to an abnormal daughter, a son who understands nothing, I know what it means to have a husband who comes home one vile day, crawls into bed and doesn't say another word, look at me, Captain, take a good look at me, look at this greying hair, these lusterless eyes, these withered hands, listen to this voice that, unluckily for me, has fallen silent, observe carefully my elderly looks despite my forty years, do you understand, Captain? the Island is me. The captain leans down to the ground, to Irene's ferns, he's about to cut a gardenia, and he doesn't, something stops him. What's wrong with Chacho? The same as with you, the same as with me, I suppose, Doctor Pinto gave him a checkup and couldn't find anything physical, he spoke of . . . I don't know, I don't know, Doctor Pinto isn't sure what my husband has. Captain Alonso squats down to watch a line of ants carrying leaves, petals, insects. And you say he never gets out of bed? The woman stands in thought for a few seconds, then smiles and says, Well, there was one day that Chacho left the bed.

Three or four days ago, early one Sunday, the bells in the great iron gate were ringing. There was no one at the door. At first I thought it might be the gang of kids that go around knocking on doors, or perhaps the Jehovah's Witnesses with their Bibles and *Watchtowers*. Yet there was no one on Linea Street. Even the gangs of kids — even the Jehovah's Witnesses! — respect the melancholy of Sunday mornings. Helena returned to work, she was very busy cleaning the bloodstains off the Cuban flag that Tingo and Sebastián had used to wrap up the Wounded Boy. A while later the bells were ringing again, and again Helena went to see, and this time she found Merengue, who hadn't gone out with his bead-encrusted white cart even though it was Sunday (great day for sales in the hospitals), looking strange and dejected and sad and silent (and he's always so rambunctious). Merengue was in the courtyard, placing a vase of butterfly sorrels at the feet of the Victory of Samothrace. Helena knew, naturally, why he was acting so strangely, why he was setting out the bouquet, so she greeted him shortly, she asked him, Have you seen anyone knocking? Merengue looked at her for a moment as if he didn't understand and then he made an effort to affect his usual tone, at which he was unsuccessful. No, the truth is, I was coming here with this bouquet and I heard the bells ringing, when I got here there wasn't anybody, not at the door, not on the street. The same thing happened to me, Helena explained, it's the second time it's occurred. Must be the wind, whispered Merengue. What wind? you woke up feeling romantic today. Merengue couldn't answer and couldn't smile; nor could he look at her. He waited for Helena to leave before he knelt down again before the reproduction of the Victory of Samothrace, to whom he wanted to dedicate a Hail Mary. The bells in the iron gate rang again. Merengue turned as quickly as he could and saw nobody. Helena returned, accompanied this time by Irene. The two women even went out into the street. Nobody. There was nobody there. At this hour, at most, a few soldiers were beginning to walk down from the train station toward the Columbia base, it was not, however, very likely to have been them (pardon me, Captain Alonso, no matter how congenial a man is, he loses his sense of humor as soon as he puts on a military uniform; in my opinion, armies come about precisely when human beings become ashamed of laughing, a soldier is a man bereft of everything but hatred and tragedy). When Helena and Irene returned to their houses, to their chores, Merengue knelt down once more before the clay reproduction of the Victory of Samothrace, joined his hands, closed his eyes, prayed, pleaded fervently for Chavito. Then he began to feel that he was levitating, little by little he was levitating from the ground. A great feeling of well-being came over him. He passed above the wooden screen, next to the Apollo Belvedere, overflew the evergreen oaks, the willows, the sacred jagüey, the red sandalwood tree of Ceylon, the mango and soursop trees (the ones that produce the biggest and sweetest fruits, and that Sunday morning their aroma was overwhelming), from up there he saw the fountain with the Boy and the Goose, the Watering Hole, Consuelo's Elegguá, he went off into The Beyond, toward Professor Kingston's house, got to the River, returned along the other side of the Island, past his own house, past Eleusis, and from up in the sky he saw Linea Street and he saw an enormous blue Cadillac turning onto it. Merengue opened his eyes at the feet of the Victory of Samothrace. He turned around with great unction. There stood, yes, there stood the blue Cadillac. He didn't stand up, he walked on his knees to the great iron gate and started moving it desperately to ring the bells that are set into it, so that everyone would come, would run over and have the joy of seeing who would come out of the blue Cadillac.

First Iraida came out, looking lovely (have you ever seen a more beautiful mulatto than Iraida?). Offspring of Spanish man and black woman, she had perfect coloring, perfect hair, perfect features, a perfect body (though they get tired of explaining it, one will never understand why it is that every inhabitant of the Iberian Peninsula doesn't run out to find a mate in the African continent — or vice versa — in order to begin to bring about — in the only way possible — the dream of a Better World). As a daughter of Our Lady of Mercy (Obbatalá), she dressed in white, wearing a simple cotton dress that revealed her shoulders, which were covered by her hair, sort of like a black woman's hair, sort of like a white woman's hair. From the moment Merengue saw her descend from the Cadillac he sensed the aroma of Cotillon perfume that preceded her, as if a legion of Iraidas were announcing the arrival of Iraida. Behind her, of course, came the Greatest Singer in the World, Beny Moré! Merengue shouted in greeting, what a great band you have! In his wide-brimmed hat, his denim overalls, and his red-and-yellow checked shirt, Beny looked thinner than usual, tired, haggard, a little sad despite the smile that never left him. At the sound of the ringing bells, the courtyard filled with people, Helena first, affable as she has rarely been in her life, opening the padlock. Everyone (except Chacho) pressed in to greet Iraida, Woman, you're beautiful, kissing her, hugging her, and there she was in the center, enchanting, smiling. He stood behind, radiant in his wife's glow, giving hugs, shaking hands, handing out smiles, with his characteristic greeting, And what about my Cuba? to which everyone replied, flatteringly, As long as you're here singing, there's nothing wrong with Cuba. Not even Uncle Rolo could hold back his admiration, and he shouted, The day you die, Beny, the Island will go under. And they passed by the wooden screen, left behind the courtyard, the comfort station, the spittoon and the hat stand, to arrive in front of Merengue's house, where the necessary rocking chairs appeared, and someone (Casta Diva, I suppose) brought rice pudding, and someone (Helena, I suppose: it wouldn't be logical to think Irene would leave the Wounded Boy for so long) started brewing coffee. Buva and Pecu hopped onto the singer's lap in a single bound, he petted them, smiled at them as if cats, too, had to be won over, as if they could have known he was the Greatest Singer in the World. Beny ate rice pudding, drank coffee, and talked about Mexico, about how his band's tour through there had gone, about his duet with Pedro Vargas. My goodness, with Pedro Vargas! *(prolonged applause).* The Mexican people really love Cubans, Beny explained, and besides, there you have Ninón Sevilla, Rosita Fornés, María Antonieta Pons, Pérez Prado, Mexico is a frightfully beautiful country, life and death working together, as they should, producing volcanoes and gigantic flowers over there, I feel good in that country, not as good as here, naturally, and I don't have to explain that, right? being Cuban means you suffer when you're away, staying in the Island is the only way . . . Silence. Silence reigned. Then, to break it, Beny struck a beat on the rocking chair arms and sang, *Oh but how deliciously lovely Mexican women look dancing mambo . . . (applause).* Fanning herself with her white fan, Iraida stood up, elated, Tell them, Beny, tell them how we met Cantinflas, an enchanting man, refined, elegant, not at all like what you see in the movies, those hilarious entanglements, no, no, a man of culture, he invited us to dine at his house, well, not his house, his mansion, well, not his mansion, his palace, filled with objects of art, so valuable, and I swear, if it hadn't been for his physical appearance and his way of talking, I would have sworn Cantinflas was English. Irene sat down again, smiling. We also met María Félix, they call her María Bonita for good reason, she's the most beautiful woman ever born on this planet, and we visited the tombs of Pedro Infante and Jorge Negrete, and we placed flowers there and Beny sang to them. Then the Singer interrupted Iraida, who was undoubtedly ready to relate every detail about their visit to the tombs, and asked again, though with a different intonation than he had used when he greeted them by the iron gate, And what about my Cuba?

Silence. Silence reigned.

Anybody would know what the blue Cadillac parked on Linea Street meant. Helena, who knew from experience what would happen, made an exception and didn't padlock the great iron gate. Then something that rarely happens, happened: the Island filled up with visitors. First Lila appeared, the fifteen-year-old with blue eyes and blond hair, with no arms and no legs, in the baby carriage her sisters used to take her everywhere. Beny picked her up from the carriage, carried her, and started whispering with her, not letting the others hear what they were talking about. Lila started to laugh and cry at the same time. The Singer hugged her tight, carefully returned her to the carriage, and gave her some chrysanthemums from the Island. Acacia, who they say is the bastard daughter of Amadeo Roldán, presented him with a musical score called *La Rebambaramba* with annotations in the illustrious composer's own hand. (Acacia apparently didn't know that Beny had never studied musical theory or notation.) Solidón Mambí, secretary to Luis Estévez (first vice president of the Republic), appeared with a golden medal engraved with the profile of José Martí, which he, Solidón, fixed to the singer's overalls. Roberto the Beautiful and Jenoveba de Brabante showed up with enormous casks of ice-cold coconut juice, which was immediately distributed to all those present. Belarmino the Poet came in singing a ballad. Also singing (Mexican country songs), Blanca la Negra entered, with her tight lamé dress and her voice that sounded just like Lola Beltrán's. Single-file, well-behaved, in uniforms, led by the teacher María Amada and the caretaker Laura, the fifth-grade students from the Flower of Martí School arrived; one of the children, trembling and wearing turtle-shell glasses, read an essay dedicated to the man *in whose voice the soul of our Country will always reside.* Councilman Genaro declared him *Favorite Son of the District of Marianao.* A little old man with filthy clothes and a wretched face, whom they called Abelardo Pennypincher, led by a bland and equally filthy guide whose name, as might be expected, no one remembered, asked the Singer to grant him forgiveness for his uncountable sins. Then there arrived Fina la Libertina, Reinaldo the Scribbler, Soleida Triste, Maruchy Manwoman, Paco López (who wouldn't stop talking), Raulito Nuviola (in his sequin outfit), Xiomara the Puppeteer, Tabares the Apostate, Unruly Raquel (Doña Bárbara), Chantal Dumán (a Frenchwoman, a marquise, and down on her luck), Gloriosa Blanco, Plácido the Shopkeeper, Elodia, Nancy, the wicked Amor and her wicked twin sons, Omar the Informer, Rirri Arenal, Alicia Mondevil . . . And they kept on arriving and arriving until, despite the din arising from the multitudes, they heard the rap of a cane and the voice of the Barefoot Countess who shouted as never before, This is not an Island but a tree-filled monstrosity, and an intense silence followed. You could hear the startled breathing of the Greatest Singer in the World.

Shoeless, wearing her blue dress and looking like an exiled empress, leaning unnecessarily on her ácana wood cane, with that elegance whose origin you can never ascertain, passing by the Laocoön, the Barefoot Countess emerged. She stood still for a moment when she entered the gallery with her mocking smile and her gaze that seemed to contain every mystery (a gaze heavy with wisdom and kindness, contradicting her smile, a sad gaze of one who *knows*), until her eyes came to rest on those of the Singer. He had gone pale. She lifted her cane. Trying to escape this solemnity, he exclaimed with feigned cheer, I was hoping to see you, Countess. She did not reply. She slowly walked forward. The crowd began to part for her as if she really were an empress. When she arrived before him, she kneeled down. He extended his hands and could not quite touch her. Why are you kneeling? The Countess was serious. Because you no longer belong to this world, Singer.

It occurred to Roberto the Beautiful, thank God, to hand out more ice-cold coconut juice. Even children know that in this Island, where the devil has installed the frying pans of hell, coconut juice helps man forget all his discomforts. Even children know that coconut juice is to the Island what nepenthe was to the Greeks.

When evening fell, Beny began to sing. He strolled through the gallery and sang, *Reality is birth and death, so why should we even worry . . .* His voice was melodious, pleasing. Even the trees of the Island held their branches still. Everyone else sat on the floor and looked at the floor. Some of them closed their eyes. Some embraced each other (whether or not they had met before). *The world is nothing but eternal suffering . . .* He sang down the path that leads to the Fountain with the Boy and the Goose. The Barefoot Countess went off to Consuelo's house. Evening depended on his voice alone. *Life is a dream and everything fades . . .* Anyone would come to think that the sky was darkening over, that clouds were thronging to the Island, as if night were suddenly about to come. Apart from his voice, someone was heard sobbing. No matter how much they searched, no one could tell who the sobs were coming from. *Reality is birth and death . . .* You couldn't see anything now; they continued to hear him nonetheless, as if he were singing into each one's ear. That voice is all that matters now, thought Casta Diva. That was the moment when she saw Chacho next to the Venus de Milo. Though he was crying, the man had a blessed expression on his face.

(The same Sunday that Iraida and Beny Moré paid their visit, almost at night, Sebastián found the Barefoot Countess in The Beyond, at the riverbank, apparently playing with her cane and a bunch of yagruma leaves. Seeing him, the Countess called him over, Sebastián, boy, listen well, remember this, what I'm about to tell you is important, did you see him? did you hear what a voice he has, how well he sang? you'll never see him again. The Countess went back to playing with the yagruma leaves, remained silent for a few seconds, then insisted, Remember that, Sebastián, it might be useful to you in the future: the most serious problem with this Island is that its gods are mortal.)

There lies the Wounded Boy. Merengue sees him with his mixed-race hair and mixed-race eyes, a mixture of Chinese and black and white, his mixed-race skin and thick, mixed-race mouth, and he feels the same unction as Irene and as Helena and as Lucio and as everyone else. Merengue brings a bouquet of everlastings, which he places in a vase on the nightstand, and then he sits down to chew his unlit cigar.

He had gotten to Regla very late, when it was already dark and Havana had stopped being The City and turned into The

Phantasmagoria. You could no longer hear the shots being fired nor the police car sirens wailing. Merengue wandered through unknown streets, past places that meant nothing to him, and almost without knowing how, he found himself facing La Rusa's huge house. He knocked on the door and no one opened. He knocked again and again felt that time was exaggerating its pauses, its dimensions. He knocked desperately. At last it was opened by a black boy a dozen years old who went barefoot and bare-chested and wore a blue skirt, earrings, a blue ribbon in his hair, and bright red lipstick. It was Mandorla, La Rusa's little brother. It was rumored in Regla that he was a girl whom Ollá, out of a dispute with Yemayá, had transformed into a boy so that the poor child would live with nostalgia for his former girlhood. Whom do I have the pleasure of . . . ? he or she (as the reader prefers) asked respectfully. Merengue replied that he was Chavito's father. Mandorla bowed, adopted a face befitting the circumstances, and said, Come in, please, our house is yours. In the enormous living room, all the furniture had been moved into one spot. Only a grand piano could be seen in one corner, where an old man, also black and red-haired, played a version of "The Swan" from *The Animals' Carnival.* Another black boy who looked like Mandorla, perhaps suffering from the same curse of Ollá, in a snow-white tutu, waved his arms urgently. When Merengue entered, the old red-haired black man stopped the music, and the little black dancer (twelve or thirteen years old) let his arms fall easily, languidly. Chavito's father, Mandorla announced in a doorkeeper's tones. Merengue was about to bow, but Mandorla stopped him by taking his hand and leading him into a room full of altars with images, with flowers, with old photographs, with candles, with glasses of water and wine, with plates of food and candy. Greet her, Mandorla ordered. Merengue greeted the Virgin of Regla and fell to his knees. I'm looking for my son. I know. I thought maybe your sister . . . I'm looking for my sister, my sister disappeared the same day Chavito did, wherever they are, they're together. What can we do? Mandorla sighed, shrugged, and straightened the Virgin's blue cape. I'm tired of asking. Merengue pointed to the saints. What do they say? Nothing, they don't say anything, the little faggots are silent. Be respectful! Respectful? Have you forgotten how they disappeared, your son and my sister? It wasn't them! It was, it could only have been them, only they have the power. Mandorla took hold of a cup of water and held it out for Merengue. He took it, trembling, looked into it and for a moment I thought the water was churning, and that my son's image was going to emerge in the bottom of the cup, I thought a miniature of Chavito was forming there. Then the water calmed and no such image appeared and the cup of water was nothing but a cup of water. We'll have to check with the hospitals, with the police. Mandorla took the cup of water back from Merengue and threw it at the Virgin, who tottered and lost her head. Her crown rolled to Merengue's feet. Don't even think of going to the police, old man, because I'll kill you, screamed he or she (as the reader prefers).

Believe it or not, Sebastián, there really is a place called Florence, and it's the most beautiful city in Tuscany, and Tuscany is the most beautiful region in Italy, and you wouldn't be capable of imagining what kind of a city it is, accustomed as you are to the hick towns and little villages of this country that isn't even a country, Sebastián, just a horrid little thing we call an Island for lack of a better word (and islands aren't countries, just ships run aground forever — and time, ay! doesn't move in ships that have run aground forever), and the city of Florence has the most beautiful cathedral you could ever imagine, it's called Santa Maria del Fiore and it's made of so many shades of marble that it looks like a piece of candy, a famous (incredibly famous) painter named Giotto built the Bell Tower, which is more than two hundred fifty feet tall, and the dome is a monument to perfection, built by someone named Brunelleschi, the teacher of another important man, Michelangelo, and don't ever think that there's no more to Florence than its cathedral, no, not a bit of it, because there's the Piazza della Signoria and the Pitti Palace, and the Uffizi Gallery where you can see Botticelli's paintings, and in that gallery (or maybe another one, I'm not sure) people go to cry before the most beautiful man in the world who is Michelangelo's David, and after crying till their eyes nearly fall out they go to the Arno, which is a river (a real river, Sebastián, not like this ditch you people like to call a river) to see the night fall, and seeing the night fall over the Arno is an opportunity to keep crying from happiness, until the next day comes and you keep crying because it's a new day in the magical city of Florence, where in the end the most important thing isn't the monuments but a rare something no one has ever been able to explain, and I swear, Sebastián, dear boy, I'm crazy about going there to cry, though I know it's pointless, why should I go if my eyes are dried up and I can't even dream.

They have passed the schoolroom, empty at this hour, and the disjointed little door that separates This Side from The Beyond. Sebastián goes in front, like a good guide; Marta behind, resting her hand on Sebastián's shoulder. Despite the fact that The Beyond is practically impassable, Sebastián knows it very well and is following the path worn by Professor Kingston with his daily walk. Martha insists on saying hello to the Jamaican. They halt for a moment before his house. They shouldn't even knock, the professor has sensed them and has come out, smiling, affable, despite the fact he seems to have taken a turn for the worse and is wearing a coat and scarf and you'd say he's trembling with cold (in all this heat!). How do you do, Professor? Holding on, dear, holding on. The afternoon must be so lovely . . . I told Sebastián to accompany me on a stroll. Every afternoon is lovely, Marta, each one in its own way. That's true, pardon me, I meant, lovely for a stroll. I only wish I could join you. And why don't you? My legs hurt, I can barely move them, you realize you're getting old when your legs hurt and you cut back on your strolls. *(Laughter)*

I can't remember how the rain fell in Jamaica, Professor Kingston says, though there is no one else in his room, nor could there be. He has entered his house, feeling cold, and he is giving his legs alcohol rubs, because they hurt on account of the humidity. Whenever I try to remember the rain in Jamaica, my memory turns up blank. It must rain there just like it does here, they're both Caribbean islands, exposed to the same horrors. The day I met Cira the sky split in two, it rained as if there had been centuries of drought. No, it had actually not been that day, Cira and he had met on a May 20, the day they hoisted the flag, a lovely day, to tell the truth, and the people were as contented and lovely as the day, and he saw Cira crying as if instead of raising the flag it were Jesus himself they were watching ascend into heaven. Cira, *it didn't rain that day, right?* The hard rain took place later, yes, the afternoon when he went to meet her at the entrance to the house where she worked. The day I first saw you it didn't rain and it couldn't have rained, it was a national holiday. *Who can forget that day?* No, I remember, as if in a dream, the bands playing, the little flags decorating the streets, the Prado all decked out, people elegantly dressed, dancing, from one side to the other, to the music of the bands that filled the avenue. And when they played taps, that was when I saw you, Cira, leaning against the columns of that building, dressed in red, blue, and white, with your beautiful black face covered with tears because they were hoisting the flag. Professor Kingston never saw the flag hoisted for the first time: he was looking at Cira and, while they were playing taps, all Havana came to a standstill as if under orders to do so, he took out his clean, perfumed handkerchief and offered it to Cira, who couldn't stop watching the flag rise slowly up the pole. You took the handkerchief, woman, without drying your tears, without looking at me, and then when the flag began to wave and a unanimous shout of jubilation went up, you realized you had accepted a stranger's handkerchief and you returned it, perplexed, frightened, begging my pardon. He continued to give his legs an alcohol rub. Humidity is terrible for the bones. And despite the heat, I'm dying of cold.

For a long time now Marta has been asking God to let her go to Florence. Of course, it isn't that Marta really wants to *go* to Florence, it's that she wants to *dream* of Florence. It wouldn't occur to anyone to doubt that there is a substantial difference between actually going and imaginatively dreaming. Marta is much, much more interested in the imagination than in actuality. She knows that, as she has gone blind, going to Florence, being there, doesn't signify much; she knows that it is better to fancy Florence, and every afternoon I sit in the rocking chair, the center of my world, and close my eyes, which is a mechanical act since it doesn't matter whether I keep them open or closed, and invoke God, I get ready to walk through those mysterious streets, past Santa María Novella, down la Via della Scala to the Piazza del Duomo, I insist on seeing the door of the Baptistery, the Paradise Gate, I insist that it be twelve midnight on the dot on Easter Saturday, I want to be there for the Explosion of the Carriage. Nothing. God (or whoever it may be) never takes pity on her, on her desires to dream. She never manages to break through that dark, nearly black, red curtain that hangs between her and Brussels, between her and Florence, between her and Alexandria, between her and her dreams.

You do well to take a stroll through the bamboo, Rolo, to look at the old watering hole and to stop for a moment in front of Consuelo's Elegguá, whom you will once more ask to open up the roads for you. He continues to the statue of that skinny woman (Chavito says it's Diana), walks into The Beyond. Look, there go Vido and Tingo-I-Don't-Get-It, flying kites. (Sebastián is going with Marta toward the sea.) You'd do well to go where they're going. Go ahead, please, and forget that Sandokán exists. After all, he isn't the only beautiful man in the world.

The fact is that Sandokán hasn't come by in days and Rolo doesn't know what to do. He can't send him a message, Sandokán has taken the precaution of never revealing where he lives. Rolo supposes that his mother must live in back of the Military Hospital: many times he has seen Sandokán taking that route, getting lost among the officers' little houses. He shouldn't discard the possibility, however, that this may be a way of throwing him off track, given that it is also true that he disappears many times down Linea Street going toward the train station, and other times, going through the pastures; there are even afternoons when you can see him cut through the Island toward The Beyond. Sandokán is clever. He knows little about Sandokán, so little that he doesn't even know his real name. Helena has warned him, It's dangerous to let that man enter your life, enter your house, enter the Island. Rolo replies, I can't help it, Helena, I can't. Of course he can't tell his sister the reason why he can't help it, even if it's easy to deduce, he can't say this man means a lot to him, he changed my life, not because he arouses my love but because of something much more serious, it's a whim, and there's nobody like him for making me feel that this wretched body to which I must unfortunately attach the possessive adjective, this worthless body of mine, is an object of desire. There has never been anybody like Sandokán to make him feel the reality and the desires of his body. Whole zones of his body had been asleep until Sandokán arrived. Whole zones of his spirit were benumbed as well, just waiting for someone like him. He met him more than a year ago, on one of those nights when desire came between him and the bed and made rest impossible. Rolo already knew that on nights like this the only thing to do was to abandon the bed and go out to the train station, in whose urinals he always could sense the urine of some generous soldier willing to let his generosity be fondled. That night, however, even though there were two hieratical soldiers instead of one in the urinals (he suspected they were fondling and smooching each other), Rolo couldn't stop looking at that unique specimen, with the profile of a Greek vase, a classical torso (he was shirtless), an athlete's legs (he was wearing short frayed pants), barefoot, crying in a corner. He produced such an impression on him that, breaking his cautious habits, he walked straight up to him. Young man, why are you crying? The young man looked up quickly and said nothing. Rolo sat down beside him. Cry if that makes you happy, but I'm advising you: tears don't solve anything, and he dared to put his hand on the boy's shoulder, atop a tattooed acanthus leaf. Do you want to come home with me? I can offer you a cup of coffee, a glass of rum, as you prefer, you could also take a shower and rest, we can talk if you'd like, I know more of life than you do, the devil's smart because he's old, not because he's the devil. The young man wiped his nose with his hands and then rubbed his fingers on the wall to dry them. He looked at Rolo with curiosity, almost smiling despite his tear-reddened eyes, and he asked with the best-timbraled voice in the world, Where do you live, old man? And Rolo wanted to say, Very near here, but his voice wouldn't leave his throat and he could only make a gesture with his hand. The young man straightened out his short pants, dried his tears, and left the station followed by Rolo. When they got to the house, to avoid people's gazes and indiscreet comments he didn't go to the Great Iron Gate, rather he decided to enter through Eleusis. It amused him to see that specimen looking with surprise and a bit of terror at the books. At the same time he felt a touch of rage. He couldn't stand to see laymen looking at books, he felt that literature was a mystery, and insofar as it was a mystery, for initiates only. With some impatience, therefore, he led the young man toward the house. Come along, you can't shower or sleep in this sanctum sanctorum. When they were in the living room, the boy sat down in a little rocker and picked up the bust of la Malibrán. You run the library? Rolo took the small bust from his hand and didn't answer. He looked for a clean towel. It isn't a library; what would you like to eat? The boy's eyes, no longer reddened, were looking dark and lively. Whatever ya got. Not what I *got,* what I *have.* Okay, a piece of bread. He was about to take off his pants in the living room, thought about it for a second, and went dressed into the bathroom. God, Rolo thought, he's more beautiful than young Flandrin. He prepared a supper (bread, cheese, sausage, ham, olives, and ice-cold beers) while getting excited listening to the sounds of the shower. There was a noticeable difference between the sound the shower made when it hit the floor and the one it made when it flowed over a body. You could tell when a person was showering and when he was soaping up. You could think that when he wasn't showering, he was doing other things. The wait was also exciting. He approached the bathroom door. Can I hand you the soap? He didn't hear or didn't want to answer. He sang, *Our kisses were like fire, romancing with desire . . .* At last he came out of the bath with the towel tied around his waist. They sat at the table like that. He hadn't dried himself well, his hair was sopping and his body was sprinkled with drops of water. He looked white and handsome, with those long sideburns that end in a perfect diagonal. His mood seemed to have changed magically. Hey, old man, this is a banquet, he exclaimed with a mouth full of ham. Rolo opened two beers. He served them in a pair of mugs that said in red letters: HATUEY, THE GREAT BEER OF CUBA. He quickly drank from his own before Rolo had time to clink mugs, so that the gesture was left hanging in the air and the word *Cheers* on the point of being spoken. What's your name? The boy smiled, evaded, ate sausage, olives, drank beer, before explaining, It doesn't matter, old man, they call me Sandokán. So you're from Malaysia, Rolo joked. No, the other replied seriously, I was born in Caraballo and I grew up in Marianao. Rolo found a washrag and began to dry his back for him. Busy eating, Sandokán not only allowed him, he even helped him by moving his torso and lifting his arms. Afterward Rolo rubbed lavender water on his neck, on his arms, especially there where he had the tattooed acanthus leaf, and in his sweetest voice asked him, Stay here tonight, I wouldn't like for you to leave, it's too late, something could happen to you, these are bad times . . . and he went into the bathroom as if he wanted to take a shower, and what he did instead was take Sandokán's dirty cutoff pants, his cotton underwear that must have once been white, and caress them, smell them: no one who's even halfway sensitive should doubt that the sweat of a beautiful man is finer than the most expensive perfume in Paris.

You do well to stay there, sitting on a rock, watching Tingo fly his kite. Anything that helps you forget Sandokán is good. Tingo, who sees you, comes running over and says, You know what I'm doing with the kite? I'm mailing a letter to God, Sebastián and me tied, you know, the paper, the letter, to the kite tails, and since kites go up and up and up we're sure He'll read them and we hope He'll write back to us right on the kites but Miss Berta told us God's too busy and He doesn't answer like that. Whose idea was this? Who do you think, Uncle Rolo? Sebastián's. Might one inquire what you have asked of God? Tingo looks in every direction, unties the letter and hands it to Rolo. Uncle opens the paper and reads: Dear God, we hope You are feeling well when You receive this letter. We, Your children, are fine, though we would like to beg You: Don't destroy the Island, don't punish us! Good or bad, this Island is all You have let us have. So just think, what would we do without it? Hoping for Your generosity, we are, Yours.

Tingo keeps on flying the kite and he doesn't know why. Sebastián told him to do it to send a message to God. Except Tingo doesn't know what a message is, much less who God is. I don't get Sebastián's message either, you know, Sebastián thinks of the strangest things. Sometimes Tingo gets tired and lets the kite fall dead. And he wonders what sense it could make to fly the kite. It's like the other day when Miss Berta said the earth was round and that it spun around the sun. Tingo doesn't get how the earth could be round, how it could spin around the sun. Nor does he get how Miss Berta could know that, much less what he's supposed to do from now on with this information. It's like flying kites to send messages to God. Before I knew the earth was round, I could walk as good as could be, now that I know it's round I can still walk as good as can be, I don't get tired, I don't get seasick, nothing's different, my father's still lying in bed not talking, my mother still cries and complains all the time, my sister Tatina laughs and pees, and all that happens with or without the roundness of the earth, and the truth is there's a lot of stuff I don't get, for example, why is my mamá my mamá? why not Helena or I-don't-know-who? why aren't I a flower or an ant? why do I have to sleep at night and not during the day? why sleep with your eyes closed? why doesn't the sun come out at night and the moon during the day? why do I have to eat just to crap it out later? why take a bath if I'm dirty, and get dirty so I can take a bath? why get dressed if they say I was born bare naked? why is it if I want to talk I have to talk? why is it if I want to be quiet I have to shut up? why do my mamá and my papá argue when they don't agree? why don't they argue when they do agree? why do trees make shade? why is it, if trees make shade, I have to live in a house? I don't get it, and everything seems to indicate that the only one who doesn't get it is me, of course, there's no difference between getting it and not getting it, otherwise I'd be different, I'd have just one eye, just one ear, just one arm, just one leg, and it's not like that, I'm the same as everybody else, I sleep, I talk, I eat, I piss and crap like everybody else, which proves that someone who gets it is the same as someone who doesn't, so I can tell you one thing as easily as I can tell you the other, you know, for me everything we see isn't what's there, it's what isn't there, I'll try to explain, what's there is something different from what you can see, that is, I'm going to give you an example so you'll understand (if you're one of the ones who understand, because what if you're like me), I see a tree, a royal palm let's say, well the truth is that this royal palm is what I can see, not what exists, what exists is something else that I take to be a royal palm, look, what I'm trying to tell you is that there's a veil between my eyes and the real stuff, which is the other fake stuff that we take to be real, get it? of course, that doesn't change anything either, it's like knowing that the earth spins, in the end, you know, what I can see is the royal palm, and what's really there behind the royal palm I can't see, so forget it, it doesn't matter.

In front of the bust of Martí, at the entrance to Miss Berta's classroom, Rolo finds a bouquet of roses and, a little lower down, a bunch of bananas tied with a red ribbon. My country, so young, how can you define it, Rolo declaims in a querulous tone, and instead of walking down the gallery he continues through trees and crotons, ferns and herbs, rosebushes and creepers, passing the Hermes of Praxiteles, the bust of Greta Garbo, and reaches Irene's house. Although the house is open, Irene is not to be seen. Nobody offering coffee? Rolo asks in a loud voice. Irene appears at the door of her kitchen, drying her hands on her apron, unsmiling, looking as if she's had a bad night. If I offer you some coffee, what will you give me in return? What you most desire: a memory! Irene is ready to embrace Rolo. An intelligent character, after all, he realizes that Irene is feeling bad, that she wants to embrace him, and since besides being intelligent he is a character who has fits of clairvoyance, he looks in her living room and finds the stuffed falcon; he knows he shouldn't ask and for that very reason he asks, Who did it belong to? knowing full well that he will provoke the same anguish in Irene as when she found the falcon, an important falcon in her personal history, but whose importance Irene has forgotten. I don't know, Rolo, you know very well that I don't know who it belonged to. What's wrong with you, woman? If I only knew . . . someone's set on making me forget, soon I'll forget my own name. Rolo hugs her. Controlling her desire to cry, Irene asks him, Come on into the kitchen, I just made coffee a little while ago.

We can spare ourselves the description of the moment they enter the kitchen to have a cup of coffee. What matters isn't that Irene and Rolo are drinking coffee from uncomfortable, sophisticated porcelain cups shaped like birds with little feet that are useless for balancing them on the saucers, what matters is that Irene reveals that this morning she forgot she had the Wounded Boy in her house, and she didn't come to give him his six A.M. treatment. Past nine o'clock, by chance she entered the room he sleeps in, and the worst part wasn't finding him there, but not knowing for a few minutes who he might be.

There lies the Wounded Boy. Sleeping, gently breathing, the perfect incarnation of the Tropical Gypsy, with a face Víctor Manuel would kneel down before. Rolo draws near as if he is in church before an image of the Descent from the Cross. He passes his hand across the boy's forehead, cool and slightly sweaty. What's your name? he asks, knowing full well he won't reply. The Wounded Boy, nonetheless, moves his right hand almost imperceptibly. What's your name? The Wounded Boy blinks, moves his lips. The window is open and it's as if the afternoon doesn't exist in the outskirts of the Island. Could someone really be playing, on some piano, to the point of exhaustion, something (Schumann?) that Rolo cannot identify? Rolo takes the Wounded Boy's hands in his own. What's your name? He opens his eyes, now he's really opening his eyes and Rolo thinks he's looking at him. What's your name? He smiles with those lips that Víctor Manuel would have to kneel down to. Scheherazade, he exclaims in a weak voice, my name is Scheherazade.

Where are you taking me? Marta asks. To the sea, Sebastián replies, we're going to sit down by the shore of the sea.

III

The Faithful Dead

The sea, Sebastián, can you hear it? close your eyes, that way you'll hear it like I do, you have to close your eyes, sight is such a powerful sense that if you don't close your eyes you won't be able to hear it, if you only knew, I used to live facing it, after the death of my father, when we had to leave Melania and the kingdom of Lalisia, my uncle Leandro brought us to his house on the beach at Jaimanitas (which we called Typee), even though my eyes were starting to dry up they were still alive then, I could see the sea, those were the best years of my life, despite the fainting spells and the constant thirst I lived with, it's bad to be thirsty all the time, Sebastián, it's like living in the desert, your mouth dry, your throat dry, thirsty, and despite that, believe me, I was happy, Uncle Leandro was the only man I had met who had ever gone past the horizon and been off the Island, and more important, his absence was called India, for me India was gigantic rivers, crowds performing ablutions and chants in the gigantic rivers, marble palaces, golden temples, painted elephants, and one man, my uncle, meditating in the middle of a downpour, with the help of a snake, the mystery of that trip persisted in Uncle Leandro's eyes, all those palaces and temples and rivers and forests were in Uncle Leandro's eyes, and that fascinated me.

And perhaps this is not the proper place to call attention (though in the end it will have to be done on some page of the book) to the fact that there's nothing so enchanting for an inhabitant of the islands as knowing that someone has dared to break through the encirclement of the sea, has overcome the fate of the horizon, someone has been *outside* and learned what the world is. For an inhabitant of the islands, *traveler* is synonymous with wizard; *travel* synonymous with good fortune.

Facing the sea at Typee, Marta first felt the desire to travel.

Sometimes they could see ships in the distance. For any islander, a ship (one that plies the seas, of course, this isn't about the grounded ship that is an island) constitutes the most sublime image of freedom. A ship cutting through the water is the symbol of hope. If it arrives, you should caress it to get the smell and the air of other lands on your hands. If it sails off, you should caress it so that the smell and the air of other lands will know our hands exist. Marta bid farewell to the ships with a handkerchief, in the certainty that someday she would be the one who would see, through tears of joy, the handkerchiefs along the seashore. She would go off, away to cities with promising names, and in Paris, Liverpool, Salzburg, or Santiago de Compostela she would finish becoming a woman. What happened, however, was that little by little the ships grew blurry in the distance, and she would ask Mercedes, What's that out there, far off? A ship, her sister would answer in surprise. The sea also faded, changing colors little by little (so calmly that it was only much later that she realized it) until it became a reddish expanse. India disappeared from the eyes of Uncle Leandro. Her uncle's eyes disappeared. As did those of Mercedes and her mother. Their faces dissolved into hues as reddish as the sea's. The sea grapes no longer were trees; before they were definitively hidden, they turned into black structures. The mirror also began to hide her own image from her. One morning there was no image in the mirror. Another morning, there was no mirror. A weaker and weaker resplendence distinguished day from night. Not knowing how, her legs adopted a stealthy pace, and her hands began to stretch out, to specialize in touch. It was as if her hands were thinking for themselves. Writing, for example, turned into something her hands did on their own, forming larger and more directionless letters every day. So it happened that one morning Marta felt she had woken up nowhere. Her eyes opened to a dark, nearly black redness, and she felt alone, more alone than she ever had. Despite the fact that being an adolescent, after all, the majority of things were not very clear to her, she somehow instinctively knew that it was unfortunate enough and imprisoning enough to live on an island, not to have to lose as well the only sense that allowed her to be aware that other men and countries existed.

That was, besides, the era when the beggars appeared. Little by little they took over Typee. The first day two arrived; by the end of the week there was a crowd. They were rowdy, boisterous, and spent the whole day singing and playing. Perhaps their mother was right, perhaps it was pleasant to live a timeless and unworried life with them. Except that their lack of responsibility led them to stink; to eat with their hands; never to comb their hair or change their tattered rags; to piss and crap in full sight of everyone; and worst of all, to relieve their burning lechery at any time, in any place. A moment came when even Uncle Leandro, who only saw his own saintliness in this world, began to grow concerned. The greatest concern took place when their mother sat down among the beggars and ended up at the foot of a bonfire singing, *I'm the woman from Lagartera and I bring Lagartera lace* to the rhythm of the beggars' part-mocking, part-kindly hand clapping. For her as well, with the passing of the days time ceased to be a concern, with all the baneful consequences that phrase encapsulates. She forgot about entering the kitchen. She never again set foot in the bathroom. Never again embroidered or sewed. Unkempt, disheveled, she now spent little time inside the house. Her life was limited to staying on the beach, bathing, and singing with the beggars. Laughing, playing with them, as she had never laughed or played with her own daughters. So it went until one morning when silence and peace were reestablished in Typee. One might have thought it had all been a hallucination, that all those beggars had never lived by the sea, next to the house. To prove, however, that it was not just illusion, one could see the remains of dinners and campfires, an unstrung guitar that their uncle found floating in the sea, two books in an unknown language, a rabbit tied to a tree and hundreds of pages of the magazine *Bohemia* strewn across the sand. The best proof, in any case, was their mother's absence. Mercedes stated that her mother had stayed up very late that night burning photographs and that much later she had heard a sound of breaking glass. In effect, they found the albums empty and the mirror broken.

Though you might not believe it, Sebastián, I saw them leave, no one ever believed it, I was blind and they said it was impossible for me to see them leave, though I had also begun to lose sleep, to fall victim little by little to insomnia, the insomnia that still torments me today and is (I swear to you) worse than hunger and thirst and blindness itself, always being awake is like living twice as much, one life is fine, but two, on the other hand, can become a torture, in those years I still went to bed at the same time as everybody else, when the sensible people of the world go to bed, and I heard how the bell of the clock rang the hours and how everyone else's breathing showed they were already soaring up to other worlds, other times, while I remained mired in reality by the weight of I don't know what punishment, and though I couldn't see it I knew reality was there, intransigent, severe, tedious, Sebastián, and that's how it's been ever since, for a long time now I don't know what it is to sleep, and the worst part isn't that the light of my eyes has gone out, or that my eyelids remain obstinately open, no, the worst is that God (that sweet way we have of invoking the devil) hasn't even left me with the possibility of imagining, of recomposing a new reality based on what I once saw, like a good islander I always wanted to see the world, go to other cities, learn what they were like, how men lived in other cities, Glasgow, Manila, Paris, Buenos Aires, Baghdad, San Francisco, Oran, Tegucigalpa, have you noticed how enchanting the names of cities are? each one suggests something different, Glasgow smells of trees, Manila is golden, Paris a crystal, Buenos Aires a great bird with wings unfurled, Baghdad smells of incense and also is a tenor's voice, San Francisco sounds like rainfall and piano music, Oran is a handkerchief, Tegucigalpa a pitcher of milk fresh from the cow, and the night the beggars left (and with them my mother) I had my last vision, I was awake, the others were peacefully sleeping, rubbing it in that I was still awake, I heard the murmuring of the sea, a strong murmuring, a swelling surf, I got up, I already knew how to behave like the perfect blind girl, I knew where each piece of furniture was, each door, each window, and when I didn't know where they were I knew that, too, because one of the mysteries of being blind is that your body doesn't need your eyes to find a path, and I went to the window, I don't know why it occurred to me to go to the window, I wasn't sure what I would see, I must have gone perhaps because the land wind caressed my face with the smell of the ocean, perhaps because the sound of the sea was more imposing at the window, the fact is that I went, the darkness dissipated as if by magic, the first thing I saw was the moon emerge between the scudding clouds, then a crowd of beggars launching rafts into the sea, rafts made from any old lumber, any old tree trunk, with sails made from old shirts and canvases tied to masts (if you could call them that) poorly crafted from branches, and they illuminated them with torches, and they sang, I remember very well they were singing, *We'll be free when we're far from this prison, we're off in search of wider horizons . . .* and there were thirty, forty rafts beginning to move off, and thirty, forty more in the sand waiting their turn to set sail, I saw my mother carrying a torch, I saw her practically naked, practically an old lady, giving orders to launch her raft on the sea, the beach was a ceaseless to and fro, I don't know if you've ever seen rafts set sail, Sebastián, I don't know if you'll have a chance to see it someday, you see those poorly tied logs, you see a man working so hard to push them toward the water, you see him run across the sand, enter the water, jump onto that little defenseless square of lumber, you see the boundless sea, the wind agitating the boundless sea, and you get a knot of sadness in your belly, that man might not get anywhere, and you think, Here in the sand I'm not going to get anywhere either, he might drown, might end his days at the bottom of the sea, I'll drown on the surface, end my days on the shore, it's all the same, except that he's carrying out an act, I'm not carrying out anything, see what I mean? there's something solemn and tragic about seeing someone set to sea on a raft, and he's got to be very dispirited, very put-upon, to go fight against the sea so humbly, without the pride of that Oriental king who punished the ocean with lashes, this is like trying to fool it, to ply the water unnoticed on little more than a piece of paper, to navigate hoping neither the sea nor anyone else notices you're navigating, it's glorious to see a ship leaving the bay, that's proof of human greatness and patience, but it's piteous to see a man, a woman, an old lady, and a child on a raft, that's proof of human poverty, hopelessness, and desperation, it's something that reminds us that in the end we're so unimportant, a raft is proof of insecurity and also of weariness, I broke down in tears watching the beggars' rafts drift away, turn into luminous little points as they moved off from the shore and melted into that dark expanse (the sea), I broke down in tears, I cried for so long, I spent whole days crying, and when

I didn't have any tears left in my eyes, Sebastián, that was when I really never saw anything again.

There are moments when running away seems like the only solution, a voice exclaims behind them, and it laughs, and how it laughs.

Vido's bare feet feel the sand on the beach. The sea, at this hour, is a steel grey, and Vido sees it motionless with only a brief surge of breakers by the shore. The sky acquires a more intense blue. He begins to hear a dog barking, so far away he doesn't know if it's a real dog or a dog from some other place and time. He greets the others, who can be seen some distance off, and he stands on a shore covered with seaweed and seashells, with miniature crabs. The sea enters the sand and forms a circle, closed off by two lengths of coral reef. There's a depression in the sand, where the water, entering, forms an ephemeral pond.

There are moments when running away seems like the only solution. Marta doesn't move. Sebastián turns and sees the Barefoot Countess coming across the sand, with her fan, her ácana cane, and her air of an exiled queen. We live in an Island, *chéri,* you shouldn't be so shocked, after all, what is an Island? have you read the dictionary? The Countess jams her cane into the sand, sits down next to them. As is her habit, she wears a mocking face. According to the Dictionary of the Royal Academy, *island* means *a portion of land surrounded entirely by water,* a concise definition, what an aseptic tone, what linguistic precision! it couldn't be so simple, right? for an inhabitant of the islands this is something profound and poignant. The Countess spreads her fan out on the sand and traces its outline with her finger. The dictionary phrase uses words that fill us with terror: *a portion of land,* meaning something diminished, something brief, a quantity wrenched from a larger quantity; *surrounded,* the participle of a verb with warlike connotations, prisonlike resonances; *entirely by water,* observe how this adverbial phrase evokes the impossibility of escape: water, symbol of the origins of life, is also that of death. She pauses for breath and caresses Sebastián's hand. Wasn't the Flood a punishment sent by God? She laughs briefly. You have to live on an island, yes, one must wake up every morning, see the sea, the wall of the sea, the horizon, as a threat and as a promised land, to know what it means.

Vido breathes deeply and opens his arms and feels his lungs filling with the breeze. He opens his eyes wide, closes them, opens them again. When he has them open, it's the sea and the sky and the horizon, clearer each time; when he closes them, another sky, another horizon, a reddish gleam. He shouts a name, his name, Vido! so that his voice, his name, will stop the bellowing of the sea.

With great caution, the Barefoot Countess takes off the straw hat that she's wearing tied beneath her chin by a red ribbon. She arranges her hair coquettishly. She says, This is something that people who live on continents will never know, they'll never know how isolated the man of the islands is. A long silence follows. The afternoon sea is calm despite the breeze; its color is intense, becoming darker and darker as it moves away from the shore and approaches the horizon. It seems to Sebastián that the sea is covered with hundreds, thousands, millions of tiny mirrors.

He undresses and it's as if each part of his body were acquiring life, or better, as if he were discovering his body, his skin, the tension in his muscles, the throbbing that runs through him from head to foot. Vido is naked and he vividly feels the sensation of the breeze. The landscape, the whole world fits in his hands, in his arms. His lungs can capture the breeze that stirs the branches of the sea grape trees. He kicks up sand with his feet and he picks and bites into the red fruits. A sweet flavor wets his lips.

The Countess throws her head back and for a moment it seems that she isn't going to laugh. This Island we live in, she says, has been and is particularly unfortunate. She takes one of Sebastián's hands. I don't know, *poveretto,* if Miss Berta has told you that when the Spanish discovered this bit of land, where a few defenseless natives could barely live, they were searching for El Dorado, and this bit of land, for good or ill, has never had a drop of gold, so that the Spanish fled from it for the continent, they just opened two or three ports here, founded a few towns (with the poorest families of Iberia), and the Island *(sigh)* became a transit point *(another sigh),* which it has never ceased to be. She sits, looking into the distance. At one moment she lifts a hand as if she wanted to point out something. Marta holds her head down; at times she touches Sebastián's back, perhaps to assure herself that he is still there.

When a first wave wets his feet, it's as if there were other Vidos there next to him, inside him. He enters the water and feels it move up his thighs, wrap around his waist, reach his chest. He feels as transparent as water, and he dives in.

The Countess's voice now sounds more serious, It's logical, *chéri,* that the beggars on the rafts would make you cry, the man of the Island always believes he's on a raft, always believes he's about to set sail and also about to founder, except that this raft doesn't ply the sea, and the moment he discovers that the Island will never move, the moment the man of the Island realizes that his raft is fixed to the bottom of the sea by some eternal and diabolical force, at that instant, he cuts logs and builds his raft and leaves forever. She lets loose a laugh. And what happens? the unexpected, the Island doesn't abandon him, he abandons it but it doesn't abandon him, there's the worst part *(more loud laughter),* you leave the Island and the Island doesn't leave you, because what the islander doesn't know is that an Island is rather more than a portion of land surrounded by water on every side, an Island, my dear Marta, my dear Sebastián, let it be said once and for all: an Island (all right, I'll be more precise), *this* Island we live on, is an illness. She picks up the fan open on the sand, closes it and looks in every direction with such a mocking face that Sebastián feels afraid. *Ah, mon Dieu,* a country could never be happy when it's founded on the homesickness of Galicians, on the nostalgia of Andalusians and Canary Islanders, on the *rauxa* and *angoixa* of Catalans, no, no place could be happy when a slaver like Pedro Blanco brought thousands of blacks there, torn from their homes, mistreated, tortured, and sold them there naked, and enslaved them, and made them work from sunup to sundown, such a hodgepodge must necessarily make for a sad people, an accursed people, and if you add to that the heat, the suffocation, the time that never changes, and the methods of avoiding all this, the rum, the music, the dancing, the pagan religions, the body, the body to the detriment of the spirit, the body sweating on top of another body, the idleness, the idleness! not the productive idleness that Unamuno spoke of, no, but the kind that is called laziness, an idleness called impotence, skepticism, lack of faith, I would like you to tell me . . . She suddenly falls silent. As the afternoon has advanced, the sea has been acquiring an intense violet color. (Nostalgic for the birth of the gods?)

Swimming along the bottom of the sea is more than a pleasure. He wants to observe this imprecise bottom and, opening his eyes, thinks he sees verdant leaves waving like miniature arms, rocks that sometimes are faces, lines of silvered fishes darting by faster than his gaze. Returning to the surface, he lies on the water with his arms folded. Above him is the afternoon sky. Something is making him drift away, but it isn't the water, rather a force within himself. He swims away from the shore, comes back again and dives. He returns to the sea bottom. Comes up with a piece of seaweed. Jumps up with it on his neck and raises his arms. Breathes strongly. The smell of the sea is strong, very strong. Again he shouts his name and he doesn't know why calling out to himself makes him laugh. He swims back to the shore, where he lies down and closes his eyes, to plunge into a new stillness that could be sleep. He brings a hand to his chest, over his heart, and perceives the strength of its beat. He also caresses his shoulders, his neck, his nipples. Though he thinks he is sleeping, his body is aware of the last sunlight of the afternoon.

From among the sea grapes they see Uncle Rolo appear. The Barefoot Countess turns and smiles. Uncle is coming at a rapid pace, as if he is about to deliver important news. Nevertheless, when he sees the Countess he doesn't speak, he sits down next to Marta, hugs her. She lifts her head, Rolo? she asks, and he smoothes her straight pageboy-styled hair. The Countess fans herself for some time. Sebastián throws pebbles at the water. The crazy woman closes her eyes and says, *Mon petit,* do you know what has happened to the poets of this Island? No, don't tell that story, Rolo suddenly interjects. There's no way to help it, Rolo, you know that. Not right now, at least not right now, Rolo begs. The Countess makes an authoritative gesture with her hand and exclaims, The first stammering poet, Zequeira, lost his mind from being the first stammering poet, he went crazy, Sebastián, he put on a hat and became invisible, which wasn't true, but it really was, as you may understand; the first great poet, José María Heredia, was fated for exile (as I told you, men flee but the Island doesn't abandon them, poor Heredia saw a palm tree growing next to Niagara Falls), he never truly left, exile killed him, nostalgia and consumption killed him (you can't deny to me that both, together, add up to a tragic destiny); they shot Plácido, the mulatto comb-seller to whom rhymes came so easily; Zenea (the first in this Island to read Alfredo de Musset) was also shot; Milanés of Matanzas, wonderful when he didn't give in to moralizing, also found himself compelled to go crazy; and what about El Cucalambé? with his simple but enchanting stanzas, he disappeared without a trace, they never heard from him again; another elegist, Luisa Pérez de Zambrana, saw her large family die while she lived on, nearly eternal, and came to know solitude in the humblest little house in the district of Regla, across the bay; and Julián del Casal, the first to read Baudelaire, the friend of Darío, misunderstood and lonely and sad, with a sense of sadness and guilt that I don't know if we'll ever understand, died at the age of twenty-nine, also consumptive, from a hearty laugh that made him cough up all his blood, he died like Keats without the glory of Keats, *I weep for Adonais* . . . (consumption was the great ally of the ephemeral nineteenth-century bourgeois against the immortal poets). And as for Martí . . . you already know: he let himself get killed on the battlefield at the age of forty-two . . .

Far, far away the white outline of a ship can be seen among the scudding clouds of afternoon. Sebastián waves good-bye with his hand. Vido, Rolo, and the Countess do the same. Marta raises her head. It's a ship, Uncle informs her. The horizon has become a fiery line.

I waited to reveal what I'm about to reveal because I didn't dare do it until I was sure. So says Uncle Rolo to Marta, the Countess, and Sebastián during their walk back to the Island. It's something so important that I couldn't take it lightly, he emphasizes. He pauses, then announces, I have received important signs in my dreams, first, in my dreams, I saw a street that I didn't know, that I couldn't remember ever actually seeing, and I knew it wasn't a street in Havana because its hues, its color, its silence were different . . . I returned to this street again and again in my dreams, and one house stood out, number 13, until one day, leafing through a book about Paris, I was shocked by the surprise of seeing the street of my dreams in a print, it was called, ladies and gentlemen, listen closely, Rue Hautefeuille, then I began dreaming that I was at my father's wake, that is, my father is dead, but my father in my dream wasn't my father, the father I always knew, understand? in the funeral wake in my dreams I was about six years old, which would argue against this dead father being any other than the father I had as such, if it weren't for realizing that the wake was taking place in another era, a wake from another era, understand? in a third dream I hated my mother, by her side I saw a man in uniform, covered with gold braid, a general, and I, like Hamlet, hated the general and hated my mother (I hated her and loved her, as is always the case with mothers), in a fourth dream I saw myself dressed up as a dandy, on a ship, surrounded by sea mist, and I felt more weariness than I could ever express to you, no matter how much I tried, understand? the days go by and I have more and more dreams that I don't want to burden you with, every day I recite phrases in French, phrases I never knew, I don't even speak French, phrases like *Là, tout n'est qu'ordre et beauté . . .*

They have left the marabú bushes behind and are entering The Beyond. Uncle Rolo looks pensive, as if he is afraid to give the news he has prepared for them. At last, he throws his head back, closes his eyes, and exclaims with some embarrassment, My friends, what I have discovered is the following, please pay close attention to what I am about to say: in a previous incarnation, I was Charles Baudelaire.

> *Addio, del passato bei sogni ridenti,*
> *le rose del volto già sono palenti . . .*

comes the voice that has been heard around the Island for the past few days. Casta Diva runs to the mirror. There's nothing to be seen on the other side.

There's a garden here now with poplars, willows, cypresses, olive trees, even a splendid red sandalwood tree of Ceylon. I know this is hard to believe. On this Island of anonymous, uniform trees, all of them boringly green, it's hard to imagine willows and cypresses, even when a hundred tireless elegists write of them, such as the hapless author of *Fidelia* or the ghoulish poetess of *Returning to the Woods.* Nonetheless, you should believe me. Does any one of you doubt that this is the Island of the unpredictable?

Many, many years ago, there was no garden here, just a grassy patch that barely kept the cows fed. They said this land was bad, unlucky, cursed by God. And, indeed, you couldn't even grow a simple squash in it. Everyone who tried growing the most basic crops, after the hopeful early period when the plants started germinating, later saw them turn yellow and shrivel up as if roasted by an invisible fire. And the cows, with their obstinate patience, would return to rule over that ugly, deceptive patch of grass that was the Island in those days. This continued up until the arrival of Godfather and Angelina. With them, this arid field was transformed into Eden itself. They called him Godfather because he had baptized the only daughter Consuelo had, a poor girl who died before the age of fifteen, before she could know the pleasures of life, from a poorly aimed bullet fired during the Little War of August. Godfather's real name was Enrique Palacio. He was born poor in a little fishing hamlet, on the sea, of course, in a region of sea mist and *saudades,* near Santiago de Compostela, around the middle of the last century, they say. His sister Angelina, who for some people became as important as he was for the Island, was born five years later. Struggling against the capricious sea and against the equally capricious land, struggling against poverty, which is always a misfortune in our world, Godfather, known then as Enriquillo, became a tough, impetuous, clever young man, practically illiterate but extraordinarily intelligent. When the War of Independence broke out in Cuba, Enriquillo enlisted with the army that would defend Spain. He didn't do it for patriotic reasons, really, it seemed like the best way of escaping that fog-shrouded and accursed land, his chance to make his fortune in the Island celebrated for its generous geography, the Island that, according to the stories they told, was another land of plenty. One fine day he bid farewell to his parents and to his sister Angelina, who was beginning a beautiful adolescence, and crossed the Atlantic in a precarious ship overburdened with healthy, rough youths, so healthy and so rough that they never bathed, and their armpits, feet, and crotches had exciting and nauseating smells to show for it. It was a slave ship loaded with Galicians, and it took more than a month to reach Santiago de Cuba. It hardly needs to be said that the Island was not what Enriquillo had in mind. It was just as poor as his little hamlet by the sea, and made worse by a savage sun that faded colors and made your body always feel like there was a lead weight on your shoulders, so that every step took the effort of twenty, so that you were bathed in sweat and thirsty and desperate twenty-four hours a day, under a sun that caused delirium and hallucinations among the troops. The Island, besides, was infested with insects. There were more insects than people. Tiny, strange insects, implacable as the sun, devilish insects, even more dangerous than the enemy troops. Therefore, malaria, plague, yellow fever, and other serious mortal and unknown illnesses wreaked more havoc than the poorly sharpened machetes of the Cubans. The Spaniards had no defense against these scourges, unlike the damned Cuban insurgents who could sleep in a swamp and get up as immaculate as angels. The Spanish troops crossed the forest (the unknown and mysterious forest, the labyrinthine forest, the sacred forest) wearing flannel uniforms more appropriate for winter in Galicia. They went almost barefoot, wearing sandals that proved ironic in the swamps, among the roots of hostile trees, through the dangerous savannas. And they went hungry; Enriquillo lost so many pounds he almost disappeared. Nevertheless, he was lucky. He took part in few battles. He was only wounded in the leg when the Pact of Zanjón was about to be signed. When he was out of danger, he left the army, settled in Havana and began to work as a bartender in the dining room of the Isla de Cuba Hotel, which stood back then right where it stands today, facing the Campo de Marte. He rented a foul-smelling little room on potholed, trash-strewn Cuarteles Street. He didn't let himself be seduced by any black or mulatta women, unlike so many Galicians who landed on the Island. Although, like so many Galicians who landed on the Island, he did dedicate himself to stashing away money. His dream wasn't exceptional: wanting to make himself rich, start a business, bring his parents and sister to Havana. He did, of course, stash money away; he did, of course, make himself rich. He couldn't bring his parents over because they decided to die, one right after the other, among the sea mist of their little hamlet by the sea, near Santiago de Compostela. Angelina did receive a ticket for passage on an opulent schooner that set sail from La Coruña one jubilant spring morning. Enrique, who knew about his sister's botanical leanings from her letters, had bought a fairly large country estate in the district of El Cerro to welcome her. She was twenty-five years old at the time, and bright as a Virgin by Murillo. When she disembarked from the schooner in the foul-smelling and festive port of Havana, Angelina looked at her brother without knowing who he was, impressed by the power emanating from that figure of a man. Enrique, too, looked at her without knowing who she was, impressed by the sweetness that emanated from that figure of a woman. He saw her dressed in discreet white linen, which she had embroidered herself, her skin clean and rosy, her hair as jet black as her large eyes, her mouth lovely and well formed, and he couldn't help trembling. She couldn't help trembling when she saw that man, whose strength did not reside merely in the vigor of his arms but came from some recondite region of his heart, and was reflected in his precise and restrained movements, and in his resolute, calculating, pitiless eyes. It was a confusion of a few seconds, naturally. He immediately discovered his mother's face in hers, and softly, almost timidly, called her, Angelina! and she heard her father's deep voice and was at the point of weeping from joy, from sadness, and exclaimed, Enrique! And they embraced, and they blushed when they embraced, and they kissed, and they blushed when they kissed, and they went to El Cerro as a pair of strangers, and not at all disposed to stop being such. She thought Havana looked like a farmyard. A rainstorm had fallen shortly before, and although no symptoms of it remained in the clear blue cloudless sky, the streets were pure mud, the walls of the houses were pure mud just like the streets, and the chickens, pigs, dogs, turkeys, cows, and sheep that ran before and behind the coaches were pure mud just like the walls and the streets. The women, singing inexplicable songs at the tops of their lungs, hurled the contents of chamber pots from their windows. Sweating mud, passersby barely escaped these urinary assaults and screamed curses, which the women returned between one inexplicable song and the next. There were lots of blacks. This especially called

Angelina's attention. Handsome, splendid animals, with the most enchantingly naked torsos she had ever seen, they gathered together to display their utterly healthy teeth and to play their disturbing music on wooden boxes, music that did not sound at all like it was being played on wooden boxes. Where have I landed? she thought, remembering, in contrast, the misty calm of her little hamlet in Galicia, and she instinctively stretched out her hand toward her brother's, while he, as if reading her thoughts, or rather, as if he were thinking the same thing, stretched out his hand at the same instant toward hers, and their hands joined, and he placed a kiss on hers, and she received that kiss on her hand and in some other unmentionable part of her body, and she rested her head on his shoulder and closed her eyes to give herself courage and to say, If I'm with you I don't mind living in this Babylon of blacks, and the phrase coincided with the moment their coach entered Cuatro Caminos and clumsily took the road, flinging mud and provoking curses, toward the country estate of El Cerro. Angelina couldn't sleep the first night. Sheets and mosquito curtains suffocated her. The heat was impossible. The flowers gave off so much perfume that there was no way for her to close her eyes. She heard singing in some foreign language. When she managed for a moment to yield to exhaustion, the heat, the flowers, and the singing joined together to awaken her with a start. Then she had to get up, strip off more and more of her clothes, end up naked, sleepless, facing the balcony where white flowers seemed to move, seemed to lean toward her. Enrique couldn't get to sleep, either. Never before this night had he felt the simmering humidity that arose from the earth and conspired with his sheets to expel him. He, too, had to strip, to go out onto the balcony. His manhood had reacted forcefully, growing and growing, throbbing, as if there were some independent, unsuspected relationship between the earth and his cock. Concentration exercises did no good; it did no good to think about the account books or the lepers who sometimes came to the door begging for food. His prick remained as erect as a spear, ready to fall only in bodily combat. The next morning, when brother and sister sat down to breakfast, they looked pale and haggard. She tried a soursop juice for the first time, and she liked it, and she felt it slipping down her throat, and she couldn't repress an exclamation, Where the hell are we! He peeled a mango with his teeth, sucked at it helplessly, let its sweet juice flow down his neck to his chest, wiped the juice from his chest with one finger, squeezed his prick, which, still full of blood and momentum, lifted his trousers passionately, and replied, Where the devil cried out three times and nobody heard him. She broke a raw egg yolk into her mouth and sighed, I'm so sleepy. I'm so sleepy, he repeated, wiping a slice of pineapple across his burning temples. She wet a napkin in the cool milk, fresh from the cow, and wiped it across her brow. He sucked on the fingers he used to stir the papaya jam and said, When you were a little girl you'd fall asleep before supper was over, and I'd carry you to bed, remember? I don't remember, I can't remember anything, ever since yesterday, since I came into this city, which isn't a city but the uproar of a delicious nightmare, a disturbance, I can't remember a thing, I'm stuck in the present present present without a past or even a future. She looked at her brother with sleep-reddened eyes. And you, who are you, looking so much like my brother, like my father? He pushed back his chair with a certain aggressivity, stood up without worrying about how his full-grown manhood was lifting his trousers. That other body, full of life, bursting with blood, was, on this unforgettable morning, the most important part not only of his body but of the whole universe. Who am I? I'm going to tell you who I am. He went over to her, picked her up, carried her to her bed, stripped her. He stripped himself and stretched out on top of her, and she sensed, emanating from his body, the aroma of flowers, the fierce heat of the morning, the curse of Havana. He brought his lips to hers, kissed her many times, ran his tongue around her teeth and tongue. Who am I? Your brother, your father, the man who has your own blood, the one who shared the same womb and who engendered you; you are my sister, my mother, the woman who bore me and who shared the same womb with me. The enjoyment she felt was much more disturbing than that caused by the soursop juice, and she exclaimed, We're moving on from wherever the hell we were, and entering hell itself. While he caressed his sister's neck, he said, The devil's still crying out, there's no way to hear him, and he went down into the dark and desirable depths of her body and began a tormenting caress at the same time that he told her, When you were little, I'd carry you to the sea and bathe you naked and you'd be afraid of that blue expanse that wanted to devour you, devour us, and you'd cling to me, and I'd calm your fears by promising that I'd always protect you, that nothing could ever harm you so long as I was with you. Squeezing his head with her hands and pushing it toward her swarthy crotch, she cried with joy and said, You were always the best brother in the world, sweet, obliging, handsome, I felt proud to have you lead me by the hand, to carry your blood, to look like you, everyone said we had the same eyes, the same lips, that I was your female side, that's why I recognized in your mouth the taste of my own, and in your eyes the violent calm of my own, and it was like I desired myself and like I was pleasuring myself. He sat up tall, caressed her face with his hardened manhood, her face so like his mother's face. She caressed it with her mouth, moving her tongue rapidly. He could barely stand it and explained, Ever since adolescence I've wanted to give myself the same caresses that you, Sister, are making me so happy with, but it's impossible, no matter how hard you try it's impossible, you just can't give yourself joy, you always need someone else, ah, what good fortune if that someone else is yourself, if that someone else is the woman you rocked to sleep in her cradle, my sister, my other self, my female side. She took out his prick. Her lips were bright red and moist. Why don't you enter me, you, my brother, the only one with the right to do so? And he entered her body while he whispered in her ear that, as a young girl, she was afraid of the ghosts of night.

They never paid much attention to the rumors that began spreading in the provincial city, the Babylonian city with the soul of a village. One morning they dismissed the parish priest who had come to visit them; the next, the bishop himself, who was scandalized (as was to be expected in a bishop worthy of his rank). They remained selfish and apart. They thought only about the world of happiness they had built. For at least four years they managed to live in that joyous irresponsibility, warding off the attentive eyes of the hypocritical city, the shameless city, living for one another, enjoying the perfect love, since they loved doubly, as lovers and as siblings. So it went, until she became pregnant. When the doctor they were forced to consult (she couldn't keep anything down, and vomited if she so much as thought of a plate of food), pale and trembling, with horror on his face, diagnosed her pregnancy, Enrique and Angelina decided to abandon the country estate and move to a remote location where no one would know them, where the gossip wouldn't affect them. They sold the country estate of El Cerro; they bought what today is the Island. In those years, before the U.S. occupation of Cuba, Columbia had not yet become a military base; Carlos J. Finlay had not yet become famous for discovering in this area the mosquito that carries yellow fever. Marianao was a small settlement famous for its benign climate, its proximity to the beaches and the Hippodrome; sufficiently close to Havana to feel that you weren't in the countryside, sufficiently far not to suffer the terror of the city. In that expanse of arid land, in that grassy patch that barely kept the cows fed, in that bad land, cursed by God, there was a large house where brother and sister went to live, and a tiny house, barely two rooms, where a lovely young mulatta named Consuelo lived soon afterward with her husband, Lico Grande, a much older black man who had been a slave of the Loynaz family. Consuelo took care of Angelina. Apart from being lovely, the mulatta was sweet, and possessed a strange wisdom or a strange power. It is said that one night, for example, soon after she occupied the new house, Consuelo came up to Angelina with a profoundly sad expression, touched her belly, and exclaimed, A son cannot be a nephew and at the same time a man like any other. Angelina broke down crying, How did you know . . . ? My dear, Consuelo replied in an old woman's tone of voice that hardly fit her face's nearly adolescent expression, the eyes of a sister who is also a wife aren't like those of other women, have you looked at yourself in the mirror? And she hugged and caressed Angelina, who let herself be hugged and caressed like a young girl with the chills. At that time Enrique had already embarked upon his obsessive planting of rare trees, of cypresses, poplars, willows, olive trees, even the red sandalwood tree of Ceylon, ignoring the advice of Lico Grande, who explained, In this land nothing's possible. At night, while everyone else slept, Consuelo came out and replanted whatever Enrique had planted by daylight. She did this, blessing the future tree, whispering prayers that she herself invented. And the trees, of course, grew as vigorously as Angelina's belly. It's a miracle that this patch of grass can grow such rare, handsome plants, exclaimed Lico Grande. No, Consuelo replied, it's not a miracle, it's compensation.

At last, one day, with Consuelo's help, Angelina gave birth. Some people say it was to a minotaur. Some say a basilisk. Others, a medusa. We all know how boundless the popular imagination can be. In any case, it's true, it was a monstrous being that Consuelo wrapped up well in black cloth and showed to no one, least of all the mother. She walked straight to the garden, where Enrique was planting a willow, and said, Your son came from the depths of the earth with a smell of sulfur, I want you to let me do it the favor of perfuming it and sending it to heaven. Enrique looked at Consuelo, not understanding, and, not understanding, agreed. Consuelo drowned the monster, sprinkled bottled essences on it, and buried it, half an hour after its birth, at the foot of the red sandalwood tree, which wasn't yet the vigorous tree we admire today. As if she knew, Angelina did not inquire about her son. All she could ask was, Could you open the windows? the smell of sulfur is killing me! That was the last thing they heard her say. Angelina fell mute for many months. She dedicated herself to helping Enrique plant the trees of the Island, which Consuelo replanted at night. It's thanks to her and to Enrique (though the actual truth of it is that we should be thanking Consuelo) that the Island enjoys the profusion of trees we admire today.

One fine day Angelina disappeared. They never heard from her again. Enrique, who went on to become Godfather, lived for a hundred years. Some people say he left the Island. Story goes, he was accursed. They say that at the age of a hundred and nine he's still around in Galicia. There, instead of planting willows and cypresses, he plants mango and soursop trees.

Did you like it? No, it's a fake story, too melodramatic, too graphic, sounds like it was told by a southern writer from the United States. Then I'll just have to tell you the story of Consuelo, you'll like that one. I'll tell it another day, right now I'm tired *(yawning sounds)*.

Of all the characters in this book, Lucio is beyond a doubt the most typically Cuban. For many reasons. For now, however, I am interested in pointing out his exaggerated need to dress well. Let's be clear about this: not in the style of Beau Brummel, no. According to Barbey D'Aurevilly's famous book, the dandy might spend three hours composing his wardrobe so that, when he steps out, he can forget all about it. The dandy abhors exaggeration and clothing that appears newly bought; for him, the man should stand out above the clothes. Lucio is no dandy. He never forgets about his attire. (The habit makes the monk, he tells Fortunato every chance he gets, since Fortunato isn't very interested in stylish clothes.) Lucio is no dandy. He never gets his clothes to attain that indispensable quality of elegance, invisibility. He is patently interested in having everyone notice that he wears suits from Casa Prado, Gregory guayaberas, Once Once socks, Amadeo shoes. He exaggerates the Old Spice (which isn't expensive, but does attract attention). He shows off his eighteen-karat gold chains, his emerald ring, his bracelet, also gold, and his Omega watch. His fingernails are trimmed and polished. For him, the image of a Baudelaire, armed with a glass-bristled brush, trying to eliminate the uncouth gloss of a recently bought suit, is little less than sacrilege. His beauty is also that of a typical Cuban. Tall, thin, muscular though not exaggeratedly so, very white (utterly and suspiciously white), his hair black, his features delicate and beautiful, or rather pretty, almost feminine. When Lucio steps out, dressed to the nines, and coquettishly dries his forehead with a linen handkerchief daubed with perfume, he is the most Cuban of Cubans. It would never occur to anyone to imagine that this extraordinary, delicate, and elegant specimen works in a vinegar factory.

He vomits. By the side of the bed, ashen, he is vomiting up a yellow liquid that smells of bile and rum. Fortunato, who has taken his shirt off for him, wipes a towel soaked in rubbing alcohol across Lucio's head and says, Fuck it, man, I don't want you to drink anymore. I would like it if the reader could note the interesting mix of demandingness and protectiveness heard in Fortunato's voice.

Like a typical Cuban, when it is time to dress up, Lucio first combs his hair. Facing the mirror, completely naked and covered with talcum powder, legs spread wide, like a typical Cuban. He arranges his smooth, black hair with generous amounts of brilliantine. With the slight palm of his hand he pats down his hardened, diligent hair. Retouches the sideburns. Looks at the skin of his face, if there are any pimples, any stain . . . observes his nose, his eyes, his forehead. He does everything he can to make the mirror show him his own profile. He wipes his forehead and nose with a powder puff to keep the sweat from making them shiny, and, like a typical Cuban, wipes his eyebrows and lashes down with a finger wet with saliva. Then, like a typical Cuban, he carefully studies his teeth (a gold molar flashes) and cleans out his ears with cotton. He continues looking at himself in the mirror, like a typical Cuban. This time his study takes in his whole body. In one swift motion, happy, satisfied, he lifts his potent and talcumed manhood, and looks at his balls, which are also talcumed, which are also large, like those of a typical Cuban. Sitting on the bed, he covers his feet, softly, caressing them, with socks. Then his clean cotton and of course starched undershirt and underpants. Like a typical Cuban, he makes sure the undershirt fits tight against his body, tucked into the underwear. He looks at himself from front and side wearing the underclothes; he admires, he verifies that his abdomen is perfect, that his chest is perfect, like any typical Cuban. He lightly thumps his chest and abdomen. Then, like a typical Cuban, he puts on perfume without taking his eyes off himself in the mirror: neck, ears, chest, and arms, not forgetting first to put deodorant on his armpits, where, like a typical Cuban, he has first trimmed his armpit hair. He smells his arms, his armpits. He smiles, satisfied. He takes advantage of the smile to study once more his exaggeratedly well-brushed teeth and to admire the sheen of the gold molar. (No, the molar doesn't shine enough. Lucio comes up to the mirror and, like a typical Cuban, takes a piece of cloth and works at it, to make it shine, yes, to make it shine, because your forehead and nose shouldn't shine, but your gold tooth should, so it can be seen at night, so everybody can see it.) Now it's time for the trousers. Cashmere. He likes cashmere. It's a fabric that caresses your thighs, and Lucio, like a typical Cuban, likes to have his thighs caressed. He puts on his polished shoes. He ties and unties the laces until the knots are perfect. With a rag he works at his shoe tips, because they should also gleam and dazzle. He studies, swiftly but precisely, the way his trousers fall over his shoes (for a typical Cuban, this is of the utmost importance). Carefully, with slow and studied voluptuous movements, he puts on his shirt. White, of course, and short-sleeved to make the heat bearable; white, starched linen, ironed to excess by Irene (even that: Lucio, like a typical Cuban, has a typical Cuban mother to make sure that her son looks like a prince). He quite intentionally forgets to button the top two buttons on his shirt; that way you can see the edge of the undershirt and the clear skin and the rough, victorious way Lucio's neck lifts high. Now it's time for the jacket. The jacket quickly adapts to his body, as if it had been given an order. He retouches his sideburns again. Studies his teeth again, especially the gold molar. Combs his hair once more. Once more wipes a finger wet with saliva across his eyebrows and lashes. Wets his lips with his tongue. Perfumes his handkerchief, which does not go into the jacket pocket but the trousers. Looks for an instant, almost mechanically, at the watch on his wrist, and contemplates the finished product. Yes, it's turned out well, it's just fine, he seems to say with a half-worried, half-satisfied expression on his face, with his pleasantly frowning brow. At last, like a typical Cuban, he tosses a mock-sincere kiss at the image on the other side of the mirror. The image, which is also that of the typical Cuban Lucio is, responds with a kiss that carries the same burden of mocking sincerity.

After he got dressed, Lucio tried to go out without letting Irene notice. His outings always had something of a breakout about them (which doesn't in the least mean that Irene didn't detect them: for every son who tries to get away, there's a mother to spy on him). So that Irene had hardly heard the footsteps in the living room, footsteps only she could have been capable of hearing, when she called, shouted anxiously perhaps (because once again she was lost, despite the fact that she was sitting right there, on the easy chair in her room), shouted in anguish the name of her son, Lucio, Lucio, and he felt for one infinitesimal instant the unpleasant sensation of having been found at fault, though the most elementary reasoning would show that there is no fault in getting dressed and going out into the Island or into the streets. Docile, though masking his docility with an air of annoyance, he entered his mother's room. Irene was in the shadows, seated on her easy chair, caressing a stuffed falcon; she raised her head and exclaimed, What a handsome son! in authentic admiration and authentic sadness, and asked, Whose bird is this, Lucio? do you know whose bird is this? and she broke down crying. Lucio knew instinctively to caress her, to kiss her, to tell her, Don't cry, please, don't cry, Mamá, after all it doesn't matter whose the bird is, because you're here and that's the only thing that's important. He did nothing, said nothing. He merely wet his lips with the tip of his tongue and made another mocking gesture with his mouth that he knew was false and that he couldn't help doing. In a halting voice, crying all the while, Irene tried to explain to him, Ay, son, I found this falcon and I swear it was important, the problem is I don't know why or to whom. Pretending annoyance, Lucio left his mother's room and entered the other one, where the Wounded Boy lay. There, between white sheets, calm and alive, the Wounded Boy seemed a hallucination. Lucio had already admired his curly saffron hair, his eyes that sometimes opened to flash with a mysterious blackness, just like his bronze skin, like his well-defined, hairless chest, like his long arms, like his magnificent hands (especially the hands, right, Lucio? especially the hands). The room was still dark; that is, Irene hadn't turned on the lights; nevertheless, a blue light, very blue, escaped from the body of the Wounded Boy. Lucio approached unctuously. Boy, he asked, who are you? what are you doing here? The Wounded Boy moved a hand imperceptibly and opened his eyes, which weren't black but green. Lucio thought the Wounded Boy was watching him from the distance of his fever. Who are you? what are you doing here? he repeated, caressing the boy's forehead (which was burning). And he had the impression that when he touched his body, the blue light burst from his own hand, and he felt a kind of current passing to his body. Rare well-being, swift happiness, unfathomable, uncontainable desire to burst out laughing, crying (two verbs that in this case covered the same joy, the same passion for life). He went out, smelled the damp aroma of the Island, the breeze carrying all the smells of night, turned onto the stone path that opens up between the bust of Greta Garbo and the Hermes of Praxiteles, saw the trees that night makes even larger, walked along touching the trees, and it was as if the trees were growing, were growing at the touch of his hands, as if his footsteps made the earth spring forth with thoughts and mimosas, jasmine, hibiscus. When he reached the fountain with the Boy and the Goose, he considered that everything he saw, and more than that, everything he couldn't see and could only imagine, everything, the world, the whole world, was the result of his creation.

"It's hot" is the phrase heard most often in this Island since the days of the Creation, It's hot, at any time in any place, the circumstances don't matter, when you open your eyes to the sluggish morning sun, or when you go outside to see what the sky is offering you today, or you await without resignation the downpour whose greatest threat isn't the black clouds but the horrendous steam that rises from the earth, and it compels you to shout, It's hot, oh yes it is hot, at Sunday dinner, at some saint's day party, when it's time to take out the tamales, to fry the chicharrones, to uncork the bottles of rum, to play dominoes under the royal poinciana, It's hot, it's real real hot, when some baby lets out its first cry, and also in the bed of liaisons, in the bed of sunken bodies (bodies sunken in heat), in the instant when they try to flee, not by sea, not by road, not by distance, but by a path of mixing salivas, mixing sweats, mixing saps, by the path of enjoyment, between one caress and the next, one kiss and the next, one bite and the next, when they spread their legs to receive another's vitality, It's hot, writing the letter, watering the roses and writing the miscellany that is the greeting of the peerless Graces of the peerless Island, It's hot at the wake, facing the burning candles, and also at the hour of the Holy Sacrament, and at the moment of jumping out the window, hoisting the flag, singing the anthem, or when you're dying in a nursing home bed, or swimming in the steaming sea, or you stop on the steaming street corner not knowing which road to take (it's a lie, the roads don't lead to Rome!), each road opens a path to the frying pans of hell, It's hot for the carpenter, the lawyer, the dancer, the tourist, the woman-of-the-house, the woman-of-the-street, the candy-seller, the bartender, the pigtailed girl, the girl-without-pigtails, the bus driver, the nurse, the high-ranking officer, the actress, the criminal, the singer, the teacher, the model, the collector, the writer, the little-shot and the big-shot, the winner and the loser, if there's anything democratic about this Island it's that, for everyone, It's hot.

Sebastián will try to write in the sand, on the seashore. Sebastián will try to write, with his index finger, that phrase he heard from the tall, suited mulatto who went one day to buy books at Eleusis. Sebastián will write, *I don't understand anything, I'm a simple soul,* while one wave after another and another will come and erase the phrase each time. For all Sebastián persists in rewriting it, each time the sea will erase it.

So the truth is, Lucio, I don't understand what you went to do at Miriam's house, or rather, around Miriam's house. If you were feeling good, if you were lucky enough to enjoy an instant of that contentment not everyone can attain (I want you to know: there are people who die without ever knowing the luck of imagining themselves for one second the creator of all that exists), what evil notion led you toward a meeting with the woman you hate? (Yes, you hate her, we should call things by their real names, don't you think?) I know, you never got there, you prowled around her house like a thieving ghost debating whether you should enter and say, Good evening (with your mellifluous voice, the best of your smiles, the politest way possible), give her father a formal handshake, give a kiss to her mother (or to the air of cheap fragrance that surrounds her mother) who will doubtless be leafing through a copy of *Vanidades,* and then kiss her, Miriam, the woman you hate, and sit down in the rocking chair to repeat, You have the prettiest eyes I've ever seen, while you know you're lying, and you consider yourself a swine for lying, while you're thinking about the festive atmosphere of the outdoor cafes on Prado. If you detest the house, the woman, the family, why did you have to go, why lose another night of your life? (I don't know if you're aware how few nights there are in your life) and, worst of all, why make her lose hers, too? why? You didn't enter, you didn't see her, it's true; perhaps it was worse to stick around on that corner, smoking in the shadows, taking advantage of the burned-out lightbulb in the street lamp, watching the lights of the house, knowing that the lights of the house were waiting for you, lying in wait, allowing a delinquent's eyes to look out through your eyes, allowing mediocre malefactor's fear to supersede your fear. Why not tell her once and for all you don't like her? Miriam is just seventeen. At that age, a disappointment in love lasts three days.

No, I don't hate Miriam, it's true I don't love her, it's true I don't like to rock by her side in the rocking chair, and that rocking chair seems like the most uncomfortable one in the world to me, and her hand the roughest, and her voice the most unpleasant, and her eyes so unexpressive (you could say she was denied the ability to look), and her teeth are dry and they don't laugh when they laugh, no, I don't like to kiss her, I detest the flowers she sticks in her hair, and the dress she wears every Wednesday for me, and the magnolia scent of her perfume, her perfume makes me want to run away, and her hands always holding the little fan and the little lace handkerchief, I abhor little fans and little lace handkerchiefs, and the women who hold little fans and little lace handkerchiefs, it's true, I wouldn't like to be next to her even in my most desperate moment, and when I'm on her big porch, sitting next to her in the torturous rocking chair, I have the impression that if I don't jump up and run away the world might come to an end, yes, that's true, but I don't hate her.

Night in Havana begins early, and that's why night is so long in Havana. Even before it grows dark, Havana is partying. Well, it is always partying, because Havana is a twenty-four-hour party, from the moment the sun rises until it sets, it's well known, here you greet dawn with the same cheerful striking of drums, the same offerings of fruits and booze as you bid farewell to night, and I know it'd be better to write: One of the mysteries that night brings to most cities (there are cities with no mystery) begins sooner in Havana than anywhere else. Lighted signs are turned on impatiently. Long before the sky darkens, before the bars make their presence even more obvious, before the lights go on in the outdoor cafes on Prado where the bands play, there's an hour in Havana that is neither day nor night. Children are still playing hide-and-seek in Fraternidad Park, still running around the bronze busts (luckily stained by the cheerful crapping of birds), still bathing in the stagnant green and venerable waters of the Fountain of the Indian, still singing, *Let's go, let's go, the fountain broke!* still jumping rope,

One, two, buckle my shoe, when the scandalous, convertible, red-painted Fords and Buicks begin to arrive, and men emerge from them wearing cotton twill, with slicked-back hair, gold-plated watch chains, and two-toned shoes; and sculpted women approach with their hair always done up to the point of despair, always with steatopygia (real or feigned), walking lightly on heels so light and so high they don't exist. The churches haven't closed yet and the gaming halls have already opened, and the parishioners hurry out of the churches and run to trade their rosaries and breviaries for rum glasses and decks of cards or dice cups. Shopkeepers haven't closed their stores yet and you can already see the bottles being uncorked. Before the bells for the Angelus ring you can hear the bands and their catchy melodies, *At Prado and Neptuno there's a chick that all the guys can't help but watch.* Night still hasn't fallen and the city has already begun the best homage ever made to a race cruelly annihilated by the Conquest: serving great transparent glasses of cold Hatuey beer (cold as can be, for cooling down your throat, for exorcising the devil we call heat). Night falls on a city where for some time now it has been night.

Night began early in Havana, and we should imagine Lucio, dressed like a typical Cuban, like a prince, heading through Fraternidad Park toward the outdoor cafes on Prado. The children of course were there at the Fountain of the Indian, except they weren't singing *Let's go, let's go* any longer, just sitting there, silent and still, unsmiling, looking somber. The first thing that surprised Lucio whenever he was about to cross Prado Boulevard was the fortunate odor that received him, the mix of odors, of fries, sweat, onions, flowers, dried cod, urine, oil, garlic, bread, beer, perfumes. The outdoor cafes were well lit and full of people, and Lucio sensed that he could forget Miriam. In the first bandstand he recognized the Anacaona Orchestra with its majestic mulattos playing a danzonete. Although a few couples took up the dance, the majority preferred to keep on drinking, laughing, talking at the top of their lungs, perhaps holding back now so they could let go all the more freely at a later hour. He stopped when he got to the corner of Dragones Street and leaned against a column. Very close to me, a blonde stirred under the arms of a man who looked like one of the bronze statues at the ends of the entrance to the Capitol; he was kissing her on the mouth as if he wanted to empty her out; to let herself be kissed, she was standing on the tips of her toes, her dress was creeping up, I swear you could see her black lace underwear, and also, since there were so many people standing around the kissing couple, a little red-haired kid was trying to pick the wallet out of the back pocket of the man who looked like a bronze statue (who was so busy trying to eviscerate the woman he didn't even notice), I saw the red-haired boy, he noticed I was looking at him on purpose, that I had seen him, and he ran off in search of another pocket, I suppose, now the band was playing, *There's a tree that grows in my Cuba, you can't cut it down unless you pray . . .* a whore with a thousand-year-old face covered by a thousand layers of makeup offered me a cigarette and I said, No, I don't smoke, my dear, I have other vices but not that one, and I pretended to look away, in another direction, though I was actually having fun watching how she studied me from top to bottom, biting her lips, as if she were looking at a piece of candy, Woman, you're the one who should be paying me. Since the whore kept on circling, Lucio left the column he had been leaning against (only one of a million or so columns in the city) and continued toward Teniente Rey Street, where a female band played, *Even Queen Elizabeth dances danzón, 'cause its rhythm's so sweet and delicious.* A ragged Chinese woman walked by, touching all the drinkers and passing judgment, This guy has a big one, this guy has a small one, this guy doesn't have one at all, protected by a chorus of guffaws. A gaunt forty-year-old in black suit and hat was announcing, An angel descended from heaven, he had great authority and the earth was lit up in his radiance, this angel told me: "It shall fall, worry not, Babylon the Great shall fall, it has become the abode of demons, the dwelling place of impure spirits of every sort, and it shall fall, you may be sure of it, Babylon the Great shall fall and not even the memory of it shall remain." Now the band was playing *The Martians have just arrived, and they came here to dance the cha-cha-cha.* A group of people had gathered almost in the doorway of the *Diario de la Marina.* Lucio stopped out of curiosity and saw an adolescent boy, grown disproportionately tall, white as could be, timid-looking, dressed only in a loincloth. Facing him, a man in a suit (evidently the boy's father: you might say, an aged replica of him) opened a suitcase full of knives of every shape and size. Now you will see a unique sight, shouted the man in a voice that tried to mask his exhaustion, now you will see something never seen before, here you have before you Sebastian of the Knives, the martyr nonpareil, he who knows-not-the-meaning-of-pain. At a distance of four or five yards from the man, with rare equilibrium, the adolescent balanced on a beam, eyes closed, arms and legs wide open, expression of waiting resignation. A little girl Lucio hadn't noticed before (she blended into the public) began beating a drum. The man took the largest of the knives. Please, gentlemen, be silent, very silent, I require the greatest cooperation from our kind and beloved public. He pointed the knife at the adolescent and stood still a few seconds, watching him with a fixity that became almost unbearable. Then he threw the knife into one of the boy's arms. The boy barely opened his lips to utter a slight groan that could not be heard. Blood rushed out quickly, as did the public's Ahh! The boy returned to his motionlessness, to the meekness of his waiting. Another knife penetrated his other arm with the consequent loss of blood, except that this time the boy limited himself to pressing his lips tight. Lucio thought the adolescent was growing paler. A third and a fourth knife struck each thigh. Blood, of course, burst from them with even greater force. The fifth ended in his breast, beside his heart, and this time the boy could not repress a grimace that opened his eyes (meek, it is true, but also alarmed). The sixth went into his gut. The seventh perforated his forehead, and the impact was such that it almost managed to knock him off balance. His face flowed with blood and with a strange blood-streaked substance. The adolescent's whole body was soaked with blood. The violence with which the father threw the knives, his face filled with hate, shocked Lucio almost more than the spectacle of the wounded boy. The public cheered, applauded ardently. One woman fainted and another began to jump with happiness. Next to Lucio a man exclaimed enthusiastically, This is the most educational spectacle I have seen in a long, long time, and he threw a bill toward the man's open box. Lucio felt sick. He kept walking down to the Theater Payret, where a Spanish zarzuela troop was performing *La Gran Vía*. Later, for the midnight show, they would screen a Dolores del Río movie. Another band, also all women, could be heard playing

A rose of France, whose soft fragrance, one evening in May . . . (to a *son* tempo). The grandiose entrance to the Payret was crowded with people. Every possible form of human being was there. Coming and going, Babelian uproar, indistinct, unbearable. Only the sales pitch of the flower and cigarette vendors could rise above that confusion. A pretty girl came up to me, wearing a dark green velvet dress (velvet on the Island, what do you think?) under which she must have been sweating like a pig, looked at me with too-feminine blue eyes, smiled with a too-feminine mouth, stretched out to me her little alabaster hand (where does she hide this beauty during the day?) encrusted with jewels, too feminine (which I kissed to make myself out to be a libertine), and exclaimed with too feminine a tone in her rough voice, May God bless you, macho! too much femininity, too female of her, don't you think? it was a man, of course, there's no woman so feminine as a man when he wants to be feminine, and women know it, and that's why they hate feminine men. Lucio looked for a flower vendor, bought a Black Prince, and gave it to her. Please, she asked sweetly but firmly, leave me alone, because you can't fool me. The girl sniffed the flower, smiled, and threw a kiss as she walked away in her green velvet dress. Across the street, by the doors to the Centro Gallego, Lucio found they had opened a side show. SHOW OF WONDERS, said the sign by the entrance. Roosters with six feet, hermaphrodite monkeys, cows with a single horn in the center of the head, human fetuses with two heads, gigantic chameleons, eyeless dogs, and the only living beings in the show: Siamese twin sisters, resolutely united, who played guitars and sang *Punto Guajiro*. Lucio walked on past the National Theater, where *Lucia di Lammermoor* was playing, thought of Casta Diva (naturally enough) and, not knowing what else to do, turned the corner into San Rafael Street. He felt tired and entered the Nautilus Bar. Luckily the bar was almost empty. On the Victrola he heard the voice of Vicentico Valdés, *Envy, how I envy the handkerchief that once dried your tears* . . . Seated at a table, he asked for a double rum and lit acigarette.

A gaunt forty-year-old, in black suit and hat, sat down in front of me, taught forehead, eyes sunk in their sockets, sunken cheeks, lipless mouth, told me in a low voice, barely a whisper, it was hard to hear it, It shall fall, worry not, Babylon the Great shall fall, the angel told me, no one wants to believe me, I saw the angel one night, last night, today, this very night, I saw it speaking, words of fire, words you could see coming out like flames from his lips, Babylon the Great shall fall, the buildings shall shatter, the sea shall rise, the sky shall fall at once to the sea, sea and sky shall unite, the union of the two is fire, fire, all hopes shall turn to ashes, all illusions to ashes, the land devastated, and that means more than devastated, understand, and the worst part: no one wants to believe me, I saw the angel who announced the destruction of Babylon the Great, I saw him just like I see you now, better than I see you know, because you are condemned to the horror, that's what I heard from a gaunt forty-year-old in black suit and hat who sat down in front of me that night in the Nautilus Bar.

Very late, when the rum was burning in his stomach, Lucio went to the Cafeteria America and asked for a ham sandwich and a mango juice. At a table nearby he discovered the adolescent of the knives, the Sebastian of the Prado, with the little girl and the father. Aside from his pallor the boy showed no sign of the spectacle of two hours earlier. The father took some fritters from a bag and distributed them among their plates. The waiter served them three glasses of water. The girl whispered something in the boy's ear (about the waiter, apparently) and the boy laughed, laughed so hard he nearly choked. Drank water and kept on laughing. To Lucio he seemed whiter, more childish. The father picked up the suitcase from the floor, opened it, took out a knife and used it to cut them each a slice of bread.

When he got to Miri's house it was maybe past three in the morning already. Lucio looked through the window and saw Manilla, black and fat, who had fallen asleep, bearlike, in one of the big living room easy chairs. He was shirtless, with his immense belly, his breasts sopping with sweat, and his santería necklaces more visible than ever. His mouth was open and a trickle of saliva dripped down his chin to mix in with the sweat of his chest. Since he came enshrouded in the vehemence of cheap rum, Lucio had no qualms about knocking insistently at the door. The big fellow halfway woke, and raised his hands in surprise (and nothing ever surprised him). He stood up with great effort. Stumbled forward, making furniture and walls tremble, to the door, and when he opened it his bloodshot frog eyes shone in a particular way. What the fuck do you want? To see Miri. Lucio smiled. You know what goddamn time it is? In answer Lucio just held out a twenty-peso bill. With astounding agility, Manilla caught the bill in the air. His huge hands were laden with rings. There'll be another twenty when I go, Lucio said. Manilla opened the door, let Lucio pass, and closed it with two turns of the lock. He also took the precaution of half closing the window. He returned to the easy chair, obviously his easy chair, because it looked about ready to collapse. Lucio took off his jacket and arranged it on the back of his chair. More awake now, Manilla looked at the boy with his eyes redder and redder, full of mocking veins. Hey, this is a decent house and every once in a while we'd rather be left alone to sleep. I had to see Miri. You don't need to take an oath on it, prettyboy. Manilla's cavernous voice sprang from a throat thirsty for rum. Manilla picked up a cigar, sniffed it, held it back from his eyes to get a nice look at it, licked his tongue over several spots, cut the tip with scissors, and lit it ceremoniously. He laughed with the cigar in his mouth. It's hot, isn't it? and to back up the phrase with a physical action he began to wipe his neck, chest, and belly with a yellow handkerchief that smelled strongly of Agua de Portugal. Havana's on fire, he insisted, I don't know how you can walk around by yourself at this hour, prettyboy. Lucio didn't answer. The only light (and the only luxury) in the living room came from a neon lamp wrapped around the gigantic conch shell that contained the altar for Oshún. This image had little in common with the Virgin of La Caridad del Cobre in the Island, perhaps only her yellow dress; her face, more mulatta than the other's, was smiling, with a picaresque expression that seemed fairly inappropriate for a saint. The altar was full of offerings: pieces of fruit, sunflowers, bowls of farina, jugs of beer, golden clothing, and, of course, candles. Manilla took several drags on the cigar, looking at the ceiling, looking at the smoke, forgetting about Lucio. He laboriously stood up his enormous humanity, lit a candle, wet a finger in the goblet of water placed before the Virgin, marked his forehead with the sign of the cross, rang a little bell, crossed himself. He turned toward Lucio caressing his concisely black belly. These are bad times, prettyboy, people are going around disbelieving, where disbelievers are you'll find Beelzebub. He collapsed in the easy chair again (the lumber shrieked) and picked up a cane with which he knocked on the floor. Miri, he called, Miri. Silence. Manilla sucked on the cigar and shook his head. These kids . . . he complained. Miri, he called louder. There was some kind of movement in the bedroom next door; you could hear a sigh or a complaint, a metal bedframe creaking. The black man again hit the floor with the cane — Miri! Lucio felt her sit up in bed, thought he knew when she put on her little wooden slippers. Her footsteps came up close to the door, covered by a curtain strung together from seashells. The child appeared, rubbing her eyes. Her body was thin and, dressed in a threadbare cotton robe, she gave the impression of being even skinnier, smaller, more of a child; as if they had disguised her as a woman. A fairly light mulatta girl, fairly pretty, she had good hair and Oriental eyes, and if it weren't for the lips you could never have told that she was Manilla's daughter. She looked at her father incredulously and yawned. Manilla turned the cigar several times in his mouth and then pointed to Lucio with it. The prettyboy wants to see you, wants to sprinkle Holy Water on you. Miri made a half turn and disappeared again into her room. From it now came, muffled, a Pedro Junco bolero (no way to guess who was singing, in any case a woman), *We, who are so much in love.* When she reappeared, more wide-awake, she had her hair pulled back in a bun and wore the silk kimono with the lotus flowers that Lucio already knew. She stood in the middle of the little living room as if awaiting orders. Manilla served himself a magnanimous glass of rum (the rum and the glass were close at hand, on the little table that also held an ashtray and a plaster crucifix). Sit down in front of him, Manilla ordered. *We, who have made of our love a wonderful new world, a romance so divine.* Not thinking twice about it, almost mechanically, Miri sat down on an easy chair in front of Lucio. Unable to focus on anything else, Lucio's and Miri's eyes met. She's still not a woman, she could be playing with dolls, and dreaming of a fairy-tale life, and hoping for a Prince Charming. *We, who are so much in love, we ought to separate now, please do not ask me more.* Manilla swallowed a sip of rum, knocked the ashes from his cigar and told Miri in paternal tones, Open up your robe. Miri obeyed instantly. She's a child, so she doesn't have breasts and barely even peach fuzz, she shouldn't have any idea what opening up her kimono in front of me is for, what a man's body is for. Hitting the floor with his cane, Manilla this time ordered Lucio, Look at her, prettyboy, she's practically a child, where, tell me, where are you going to find a girl who'll open up her robe to let you look? Manilla's words roused two opposing sentiments in Lucio: on the one hand, a wave of indignation; on the other, a rush of blood (roused by that very indignation) that made his member harder. He wanted to get up and hit Manilla; instead of that, he massaged his crotch. The record was stuck: *We ought to separate now, we ought to separate now, we ought to separate now.* After another drink of rum and another blow of his cane, Manilla asked her, On your feet, Miri, take off that kimono, let him get a good look at you, let the prettyboy see the fresh meat he has in front of him. The girl obeyed. She let the kimono fall off and turned around several times so Lucio could see her body from every angle. Lucio wanted to unbutton his fly; raising his cane, Manilla stopped him, You don't need to rush things, Miri's here to do that, prettyboy. When she fell to her knees in front of Lucio, the stretched-out candlelight projected the image of Oshún on the wall. Interested, Manilla left the cigar in the ashtray, took a long sip of rum and half closed his eyes; his voice sounded warm, Unbutton the trousers smoothly, Miri, as smoothly as you know how, at first it should be smooth, real smooth, so he can't feel your hands, so he can't tell what's going on, so what you promise will be bigger than what you do, never forget, the pleasure they enjoy the most is the one that never quite gets there, waiting for pleasure is more seductive. The girl unbuttoned Lucio's shirt, his fly, his underwear. Her little hands wavered in the air as if awaiting fresh orders, her eyes stared at some place that wasn't in Manilla's living room. The black man caressed his belly. Good, Miri, let's get that prick into the fresh air, it's dying to come out, look how it's stirring in his pants, look at it and never forget: delicately, leave roughness for the end, like that, little by little, take that sausage out like it's made of glass, that's it, my girl, very good, you're doing it real good, now look at it, take a good long look at it, the prettyboy bastard has a nice big prick, and every time you're in front of a big prick, stop to look at it, that really makes them happy, because big fat pricks are like movie stars, there's nothing they like more than always having people look at them, and if you're in front of a little prick, look at it for a long time too, that way it'll think it's big and it'll get excited, besides, the prettyboy's crazy for you to do something with it, and you'll be smart and take all the time you want so he'll go crazier and crazier, take out the balls, my daughter, they're also a part of what you're doing, remember, those tense balls hold the cum, and the cum is what you're aspiring to, the Holy Water. Manilla wiped off his sweat with his huge yellow handkerchief, which again filled the living room with the smell of Agua de Portugal. Afterward he began to caress the end of his cane. It if weren't for the singer who repeated endlessly, *We ought to separate now, we ought to separate now,* it seemed that nothing would break the quiet of the room, as if for a few seconds nothing would ever happen. Come on, Miri, Manilla asked persuasively, run your tongue around the prettyboy's balls, give the balls some pleasure, forget about the rod, don't pay any attention to the rod, don't even look at it, concentrate on those balls, that's your objective now, the more desperate the prick gets for your mouth the better, trace figures with your tongue on the balls, put them in your mouth, without hurting them, pleasurably, no rush, you're not in any hurry, you have all night to give yourself pleasure and give the prettyboy pleasure, look, take a look at the little mole it has there, suck that a little, just a little, lightly, don't insist too much, now start moving up, Miri, my girl, start moving up, stop right there, at the base, stay there, take your mouth away, touch it, touch it like you're putting your hands on the Virgin's robes, softly, my love, so he can barely feel the pressure of your little hands, touch it and let your mouth fill with saliva, because you're going to wrap your mouth around the big head of the prettyboy's prick, because that's what the son of a bitch is waiting for, come on, little by little, so the prettyboy's rod, his cock, his prick will finally enter your mouth. Manilla struck the floor with his cane. Not like that, Miri, that prick didn't go in right, not like that, hold it from underneath and let it penetrate your mouth like God meant it to. Another blow of his cane. Fuck it, Miri, I told you not like that, try it again, remember, when the prick enters your mouth that's a magical moment, come on, don't give up, my daughter, the key to a good suck is getting the hang of it, the only rule for giving a good suck is liking to suck, come on, now your tongue, let your tongue come alive, let it move, let it move a lot, Miri, all over the head, concentrate there, on the underside, understand, that's where the prettyboy's feeling impatient, faster with your tongue, Miri, faster. Again Manilla hit his cane on the floor and wiped off the sweat with the yellow handkerchief. If you don't put in something for your part, Miri, you've lost. Once more, like that, like that, my girl, like that, move your tongue real fast, come on, so the prettyboy'll always remember the cocksuck you're giving him, so his rod won't think that just because it's big it's better than you, so it'll always be thinking about your mouth, so it can't forget your mouth, Miri. The girl lifted her head, her eyes were red and two tears were about to fall. What's the matter, Miri? Manilla asked in a loud, imperative voice. The girl did all she could to keep from sobbing. The black man stood up from the easy chair, went to the altar where the candle was starting to go out, lit another, wet his finger in the goblet of water and again made the sign of the cross on his forehead. You're hopeless, he exclaimed, helping Miri get up, stand here, it's time you learned how it's done. With tremendous effort Manilla prostrated himself before Lucio. You do this with lots of love, Miri, with lots of love, he took the boy's member and carried it patiently to his mouth.

Stealthily, with the utmost care, Miss Berta enters the room and, without even turning on the light, stands in front of her mother's bed. Doña Juana is sleeping, as always, her insuperable sleep. The candle she had placed next to the nightstand, in front of an image of La Caridad del Cobre, has been consumed, so Miss Berta lights another one, white and Solomonic, and crosses herself.

It should be kept in mind that such a candle will play a decisive role in the history of the Island. Though this is not the occasion for getting ahead of events. If the things in life lack a proper order and timing, that's why we have books.

The great breast, the great belly of the ninety-year-old woman rise and fall with jubilant regularity. It's been years since Doña Juana last deigned to wake. For years she has remained wonderfully asleep, in her white nightgown, her rosary between joined hands, as if she wanted to anticipate death.

Though it seems like it, it isn't two in the morning (it's well known the Island can fool you), the clock actually shows six-thirty in the afternoon, but since October is like this in the Island, it got dark too soon. Miss Berta is trying to read *Figures from the Lord's Passion* while picking her nose and lightly marking the words with her lips. At this instant, as might have been expected, she feels she is being observed. For several days now the gaze has not returned to bother her. Now she suddenly experiences the force of the eyes hitting her, she stops understanding what she's reading and turns the pages desperately, because she's not conscious of anything but being observed by someone she doesn't know, and she doesn't know where he is, she has no idea why he has decided to torture her with this persistent gaze. Indignation rises in a wave of blood to her head and compels her to hurl the book furiously against the wall, to confront resolutely the open window, the painting of the Sacred Heart, the graduation portrait that shows a young Berta full of grace and high hopes, yes, high hopes, why not? at some time you have to be young, ingenuous, and believe in impossible things, there's a reason why you're mortal, and I want you to tell me, what do you want to know? why are you worrying about me? if you know everything that happens in this damned, injurious Island, created for bitterness, if you know everything that happens on this accursed planet, why do you want to be so wicked with me? why not leave me in peace and forget about me? yes, I'd advise you, forget about me, I'm nothing more than the miserable ash you made me with, leave me, leave me ash, don't look at me, don't turn me into anything else, not better and not worse, allow me to scatter in the gusting wind you like to use to punish this wretched land foundering in the middle of a sea as lovely as it is corrupt, I'm dust and want to keep on being that, I don't aspire to anything, not even to your gaze, don't stare at me, let me die peacefully, a little bit each day, let me die without having your eyes stab into me like knives. Miss Berta goes out into the Island ready to meet up with someone (with Someone!), ready for anything; what receives her, however, is the wall of exotic trees, the damp and perfumed breeze smelling of pine trees, mango trees, acacias, soursops, smelling of the red sandalwood tree of Ceylon, what receives her is the precocious shade of an October night, the immense solitude of the hour when everyone retires as if in response to orders from above. There's nobody, of course, there had to be *nobody,* I mean n-o-b-o-d-y, God, Nobody! Though for all that, she doesn't stop feeling like she is being watched, as we know: a gaze is and will always be a mysterious thing, it doesn't have to come from anyone's eyes at all; for Miss Berta (or for any one of us) to feel watched, she doesn't need to have anybody watch her.

Almost without saying hello, Miss Berta walks into Irene's house. Irene starts explaining, I've thought a lot about that question you asked me, I've thought a lot about God and I've come to the conclusion . . . But Miss Berta interrupts her: They're watching me, she complains. They're watching me. And without waiting for Irene to invite her, she goes into the Wounded Boy's room.

There lies the Wounded Boy. Like one of the prints of Christ that she buys in that store on Reina Street. His Nazarene face, the sharpened profile of a dying man. His long, bony hands on which she thinks she sees the marks of the nails. Miss Berta comes close, takes one of the hands and kisses it, there where she thinks the wound is, where the coagulated blood has a slight taste of iron. The Wounded Boy's eyes, however, remain closed. She steps away, desperate, yells, Who's watching me, fuck it, who's watching me? Irene runs in, What's wrong, woman?

The path that opens up between the Hermes of Praxiteles (in truth, the Hermes of Chavito) and the bust of Greta Garbo is sown with lemon and orange trees, always full of flowers and fruits, I pick an orange blossom, arrange it in my hair, keep walking up to the fountain of the Boy with the Goose, I stand there angry as if the clumsy statue of the Boy were implicated somehow in my misfortune, as if he were the one dedicating himself to watching me and watching me with an insistence that's going to drive me crazy, afterward I keep walking toward the courtyard and Merengue's pastry cart, snow white and covered with decorations, prints and colored ribbons, it looks more like a small carnival carousel than a peddler's cart, Lord, don't look at me, by Your Sacred Mercy I beg of You, don't look at me, forget about me, leave me forgotten, off in some corner of this poorly created world of Yours, I'm, Lord, and You know it, given that You know everything, I'm not responsible for your mistakes.

On the streets it hasn't grown dark as it has on the Island. On the streets there's still a trace of sun sweeping weakly up toward the higher reaches of the walls, toward the rooftops. A few nearly naked children, mounted on stick horses, are playing war between Indians and cowboys, firing stick pistols, bam-bam, I killed you. Miss Berta passes by Eleusis, where Rolo receives her affably and informs her he is about to close. She gives no reply. She searches among the books with a nervous gaze. She doesn't even say good-bye when she leaves the bookstore and again faces the street, which the light is turning blue. A sailor approaches. A young man, about twenty . . . (the same one Rolo met a few pages back, the same one Sebastián thought he saw the night they found the Wounded Boy, the same one who'll play a decisive role in this book; no need to describe him; the reader has met him; and even when it doesn't occur to the narrator to describe him, the reader will always find him young and handsome; a sailor will always be, above all, young and handsome; the reader will also be inevitably reminded of Cernuda and Genet; and that is fine: those great writers, each in his own way, gave the sailor divine rank, and they deserve that every time good luck puts us in front of a sailor, in front of The Sailor, we should pause for a minute of silence, of remembrance, of fervor). Since she is not very sensitive to human beauty, male or female, Berta doesn't even glance at him. She knows he's a sailor because of his white outfit, his wide collar circled with blue stripes.

The parish church is closed. She knocks on the door, desperate. No one opens. The sacristan, is he deaf? he must be deaf. The priest is off giving extreme unction, since this is a diabolical era, people are dying like flies and there isn't enough holy oil to go around. She circles the church several times. No window, no bit of stained glass lets out any light. The priest's house, too, is so dark it looks abandoned. She sits down on a granite bench, right beneath a street lamp (the only light at the parish church), near the image of Saint Augustine, feeling she's being observed, minutely observed, judged (after all, the characteristic property of any gaze, even the most ingenuous, is that it evaluates, it judges). She doesn't know what to do. Sitting at the top of the wall of the parish church, a little girl observes her. Berta leaves the bench, goes toward her. She approaches her slowly, as if she were afraid to scare her away. What's your name? The little girl smiles and doesn't answer. You're pretty, where do you live? The girl's eyes, half closed from smiling, shine ingenuously. She lifts a little arm and points vaguely toward a place, any place. Have you been watching me for a long time? The girl neither nods nor shakes her head, just plays with the ribbon in her braid. Yes, Berta exclaims, I know, you've been looking at me for a long time, and she spreads her arms to take the girl into them, hug her tight, Come on, you could fall from here, she goes back to the bench holding the girl, who is not laughing now. I want to know why you were watching me. The girl hangs her head. Tell me, please, I beg you, it's important, why were you watching me? She hugs her, grasps her, tightly to herself, tries to look her straight in the eyes. It's impossible: the girl won't stop playing with the ribbon in her braid. If I give you a piece of candy, will you tell me why you were staring at me so much? The girl starts crying, crying disconsolately. She pushes Berta, escapes her arms and runs away, still crying.

Although the market plaza is closed at this hour, it is still full of light. The vendors don't place too much confidence in the night watch. So they leave the lights on in their stalls to scare away thieves (there are so many of them in this era, more every day, will the time come when we start stealing from each other?). Berta goes inside the illuminated, deserted market, where the only ones you can see are a few beggars stretched out on the floor. She walks slowly up the aisles that are impassable by day, they're so crowded, there's so much coming and going, so much merchandise, fabrics, flowers, vegetables, plaster saints, wickerwork, fake jewelry, leather goods, live animals, and butchered animals. Since nobody's hawking their wares, since nobody's promoting their merchandise with boorish insistence, since the beggars seem to be sleeping, a great silence prevails inside the market, so that Berta's footsteps sound even more grandiose. The eyes continue watching her, ironically, sarcastically, making her experience the sensation that she is nobody, that she is no more than a bit of dust among the dust. Then she hears a laugh, Lord, if that is You laughing,

I beg You not to mock this, Your humble servant, do not distinguish me with Your gaze, if I really am nobody allow me to disappear among the crowd of nobodies that surround me. Much clearer, much more mocking, the laughter returns to wound the silence of the market plaza. Berta looks furtively in one direction and another. She discovers an old man asleep, dressed in a suit, dirty as all get-out, sitting on the floor and surrounded by bags full of God knows what, accompanied by a dog and by a pewter jar at the bottom of which you can see coins. Deeply unsettled, Berta comes closer; little by little she comes closer, hoping her footsteps won't wake him. When she's next to him, she kneels down with great difficulty. Dirty white, wagging its tail unenthusiastically, ears fallen, the dog lifts its head, which was resting on one of the old man's thighs, and observes her with sad watery eyes. Berta brings her index finger to her mouth to beg it to be quiet. The bald, toothless old man has his mouth open. A trickle of saliva drips down his chin. Not one more wrinkle could fit on his face. He doesn't sleep placidly, he chokes, coughs, brings his dirty hand to his brow as if trying to scare away the nightmares that must be tormenting him. Berta comes a bit closer. The stench of his body, covered with sweat and dirt, is remarkable. Also the other stench escaping from his toothless mouth, his empty stomach. For Berta, however, none of this matters. She takes one of the old man's hands between her own and stands there for some time, until the old man wakes up. The old man's hands pull free of hers and stretch up as if they were trying to touch the sky. His pupils are blurry, his eyes are two pebbles of white glass. Who are you? The anemic movement of his lips makes the trickle of saliva drip faster down his chin. She drops some coins into the pewter jar, unfastens the orange blossom bouquet she wears in her hair and places it carefully in the lapel of his threadbare coat.

Dark, empty, silent streets. You would be nobody, nobody at all, if it weren't that you keep feeling yourself observed, and you think you discover at every footstep, behind the lace curtains on the windows, behind the trees, in people passing by, the eyes that pursue your footsteps, your movements, your thoughts, yes, your thoughts (you're well aware that the eyes go beyond tangible reality, you're aware of the power of the piercing eyes that meet all and know all).

A strong wind has picked up, bringing, mixed with a smell of trees, a strong smell of the sea (in the islands the wind always carries a smell of the sea). You're going down toward the Island and you don't want to get to the Island. If you shut yourself up in your house, you wouldn't be able to sleep with the maddening awareness that the eyes are on you, pursuing you into the most unimaginable corners. Do you remember, Berta, the picture that hung in your house when you were little? Do you remember that old man with the long white beard and the stern scowl (always long white beards, always stern scowls!) writing with a goose quill on parchment? do you? Gilded gothic letters, saying God hears all, God writes all, God sees all, God knows all. Profound rage compels you to turn around. There, near you, look, a shadow, a man's shadow, yell at him, don't be afraid, yell at him, Don't You think it's terrible to waste eternity hearing, writing, seeing, and knowing everything? with all the lovely things there are to do, why start it with poor mortals like us? besides, what are we that You should pay any attention to us, if after all You made us from a bit of clay, another bit of ash, and a breath? No, Berta, calm down, keep on walking. It isn't a man's shadow. Come over, see for yourself, it's not a man, just a scarecrow in a garden.

In the Fair of the Century there are people, cheerfulness, a constant coming and going; balloon vendors; children eating cotton candy; drinkers; carnival barkers; hawkers; more children, on roller skates; couples; the couples walk slowly, calmly embracing; singles looking for someone to embrace; lovers kissing furiously in dark corners that aren't so dark; music, a lot of music coming from every direction and forming this great hubbub: the carousel is playing something vaguely reminiscent of arias from the *Cavalleria Rusticana,* and the old woman in the shawl that no one notices is cranking her hand organ and singing in a poor soprano, *Watch out, boy, 'cause the Virgin sees everything and she knows how bad you've been . . .* In the Fair of the Century there are card readers, singers, sword swallowers, improvisationalists, fortune-tellers, magicians, clowns, rumba dancers, acrobats. Here is the famous Pailock the great, the famous, the great prestidigitator, celebrated for making his wife, the divine Asmania, disappear.

With her orthopedic shoes, her crocodile skin purse, and the fan she just took out because, although it isn't hot, for her the heat tonight is becoming unbearable, Miss Berta stops next to a group of people surrounding a man. This is a man who is getting on in years, who wears gilded damask trousers that contrast with his red turban, and whose aging chest is bare, displaying his skin, reminiscent of the crocodile skin of Berta's purse. Strange, indistinguishable music barely emerges from a horrible-sounding Victrola, it could as easily be Mozart's *Requiem* as a danzón by Antonio María Romeu (the music mixes with all the other indistinguishable music at the fair, but through it all prevails the old, fluty voice, *Watch out, boy, 'cause the Virgin sees everything* . . .). From a table covered with swords, the man ceremoniously selects one. Raises his head, brings his right hand to his chest and holds it there dramatically; the left, the one grasping the sword, lifts even more dramatically. Opens his mouth, closes his eyes. Begins to introduce the sword into his mouth. The sword slowly enters the man's throat. The audience, in suspense, can't believe what it's seeing. When the sword grip, which isn't very golden, or very pretty, is all that's left visible, the public lets out a unanimous Ahh! Applause. The man quickly pulls the sword out of his mouth and looks at the audience without laughing, with a scowl on his face, as if great pain kept him from continuing the spectacle, as if all the organs in his body were run through, wounded, injured. His eyes, annoyed and defiant, wander across the people surrounding him, stopping at Berta for an instant, and she knows that the annoyance and defiance aren't real. At the bottom of his eyes is a great desolation, similar to that which she observes in her own eyes when she looks into the mirror.

They've taken the fire-eater to the hospital. His act went bad and he was burned. Several people make comments about it. One gentleman in a suit, getting on in years and holding a little dog in his arms, tells the story, unable to hold back his raucous laughter, that's right, the flame didn't go into his mouth, I don't know why the little guy closed his mouth, his cheeks were burning like they were made of paper, but the funniest part was when his hair caught fire, it made him look towheaded, it looked like henequen rope, I never knew it would be so funny to see a man's scalp on fire, and his eyelashes, did you catch his eyelashes? those tiny little flames on his lashes . . . He keeps on laughing, laughing, doubling over with laughter. The little dog barks.

Like the sword swallower, the magician is surrounded by a crowd. He does not, however, resemble the former. The magician is a well-built forty-year-old with interesting grey hairs beneath his bowler hat, wearing an impeccable tuxedo, leaning on a cane. He isn't a trick magician, no, not at all, isn't one of those who make rabbits and handkerchiefs appear or disappear, one of those who hide women in boxes and run them through with swords or do sleight of hand. He is much more serious. He dedicates himself to observing those before him with terrible shining eyes. He divines their names, their ages, what they do and want and keep in their pockets. Berta is staring fascinated at the magician's eyes. What if those were . . . ? Now the magician is fixedly observing an adolescent, a tender youth with blond hair and blue eyes, girlish face and the handsomely gawky body that all adolescents have. The boy stares into the magician's eyes. The timid smile that had been on his lips disappears. The adolescent keeps his sight fixed on the magician's shining eyes. Taking a few steps back, the magician raises his arms. The adolescent steps forward. Come on, Adrián, don't be afraid, the magician tells him, also serious, also concentrating on Adrián's magnificent eyes. You can still hear the hubbub of the fair, and above all the noise, the voice of the old organ grinder, *Watch out, boy, 'cause the Virgin sees everything* . . . The adolescent then closes his eyes and cries. Falls to his knees. Joins his hands in front of his mouth. The magician comes closer and puts one of his hands on the boy's head. The magician is frowning, you'd say he could also start crying. Who am I to you? For an answer Adrián, the adolescent, just exclaims out loud, Our Father who art in heaven . . . The audience raves with applause. Miss Berta pushes her way through the crowd around the magician. She stands in front of him right when the adolescent stands up, disconcerted, his eyes filled with tears, his forehead covered with sweat. The magician, for his part, has taken off his bowler and is daubing his hair with a large red handkerchief. The sweat makes his makeup run. The magician notices, with confusion, the woman's untimely arrival. Berta begs him, Look at me, look at me! He obliges her with restless eyes, dismayed, indecisive, irritated eyes of indefinite color, the vulnerable eyes of a tired, sleepy man desperate to get back home, jump into bed, wait for tomorrow night when he'll have to come back to the fair to earn a couple more pesos to keep living, that is, keep wearing a tux, bowler, cane, large red handkerchief. Blushing, Berta draws back among the crowd surrounding the magician, saying, I'm sorry, I'm sorry, I didn't know what I was doing.

I pay twenty-five cents to a hunchbacked old man sitting in a wheelchair, go into a black tent embroidered with yellow stars and half-moons, go into a dark place where fortunately I feel invisible, free from those gazes (if only for an instant!), they told me this card reader is the best in the fair, bald head and witch's face, this woman must be more than ninety years old, gypsy costume, sitting at a table, she has the table covered with a dark blue velveteen tablecloth, everything's dark here, the only light comes from the two candles on the table, the old woman raises one of her wrinkled hands, the nails are impressively long, and black, she doesn't invite me, rather she orders me to sit, I do it, of course, on the edge of the seat, above the table, between the candles and a glass of water with a jasmine flower, there's a pack of cards, one of the card reader's ancient claws falls on the pack, she moves her lips, I think she's praying, imploring someone's favor: I can't be sure of this: all I see is the movement of her lips, I don't hear anything, the card reader watches me with tiny, watery eyes that are almost shut. Cut! she orders in a surprisingly vigorous voice. The card reader joins the two halves and places three cards on the blue tablecloth. These three cards are your life, she says, this one here's for the past, this one's for the present and this one's for the future. She turns over the card that sits on the right: You see this figure with wings, you see this angel? it's number fourteen of the Major Mysteries and it's called Moderation, as you can see it has two amphoras that contain the essence of life and symbolize frugality. She pauses, lifts a hand to her forehead. Your name is Berta, right? mine is Mayra, I know you were a nun in another life, a servant of the Lord, in a certain way you have continued to be that during this transitory life you are leading now, a nun and a servant of the lord, and you have led a moderate, patient, harmonious, adaptable life, you have nothing to repent, Berta, the Lord looks on you with approval, I don't know why His holy gaze bothers you. She wets a finger in the water that is in the glass, the jasmine water, and wets her forehead. She turns over the second card, the one in the center. The present is represented by card number sixteen of the Major Mysteries, the Tower! a tall tower crowned with four battlements, look at it, see? it's being struck by lightning, House of God, Hospital, Celestial Fire, Tower of Babel . . . men fall to the ground, the past is past, it's over, Berta, it's over and we don't even know it, from now on it will be destruction and change, I see you and I see myself, you and me and everyone else, everyone walking around out there and beyond, we're all falling from the Tower, headfirst to the ground, old beliefs are crumbling, families and friendships are breaking up, destruction is upon us, this is bankruptcy, the end, loss. The card reader crosses herself. Berta does, too. The former holds out one of her ancient hands with the long black nails, and Berta understands that she should take it, squeeze it. The card reader turns over the final card. Number fifteen, the devil, the bat-winged Demon. The card reader lets go of Miss Berta's hand, points to the ground, lowers her head. Fire! she shouts with an even stronger, more powerful voice, a young and even lovely voice, My daughter, you will, though unwillingly, contribute to the fire, I see trees burning, houses burning, I see the past burning and the present burning, a garden devastated. At once Berta jumps to her feet. What should I do? tell me, what can I do to keep this destruction from taking place? The card reader cleans her forehead and neck with water from the glass, picks up the cards, yawns, nods her head, closes her eyes.

The Sailor. Again. He emerges from the crowd at the fair. Approaches and says in his magnificent deep voice, in a shockingly self-assured tone, You are looking for me. She looks into his eyes for an instant, his large and beautiful eyes in which she cannot find the least sign of pity, and replies angrily, Get out of my way. She tries to keep walking. He blocks her path. I know that you want to meet me, and the Sailor's voice becomes more sensual, more lovely, more sure of itself, Here I am, don't lose your opportunity. Miss Berta is almost dumbstruck with indignation, but that doesn't keep her from riposting, I could be your mother, and I think even your grandmother. The Sailor bursts out laughing, shrugs, and starts moving away, moving away (it would almost be proper to write: "fading away") without turning his back on her. Suddenly, he's gone. Yes, he's gone. How is that possible? He's gone. As if she had never seen any sailor! Miss Berta breathes a sigh of relief. That's sailors for you, they appear one minute and disappear the next.

At the back of the fair they've put together a movie theater. CINEMA ANTAEUS, says the pretentious sign. When the fairgrounds are about to give way to brushland, to wilderness, take a few posters of smiling women advertising Cerveza Cristal, folding chairs, a stained yellow screen, and a door in red: CINEMA ANTAEUS. The poorly drawn sign at the entrance announces Bette Davis in *Jezebel* for the second screening. Berta pays the five-cent entrance (Just five cents, today is Ladies' Day), and lets herself be guided by a bored young woman with a flashlight. The flashlight and the young woman are both unnecessary: between the light from the screen and the sky white with stars, Berta can see the improvised theater full of laughing people. Why are they laughing, why so heartily? Berta feels ready to remain unconvinced; she has never found funny movies funny. She prefers a good drama with Joan Crawford, Olivia de Havilland, or Lana Turner. Not to mention Vivian Leigh in *Gone with the Wind*. But she'll have to wait a bit to enjoy Bette Davis in *Jezebel*. First, the viewer is forced to consume one of those stupid fillers . . . After making herself comfortable, studying her surroundings and feeling relieved (apparently the gaze has offered her a kind of truce), she begins to fan herself. Her eyes come to rest at last on the screen. A group of people are arguing at the door to a shop. Every time one tries to hit another, the other one quickly avoids the blow, which hits a third one in the face. More and more people join the brawl. Berta recognizes among the group the unmistakable figures of Laurel and Hardy. The fat one tries to hit the thin one; the thin one jumps nimbly away; the blow lands on a dignified woman in a little hat who is passing that way by chance; the woman's husband, also dignified and well-dressed, joins the fight, tries to hit someone who doesn't let him so that he ends up hitting another dignified woman in a little hat who is passing that way by chance and who also has a well-dressed, dignified husband. Endless situation. There's no stop to it. The audience laughs, laughs, laughs till it can't laugh anymore. Not Berta, Berta doesn't laugh, though she does smile at least, the truth is it's funny to see those high and mighty women get hit (actually what's funny isn't seeing them get hit, but seeing them lose their dignity). When the fistfight has spread to a whole crowd, when it stretches down the street, Laurel and Hardy manage to scramble out of it. They, who created the problem, manage to escape, leaving the melee running in the street, hundreds of people hitting people they didn't need to hit, while they walk off smugly. Then the thin one's face completely fills the stained, yellow screen. For an instant, the one fleeting instant in which he looks at the audience in the theater, he scratches his head and smiles. The brevity of the smile doesn't keep Miss Berta from experiencing a shudder (or as she will later say when she tells the story to Mercedes and to Irene, keep her heart from "skipping a beat"). Something in his smile perturbs her, moves her to tears. That is why, come what may, that is why she jumps to her feet and screams, screams without caring if everyone else gets indignant, hisses at her, tells her to shut up. She doesn't care. It makes no difference to her that the bored usherette tries to force her from the theater. The only thing Berta wants is to hold on to the smiling image of Stan Laurel, that flash of lightning (ephemeral as any revelation), which for one second makes her feel the conviction that she is saved.

I don't know if you're aware, Casta Diva, that tonight they opened the monumental doors of the Paris Opera, and the City of Light (which doesn't let itself be dazzled by any light but its own) was dazzled. The theater was witness to a historic, unparalleled happening. Maria Callas, the Divine, gave a concert. Early on she was seen arriving, dressed in white, in her black auto, followed by a crowd of fans and hundreds of photographers from newspapers the world over, who had traveled from the most distant parts of the planet to report on the event. The police had to escort the Diva so she could enter the theater without mishap. Despite the fact that her lovely Greek eyes (the eyes she had also learned to sing with) looked exhausted, she smiled in greeting to the throng who applauded her. She shut herself in her dressing rooms for hours, accompanied only by her attendants. She usually meditates, *comme il faut.* Meanwhile, when they opened the monumental doors, the most illustrious men and women arrived, Marian Anderson, Edith Piaf, Alicia Alonso, Serge Lifar, Anna Magnani, Leontyne Price, Marc Chagall, Pablo Picasso, Coco Chanel, Katharine Hepburn, Joan Miró, Margretta Elkins, and many, many, many more that I cannot cite because the list would be enormous. Non-illustrious people also arrived: many members of the European nobility, hundreds of old women whose importance lies in the fact that they are encrusted with jewels and hold titles like Princess, Countess, and Lady I-don't-know-what-all (you are familiar with human idiocy). There were also some frankly despicable little characters arriving, such as Monseigneur le Cardinal and Monsieur le President (chief of Church and chief of State, that is, two wretched administrators who think they have the right to give the orders in everyone else's lives). At nine o'clock sharp the musicians began entering the stage. At three past nine the orchestra conductor, Tullio Serafin, entered, who as you are well aware is the conductor of the Scala in Milan and who came to conduct the Opera at the Diva's request. At four and a half minutes past nine Maria Callas went out on the stage. Radiant, smiling, her beautiful Greek eyes looking not a bit tired. She wore a black dress that made her look even more graceful. Not a single jewel (an artist, after all, has no need of tinsel; her finest jewel: her voice; you should know that when she began to sing, the emeralds and diamonds and rubies that so abounded in the boxes and the pit ceased shining). Ovation. You have only to see her to know she's worthy of an ovation. She, smiling, not timid in the slightest, sure of herself, with the conviction that she deserves this ovation more than anyone. What do you think she began with? Of course, Bellini, *Norma,* "Casta Diva," which she (pardon me) sings as no one else could. Then came "Regnava nel silenzio," "Surta è la notte . . . Ernani!," "Vissi d'arte," "Je suis Titania" . . . At one point no less than Giuseppe di Stefano came onstage, and together they sang the unsurpassable duet of Amelia and Ricardo from *Un Bal Masqué.* Another duet that even came close to moving the Army Chief of Staff (!) was the "Miserere" from *Il Trovatore.* The real climax, however, came later; the audience actually levitated (I'm not exaggerating: people floated up from their stuffed seats) when they heard that unique voice, that voice sent by God for our redemption, singing "Mon coeur s'ouvre à ta voix," the aria from *Samson and Delilah* that Saint-Saëns composed shortly before the bicycle accident. They say that even Queen Elizabeth of England, who had not cried since childhood and who was listening to the concert on an RCA-Majesty radio set, cried with emotion. They say that Monsieur le President took his wife's hand, caressed it, and signed a bill that night to help the *clochards.* They say the Cardinal did what he had never done: rebelled against the Pope by sanctifying love. They say the marchionesses and countesses gave away tiaras when they left the theater. They say that Generalissimo Francisco Franco recited a poem by Lorca from memory. They say Picasso painted a marvelous painting and didn't sign it so that it would remain anonymous, like the Spanish ballads. That say Joan Miró helped Picasso paint the anonymous painting. They say that for days there weren't any pointless debates in the United Nations. They say the comrades in the Kremlin were about to start thinking about the happiness of the people. They say there were no murders recorded in New York City, and that the poorest blacks in the city attended a cocktail party at the White House. They say the Island broke loose from the sea floor and went wandering over the seas on the night of the marvelous concert. What is for sure, Casta Diva, is that after the concert at the Paris Opera, it was established at last that, like Christ, Maria, the Divine Callas, had divided the history of the world in two.

Casta Diva has opened the secretary and taken out and dusted off photographs, postcards, makeup, costume jewelry, scores, and outfits, and has spread it all out on the bed, and has stood staring at it as if these were the remains from a shipwreck. And what are they but the remains from a shipwreck? she asks Tatina, who, as might be supposed, laughs. The photographs have lost their clarity and it is very hard to make her out dressed as Traviata or as Louise. The writing on the scores is illegible, the outfits have lost color, time has tattered them, the jewelry looks more like bits of glass than ever, and to think that this was my soul, Tatina, that this secretary contained me, especially this little white dress with tulle and pink ribbons (though you might not believe these ribbons were pink) in which, when I was just twelve, I stood before the great musician, before Lecuona, singing *El jardinero y la rosa,* and the great musician came up to me, deeply moved, and said, You will be a great singer, and even Rita Montaner gave me a kiss on my forehead and predicted I was sure to succeed. When Tingo enters, his mother is hugging the little dress with tulle and pink ribbons. Casta Diva sees him and comes up to him, fascinated. I was your age when Lecuona heard me sing. And she undresses Tingo and puts the little tulle dress on him. She places a ribbon in Tingo's hair so the likeness will be better. Now she moves her hands in front, and orders Tingo, move your hands, I'm going to sing.

Sebastián has written on a leaf of notebook paper: God Almighty, I hope You are feeling well when You receive this letter, we aren't doing so good, we're writing You because we'd like the Island to stop being one, if You'd put in a little on Your part You could take it and carry it off to Yucatan, off to Florida, or off to Venezuela, just imagine, God, how happy You could make us, Your not so sinful children (at least not so sinful as You think we are), if You felt like it, by letting us walk from one country to another without worrying about drowning to death, we trust in Your generosity, hoping for Your reply, Yours. Sebastián has put the letter in a bottle and has thrown it into the sea.

Returning from The Beyond, almost at the doorstep of his house, Professor Kingston has found an orange, large and golden. He bends over with tremendous effort to pick it up. It is such an effort I'm sorry I ever saw it, I ever stopped, though I'm picking it up no matter what, even the simplest things are turning into a question of honor for me. He enters the house, finds a knife and slices the orange in two. He sits in the little rocker to suck on the orange. What a disappointment, the orange has no flavor at all, its abundant yellow juice is as insipid as water. Is it my problem or the orange's? *I don't know.* Then he goes and pours himself a glass of milk, which likewise has no flavor at all. He slices a piece of processed ham and chews it just to check on how it tastes, and the processed ham is equally flavorless.

⋆ ⋆ ⋆

There lies the Wounded Boy. Sebastián has sneaked into Irene's house and has slipped through to the room where the boy sleeps. Is it a boy or a girl? Sebastián isn't sure. He stretches out a hand to touch his (or her) hands, which are crossed over the stomach, the way Sebastián has seen them arrange the hands of the dead. It's night, so Irene has turned on the lamp on the little table next to the bed. Nevertheless, Sebastián thinks he notices that the lamp is unnecessary. The Wounded Boy's body is lit up by a light shining down diagonally from the ceiling, though Sebastián checks and sees that no light is shining down from the ceiling in any direction, that there's no light in the ceiling, he even thinks it's possible that the light is flowing diagonally from the body toward the ceiling. To check this, he turns off the lamp and sees that, indeed, the Wounded Boy's body stays on as if it were no big deal, as if the light were its own business. The room in darkness. The body shining in the middle of the room in darkness. What are you doing here? he asks the illuminated body. The Wounded Boy opens his eyes and looks at him. I came for you, he says in a voice that could be a man's or a woman's, you can't tell. What do you need me for? It's me that *you* need. What do I need you for? Be patient, Sebastián, everything in its own due time, you know? Men have forgotten the value of patience. You're going to take me somewhere? Perhaps. Why do you talk so funny? What's your name? The hands uncross and one of them sketches a tired and luminous motion in the air. The proper place and moment will come for those details, tell me, is there a piece of paper on the nightstand? Sebastián nods. Is there anything written on it? Sebastián nods again. Read what it says. Sebastián takes the paper and gets ready to obey. There's stuff I don't understand. It doesn't matter, read it without understanding it, read it as if you understood it. Sebastián reads: Lucretius, *De Rerum Natura;* Apuleius, *The Golden Ass;* Carlyle, *Sartor Resartus;* Renan, *The Life of Jesus;* Michelet, *The Witch;* Lessing, *Laocoön;* Vives, *Dialogues;* Jacobus de Voragine, *The Golden Legend;* Boethius, *The Consolation of Philosophy;* Fulcanelli, *The Hermetic Symbolism of Cathedrals.* Very good, Sebastián, it's an unbeatable list, now fold up the paper and keep it in your pocket, don't lose it. Why do I need it? Men have forgotten the value of patience! The Wounded Boy sighs, all you should have to know is that you will need it, now go, you ought to sleep and dream, and as for me . . . I'm so weak! Sebastián did everything the Wounded Boy asked. The boy closed his eyes and the light from his body began to disappear, until Sebastián again found it necessary to turn on Irene's lamp.

One of the virtues of literature is perhaps that through it one can abolish time, or rather, give it a different meaning, jumble the three known tenses into a fourth tense that covers them all and induces what could be called simultaneity. Isn't it one of the great ambitions of any novelist to have Past, Present, and Future mix together on one page, just as in a single painting by Luca Signorelli it is possible to see the Stations of the Cross, the Crucifixion, the Descent from the Cross, and even the Transfiguration? So it should be possible to narrate briefly, even before it has occurred, the dream Sebastián will have tonight. It would have been ideal to narrate this future dream in the present in which the Wounded Boy is speaking. While the Wounded Boy speaks, Sebastián dreams. I suppose, however, that such effects are too sublime and beyond the limited means with which this book has been written. Undoubtedly, the novelist who achieves simultaneity will have made that conquest on behalf of everyone and will be termed a genius. This book's more modest author is now ready to tell Sebastián's dream as it will happen, after Sebastián slips out of Irene's house in the middle of the strange night of the Island.

Sebastián will be in a garden, next to a man. The man will be about sixty years old and have handsome eyes on either side of an ugly nose. With a mocking mouth he will say his name is Virgil. Not really knowing why, Sebastián will revere him as a master, and will call him Master. Whenever the Master walks forward, no matter where he goes, Sebastián will follow his wary steps. In the dream, they will be walking through a garden. They will stop next to the gate that separates the garden from darkness. The Master will ask him, Do you want to go on through to the other side? Ingenuously, Sebastián will reply, I'm afraid. Logically, the Master will observe, I didn't ask you whether you are afraid, I simply asked you whether you want to go through to the other side. Isn't it dangerous? and Sebastián's question is loaded with innocence. Of course it's dangerous, but remember, some dangers are delicious. Then the Master named Virgil, to set an example, will go through to the other side. Explosions will be heard, and the figure of the Master, burning, will disappear into the darkness. Could it be necessary to detail the loneliness Sebastián will feel after the disappearance of Virgil, of the Master? It's terrible, the grief that dreams can cause . . .

After Beny Moré had left, Chacho returned to his bed and to silence. Casta Diva, who had gotten her hopes up when she saw him appear among the trees, when she saw him nearly cry, listening to the Greatest Singer in the World, felt swindled when she saw him go back to bed and lie down in it again, and she cursed him up and down, shouted at him, A bad father, a bad husband, even if you have an idiot daughter and a useless son, aren't you planning to go to work? Captain Alonso was here asking why you haven't gone to the base, because they're going to give you a dishonorable discharge from the army, if you don't work what the hell are your children and I going to live on? He closed his eyes and it was as if he hadn't heard, he didn't move a single muscle in his face, didn't raise a hand to indicate she should lower her voice, as he usually did when they argued. Chacho didn't do a thing. Despite her rage, Casta Diva realized that her husband couldn't do anything but stay in bed, maintaining that silence that drove her to desperation, and she went from rage to compassion, and felt a boundless fatigue take over her body, and she lay down next to him, and also closed her eyes, and it could be she even fell asleep.

For days, the only proof Chacho gave of being alive was his breathing and his eyes, which opened at times to stare up at the rafters. Tatina could be laughing out loud for hours; Tingo, asking questions over and over again; Casta Diva, fighting and crying: he seemed not to hear them. It was as if, while living there, Chacho were living somewhere else. He never sat at the table, never was seen to drink a glass of water, never seen to satisfy any necessity. It seemed as if his bodily functions were paralyzed. The only things that gave the impression of continuing the normal course of life were his beard and nails.

And suddenly now, on this morning that has dawned with drizzling rain (or so it seems: as you know, in the Island things aren't always what they seem), Chacho gets out of bed, walks over to the ancient gramophone and looks through the records. He puts one on the platter. With a loud noise, the room, the house, the Island fill with the voice of Carlos Gardel, *Her eyes closed and the world continued spinning . . .* The voice of Gardel entered Helena's house, and she didn't know at first where that miraculous voice was coming from, wailing, *Her lips that once were mine will never kiss me again . . .* and Helena went out into the Island and it seemed the voice was coming from every tree, from every corner, from every statue. And Rolo, who was in Eleusis straightening out the books, knew it was Gardel (a knot formed in his throat) and left the books, of course, and went out into the Island and met Merengue next to the wooden screen and the Apollo Belvedere, and they both saw Helena, and none of them knew where the voice was coming from, because the voice was beyond a doubt emanating from all over the Island, *I'll never hear the echoes of her rich laughter . . .* Irene was at that moment treating the already healed wounds of the Wounded Boy with hydrogen peroxide and was also surprised, and went outside to find out and saw Miss Berta sobbing next to the bust of Greta Garbo. It was Marta, who was walking along touching the walls to guide herself and not trip, who informed them, Gardel is singing at Casta Diva's house, *And this silence is so cruel, it hurts me so much . . .* And they went to Casta Diva's and saw that she and Chacho, sitting on the ground next to the speakers of the ancient gramophone, were hiding their faces in their hands.

This is how he got me to fall in love, Casta Diva explains, one January 6 I was walking down the Calzada Real with my sister Luisa, who was just a girl, when I saw him coming in his soldier's uniform, twenty years old, he had such cheerful and sad eyes, and when we passed he followed us, singing *Noche de Reyes,* one of the most beautiful tangos I have ever heard, and he sang it so well, and every time he saw me he sang the tango, and I waited and waited, I needed to hear him sing so much, until one afternoon he took me by the arm and led me to a bench in the little park in front of the church, and he swore, I'm so happy that you're happy to be my sweetheart, and I couldn't respond to his daring except by saying *happy* isn't the word, there's no word for my happiness, and that's how it's been, believe me, up to today.

Vido is sucking on mangos under the tree. It has suddenly gotten hot again, as if it were August. Vido sweats, sucking on mangos under the tree. The flavor of the mango is sweet, and its juice is so abundant it escapes from his mouth and a trickle of juice runs down his neck, down his chest, mixing with the sweat. Vido uses his finger to pick up the juice mixed with sweat, and he brings it to his lips. The sweetness of the mango is now complemented by a delicious salty touch. The smell of the mango is intense, as is the flavor. So is the smell of his sweat. Vido smells his armpits and enjoys it, and wipes the mango in his peach fuzz–darkened armpits, and then sucks on it with that pleasant touch of salt.

Another Sunday (not the Sunday of Beny Moré's visit), at midday, shortly after lunch, Mercedes leaves her house and passes by the schoolroom, the little gate into The Beyond, leaves behind Professor Kingston's house, enters the marabú grove and, not knowing how, reaches the seashore. Mercedes is surprised to find herself there, she was walking along thinking, God, what I wouldn't give to be a character in a novel! She just finished chapter eight of *Honorable Women,* the chapter in which Victoria can't help but yield to Fernando, and she is feeling unsettled. Her body has woken up.

My body woke up reading in one of the rocking chairs in the living room, facing my sister, who was asleep, or seemed to be, I was feeling as if each part of me reacted to the reading, and suddenly, just like that, I felt desperate, I went to the bedroom, I took off my clothes as quietly as I could not to wake up Marta, I went into the bathroom, filled the bathtub with warm water and let my body be blessed by the water, picked up the sponge, soaped up, the sponge was good, rubbing my body like a man's rough hand (men's hands should always be rough and delicate at the same time), I observed the skin on my arms, on my legs, I discovered it was white, refined, tempting, my skin, I closed my eyes tight and let the sponge, that is, the rough and delicate hands, do the rest, with your eyes closed you can imagine things more powerfully, I usually take off my clothes and stretch out in the tub full of warm water to have someone come in and soap me up, the bath is one of my secret satisfactions, no one knows it, no one will find out, a different man comes each time, from Lucio to the conductor of the red bus, that tall, thin mulatto who wears khaki pants, too tight in the crotch, and he seems to be proud of the way it sticks out there, also the soldier who stands guard at the entrance to Columbia, not so tall, but straight, a tin soldier, white and handsome, in his yellow uniform, I'll never get tired of watching him when he walks down the street, with his majestic pace, or when I see him in civvies drinking solemnly in Plácido's bodega, shooting pool, he doesn't notice me, he's never looked at me, I don't exist for him, sometimes Chavito enters, Chavito is also handsome, except in this case I shouldn't say it, what would they think of me? Chavito is black, as black as Merengue, I don't care, the truth is I find blacks beautiful, but today who was by me in the bath? Fernando, how can you come if you're a character in a novel? Fernando, yes, one of Carrión's characters, he came to the bath today and found my body awake, sat on the edge of the tub, first he looked at me for a long time, I kept still, as I was supposed to, pretending I was only interested in being there in the water, he smiled with superiority, passed his fingers over my damp cheeks and started lowering them little by little, slowly, Fernando, slowly! down the neck, down the breasts, take your time on the nipples, torture me, I'll keep on meanwhile trying to feign indifference, though I barely can, I'm going to scream, I'm going to scream! don't let your hand pay any attention to me, let your hand go on undaunted to caress my navel and farther, farther down, just a little farther down, that's it, wisely, Fernando, it doesn't matter if you're a character in a Carrión novel, be aware of the pleasure you're causing by taking your time, now I understand Victoria, where did you learn to be so wise? I'll open the legs to receive your fingers, what big fingers! your fingers, like that, entering me, and now that I feel so happy, I'm going to make you a confession: right now, I am nothing but the dampness your fingers are entering, Fernando.

Mercedes is sitting on the seashore. The sun is in the very center of the sky, at the point where shadows do not exist. The light is like the water that reaches Mercedes's feet. No, the light isn't like the water, but worse, much worse, the water comes, the tiny wave arrives, wets her feet and recedes, rejoins the whole from which it emerged, while the light on the other hand, wiser, remains on Mercedes's body, enters through her skin, reaches her bones, destroys everything that resists its progress. Each beam of light is itself a whole. Mercedes feels herself disappearing as she is inundated by the light. Mercedes feels she herself is light. She looks at her hands, her gaze passes through them toward the sea, toward the horizon. The sea is a mirror, a thing put there just to reflect light. The sand is another sparkling expanse. Mercedes is so illuminated that she incorporates the light, she is one more gleaming, she disappears.

Everything in the past was better, this is my motto, but it's a motto that has come to be stupid: what past am I talking about? how can I say that the past was better if I can't remember, if I don't know what past I'm talking about? how are you going to understand me, Wounded Boy, shot with arrows, lying there in bed not knowing anything about reality, your mission now is to sleep while I tend your wounds and finish saving you, as is my duty, meanwhile, here you have Irene the Memoryless, poor Irene who's forgotten everything that ever happened to her, at most I know that my name is Irene, that's enough, maybe it's enough to know my name, my name and my face in the mirror, my son Lucio came today to tell me that February 17, my birthday . . . it doesn't matter what he said, the date kept spinning around, so my birthday is February 17, then . . . isn't that the date of my mother's death? or could it be that my mother died right on my birthday? that kind of thing doesn't happen, it only happens in Félix B. Caignet's radio soap operas, and I felt ashamed to ask him, Lucio, what day did your grandmother die? what did your grandmother die of? I feel ashamed, besides, what would I do with that information? what good would it do me? I'm a woman with an empty head, and some people might think that's a lucky thing, I don't, I consider that every man's worth comes from his past, it will be the past that redeems you or condemns you, I know, don't tell me, the past is woven from the threads of the present, observe, however, Wounded Boy, shot with arrows, that when a woman knits her past she has two threads, just that, just two threads, and only what stops being the present, what becomes the past, turns into cloth, the present is only good for making, that is, for the shocks and the uncertainties, while the past is what's made, whether good or bad doesn't matter, it's made and therefore it's certain, it's firm ground, let's not even mention the future, the future's an illusion, man invented it to fill up the hours of tedium that lead to his death, the future is death, and I don't know what death is, I just know what the future is, now tell me, Wounded Boy, what am I doing in the Island without a history to tell, you should know that what's important about the past isn't what it teaches (a woman knits a bad stitch, she stops, undoes it and reknits it right, no?), it's what it gives you to tell, to make the story of your life, and if you don't have anything to tell about yourself, who are you? nobody, no matter how you spin it, nobody, even if they see you, you can't tell them I was born on a February 17 in Pijirigua, Artemisa, my father worked as a farmhand for some big landowners, my mother was the washerwoman for the street, we were so poor my mother made my shoes from palm bark and jute sacks, I was a girl who started working at the age of five, I remember they'd set me up on a box so I could reach the kitchen sink, I cared for my brothers and sisters like a mother, and despite all the calamities I'm telling you, I was happy, and if you can't tell the story I just made up (and it may well be true, if only!), then no one else can know what my dreams, my fears, my joys, my woes, my obsessions are and were, the main problem, dear Wounded Boy, is that we have to understand once and for all that life can't be just for living, my opinion is that God also gives us life so we can tell it as a story, a history, that will entertain and be useful to others, don't you think?

Luckily, today Chacho hasn't put another Carlos Gardel record on the gramophone. The voice of the so-called Latin Warbler came to be so persistent in the Island that for several days you couldn't hear the shrieks of the bamboo, or the jubilation of the casuarinas, or the laments that lately are heard louder and louder. The Island was reduced to a voice that repeated the same tangos over and over again, to the point of exhaustion. Today Chacho got up early and went straight to the wardrobe and took out the military uniforms, the medals and diplomas earned over long years of service as a radio operator in the Signal Corps. He tied them into a bundle and went out into the Island.

He didn't stop to look at the cloudy late October sky. Nor did he take in a deep breath of the balmy air of the Island. He set off down the little stone path leading to the fountain with the Boy and the Goose, and reached the old watering hole. There he threw down everything he was carrying. He sprinkled alcohol and lit a match. Uniforms, medals, and diplomas rapidly caught fire. It would be correct to suppose that by then Chacho was already thinking about the rabbits.

What day is today? You already know, it's November 2, day of the dead. That's why they've set a long table in the Island, an old table, rickety from all the downpours and the sun, but dressed up with Casta Diva's best lace tablecloth, a tablecloth her mother made for her daughter's wedding and, according to Irene and Helena, a beauty, a real beauty. Covered by the lace, the table no longer looks like what it is. So you're wrong if you think the habit doesn't make the monk, observes Rolo. The table looks pretty as could be. The tablecloth almost reaches the floor, hiding the rough walls, gnawed by termites. In the center they've placed a large bronze crucifix, one of Miss Berta's greatest prides. It's a simple, unadorned crucifix, so clean it gleams like gold (though it isn't), and its greatest value, according to Miss Berta, rests on the fact that it stood watch over the death of Francisco Vicente Aguilera on his estate of San Miguel de Rompe. And Miss Berta swells with pride looking at the crucifix, and she begins to tell the story (who knows how many times she's done it) of her father's friendship with Aguilera and with the first two presidents of the Republic in arms, Carlos Manuel de Céspedes and Salvador Cisneros Betancourt, Marquis of Santa Lucia. Someone, probably Helena, interrupts her delicately, subtly, so that Miss Berta won't feel offended, it's just that she needs to be interrupted, otherwise she'll go through the whole story again of the war and exile, and again she will praise her father's heroism, Doña Juana's fortitude (that she is still sleeping, dressed in her white linen nightgown, the rosary in her hands and the white candle lit on the nightstand before a print of La Caridad del Cobre). When Miss Berta falls silent, understanding perhaps that the others aren't up to long-winded speeches, the women, Helena, Irene, Casta Diva, continue arranging the table. In each of two vases they place bunches of artificial flowers (which are truly surprising: they don't look like artificial flowers imitating real ones, but like real flowers imitating artificial ones). They admire the bouquets and line the edges of the table with the candlesticks and candles that each one of them has brought. Candles of every description. Cheap ones, two for a nickel, that burn out right away, and others, the most beautiful kinds, red, blue, yellow, pink, in the shapes of saints; there are tall ones, very tall ones, altar candles that will stay lit all night long if the wind permits; there are also thick candles furnished by Professor Kingston, which according to Miss Berta's way of thinking shouldn't be used given that they are heretical candles, since they have six-pointed stars impressed in them. Yes, the professor humbly explains, a Jewish friend gave them to me. Rolo makes clear that the stars of David don't matter, the important thing is the light that our deceased receive, besides you must keep in mind that the stars will slowly disappear as the night advances. They place the candles furnished by Professor Kingston in the largest candlesticks (and end of subject). On the floor go the natural flowers ordered from Le Printemps, an elegant nursery, where they've made five bouquets of black princes, with ribbons and bows and cards advertising the store. Irene has also prepared her bouquets (you have to admit that Irene's bouquets are even more beautiful) and has scattered about miniature palm fronds and pine branches. Two marble angels. (They actually aren't marble, let's not fool ourselves, they're clay; there is as much difference between clay and marble as between ourselves and God.) And the sad angels unctuously embrace, looking heavenward with pupilless eyes. The angels give the final touch to the table. Casta Diva almost bursts out crying. Irene compels her to control herself with a gesture and says, Don't forget that today is the day of the faithful dead. Casta Diva cries, Yes, today is my day. Mercedes hugs her, Don't get like this, Casta, you're live as can be. No, Mercedes, don't kid yourself, I'm more dead than alive. Rolo claps his hands twice with an inexplicable smile (mocking? benevolent?), claps his hands twice and declares they should bring the photographs. Each of them returns with the photos of their dead. The table fills with framed photos. Gilded and silver-plated frames, Bakelite frames, frames of wood and of glass, frames of ebony and of cardboard. And the photographs . . . the most varied kinds you can imagine. Studio photographs and cheap snapshots, color photos and black-and-whites, posed photos and candid shots. Their faces look different, suddenly (and this shouldn't be written, it sounds like blasphemy, what can you do! among other things novels are written to blaspheme), suddenly, I repeat, the table looks like a carnival stand. The following photographs stand out on the table: girl with ball in hands; toothless old woman, smiling; young man in suit; couple dressed in 1920s' style; young soldier, sea in background; months-old baby in carriage; extremely serious gentleman, with straw hat, leaning against medallion chair, in which seated lady pets white lapdog; little lady in long dress leaning languidly against Doric column; woman in pants, carrying walking stick, smiling, amid underbrush; young woman, who bears a fair resemblance to Irene, with child in arms; woman with hat, scarf, and overcoat in middle of snowfall; smiling black man playing tumbadora; sad clown; old woman at microphone; policeman; man on horseback, with leggings, machete, rebel uniform from the War of Independence. There are many faces, faces of every possible shape, with the most varied expressions, even a photo of a smiling Stan Laurel. Sebastián is struck by the photograph of a little boy on a wooden horse. It's as if they had put a photo of himself there, of Sebastián, because even though the photo is old (you can even see the date written on one corner), it's as if it were Sebastián riding the wooden horse. And he is even more struck when he finds out it is a photograph of his uncle, Uncle Arístides, who died a terrible death. He died, Irene tells him in a whisper so that Helena won't hear, on his way to a baseball game, because your uncle was polite and an old man sat down on the fender of the truck and he, being eighteen magnanimous years old, offered his space on the seat and went to sit on the fender, and fifteen minutes later when the truck overturned, your uncle Arístides was flattened by the truck, just eighteen years old, your uncle, Sebastián, your spitting image, you can bet his spirit wanders near you and helps you, your guardian angel is your uncle Arístides. Irene walks off as if she hadn't said a word, and bends toward another ear and points to another photograph. There are so many (fifty, sixty, a hundred) that the table isn't big enough. And Miss Berta has brought a bust of Antonio Maceo and another of José Martí, The distinguished dead, she says. They bring pages from the original score to the national anthem. They bring a bloodstained piece of Plácido's shirt. They bring Zenea's spurs. They bring an original oil painting by Ponce. They bring a book by Emilio Ballagas. They bring bits of wood from a certain ship that sank. Mercedes appears with a photograph of the woman who was drawn and quartered, poor Celia Margarita Mena. Casta Diva places a photo of a very pretty woman, with a high comb in her hair, a red flower, black mantilla, passionate gaze, lips half open. Also Merengue has appeared with a photo of Nola, his wife. Merengue has also brought the photo of a stern black man, a photo so old it seems a daguerreotype. Nobody objects to this, either. They know it is Antolín, the black man, the saint, the spirit protector of Merengue. And they light the candles. Mercedes goes around lighting them, and when they are all lit the smell of paraffin spreads through the gallery. Falling to her knees, Miss Berta sings, *The Lord is my shepherd, I shall not want* . . . in a defenseless contralto voice. Little by little they all fall to their knees. *He maketh me to lie down in green pastures* . . . Helena covers her face with her hands. With hands joined and eyes closed, Casta Diva joins the song. *He leadeth me beside the still waters* . . . Irene holds the rosary between her hands. *He restoreth my soul: he leadeth me in the paths of righteousness* . . . Rolo lowers his head till chin touches chest, Our lives are the rivers . . . he muses. Lucio has placed one knee on the floor and rested his forehead against one hand. Mercedes covers her face with a black veil. On the floor, Merengue has removed his hat. Professor Kingston concentrates on the palms of his hands. Hieratic as a sphinx, Marta rocks in a rocking chair. A heavy white bird flies by. They cross themselves.

(Every time an owl flies by, the characters in this novel cross themselves.)

Mamá, I don't get it, whines Tingo-I-Don't-Get-It, searching for refuge by Casta Diva. Looking at him in ill humor, his mother orders him to shut up. Tingo interrupts the psalm Miss Berta is singing. Why, Mamá, why? Shut up, boy, shut up. No, explain it to me, why? I don't get it, I want to know. If only we knew, Rolo says with double meaning, there's nothing to be known. Today is November 2, the day of the faithful dead. And that, what difference does that make? They fall silent, forget their prayers, look this way and that in perplexity. And that, what difference does that make? Why this table, these photographs, these candles, these flowers? Miss Berta interrupts her singing. They all stand up and without talking to each other move off in different directions. Why, why? Tingo asks again and again, tirelessly. No one answers.

It is the night of the dead. Late, clear, cool, full of stars, no heat, no threat of rain. Illuminated by the candles and by the photos of the dead, the table still stands in one corner of the gallery. Men and women have gathered before it, sitting in rocking chairs, fanning themselves. Once more they hold wake for their dead. Each year, on a day like this, the dead again have their wake. They make sure that the candles don't blow out, that the light reaches them, yes, that the light ascends and mixes with the light of the luminous spirits, that it illuminates the dark spirits. From time to time they change the water of the natural flowers, in the great goblets dedicated to Saint Claire. At times an Our Father can be heard. At times, a Hail Mary. They recite the rosary. Also, sometimes, they let the silence grow (the silence of the Island, of course, which is populated by the unknown language of the trees). The silence of the Island and of the late, clear, cool night of November 2, day of the dead. Over there by the courtyard, by the wooden screen, next to the Apollo Belvedere, you can hear from time to time the cane of the Barefoot Countess.

What is death?

When I was a young boy, they took me to the cemetery every day of the dead, there, my mother explained, was where the only important thing remained, the only enduring thing we had, the ashes of our great-great-grandparents, of our great-grandparents, of our grandparents, of a few uncles, I always enjoyed it when the day of the faithful dead came around, my mother fixed up one basket with candles, another one with corn fritters (always corn fritters), and she and I would go down from the town toward the cemetery, it was the only day of the year they'd let us into the cemetery at night, when we passed by the church and turned the corner onto Céspedes Street you could see far off the tall walls and the radiance that floated about the tall walls, a halo that always intrigued me, I knew that golden nimbus came from the light of all the candles, but at the same time (and I don't know how to explain it) I didn't know it, and it always intrigued me that the place my mother pointed out and named, the cemetery, should be a luminosity, a resplendence shining in the night, a resplendence that on this night made the only dark place in town brighter than bright, and I remember that when we got there we'd find vendors of saint's images and candles and prints and medallions and prayers, we'd find the people who had made vows, on their knees, begging by the love of God, by the Most Holy Virgin, by Saint Rita of Cascia (Patroness of Impossible Cases) for a coin, a bit of charity, so my mother always gave me something so I'd be the one they'd wish, May God bless you with good health, and now I can't help seeing myself entering the carnival that the cemetery had become, every vault, every tomb full, the whole family gathered there just like they'd gather on their porches on other days, conversing, laughing, sipping coffee, hot chocolate, and even cheap rum, telling stories, calculating the year So-and-So died, the year What's-His-Name became consumptive, and huge vases stuffed with dahlias, roses, gladiolas, lilies, with palm fronds and murraya branches, and I'd light the candles at our humble family tomb, and my mother would tell me about Grandmother Emilia's cirrhosis, and about the consumption of both grandfathers, Ramón and Berardo, and my father's cirrhosis, that the very day he died, in the morning, they had planned a trip to Guanabo, he wanted to swim in the sea, and you didn't say any of this sadly, at least not with the sadness that stories of the dead acquired on other days of the year, there was something joyful about these stories on that night, as if death were a party, dying was something joyful, an advantage that they, the dead, had over us, and we'd toast each other with sodas, and the families would trade the food they'd brought in their baskets, and the little girls would put their dolls to bed on the tombs, and the little boys would lie down themselves, and we'd play at dying, which is an astonishing game (especially because it was a game), and we'd walk around the earth, the earth full of earth, the earth and more earth on top, and we'd start singing, each one there would intone a different song, Babel, confusion of tongues, which no matter what God, up there, must have understood.

* * *

What is death?

Do you know the story of the young man who was going to marry a beautiful maiden and found a corpse on the path? If you don't know it, you'll never understand why it is that on days like today every theater in Spain puts on a performance of *Don Juan Tenorio* by the vilified, the none-too-easy Zorrilla.

On a certain occasion it happened that a young man, on the eve of his wedding, walking down a path, found a skeleton. As a joke he asked the skeleton, Why don't you come to the wedding banquet? And he continued on his way. The skeleton, however, did attend the banquet, to the surprise and horror (I suppose) of all present, and ate and drank with the best of them, and when it had finished came up to the youth and told him, I want to give you a present, I beg you to come with me. Trembling, the youth followed the skeleton a long ways, for a long time, and they climbed mountains and passed rivers and settlements until they arrived (at night, of course) at a wide valley full of little lights. The youth discovered that the lights came from thousands of millions of candles all lit in the valley. Some had just been lit, some were half done, some were about to be extinguished, some were already out. What do all these candles mean? the youth inquired. Each one represents the life of each one of the men living on earth. The youth looked around and almost in a whisper asked, Which is mine? This one! exclaimed the skeleton, raising one up, it blew on the candle and out it went.

What is death?

Look at me, take a good look at me and don't forget me, take a good long look at me until you're tired of looking at me, and then you'll stop asking the question, what is death? death is a night when you have no one to see and no one to tell that you have no one to see so you could tell them you have no one to see, look at me, take a good look at me, life is a journey, death is another journey, the goal is the horizon, the horizon is a line you can never reach, no matter how much you push yourself you can never reach it, because if you reach it, it stops being a horizon, couldn't it be that one journey (the journey of life) and the other journey (the journey of death) are the same journey and we just don't know it? couldn't it be that the words life and death designate the same thing? come on, answer, have you ever waited for someone for a long time, so long you forgot you were waiting for someone? waiting, waiting, waiting, waiting, waiting, to the end, and the funniest part is there isn't any end, sitting in the living room as if a catastrophe had occurred, *as if it had,* and I emphasize that because, forget about catastrophes, the earth is calm and quiet, it turns and turns, as the tango says, and no one but you waits and waits, nobody knocks at the door, ay, God, it's horrifying, you complain, yes God exists, but He's deaf, and who dares to emphasize the difference between a live man and a dead man, don't come to me with that nonsense about how a living man breathes and a dead man doesn't, and the carrion?: an insignificant accident.

What is death?

Young man, my boy, if I could sit down one day and tell you the story of my life from the first cry I took up to today, you wouldn't be bold enough to ask me a question like that, you wouldn't allow yourself to be so ingenuous, at the beginning one thinks one knows what death is, you're even able to define it in so many words, sensible words, apt words for the inept, I've seen death so often and so close up, I've dreamed it, repudiated it and yearned for it so many times, it's circled me and I've circled it so persistently that by now I know any attempt to define it is foolish, the closer it is the farther off, the horizon, I said and I'll say it again, so now you all think this is a special night, the night of the faithful dead? poor people, could this be the night when our dead feel, more intensely, the happiness of being dead? I'm telling you that today is our day, that they're the ones holding wake for us, yes, I know, those are words, one gets into the habit of words, let's pull out our tongues, cut off our hands, rip out our rotting hearts, it'll be a better world, me, for example, I love to sleep, sleep is a foretaste of death, a preparation, a lesson, my conclusion, everyone dreams what they really are though no one understands it, do you dream? do you have nightmares? let me say once and for all that I hate foolish questions and foolish answers even more, anyone knows that living and dying is the same thing and both mean dreaming.

What is death?

One day I went to the cemetery, they were removing the remains of someone I had loved dearly, someone who must be in heaven (if such a thing is possible), and the gravediggers had made a mistake and accidentally (or on purpose, gravediggers love errors) opened a tomb which wasn't the tomb of that someone I had loved dearly, they removed the splendid and recent cadaver of an eleven-year-old girl, I saw her, yessir, I saw her with these same eyes that will someday fall from their sockets, the girl had turned into a trembling mass of pus and worms that didn't keep still for one second, in some places there were bits of skin, what must have been a lovely eleven-year-old skin, and the gravediggers told me she had been a pretty corpse, the prettiest corpse, but when I saw her you could never have told that, and I won't even mention the stench, no, there's no stench in the world more unbearable than that of a human body when it dies, I swear, I remember especially the eyes, they had already lost the lids and were two puddles of green liquid that flowed incessantly like tears, and running all over that body (I say body so you'll understand me) were giant white cockroaches, like none I'd ever seen or have ever seen again, I suppose until I putrefy myself, and there was strange laughter from the mouth, there's no laughter so persistent, thousands of flies arrived from every inch of the cemetery to hum on the gelatinous mass that had been a girl of eleven years, and at her feet, intact, untouched, clean, perfect, a lovely blond blue-eyed doll that when we moved it said Mamá.

What is death?

Shut up, serpent, close your filthy mouth.

Fine, I'll close my mouth, *mais vous serez semblable à cette ordure, à cette horrible infection, étoile de mes yeux, soleil de ma nature.*

Shut up or I'll turn you into carrion long before you're ready.

Please, ladies and gentlemen, respect the memory of the dead.

Man is the only animal that warehouses its dead, the only animal, the only.

Give us refuge in Your bosom, merciful God.

Yes, give us refuge in Your bosom of horror and putrefaction.

Listen, I'd like to take a step, open a door, take another step, and that's it.

That is, nothing, one step and dust.

Dust, nothing.

Don't tell me, so you believe that we like to be kept in boxes, enclosed in vaults, and abandoned to putrefy?

Ay, fuck it, it drives me to despair to think they'll close me up and cover up this flesh, full of desires, cover up this, all that I am, with a marble slab.

Don't bring me flowers, did you hear? don't bring me flowers.

What is death?

Do you remember, my friend, that man we saw drowned one day when we wanted to have fun, drink some beers by the mouth of the river, down by the sea? remember? a magnificent young man, that is, a young man, other magnificent young men pulled him out, he wasn't stiff yet, and his body resisted understanding that the blood no longer flowed through it, his body refused to forget the sky and the seagulls and the ice-cold beers we were drinking, you told me, In one instant man ceases being man and turns into a thing, and, do you really think that that lovely dead man was a thing, one more thing among other things? we didn't want to look at it, we did want to look at it, we didn't look, we did look, and you have to admit: the drowned man had added to his physical beauty, the beauty of indifference.

What is death?

The Island.

Have you all noticed the Island? immense tombless cemetery,
gigantic cemetery of the Island,
wandering souls rove about the Island,
and when did these poor islanders die?

Among the Balonda, they say, the man abandons the hut and garden where his favorite wife died, and if he returns to that place, it is to pray for her.

To die is to enter the second life, the better one.

I don't want any more life than this one, let them leave me in this one forever, cheap rum, corn candy, and if possible a Ñico Membiela or Blanca Rosa Gil record, and another with Esther Borja singing *Enchanting maiden, maiden, I'll die for you.*

Yes, let them leave me here drinking Hatuey beer, eating El Miño sausages, roast suckling pig, boiled squash and malanga with islander sauce, understand me, there are some things that aren't meant for tonight.

Man is a suit of clothes, an old rag somebody hung on a nail and forgot, time passes and when you look again, nothing,

a bit of dust on the floor you have to sweep up.

Have you ever gotten lost in the Island?,

ah, getting lost in the Island, at this precise Island time when no one can say exactly what time it is,

waking up not knowing who you are, or where you are, or what you're going to do,

remove the layers of earth they've thrown over you, get up for nothing, look around you when there's nothing to look at,

no, dying is a fiesta, a dance with the Florida Maravillas,

with the Belisario López Orchestra,

a son, a mambo, a cha-cha-cha, a bolero,

for the sake of our love and for your own good I'll say good-bye

good-bye, good-bye, good-bye, how sad was your good-bye, what tremendous loneliness I feel without your love.

Ladies and gentlemen, please, a little respect.

What is death?

Maeterlinck, Maurice Maeterlinck, know who he is? said that utter annihilation was impossible, that we are prisoners of an infinity with no way out, where nothing perishes, everything disperses, but nothing is lost either, he said that neither a body nor a thought could fall out of time and space, from which you can deduce, my friends, that I won't die! ever! I'll never die, when the hour comes for death rattles and last gasps and dying breaths, when hands that think they're being pious come to close these obstinate eyes, by then I'll already be transformed into the fruit that some adolescent is eating, into the water that cools your bodies, into the bread that satisfies hunger, into the wine that wipes out sorrow, into the shade tree that allays the beastly sun of the Island, into the beastly sun of the Island, into every laugh with which we like to scare away the horror of the Island, into every word, I'll be in every word, I'm a combination of words, I'm all the words, my words, ascending to the stars and from there we should direct the destiny of mortals.

Are you finished? too much rhetoric for my taste.

What is death?

Vido calls over Tingo-I-Don't-Get-It and asks him, Listen, do you want to see a dead woman? Although he is shocked, Tingo nods yes. Come, I know a dead woman and I'm going to show her to you, and I'll also show you how to revive her. Vido goes running out through the gallery and ducks in behind the Venus de Milo. Tingo follows him. The night of the faithful dead is clear and the trees are sharply visible. The voices, the songs, the psalms remain behind them. By the Laocoön, surrounded by the fig trees and the charcoal ebonies, Vido stops. It's here, he says, kneel down. Why? Because, idiot, because you have to kneel, otherwise she won't show up. Not getting it, Tingo kneels down. Now close your eyes, concentrate, say to yourself, May the dead woman appear. Vido loosens his belt and lowers his pants. Open your eyes! and there is an imperious, impatient tone in his voice. Tingo opens his eyes. Vido is fondling himself. She's dead, see? Tingo is about to stand up but Vido stops him: Touch her, go ahead, touch her and make her revive, if you get her to revive you'll have to kill her slowly again.

The night keeps getting later and later, really night, really clear. They are constantly having to relight candles that have blown out. When they're lit, by the light of the tiny trembling flames, the photographs look like images of saints.

And after all, can anyone finally tell me, what is death?

Very late, when night is really night, when no one can or no one feels able to tell what time it is, the narrator decides a miracle should occur. It's not actually a miracle. The narrator (who has the defect of grandiloquence) wants to dress it up in an atmosphere of greatness, of wonder. The narrator has his theatrical streak, which, much as he wants to, he cannot part with. Impatient, like any self-respecting reader, the impatient reader wants to know what this miracle is.

And the miracle is that the Wounded Boy appears by the table of the Dead, dressed in Lucio's pajamas, his hair a mess from all his days in bed. None of the characters who live in this Island have ever seen God (at least not the way they imagine Him, given that, as you know, God is visible throughout Creation, we see Him every day in many ways we cannot comprehend). These characters all fall to their knees because they think they're seeing God. They don't think it like that, so explicitly, but in an almost inexplicable way, which almost gets confused with the happiness they feel at seeing him live and well, when they had thought at any moment he might not live. Darkly, however, something tells them that this Wounded Boy has something to do with their destinies. And he, like a good father, goes up to each of them, strokes their heads, mentions their names as if he's known them all his life. And it turns out to be lucky that they're holding their heads low, and can't see the look of pity that is coming now into the eyes of the Wounded Boy.

IV

Finis Gloriæ Mundi

And the light of a candle shall shine no more at all in thee.

— Apocalypse 18:23

The path over here was always bordered by royal palms, that's why they called it the Palm Grove. They said the palms had been here for years, since long before Godfather arrived to buy the land and build on it. They said that Godfather didn't destroy them on account of Angelina, because she defended the royal palms, though Godfather had only wanted evergreen oaks. The evergreen oaks reminded him of the oak trees of Europe, please recall that Godfather came over as a young man, practically an adolescent, and grew rich here, but never could forget Spain. Tonight the royal palms aren't there. And night has paused above the trees. Red night, above black trees. But the royal palms aren't there. There's no wind, and since there's no wind and no palms, no one can hear their whispering (which makes them sound not like palms but like pious old women during the parish novena). The world stands still tonight. Night itself is in danger, as if the sky were about to join with the earth at any moment.

And the sky seems to join with the earth. It's just a moment, maybe one second, not long enough to count. Irene went outside, the laments were torturing her. All night long she'd been listening to laments. No telling if she went toward The Beyond or toward This Side, the Discus Thrower or the Laocoön. She picked up a flashlight and went outside. She met Helena and Merengue, as was to be expected; they were also feeling tortured by the laments, the whimpering that gave the impression the Island was full of wounded folk. As might be supposed, the three of them knew all along that there were no wounded, that this was just another one of the Island's tricks. No sooner had they started for one corner, toward the Moses, for example, than they heard the wails coming from around the bust of Martí; when they got to the bust of Martí, they heard the wails coming from the fountain with the Boy and the Goose. Enough to drive you crazy. It's the wind, Merengue asserted. The wind, yes, the wind,

Irene repeated. Has to be the wind, Helena categorically affirmed. But what wind? When it seemed as if the earth had come to a standstill tonight in the midst of its revolving, as if the earth were a dead center in the middle of so much Universe. The trees looked nice and still, like on the canvas of a poorly painted landscape. Anyone would have said you could have touched the sky, the red sky, just by raising your hands. And it wasn't just the groans, in fact, but the disagreeable odor that grew more and more intense after midnight, until it seemed almost impossible to breathe. A smell of exactly what you couldn't tell, nor could you determine where it was coming from. And they found Rolo around the watering hole, crossing through the bamboo, worried about the disappearance of the palms. The strangest part: there was no sign they had been cut down. There were no traces of the palms on the ground. There never were any palms and that's that, Rolo exclaimed with an irony that was so serious it had ceased to be irony. And now is when I say the sky seems to join with the earth. The red sky comes down so low over the Island that the Island is covered by a fog, also red, so red and so foggy the Island disappears and they themselves don't know where they are or where they're going, they too disappear and if they can still believe they are living beings it's because they continue thinking (therefore they exist) that they have to find some way to get back to their houses, though, to tell the truth, you can't even see your own hand in front of your face. It makes no difference whether your eyes are open or closed. The flashlights make no headway against the dense mist. It seems they're not stepping on the ground. They cease feeling the weight of their bodies. They can no longer tell for sure whether every part of their bodies is responding to their brains' commands. Their voices die before escaping their mouths. The silence becomes as complete as the mist. Nor do they know whether time continues to pass or whether it too has stopped; like everything else in the Island, they have lost even the slightest sense of time. The red fog confuses their senses to such a point that long after it has dissipated and allowed the sky to return to its proper place, these poor characters continue thinking they are lost.

And this is where the Virgin of La Caridad del Cobre becomes the protagonist of a remarkable deed. The humble image, sculpted in wood by an anonymous artist, isn't in its place. Its glass case, between the Discus Thrower and the Diana, is empty, its glass and the vase before it broken. Helena's sunflowers are trampled. Irene discovers it is missing. She shouts and the others come running. There's nothing that can be done. There's not a trace left of the Virgin. Well, yes, there are traces: one of the wooden waves that had tried to drown the young men appears about two yards off, practically at the feet of the Discus Thrower. Faced with the disappearance of the Virgin, the characters in this book must experience a profound sensation of helplessness. This is logical, if you keep in mind that the characters in this book are Cubans. Like any Cubans, the characters in this book have never learned to live alone. Cubans don't want to know that men are all alone in the world and that men are solely responsible for their own acts, their own destinies. Cuba is a nation of children, and children (as everybody knows) like to get into mischief when there's an adult who'll see them, a father or a mother who's watching them, and will applaud when they're cute, and punish them when they go too far, and (above all) will rescue them in case of danger. That is why, when they discover the disappearance of the Virgin, the characters in this book fall (bereft) to their knees, and implore the heavens hidden behind the trees.

No matter how customary it is, it's still disturbing to hear weeping in the Island. Especially if you think the weeping doesn't belong to anyone, that it's an old weeping sound that got trapped there between trees and walls, resigned to never disappearing, a useless weeping, conscious of its pointlessness and by that very token all the more mournful, weeping all the more. And the worst part is when you hear the weeping after a night of lamentations. Then you really do despair and you're not sure whether to run and hide or to start weeping yourself: either course would be equally vain.

This weeping tonight, however, isn't of the wandering variety, the kind without a cause, or with such a distant cause that it has forgotten why it's still drifting from place to place. This weeping comes with eyes and tears, and the eyes and tears are Marta's. She has been daring enough to go out to the Hermes of Praxiteles (in the way she's able to walk, by gripping the trees, weighing each footstep as if at each footstep there were some abyss). Sebastián has discovered her and has run over. Why are you crying? He sees her looking shocked, takes one of her hands and realizes she's trembling. Clinging to the thighs of Hermes, Marta sobs. Sebastián lets her calm down. He leads her then to the gallery and sits her down in a rocking chair. She lowers her head, sits for a long time in silence. If you didn't know she had gone blind, you would think she was looking at the palms of her hands.

Just a little while ago, the Wounded Boy went to see her. When she sensed his footsteps, Marta knew it was he by that aroma that accompanies him, that strange aroma of dried flowers, old letters, dresser drawers stuffed with photographs, books, and memories. She also knew it because the footsteps didn't belong to any of the inhabitants of the Island, and she had come to recognize who was who by the sound of their footsteps. He announced to her, I want to give you a gift, Marta, and his voice had the timbre of tall, strong men, still a little childish but all men anyway, I know it has been your lot to suffer and I want to give you a gift, and that voice, there was no doubting it, had to belong to a dark blond man with clear white skin, a man with large eyes and hands, who knew very well where he was going and how he was getting there in life. As you might deduce, she did not speak. He seemed to know Marta's desire, her need to travel (even though it was only in dreams) to those cities that must exist beyond the horizon (even when she sometimes came to doubt it). He stayed there a long time telling her of remote cities, speaking of civilizations that had disappeared and civilizations yet to appear, telling her of times past and times still to come, and when he decided to leave, he left her even more desperate than ever to open her eyes before Giotto's Bell Tower, the Paris Opera, the Paseo de Gracia, the Hagia Sofia . . . But after she had been alone for a while, Marta noticed that her eyes could see. You shouldn't imagine a sudden recovery of her sight, but a slow process through which things began to appear before her eyes, the naked and faded walls of a room that she wasn't sure was her own, pieces of furniture worn out with use, a morning without radiance entering timidly through the possible frame of a possible window, to fall on a clock without numbers or hands; everything seeming dimensionless, as if it were some blurry print from an encyclopedia.

I went out into the Island, I saw there weren't any trees there, the great rectangle that is the Island consisted of a patch of sand, the houses were there, true, but empty, without windows or doors, without furniture, without people, without the smells of the kitchens, without the chattering that sometimes makes the Island the capital of noise, I tried to find somebody, it was all pointless and then I went into the street and found a pile of trash, a mound of papers flying in the wind, and I didn't know which way to turn, I didn't have any reference points, the tower of the parish church had disappeared, for instance, and what I did was walk and walk not knowing where I was going, the trees had no leaves, like in winter (in the countries where there is a winter), and the earth had turned to sand, and there weren't any flowers, I noticed they were dried up on the ground, and the sky was steel grey, as the sky of the Island rarely is, and the smell that came on the wind was a smell of putrefaction and how couldn't there be a smell of putrefaction if there were piles of trash everywhere, mountains of garbage, of junk, at times you could hear gunshots, at times I thought I saw the radiance of fire, and I asked myself, is this the dream I can dream? is this the city my eyes have access to? there was one moment when a whirlwind dropped down, dragging along dead birds, and another whirlwind dragged furniture, photographs, I saw a coach pass by without coachman or horses, by itself, as if that stiff wind were carrying it too, a lady dressed in clothes from another era was seated in the back, though when it came closer I saw it wasn't a lady but a dress torn to shreds, and I felt chilled, so chilled. Marta cried out several times. No one ever responded. She wanted to return to her rocking chair, to her blindness, to her unsatisfied desires, to return to those long barren afternoons when she at least had hope to nourish her. She thought she was sitting down to cry beneath what she took to be a tree (and actually was a guillotine). She thought she sat there crying for a long time. She felt night was falling when it had already fallen. She felt they were touching her on the shoulder when the child had been calling her for a long time already. Who are you? The child didn't reply, he only signaled me to follow him, and I of course followed him without stopping to doubt, that child was the only living being

I had seen since I left the house, and we walked and walked without talking, without talking we went down toward a kind of cave, at a certain point he ordered me, Wait for me here, and I had no other choice but to obey his order, I didn't care if he was a boy or a devil, what I cared was that there were someone by my side, it's worse to be alone than to be in bad company, you'll learn that when you find yourself lost, surrounded by sand and by garbage, when he came back to get me we began entering through dark little passages, through narrow little passages, until we came to a library, don't ask me how I knew it was in a library, I suppose because of the shelves where there must have once been books, and because of a certain religious air, I mean, an air of true religiosity, though the place was full of beds, of children, of women, of old folks, and then it didn't seem like a library but a hospital, and in fact I was in a library converted to a hospital, you could hear laments like you do here, like those in the Island on days when the wind comes from the south, and I lay down on the bed that the child pointed out to me, and I suppose I fell asleep. She fell asleep to defend herself, to escape, to make the time pass, to be unaware of the passage of time, so that when she woke up and they were taking out the refugees, it would be easier to join up with the group without understanding, without asking idle questions. They led them down long paths (the word *path* here is a euphemism). They led them through desolate places during a single, very long night. They must have reached the sea (if that's what we can call the red expanse that vaguely recalled the sea). Moored to a dock was a ship. Well disciplined, we climbed aboard, I was struck that before boarding, each one turned for an instant to look back, I did so too, I saw a city, seemingly made of glass, or not even a city, but an accumulation of reflections, a series of miniature pieces breaking up into flashes of light, and I felt like crying, and I saw that everyone was crying like me, we had to set sail, we didn't want to set sail, a sensation of anticipated nostalgia was overcoming us (don't ask me nostalgia for what), we could hear the sound of the ship's whistle, and it was pulling out from shore leaving a wake of dark red foam, I figure it was then that I heard that sound, a sound I couldn't compare to anything else for you, a unique sound I couldn't begin to describe, I turned, I saw a beautiful and terrible spectacle, the city blowing to bits, flying apart in countless, swift, luminous particles, the way I always imagined galaxies were destroyed.

There should perhaps be no doubt, the Wounded Boy explains, the saint who has caused more canvases to be painted is that officer in the Emperor Diocletian's praetorian guard, that convert to Christianity, the dashing young man whose almost naked body we see always covered with a greater or lesser number of arrows and darts, that benevolent patron of archers and tapestry-workers, Saint Sebastian, whose feast is celebrated on January 20, from the fifth century to the present hundreds of painters have concerned themselves with him, why it is that of all the ordeals, of all the martyrdoms there have been in the world, it has been Saint Sebastian's that has done the most to trouble the artists isn't very difficult to understand. The Wounded Boy speaks softly, as if to himself. No doubt various hypotheses could be put forward, the one that seems to approach the truth most closely isn't the purely aesthetic one, naturally, stoning, emasculation, beating aren't as beautiful as martyrdom by arrows (I won't take into account here any Freudian interpretations, the phallic metaphor — worthy as that is, of course), it is obvious that the image of a nearly naked lad, tied to a tree or to a column, receiving arrows with the ambiguous and tear-stained expression of someone begging for clemency, is extremely tempting and cries out for pictorial representation, nor need it be said that, were Sebastian an eighty-year-old man, he would not be so captivating, youth, martyred beauty, is more moving than anything else could be, an ugly tortured body isn't the same, unfortunately, as a beautiful tortured body, nor is a handsome triumphant body the same, unfortunately, as a handsome tortured body, the beautiful and wounded body gives the double satisfaction of pleasure mixed with pity: supreme joy! a body that makes us feel we should save it before possessing it is the body to which we aspire (whether we recognize it or not), it must finally be concluded: what's most fascinating is the component of torture that beauty acquires here, as far back as the Renaissance, or perhaps even earlier, Western man has given in to the enchantment that the pain of others provokes in him, if men such as Van Gogh or Kafka or so many others had been happy we wouldn't admire them so much, pain consecrates, that is likely why (I speak only in terms of probabilities, I don't guarantee anything) so many ideologies have proliferated that exalt hunger, sacrifice, pain, as a means of redemption, the main problem consists in the fact that it isn't so much the sufferer who is saved through pain as those who watch the suffering; suffering, insofar as it is a spectacle, acts as a cathartic, the great ideologues of suffering, the great political figures, the great religious reformers, don't suffer in their own flesh and bone, instead they watch the suffering of their people with tearful eyes and they declaim, This is the path of salvation, moments before sitting down to a generous table, it's comforting to know that you're capable of being moved by the pain of others when you're about to go off and sleep sweetly on feather mattresses, to think that others are dying of hunger and recognize your own generosity in thinking of them, this makes the ideologue of pain feel satisfied with himself and prepares him to continue enjoying his existence.

Of the hundreds of Saint Sebastians there are to see in the art galleries of the world, the Wounded Boy continues, some are unrivaled, look here, consider this one by Perugino, between columns, under Renaissance arches, with just two arrows wounding his body and that peaceful landscape in the background, here you see the one by Antonello da Messina, and the one by Andrea Mantegna, literally riddled with arrows, that of Luca Cambiaso, with this nervous outline that intensely communicates the sensation of suffering, while he sees angels arriving, all these angels, bearing the crown of martyrdom, this one by Luca Signorelli, who, taking enviable advantage of simultaneity, allows us to see the saint being brought by his enemies and later shot with arrows by them (observe: his enemies — what an interesting detail — aren't the saint's contemporaries, but the painter's), here are these two engravings by Dürer (with that strength of his), this one tied to the tree is my favorite, but you should keep in mind these particularly enchanting three: by Giovanni Antonio Bazzi, nicknamed Il Sodoma, which was even admired by Vasari (who didn't admire Il Sodoma); by El Greco, robust and real, very alive given that only one arrow has pierced him, right below his heart; and by Honthorst, perhaps the most beautiful one, in which Saint Sebastian seems dead (just seems it, you should know that Saint Sebastian didn't die from the arrows), look at him, defeated by pain, bearded, human, your contemporary and mine, with a body so perfect it makes you want to cry.

So speaks the Wounded Boy to Sebastián, sitting in the gallery, in Irene's rocking chair, with a notebook open on his lap in which he writes from time to time. From the notebook emerge the prints of the various paintings of Saint Sebastian, on which he has been noting the galleries where they can be seen.

(Sebastián sees the Wounded Boy writing in the notebook. What are you writing? Notes. What for? For continuing the story.)

No, old man, don't make literature, you don't have and you won't have even a little laudanum to relieve your staying up late, *you won't have it.* The best thing for you to do is finish giving your legs an alcohol rub and go outside to see if you can find Helena, Irene, Merengue, somebody, anybody, to alleviate your loneliness. Because now, I don't know what's happening with me, I feel this loneliness more than ever, it must be because I'm waiting, though it shouldn't be because of that, I always waited, I've always been waiting, and I've never known for what, waiting for something when you don't know what it is, that's the worst kind of waiting, the perfect form of waiting, yes, and by the same token the most maddening form. Professor Kingston finishes the alcohol rub and wraps up, he's cold, very cold. He leaves the volume of Coleridge on the nightstand, unread, and discovers something of monumental importance: on top of the sheets, the footprints of a cat. It goes without saying, he is deeply shaken. The tracks mean many things, the most important of which is that what he took to be a dream wasn't one, no, so it wasn't a dream, *it wasn't a dream.* And if it wasn't a dream . . . Professor Kingston observes the tracks as if a real dream were taking place.

He was lying down, it was still night. Since he had left the bathroom light on, it wasn't totally dark. He opened his eyes. Sitting in the little rocker, there was Cira (it had to be Cira, that woman dressed in black and wearing gloves and whose face was covered by a veil). Cira, he called. It seemed to him that the woman smiled, though it was hard to tell. She petted the cat she had on her lap. Not any cat, but Kublai Khan, the cat that accompanied her until her death. Cira picked up the animal, and the animal jumped to the bed, walked across the sheets, started purring by his side. Professor Kingston closed his eyes before asking, Why did you return? She didn't answer. When he thought he opened his eyes, neither she nor the cat were there.

There are the tracks, *the cat was here.* Still incredulous, Professor Kingston wipes his fingers across the dirt the cat's feet have left on the sheets. Then he realizes that, more than ever, he needs to find somebody, anybody, he wraps the scarf around his neck and goes out into The Beyond, where it is intensely cold and it's nighttime, how could it be nighttime? I thought it was dawn, I saw the dawn light coming in through the cracks in the window, it's nighttime and not just that, the sky is red and threatening, it looks like it's trying to join with the earth, and if it does, then what? a catastrophe. Professor Kingston moves forward through the undergrowth with difficulty, partly because his body aches but mainly because he has forgotten the path. He turns down, to the left, looking for the disjointed little door that takes him into The Beyond, but he walks and walks and doesn't find the little door. He thinks: It's better to orient yourself by Vido's father's carpentry shop. So he walks straight ahead, as if he's going toward the river, which he doesn't hear, which has disappeared, the carpentry shop doesn't appear either, Professor Kingston goes in circles, wanders aimlessly, gets lost among unknown scrub. At times he thinks he sees a waterfall, at times a group of men in the sea, at times a white house, far off in the distance. He knows, however, that all this comes from those persistent memories of his childhood, I have three recurrent memories of Jamaica: one of Dun's River Falls, those mysterious waters that never stopped falling, with their deafening, insistent sound; one of a group of elegant men, in suits, with the sea up to their waists (on one occasion my mother explained it to me, it was a Christian baptism on Gunboat Beach); one of a meadow, a snow-white house in the distance, atop a hillock. That's all the Jamaica I have, all the Jamaica I keep with me, *that is all the Jamaica I need,* apart from English, and knowing I was born in Savanna-La-Mar (not in Kingston, as everyone believes), hundreds, thousands of years ago. You're cold,

Professor, and you're getting tired from walking around lost, from not finding the little door that will lead you to The Beyond, the red sky frightens you, that sky that you'd say could fall to earth at any moment (the catastrophe draws near). You're cold, Professor, and your bones ache, and you can't hear anything but the echoes of your own thoughts. If you could just get back home . . . Professor Kingston tries to trace his path back, to find his house. All he accomplishes is to get to a rocky piece of land, where a man is sitting on top of a dead tree stump. It's him. He doesn't have to see him to know it. It's him. The Sailor. Picking up his courage, Professor Kingston approaches. There you are again, young man, ever young, impeccable sailor's uniform, black curly hair, large eyes, perfect mouth, there you are again, waiting for me, this time it's me you're waiting for. I'm looking for my way back, the professor says, exaggerating his Jamaican accent without realizing it. Standing up, the Sailor reveals his superior height; extends his hand and takes him by the arm, leads him to the beach. There is Cira, and he points to the woman in black dress and veil, with the sea bathing her bare feet. Gracefully, Cira says good-bye. Professor Kingston approaches. The woman lifts her veil, smiles. There is Cira, young and beautiful, without the marks the leprosy had left on her. I'd forgotten your face, he exclaims with embarrassment. She keeps on smiling. At the moment he takes off her gloves to see Cira's hands, the hands she would never let him see, it begins to drizzle. You were missing from my life for so many years, he confesses, that a moment came when I didn't know if you were ever really there, I remembered Kublai Khan better than you, some absences are unforgivable, I never understood what you had come into my life to do if you were going to leave it so soon, later, little by little, *as you learn all things in life,* I began to realize that you had come so I would understand what it is to be alone, the learning experience that was reserved for me in this existence was, it seems, to get to know loneliness, and getting to know it after living with you was the most complete way to get to know it, when you left I went to New York, I found Havana suffocating, Havana was you, and you weren't there, New York is the loneliest place you can be if you're alone, because in New York you're nobody, just a bit of ash, and that's what I am, what we all are, and that's what it's so hard for us to learn, a bit of ash that someone could blow away at any moment.

Dear Professor Kingston: the Sailor will approach in a rowboat and will help the two of you to board. Being experienced (God knows how many boats he must have guided in his time), he will row with agility and the boat will head rapidly for the high seas, for that horizon you don't know. It will continue drizzling, a fact that both you and Cira will interpret as a good omen. You will continue expounding to that woman (let's say) a slightly pessimistic, slightly sentimental philosophy. Pessimistic and sentimental, she will be enchanted to listen and will keep on smiling. Actually the conversation won't be so important, and the two of you will know it. The important thing will be what always was important: that you'll be facing each other, as you did in those happy times when you met. No one knows for certain whether at death you meet the dear ones who preceded you in death, so you and Cira should feel satisfied that fiction can, in this case, easily resolve such a delicate matter. Dear Professor, you will begin rejuvenating. Without realizing it you will become again the elegant black man you were so many years ago. Thus the couple you and Cira make will become a handsome couple of two twenty-year-olds as the boat pulls away from the shore. Dear Professor, if you were curious, you should turn to look, you should notice that the shore is out of sight. You should note, besides, that the young sailor no longer sits in the boat. But you will not be curious, nor will you pay attention to such details. The moment will come when you no longer sense the beating of the oars, nor the boat, nor the sea, nor the night. You will only recognize the presence of Cira and the happiness of believing you are traveling together to a place where no one can disturb you. We fervently wish that everything you two imagine be real, and that you have a good trip. *Godspeed!*

There is so much light in Havana that it gives the impression of being a city submerged in water. There are no colors in Havana because of the light. Aside from blinding us, from keeping us from looking at the city straight on, the light turns Havana into a radiance arising among mirages. It makes us feel that everything here is nonexistent, invented and destroyed by the light. The realness of Venice, what makes one live it so intensely, is rooted in its water and its light, which far from blurring colors, emphasizes them, so that the real Venice is always superior to the Venice of painters. Havana is the opposite of Venice. The basic problem is that, rather than being a city, Havana is an illusion. Havana is a trick. A dream. This last word (dream) does not appear here in the poetic sense of fantasy, of hope. We could correct, rewrite, the sentence: Havana is a case of torpor, of lethargy. Its light assumes such vigor that Havana lacks materiality. One of the functions of light in this hallucination is to erase your sense of time. You wander between past and present, back and forth, never coming to glimpse the future. The future does not exist. The light is so overwhelming that time in Havana is motionless. There is no time, though this hardly means that Havana is eternal; quite the contrary. There is no time, so Havana is the city where you comprehend, with almost maddening intensity, what it means to be ephemeral. And a man walking around Havana is as lacking in materiality as the city. This is why bodies search each other out in Havana like nowhere else. Physical encounters, bodies touching one another, become the only act of free will that can restore your sense of realness. In an ever-disappearing city, the need for a physical encounter becomes a matter of life or death, or rather, of appearance or disappearance.

Looking for someone who's gotten lost in Havana must be an act of insanity. Everyone's lost in Havana, everyone's succumbed to the harshness of the light. Nonetheless, how could these arguments convince a father who has lost his son and who's going around looking for him in every nook and cranny of the city? In this book, this father has a name, Merengue, and the places he visits are the most popular ones, let's say for example that he's spent an entire morning in Fraternidad Park, among the crowd, back and forth, sitting among the beggars, among the drunks, showing everyone a photo of Chavito, who is a twenty-year-old black man, therefore similar to the million twenty-year-old black men who wander the city. Nobody's seen anybody, of course. Let's say Merengue has gone to the beach at Marianao, that he's spent a whole afternoon at the Coney Island on the beach at

Marianao, that he has walked the Malecón from Castle to Castle, from the Castle of La Punta up to La Chorrera, that he has prowled about the Stock Exchange, around the port, that he has pretended to have a drink in Dos Hermanos, that he's pretended to have another in Sloppy Joe's, that he has sat from dawn to dusk in Prado Boulevard near the statue of Juan Clemente Zenea, that he has fallen asleep with exhaustion on the Ferry of La Playa, that another dawn has surprised him in Guanabo, on the sand, by the sea (surely the realest thing about Havana), and that he has gone through the nearby towns: Bauta, Santa Cruz del Norte, Bejucal, Güira, San Antonio de los Baños, El Rincón, the latter being a holy town, a town of lepers and of sanctuary, where he has prostrated himself before the miraculous image of Saint Lazarus and cried and prayed, and begged the saint to return him his son, and if he does this miracle, he will come on foot every December 17 in pilgrimage from the Island, dragging an anchor behind him. Merengue has done all this and still more that it is better not to detail here, though it would be impossible to overlook his visit to the hospitals and clinics, his visit to the morgue, where he recognized in the end that death is something that man, in this life, will never come to understand.

A knock. Another knock. Merengue opens his eyes. He is sitting in the rocking chair and he opens his eyes and sees nothing because he hasn't turned on the lights. The candles, before the Saint Lazarus, have dwindled so low they are two nervous little points that can do nothing against the darkness of the Island that has taken over his room. Merengue realizes he has just dreamed that someone was opening the shutters of the window that looks out on the gallery. He rises and stretches, lazily. Smiles. Nobody could open that window, I locked it, intruders don't come in through locked windows. The cigar is on the floor, gone out. Merengue is going to pick it up when he hears a knock and another knock. It's the window. The wind is opening and closing it as it wishes. So it must be true that somebody opened the window, that it wasn't a dream (just because it's impossible, that doesn't mean it's not possible). Urgently, fearlessly, he grabs a machete from under the mattress. The hand grasping the machete raises up, ready to strike, and he stealthily approaches the window. Outside, the

Island, night. Merengue opens the window wide, avoiding a fresh knock of wind. There's nobody in the Island. The world has gone inside early. He hears the hooting of an owl. Merengue crosses himself. What time is it? He looks at the clock he has placed on top of the dressing table. Five past one, that means it's broken or needs winding; it couldn't possibly be that late, but it couldn't be morning yet. More certain, he goes to the door and opens it, goes out into the gallery. One knock and another knock and he opens his eyes. He realizes: he's been dreaming, and he gets up, smiles at his dream, sees that indeed the window is open, and thinks somebody must have opened it, otherwise . . . He picks up the machete, which isn't under the mattress but in the sideboard drawer, and observes the Island, empty and full of restlessness tonight. There's nobody there and most likely he just thought he had locked the window but hadn't, it's nothing out of the ordinary, you spend your life thinking things are one way when they're really another. And he goes right up to the very boundary where the gallery ends and the land of the Island begins. Something's shining among the mourning brides that Irene planted. In the instant that Merengue is going to stoop to see it better, he has the impression that a white shade passes swiftly behind the Discus Thrower, heading for the Diana or the David. Merengue runs through the Island. He doesn't shout, to keep from alarming everyone. He raises the hand holding the machete, ready for come what may. Pushing branches aside, hurting his feet, he's barefoot, he follows something he cannot see, something he can't even be sure exists. He passes the Discus Thrower, reaches the Diana and enters an area of pines where he becomes disoriented, not knowing which way to turn. He hears a knock and another knock and opens his eyes and realizes: he's been dreaming. He gets up and sees that the window is open and thinks, Maybe that's how I left it, I probably shut it in my imagination, not in reality, and he takes out the machete, which isn't under the mattress nor in the sideboard drawer, but in the suitcase where he keeps the pliers and the spare parts for the pastry cart. Out of curiosity he goes into the Island. He knows that there is no link between a dream and reality other than that of a sleeping body. A sleeping body is a dead body. When men aren't awake it's as if they were dead. And in the gallery he sees something shining among the mourning brides that Irene planted and when he stoops he sees it's the key to the lock of some chest. It isn't an everyday kind of key; it's a large antique one. And although he doesn't see any white form running behind the Discus Thrower toward the Diana or toward the David, he goes in that direction, and he reaches the pines and doesn't get disoriented, instead he keeps on pushing branches out of his way, hurting his feet, he's barefoot, and he stops next to the narrow little wooden door that separates The Beyond from This Side, and stands there in silence for an instant, trying to hear, to discover some strange sound in the Island. Of course, the night wind is so strong it makes the sounds of the Island strange, and you think there are thousands of strangers, white forms running from one side to the other. Merengue smiles to think the statues must have gotten tired of their uncomfortable positions and run off at last, they're running away, well, maybe. And he opens the narrow little gate that separates The Beyond from This Side and crosses into The Beyond that looks impassable and goes straight to Professor Kingston's house where he sees, hanging from a marabú branch, a bloody handkerchief. He hears a knock and another knock and realizes, with relief, that he has been dreaming and he gets up smiling; there's nothing that makes a man happier than waking up from a bad dream. The bedroom is dark, he hasn't turned on the lights, the candles for Saint Lazarus have burned down so far they are two nervous little points that can do nothing against the darkness of the Island that has taken over his room. The window is open, shutters spread wide, at the mercy of the wind that brings a smell of damp earth and of sea, on rainy days the sea seems like it's just around the corner. Merengue is going to shut the window and he realizes that he's holding something in his hand. What he's holding is a key, an unusual key. He isn't afraid. As a cautious man, however, he looks for the machete, which isn't under the mattress, nor in the sideboard drawer, nor in the suitcase with the spare parts for the cart, but right on the altar to Saint Lazarus. He goes out into the Island. He heads without hesitation toward The Beyond and realizes that the narrow little door that separates the two parts of the Island is open, as if someone had passed through there. Indeed, dangling from a marabú branch there is a bloody handkerchief. He picks it up as evidence, continues down the narrow path that Professor Kingston wore with his daily walk. Continues toward the marabú trail. The stars and the moon are shot to hell. There's a smell of damp earth, of sea, the sea is right there, just around the corner. It's threatening to rain. How long has it been threatening to rain? Merengue continues barefoot through the marabú grove. The Island here is wilderness. The wilderness. And are those voices? No, it's your imagination. There are no voices here now. That shout, that lament, are nothing more than the wind sifting through the foliage. Merengue wonders whether what the Barefoot Countess says might be true, that crazy woman is full of surprises. And even though the Island is deserted and you know it, you walk through it as if you could bump into somebody at any moment. That's how the Island is. And now it's darker than dark ever is on earth. And without realizing it Merengue reaches the seashore, which is neither blue nor black, but red, a threatening red. And the sea is restless, as restless as the wind and the sky. Merengue falls to his knees in the sand on the shore, when he hears a knock and another knock and opens his eyes and this time he really is still there, kneeling at the sea's edge, waiting for something, for he doesn't know what. The clouds open. A very vivid light escapes through them and falls on a small portion of sand. Merengue first sees a shade, or not even that. At the light's contact, the shade takes on the form of a man. Merengue sees how, in the light, two legs emerge, a torso, two arms, a head. For a moment it is no more than this. Little by little, the outline takes shape. The legs and arms are a man's legs and arms. On the head the eyes take shape, the nose, the mouth. Merengue would like to hear a knock and another knock to awaken him, to get him away from the shore, to take him out of the chills that are attacking him as intensely as the waves knocking against the shore. It's Chavito, he thinks, and his heart skips a beat. And he tries to look with all the power in his frightened eyes. And Chavito raises his hands to his eyes, looks at them, apparently with surprise, and then laughs. He starts walking. Followed by the light, he sets out for the shore. One couldn't say he's entering the water; rather, to be clear, he's stepping up on top of it. Chavito has begun walking across the water, and the sea, as if by miracle, calms down to receive him. And his footsteps become firm and sure as they leave the shore and set out for a horizon hidden by the night, a horizon Merengue was never sure existed.

And if the sky joined with the earth, then what? Nothing. We'd be walking among the clouds, nice and happy. Look, over there, see that big evergreen oak? See it? Did you see the big old branch that looks like the foot of a giant chicken? That's where Carola hanged herself, the beautiful daughter of Homer Linesman. Who told you that? My Uncle Rolo, cause he saw her hanging there all black and blue, he says. You're a liar and your uncle's a triple liar; besides, shut up, they're going to notice we're here. Now the evergreen oaks are singing, yes, singing religious songs, lullabies. Tonight looks like it'll never end, dawn'll never come again, we'll always have to live in this night, this eternal night, a simple pretext for the sky to join once and for all with the earth and then we'll have to walk in the constant bland darkness of the clouds, with the angels and the saints, and God with His scepter, all comfy up in His enormous easy chair upholstered in His favorite blue satin, telling us what we can and can't do. Lay off the nonsense . . . Tell me, is it true Carola hanged herself there? Fuck it, my God. And why did she hang herself if they say she was pretty? That's why, because she was pretty.

Carola, the prettiest woman ever born in the Island, lived happily with her mother and her father, Homer Linesman, and they lived in the little house that's falling down over there, same way the old man's falling down now, all alone and sad, 'cause he walks between the tracks dragging a life that isn't his own behind him, the little house used to look beautiful, painted blue with yellow doors and windows, and lots of flowers because Carola and her mamá and even the linesman liked flowers, and Carola, the prettiest girl ever born and possibly the prettiest who ever will be born in this Island, sat down every evening after her bath, dressed in clean clothes, wearing a perfume she prepared herself from the flowers in her garden, sat down, I say, beautiful as could be, to do embroidery by the window from which she watched the trains pass by, coming and going, and waved good-bye to the passengers, they say the passengers knew when they were coming up to Carola's house and they'd get ready to wave good-bye well in advance, and they say the men tightened their ties that had been loosened by the exhaustion of all those hours on the train, and they put on their hats, and the women fixed their makeup and straightened their hair before they passed Carola's house and waved to her, good-bye, good-bye, with their handkerchiefs, what I'm telling you is as true as we're standing here, well, even truer, because I'm not sure I'm even here. Why did you stop talking? Where are you taking me? Now we're entering The Beyond. I know that, where are you taking me? You'll find out soon enough, look, there's Professor Kingston's house. Right. The little wood is behind us. The yellowish old building where the Jamaican lives reminds you of a castle tower rising precariously among siguarayas and mastic trees and casuarinas and the impassable marabú grove. A bit to the left, in a clearing in the tangle of vegetation, the dog cemetery, with nine tombs and nine tin gravestones. Where are we going? Stop asking, tell me, what happened to Carola? Can you see okay? Doesn't it look foggy? There's no fog at all. Walk slower, you're going to fall. We're getting there now. What happened to Carola? Poor girl! Folks started coming from all over the Island. From all over the Island, what for? Just what you heard, from Cape San Antonio to Maisí Point. Folks coming from far off, whole families coming to see Carola. What for? To see her, just to see her is all, her beauty was getting famous because so many trains used to pass through here. Families came from the mountains in Oriente, and from the plains in Camagüey, and from the Escambray, and from the Ciénaga, and from the Isle of Pines, and from all the big and little cities on the island, because there's hundreds of cities in Cuba, don't you know? There's exactly three hundred twenty-seven, or something like that. People came and came, more came every day. They'd hang out around Homer Linesman's house. Camping out there, in the fields, because they say there weren't so many houses back then as today. And they'd hang out just to see Carola when she came to the window, to embroider, so pretty. Of course Homer's daughter wasn't just pretty, she was super pretty, and folks weren't happy just to sit and watch her, and so one day they wanted to touch her, and since she wasn't just pretty but nobody had an edge on her in goodness, she let them touch her, smiling, she'd kiss the babies, hug the old folks, every day more families came from the farthest places, and not just from this country, the fame of her beauty also traveled by ship, crossed the seven seas, and they heard about Carola far far away, they even heard of her in Peking and in China, they say, and the people didn't even fit around here, the crowd spread across all Havana and reached Batabanó, and if it didn't keep growing it's just because the island of Cuba stops there, they wanted to see Carola even though they couldn't all see Carola, and then some people died, lots of people killed to see her, there were men who challenged duels just to get a few steps closer to Carola's house, women who collapsed from exhaustion and hunger, children who couldn't take the sun by day and the stars by night, or the rain, or the hurricanes that came through (and there were several), old people with weak and anxious bodies who fell from emaciation and anger since even in their final moments they couldn't see the magnificent, divine face of Carola, the daughter of Homer Linesman, and she, who nobody had an edge on in goodness, stood up and went out through the crowd so they'd get a good look at her, they say she put on her best dress, of the finest tulle and organdy, and she adorned her golden blond hair with flowers, and she wore satin slippers that they keep over there where the Pope (the miserable king of the Church) lives, in a glass case, and Carola walked and walked through the fascinated crowd, for months, for years, walking, smiling, waving, kissing, hugging, they say that when she came back no one could recognize her, all skinny, drawn up, wrinkled like a little old woman, the flowers in her hair had rotted along with her hair itself, she had lost her teeth, and she had lost her eyes too, gone blind, you know, they say that when she came back it looked like hundreds of years had passed for her, centuries had crawled into her body like bugs and ravaged her skin and bones, she came back by pure instinct, the crowds had already dispersed because the rumor had gone around that in Athens, a real faraway city that has ruins on top of ruins, there was another girl prettier than Carola, they left in steamers and trains for Athens to see the other one, it was the survivors, of course, who left; the land around her house, for several miles all around, was transformed, just like Carola herself, the land looked like an enormous desert where not even grass could grow, the very night she came back home, Carola kissed her mother and her father, said good night like she was going to go to sleep, and hanged herself there, in the evergreen oak I showed you.

And we can take advantage of Homer Linesman's appearance to point out that, after Carola's suicide and the death of his wife, the good man tried to find comfort in the raising of rabbits. And he didn't raise them to sell them, nor to eat them, not at all, he raised them just because, the same way someone might raise a dog, a cat, a parrot. And he had them by the thousands, in enormous cages where several human beings could live. You could say that Homer's life is well balanced between trains and rabbits, and whatever happens in the rest of the world is of no concern to him. Chacho and Homer were always good friends. As good friends as you can be, that is, with a man who practically stopped talking after his daughter's suicide. But in their own way, they've really understood each other. And it so happens that, Homer having learned from Casta Diva that Chacho was spending his days lying in bed not talking, that he had later taken to playing Gardel records tirelessly on the gramophone, and lastly, unexpectedly, had burned uniforms, medals, and everything that reminded him of the army, it so happens, I repeat, that one morning Homer appeared in the Island with a little rabbit. A gift for Chacho, he explained to Casta Diva, about the same time that he disappeared again behind the wooden screen in the courtyard. To Casta Diva's surprise, to my surprise, Chacho cared for the animal that I put in his bed, and he sat down, picked it up in his hands and I swear he looked tenderly at it, brought it up to his cheek, and when he lay down he did so next to it, next to the grey and skittish rabbit, and for days he didn't part from it for one second, he just lived for the animal's sake then, to pet it and feed it grass, to stare at it for hours, to pamper it and tell it things I couldn't manage to hear even if I tried to with my whole soul. In order to find a bridge, no matter how small, of communication with her husband, Casta Diva also attempted to pamper the rabbit, except that Chacho pushed her hand away brusquely. That same afternoon he went to Homer's cages, and stood there watching the rabbits, one by one, as if they were animals he had never seen before, petting them, feeding them grass, telling them those things no one could hear. He never went back home again. He seemed to have forgotten about

Casta Diva, Tingo, Tatina. Homer arranged some blankets for him in one of the cages, where a white rabbit that had just given birth, named Primavera, watched over her abundant brood. Chacho never left the cage again. He ate the same grass Homer served for Primavera. One afternoon after another, Casta Diva would come to see him and would talk at length about their children, about the days when they had been happy, about the tangos he used to sing to me, about how we used to go on excursions to the beach at El Salao, with the cooler full of beers and the pot of chicharrones, about how we had suffered when Tatina was born, and we had longed for her so much, and the doctor had told us she was an idiot, about how we had run around with her trying to cure her, about how fruitless those attempts had been. And when she realized that words no longer had any meaning, she even brought Tatina and Tingo so that he could see them, and one day she went so far as to install the old gramophone in the cage and put on one of the Gardel records. And it was useless, the truth is that there was nothing she could do to get Chacho to abandon the cage or his attitude, up to the very moment when he disappeared almost between Casta Diva's hands.

Is it really true, Oscar Wilde, that lust is the mother of melancholy? Sitting on his ivory-colored moiré easy chair, under the floor lamp he had recently bought at clearance sale at Quesada Lighting, Rolo turns and re-turns the pages of Samuel Hazard's *Cuba in Pen and Pencil.* He doesn't read. He doesn't even pause to look at the illustrations. He's turning the pages mechanically and thinking, That's what you say, Oscar Wilde, because at bottom you weren't in agreement with yourself, you had a secret awareness of sin in you, a sense of rejection, which you hid behind your scandalous attitude. Rolo feels sad. It's past four in the morning. It's been approximately an hour since he got back from the Leech's house and he feels as if his skin were covered by a crust of earth, despite the fact that the first thing he did when he got home was to take a long bath in hot water, with lots of Cologne 1800. He leans his head against the back of the easy chair, looks at the handsome reproduction of Velázquez's Christ hanging on his wall, above the sideboard, and continues turning, not reading, the pages of his book.

He got to the Leech's house about seven o'clock, too early, to be sure. He actually just wanted to say hello, leave a couple of kisses on the Leech's aged and odiously perfumed cheeks, tell him a few witticisms, several jokes (perhaps the same ones as last year), congratulate him, May you celebrate many more, Havana would be such a sad village without you, and run out of there, eyes watching you go. Nevertheless, from the moment he turned from Consulado Street onto All Souls (it should actually be called Souls in Torment) he knew that, like every other year, he wouldn't leave, a strange force (not so strange, that's a lie, I don't know why I'm getting so rhetorical) would keep him there to the very end so that he could come back home nice and late, filled with disgust, as sad as ever, feeling that contempt for himself that he would sum up in the question he would, invariably, ask of Oscar Wilde. He thought that if Sandokán had come, he would perhaps have overcome the temptation to stay for the party. Except that Sandokán hadn't shown his face for more than a week, and anyway it would have been the same with Sandokán, after all, *la chair est triste, hélas!* He slowly climbed the stairs of the house marked with the number 98 and the bronze inscription, ELIO PECCI, DEALER AND DECORATOR (a flagrant lie, the bit about Elio Pecci: that isn't the Leech's name, it's Jorge Tamayo, and he wasn't born in Trieste as he ostentatiously claimed, but in Bayamo). He climbed the stairs as he always did; that is, with a mixture of repulsion and fascination, as if he thought he could resist at any moment, though he knew at the same time that he wouldn't go back, that he would rest on the landing where you could appreciate an excellent reproduction of a seascape by Romañach, and at last would touch the enormous knocker that imitated one of the frightening gargoyles from the cathedral of Notre Dame. Two timid knocks. Followed by seconds of absolute silence. Rolo reasoned there was no better time to head back into the noisy streets where night was swiftly falling and where the clamor, the uproar, the boleros, the cha-cha-chas sung at full volume seemed to be in some mysterious relation with the shadows. Havana lived by night, the darker it was the more alive, a constant party, a stranger to profundity, to metaphysical speculation, to poetry (my God, Rolo, how pedantic you get, and how you like looking for pears on elm trees). No, he didn't leave the spot before the door. In the first place, he didn't actually want to; in the second place, the door opened to display a splendid specimen of the human race, a garçon more than six feet tall, a blond such as only a country with this much racial mixing could produce, because, even with his straight and dazzlingly yellow hair, with his aquamarine eyes and his skin as white as you could imagine, something suspicious, remote, and imprecise distanced him (thank goodness!) from the exotic reality of the Scandinavian. Rolo told himself that you'd have to seek the key not in his physical appearance but in another ineffable quality about his caressing eyes, about the audacity of his smile, about his attitude of yielding and rejecting at the same bewildering time, the way, as feminine as it was manly (if you could have seen him, Plato!), he said good evening and extended his strong, delicate arm in a dancelike motion to invite you in. He wore matador pants, marvelous silk embroidered with gold and silver, which fit his abundance of legs and thighs perfectly, his abundance of everything in that abundant body. As it was clearly too early, he hadn't finished getting dressed and his torso was naked; one of those wide, powerful torsos that you shouldn't look at if you're interested in keeping your heart still. Whom should I announce? the garçon asked, still smiling, inflecting his voice with a half-authoritative, half-submissive tone (really, that boy's a living paradox). Say that Rolo Pasos is here, he replied with an arrogance that revealed his defenselessness. Have a seat, please, Señor Pecci will attend you as soon as he is able. More than ever, Rolo felt like a caterpillar watching a butterfly. He crossed to the living room, thinking: They've got you well trained, boy, do you really not know that as soon as your skin loses its shine, as soon as wrinkles sadden your shameless eyes and your whole body sags from the terrible force that emanates from the earth, they'll give you a kick in the butt, leave you in the street without a latchkey, and some other splendid specimen will take your place? He felt avenged for an instant; almost immediately he replied, That doesn't matter, enjoy your privilege in the meantime, so long as the Lord was so extravagant with you, you might as well take all the advantage you can of God's glorious injustice. And so, with a mixed feeling of wonder and envy, he sat down in an Art Nouveau easy chair, upholstered in a floral motif, as lovely as it was uncomfortable. There was no doubt about it, Señor Jorge Tamayo, alias Elio Pecci, alias the Leech, didn't act like the upstart he was. Despite his illegitimate birth in Bayamo, he had exquisite taste. His salon was very smart, *très chic*. Rolo had to recognize once more that, apart from all his defects (the first of which was called frivolity), his old friend had managed to establish in the very heart of the Caribbean Sea a Proustian house if there ever was one, as Proustian or more so than the very house of the author of *A la recherche* . . . insofar as Monsieur Proust had never set out to be Proustian. And speaking of Proust, there he was, presiding over the living room, above an Emile Gallé vase, lapis lazuli blue with mother-of-pearl lilies, on his deathbed, an immense reproduction of the famous Man Ray photograph. The photograph repulsed Rolo, he didn't like the image of the bearded genius, his eyes half closed, watery, his Jewish nose even more sharply profiled in death. He didn't like it, he didn't want to think that this was the author of the most passionate novel in the history of literature, a phenomenon that, as Conrad said, can never be repeated. Then he thought, Could the Leech have read Monsieur Proust?

He closes the book by Samuel Hazard. His gaze runs over the living room, the cheap furniture bought on installment at Orbay y Cerrato, the old worm-eaten bookshelves, the antique RCA Victor that you can barely hear now, the faded walls on which reproductions of famous paintings, stained by the damp, collect dust. My life is a failure, my life is a failure, my life is a failure, my life is . . .

A door opened grandiloquently, and the Leech appeared. Rolo stood up, smiled, said, Your entrance was announced by clarion calls. Ah! *mon cher,* what a delight to have you here, he exclaimed in a countertenor that scarcely fit his thickset body, his round, bald head. They embraced. May you live to be one hundred, my dear, for your own sake and for the sake of this city that needs you so badly, Rolo said, unconsciously adopting the Leech's own theatrical tone. *Ma non tanto,* a hundred years is more than I need, though perhaps ninety-nine. *(Laughter)* The Leech smelled strongly of perfume, some expensive cologne, and looked clean, snowy white, almost blue, freshly shaven and bathed. Rolo told himself he had grown older since the last time they saw each other, that his double chin had grown, his cheeks were more flaccid, and he had grey rings in his pupils. He wore a brown silk robe, dark pants, slippers of the finest leather. In his hand, a cigarette holder and unlit cigarette. Sitting on the edge of the great easy chair, as if he were in a rush, the Leech watched Rolo with eyes that expressed a generosity that must have been false. Every time my birthday comes around, he explained in equally false distress, I get sad, you, my friends, are the ones who help me keep on living. Rolo observed that, with the years, the Leech was coming to look like Benito Mussolini. I have come early and I hope you will forgive me, I only wanted to wish you a happy birthday, I ought to be going, my sister is ill. The Leech closed his eyes and touched his chest as if it ached. I'll have none of that! You can't leave, you have to accompany your friend in this difficult juncture, when death is capturing another piece in the terrible chess game it plays with our lives. He allowed a prolonged pause to extend, evidently impressed by what he had just said. Rolo realized that he felt he had been witty, intelligent. How witty, how intelligent! he exclaimed, you're a genius and a character . . . Lowering his eyes with embarrassment, the Leech added in a tone with a certain pathos, You can't abandon me today, this will be my last birthday on the Island. Rolo showed his surprise by leaning and opening his eyes wider. Yes, Rolo, with pain in my soul, I must leave; as you know, Havana is the only city in the world for me, anything else is just a village, it's only here that I feel like a fish in water, I know better than anyone does that I won't find a Prado like our Prado anywhere else, no matter what the people of Madrid might say, I won't find this many pretty buildings anywhere else, these opulent houses, the Malecón where you can never take a stroll by yourself, this sun, this sky, the palm trees, ay! the delicious palms, the sea! where have you ever seen a sea like this one, with these colors, this sea full of emeralds? how well I know, Rolo, that I won't find men like Cubans anywhere else, Cubans are a compendium, a happy compendium! of racial mixing, it's not that they're prettier or more elegant or what have you, it's that they are graceful, child, that's the word: graceful! graceful like no one else, graceful in every color, graceful blacks, mulattos, dark blonds, blonds, albinos, dwarfs, and giants, they talk gracefully, they move gracefully, they fall in love gracefully, Cubans won't dress like Beau

Brummel, they won't calculate like Einstein, they won't write like Montaigne, they won't think like Hegel (thank God!), but then, and thanks to fact that they don't write or think or calculate, they're graceful . . . God! and why, tell me, why would a girl want to stick around poor old Bertrand Russell's side, how could you compare Ortega y Gasset with a sweaty mulatto dressed in white, red handkerchief in hand, dancing guaguancó in a seedy little cafe on the beach at Marianao? why should a girl care about a couple or three truly serious philosophical problems at the divine moment when you kneel down in front of a man of Havana who'll open up his breeches? (he said *breeches* instead of *pants,* as we usually say in Cuba. Pedant!), have you ever seen a photograph of Jean-Paul Sartre? he's cross-eyed. The Leech allowed a convenient silence to grow. Slapped his right hand against his right thigh. Fake cough. My business dealings are calling for me, my dear, my business dealings in Paris await me, and I've already rented a little flat, nothing pretentious, as you can imagine, in Saint-Germain des Prés, nothing out of this world fortunately (I don't want to have anything to do with the next world), a modest little thing, *bon marché,* that's all my finances could handle. Always crying, you fucking faggot, thought Rolo, you talk in a way that I'll interpret everything you say backward. Did you know José K.? Rolo moved uncomfortably in the uncomfortable Art Nouveau chair. The Leech lowered the tone of his countertenor voice and put one of his pudgy hands around his mouth as a megaphone, His name isn't José K., of course *(titter),* but he doesn't want his real name known *(lowering his voice even more),* he's from a good family, *pedigreé,* my love. And calling out: José K.! he made the blond reappear, even more beautiful than before (as if that were possible, as if back there, in one of His rooms, God were puttering around retouching any possible defects in Creation). The Leech turned to the boy with a tender grimace, Look here, Pepito, this is one of my best friends, what am I saying! my very best friend, a first-class writer, a genius. Rolo smiled, shook his head no, Don't you believe it, sir, he loves to exaggerate. Exaggerate? the Leech protested, Then who wrote that marvelous poem that says, *Carried off with the still waters / goes the love I thought was mine . . .* No, that's not it, Rolo replied, horrified, *Carried off by restless waters . . .* The

Leech, however, paid no attention to him, had turned back to the young man, was saying, Pepito, sweetness, why don't you bring Rolo a little drink of something? And turning to Rolo, What would you like? a little vermouth, a Campari, a whiskey, a little rum, a beer? ask for whatever you'd like because Pepito is obliging as can be. Perhaps a vermouth, Rolo conceded, giving up. The Leech looked at the boy with Marilyn Monroe eyes and blew him a kiss. With a mocking bow, the garçon disappeared. Did you see how cute he is? and look . . . He made a hand gesture to indicate an enormous size. A beauty, I took him with me to Paris, my dear, because France is France, which is one thing, and the French are the French, which is something else, if I were the president of the United Nations I would compel the French to live at least a hundred kilometers from Paris, such a lovely city, child, they ruin it, they're vulgar, ugly, uncultured, all that about French rationalism is a lie, they aren't all Albert Camus, not that cross-eyed philosopher, not that lady with the frigid womb, Simone de Beauvoir, besides, I took Pepito with me because, like I told you, a man, what you mean when you say man, what is universally meant by the word man, the Platonic idea of man, can only be found on this mysterious and terribly ill-fated Island, let me tell you I've been all over the world like Western Union, and beyond that, *mon amour,* I'm getting to be an old girl, thirty-seven, that's no joke, Rolo, that's a lot of years. Rolo didn't even blink when he heard thirty-seven years, to which you'd have to add, at the least, another ten. He felt a certain anger that he could barely control to think that this fat and Duce-like faggot got to sleep with the most splendid beauties in Havana. You're very lucky, was the spoken summary of his thought. You're very lucky, he repeated, trying to eliminate any burden of envy. God has been generous with me, because to tell the truth, I don't even go off looking for them, they're the ones who come knocking at my door; of course: a girl has to have her *cachet,* pardon me, I'm telling you this because I know you're happy for my fate and because there's never been the slightest trace of envy between you and me. And after a sad and extremely long pause: Don't mind me, Rolo, they cost me enough money. Rolo thought: You've told the truth for the first time tonight and probably for the last. The Leech stood up, recovering from his brief weakness, Now pardon me, my love, I must dress. And he disappeared with the same art with which he had arrived.

Some time later, the notes of Carl Maria von Weber's *Invitation to the Waltz* rang out, and the false matador, the false but truly beautiful José K., Pepito, received the notes with an amusing dance step. It seemed as if the guests had been waiting to hear those fiery strains of music.

Dwarflike and scraggy, dressed as a gentleman in the court of Philip II (and named The Viking), a tiny black man served as doorkeeper. Standing ramrod straight by the door and hitting the floor with his staff, he announced the names of the guests as they arrived: Carmen Miranda, Marie Antoinette de Habsbourg-Lorena, Stalin, Madame Butterfly, Gilles de Rais, Henry Miller, The Girl with the Hair Combs, Solomon and the Queen of Sheba (actually, poor imitations of Yul Brynner and Elizabeth Taylor), Douglas Fairbanks (Junior), Eleonora Duse, Cardinal Mazarino, Cecilia Valdés, Conchita Piquer, Theda Bara, The Gentleman of Paris, Jean Antoinette Poison Le Normand d'Etiole, and almost every celebrity in the world. The Leech's roomy apartment filled up until it seemed impossible to take two steps without bumping into somebody famous. The waiters serving the appetizers and drinks sported splendid scarlet velvet robes worthy of the *Satyricon*. Nevertheless, the trays offered slices of roast suckling pig, fried plantain chips, yuca con mojo, malanga fritters, tamales, chicharrones, and every other sort of typical Cuban food in surprising abundance. The drinks did turn out to be more diverse and international, so that you could see Anacaona the Indian Princess drinking a cup of Napoleon brandy next to Lorenzo the Magnificent with a bottle of Hatuey. Rolo felt uncomfortable among these guests, as illustrious as they were unexpected. It hadn't occurred to the Leech up until now to celebrate his birthday with a costume party, though it was true that his parties were always extraordinary. Only Rolo wore no costume, which made him feel ridiculous, like he was sticking out. But around nine in the evening, fortunately, a proper gentleman appeared, dressed in suit and tie, a briefcase that denoted he worked as a solicitor, maybe a notary, perhaps an attorney. Rolo felt the relief of seeing someone dressed normally and he found a way to approach, greet, introduce himself, invite him to have a drink. The man rejected him without speaking a word, with inexplicable brusqueness. Joseíto K., who had observed the whole to-do, approached, spectacular in his bullfighter's outfit and with a mocking glint in his aquamarine eyes. Don't mind her, he said, that's Martina Tabares, the most famous dyke in Luyanó. Rolo tried to become invisible in a corner. He didn't want to drink and lose his clarity, though he felt dizzy as if he had already drunk a barrel of beer. From time to time he allowed himself a piece of chicharrón, not to slight the lads serving the intricate silver platters. There, in the corner, beneath a languid country folk painting by Antonio Gattorno, he stood back to observe thickly bearded empresses, feminine knights, cross-bred gentlemen, bishops, and ambassadors of equivocal sexes and conversations. The music went from the romantic to the baroque, and from there to the danzón, until at last it got to Pérez Prado, Beny Moré, the Sonora Matancera with Celia Cruz's loud, proud voice, Daniel Santos, Panchito Risset's weepy voice, and finally to Toña la Negra, divine Toña, the divine black woman singing, *Pity, pity for one who suffers, pity, pity for one who weeps, and just a little warmth in our lives . . .* Cleopatra danced with Fanny Elssler, Alexander the Great with Gerardo Machado, Joan of Arc with Mariana Alcoforado. The temperature of the party slowly rose. The time came when they weren't just dancing, Queen Victoria began to kiss Dunia the Taina Indian desperately, in what turned out to be an apparent order to awaken the phantoms of lust. It would have been around ten o'clock. Rolo began to feel better. No one was paying him any attention, so his lack of a costume stopped bothering him. Besides, Pepito K., such a generous fellow, handed him a mask, behind which he could hide his timidity. So many days of sexual abstinence, he thought, must come to an end on such a propitious night. He laughed at poor Sandokán, who must be imagining, in his little hut in the neighborhood of Zamora, a weepy Rolo, desperate at his absence. You idiot, you don't even know the worlds I rub shoulders with, he said out loud.

And I started staring brazenly at one of those little Trimalchios serving the yuca con mojo, a little mulatto-looking he was, and perhaps that was the very reason he looked heavenly, and I smiled at him, he smiled back, and when he came closer I exclaimed in my best voice, And you, beauty, don't you have anything to offer but yuca? (I surprised myself with my boldness.) The little mulatto smiled a smile Franz Hals would have fallen in love with, and was even more brazen because he stated, Sir, I offer whatever they ask of me, but I can see that there's not much you need, and pointing to my right, he disappeared, I looked at the place he had indicated, a man (he must have been a man: he was close to six feet tall), decked out in a domino that covered him so well you couldn't even see the eyes behind the holes in the mask, was standing almost by my side in an obviously provocative pose, I mean, he was caressing the sacred region where a promising bulge was growing visible, I thought I'd stay there, get into the game, except I started thinking, I have no idea who's behind this domino, what if it's some sort of monstrosity, one of those unpleasant men who would have some reason to resort to such a mask . . . and as for the servant, his fresh, smiling little face was out in the open, you could see his handsome, nicely shaped arms, not puffed up with showy muscles from pumping weights, so I forgot about the giant in the domino, I decided to follow the little mulatto who was serving the yuca con mojo, I picked up a glass of who-knows-what from a tray, not to drink it but because I'd feel less different if I had a drink in my hand, he tried to make way as best he could through all those famous characters, and possessed by lust, trying by every means possible not to lose sight of the little mulatto, he tripped and spilled the entire contents of the glass on the costume of someone dressed as a sailor. Rolo lifted his head. The word *pardon* fell silent on his lips. No, this was no costume.

Do you remember, Rolo, the Sailor you met that strange night in the Island, that October night when the Wounded Boy appeared, and much earlier than that you had gone to the train station and seen a duffel bag there, and then you saw the Sailor leaving the bathroom and buttoning his fly, practically an adolescent, tall, thin, dark skin, a mouth (the mouth really impressed you) that was almost thick, but not quite, elegant motions, the motions of a dancer, not a sailor? remember? Again you have those great shining eyes, close up, staring at you, eyes the color of honey, in which you couldn't discover a drop of pity. The Sailor, who wore no mask, smiled. No, don't worry, it doesn't matter at all. What a voice, Rolo, what a voice! Strong, well-timbraled, it seemed not a voice but a hand caressing your cheek. You believed you were begging his pardon. Actually you were dumbstruck and pale, and the Sailor must have realized it because he stared intensely at you, a little mockingly, very wisely, knowing (and he, so young) everything that was going on inside you (so old). And all you managed to do was to take out your handkerchief, wipe it over the young man's thigh; he, more quickly, squeezed your wrist tight, No, sir, don't bother yourself, it's been a pleasure for me to run into you, to see you again. Which left no argument that it was the same man and that, besides, he remembered you. You smiled (or believed you did) and stood there, paralyzed, feeling that something definitive was happening within you. And just at that moment the lights went out. Well, the electric lights went out, because a scant few lanterns offered brief glints of light around the salon. The music stopped. The couples separated as if under orders. The notes rang out to the great march from *Aïda,* a door opened, and the unexpected occurred: Jorge Tamayo, the Leech, appeared. And it wasn't the Leech, but a constellation. His bald head was covered by a grandiose wig with gilded ringlets. His Benito Mussolini face was made-up and smiling. His hands were gloved. His dress was long and wide, with endless layers of tulle in which hundreds of living, pulsating green lights flashed, surely neither real nor costume jewelry. There was a first second of shock, an Ahhhh! followed by an ovation that compelled the Leech to raise his arms and take a ceremonious bow. The guests made way. He stepped forward slowly, majestically, his outfit shining, his smile shining, dabbing his eyes with a little embroidered handkerchief at every moment to dry the tears that were not flowing down his cheeks. Only when the lights went on again and the great march gave way to Olga Guillot, *Now I'm living off your lies, I know your love is not sincere . . .* could Rolo tell that the Leech's dress was covered with fireflies trapped in little bags of tulle. Rolo turned toward the Sailor: he wasn't there. He searched among the crowd that was returning to the dance and the smooching. The little mulatto of the yuca con mojo approached with a tray full of tamales: Just so you can see I have other things to offer. Rolodidn't even listen. Among the mortarboards, sun hats, crowns, cocked hats, tricorns, buns and bows, he tried to find the blue-ribboned Navy cap. He couldn't. Smiling, trying to hide his agitation, he continued his march through the dancers, back and forth, from one corner to the other, on an ever more fruitless, desperate quest. At one moment Pepito K. came up to him and asked, not so much with his lips as with the mocking glint in his aquamarine eyes, Have you lost someone? I can help you in whatever you desire. Rolo wanted to keep on smiling. I think I'm looking for myself, he replied, satisfied at having ducked the banderilla this fake matador had tried to pin him with. He then stood in a corner, this time under a Víctor Manuel landscape (where could the Leech have gotten this painting? Víctor Manuel hardly paints landscapes, could it be a forgery?), and repeated, Calm down, yes, calm down, and thought the time had come to leave, even if he did so with that desire inside him, with that distress that would have been the delight of Freud or Sandokán, in Vienna as in Coco Solo. Again, beside him, the giant in the domino caressed his promising sacred mound. No, I'm not going to pay any attention to you, don't even think of it, I'm not so desperate as to let myself get seduced by a mask, besides, I'm not lost yet, I can still get out of this hellhouse and take a stroll down Prado, something always turns up, don't worry, there are more fags than royal palms in Havana. Nonetheless, when the giant in the domino came so close their bodies touched, Rolo didn't even move. He let the other one caress his back, his bottom, his thighs. He searched for the promising lump and found that it was no mere promise, but a bloodcurdling and powerful reality. Let's go, the giant ordered. Rolo liked the peremptory tone, the sureness with which he squeezed his arm. *Noli me tangere,* Rolo exclaimed with a smile he knew was full of acquiescence and humility. Let's go, repeated the other one, who by all appearances neither had understood the phrase nor cared. Rolo felt himself transported through the crowd, with an agreeable sensation in which fright mingled with desire. They entered the bathroom. Next to the door, Comrade Stalin was kneeling down, caressing the magnificent cock of Eugenia de Montijo. Neither the comrade nor the empress blushed at the arrival of Rolo and the giant. Rolo too fell to his knees, filled with unction, as he had in the days when, receiving the host from the hands of the priest of the church of San Rafael, he had felt that a crowd of angels were guiding him toward the kingdom of happiness.

After attempting a frustrated trip down the river, Sebastián returns to the Island, which is now a gigantic and empty forest, peopled only by Dianas, Hermes, Thinkers, and Laocoöns made luminous and spectral by the lack of light. Not brave enough to enter in, at a standstill next to the Apollo Belvedere behind the wooden screen in the courtyard, Sebastián observes the trees, twitching as if they ache to run away, and the ever-lower, intensely purple sky that has been foreboding rain for hours now. Though he wants to go back home and shut himself inside to read, he desists because he suspects that at this hour Helena must be jotting down numbers in her interminable account book, and it's likely, besides, that it will occur to her to sit him down in front of her with the morality and civics textbook, or the religion one. That's why he walks slowly down the gallery, away from his house, hoping the time will fly swiftly. And he skirts the Island without making up his mind to set foot on the grass, though without ceasing to stare, enchanted, at the thicket that attracts and terrifies him. He plays with Buva and Pecu, Chavito's cats, which have jumped up on the belly of Christ in the Pietá; he continues toward the imposing Moses that rises where the left wing of the building comes to an end, where Consuelo's room begins. Now, around Merengue's house, he thinks he sees a figure amid the foliage. And what he has seen is imprecise, almost nothing, a shadow behind the oleander, someone who stops for a second and then disappears in that last region of This Side, practically on the border of The Beyond, which is darker than any other because the schoolroom and Consuelo's house have no lights. After all, Sebastián can't affirm categorically that there's anyone out there prowling around. An owl flies heavily by and disappears among the poplar trees. The Island is full of mirages, of illusions. The statues and the wind and the night and the branches of the trees are conspiring to bewilder you, to make you think things are what they aren't and cannot be. And there are long stories about the confusions that have taken place here. Many stories, endless stories. And I don't want to fall for those mistakes, I don't feel like letting the Island make fun of me, and that's why I make up my mind, the fear can go to hell, and I head into the trees by one of the many stone paths that lead to the fountain with the Boy and the Goose, and I hear footsteps around me, heavy footsteps as if someone were dragging himself along, and the dry leaves crunch and you can hear branches cracking, I don't let myself get fooled, it's the wind, nothing but the wind tonight, the wind wishing to pull the trees out by their roots, and I reach the fountain and see for myself that there's no white figure standing there. Instead, Lucio is here in his Prussian blue cashmere jacket, very elegant, dressed up like he's going to a party. He's got one foot resting on the edge of the pool and his arms crossed on top of his raised knee. A cigarette burns down between his fingers. Pensive, he watches the water of the pool and, typically, doesn't notice Sebastián's arrival. Silently, out of respect or out of fear, Sebastián approaches him and stands by his side. Lucio takes a red handkerchief out of his pants pocket and wipes it across his dry forehead. The smell of the cologne in the handkerchief is more penetrating than that of all the trees, than the smell of damp earth that the wind carries tonight. Sebastián comes closer, made confident by Lucio's silence. Without taking his eyes off the stagnant water, the man puts his arm around Sebastián's shoulders, embraces him, embraces the boy, brings him closer, so close Sebastián feels the fire of the other's breath. Lucio speaks slowly now, as if it were hard for him to find the meaning of each word, I don't understand, Sebastián, I don't understand, and he looks at the boy with a scowl and he asks him, Do you know what it means not to understand something? And of course Sebastián nods because he doesn't understand this very question. And Lucio flings his unsmoked cigarette off, into the water, and lowers his foot from the edge of the pool and stands up straight, and his face lights up again with his usual smile (in which a gold tooth shines), the smile that has made him so famous among the students at the Institute, and Sebastián still feels the weight of the other's arm around his shoulders when he hears, Don't pay any attention to me, boy, don't pay any attention, I'm an ignoramus who doesn't know a thing, and he walks off smiling, though the smell of the cologne lingers in the fountain as if Lucio had split in two.

Someone is crying. There's no doubt about it. Sebastián believes the sobbing comes from around where the Elegguá is, and he heads that way without thinking twice about it, and skirts the fountain, and passes the sacred jagüey, and reaches the place where the bamboo surrounds the empty watering hole (a green shade still indicates where there once was water), and at last sees the great stone with seashell eyes, striped cheeks, and a smiling mouth that reveals teeth that are white river stones. Lying on the ground, back propped up against the Elegguá, here is Tingo. And he's the one who's crying, crying uncontrollably, a cry that seems to have had no beginning and to have no end, since when Tingo cries it seems he's crying forever and ever. Sebastián sits down by his side and tells him, Tell me, why are you crying, what happened to you, come on, talk. Tingo goes on like he hasn't heard, like crying is his only possibility, his only salvation. Listen, look, here I am, look at me, I'm Sebastián, your friend, look at me, and Tingo cries and cries. Cries unstoppably. And sobs. Sebastián strokes his head, Come on, boy, it's not that bad, tell me, what happened to you? And when Tingo feels Sebastián's hand stroking his head, he shudders, he visibly shudders, and lifts up his eyes, made more beautiful by crying, to look at his friend, and little by little he calms down, stops crying, and though he sighs, and sobs a few times, he tries to control himself until at last he does so and dries his cheeks with the back of his hand. Silence reigns between the two. A silence that isn't silence because in the Island, which is ablaze with wind, it sounds like there's a whole crowd shouting insults; naturally, as soon as you listen closely you realize it's not a crowd and they aren't insults, just the branches of all these trees. And Tingo, in a faltering voice, speaks without looking at Sebastián, with his eyes lowered as if he were talking to himself, as if only he should care what he said.

When Miss Berta told us we could go home, that the afternoon classes were over because it was going to start raining at any moment, I still hadn't finished copying down the theme about the Alps from the blackboard, it's so hard for me, you know, I don't get it and I couldn't tell you why, I write slowly and there's no way I can get myself to write faster, even when I rush and try to catch up with them, well, you know, you see me writing fast and still finishing after, way after everybody else, and that's what happened to me today, and the more I tried to rush the longer it took, and so you guys left, and Miss Berta looked at me with those strange eyes, like when she's tired of waiting, you know, and she comes and tells me, Tingo, I'm going because I don't want to get caught in the downpour, and I tell her, Miss Berta, I'm almost done, I'm almost finished, and she says, No, that's what you always say and you never do get to the end, so you just stay here, finish up, turn off the lights and shut the door, and I stayed there all alone with those words up on the blackboard that I never did get, that I never understood, do you know what the Alps are, Sebastián? of course that doesn't matter, the thing is that I finished at last, and if you want me to tell you the truth I didn't finish, I skipped a few words and put a period when it wasn't, you know, the end, and I turned off the lights and closed the door and went out into the Island happy to go home early and throw down my books and go out to look for you, I went out into the Island and saw that it did look like there was going to be a downpour any second, it already felt like rain was falling, there was a little sound of water and water and you couldn't tell where it was coming from, even though the Island was still dry, and what do you know, Sebastián, but that's where what happened started happening and you'll never believe me and I hope you'll believe me, even if you don't get it and I don't get it either, what I'm going to tell you is the absolute truth, and I'll start by telling you that the statue of Martí wasn't there, not where it was supposed to be or anywhere else, it just wasn't, and I couldn't believe it, how is it possible that the monument with the bust of Martí could disappear if that morning, you know, I put roses there and everything, and I walked a little bit, and thought maybe Chavito moved it around, 'cause that's how Chavito is, and I took a few steps, took ten steps and that I can swear because I counted them, and that was the worst thing I could have done, I bet you couldn't guess what happened to me then, well, I got to a place with these real weird plants I'd never seen before, with big leaves bunched up at the end of the branch, all a dark, ugly green, and a smell I couldn't describe, and since I'd never seen any plants like that in the Island I turned back, ten steps back to get to the schoolroom again, and I realized there wasn't any schoolroom there, that it wasn't just the bust of Martí that had disappeared but the schoolroom was lost too and I found myself in a place that was just like the one I had left, with the same plants with the big, dark green leaves bunched up at the end of the branches, and I thought that if I went off a little bit to the left, walking straight to the left, I would have to get to the door to The Beyond and then I could orient myself by Consuelo's house, or if I went the other way, off to the right, I could get to Marta and Mercedes's house, and then there'd be Miss Berta's house, and then Irene's and then mine, but the more I went into those weird plants I didn't get anywhere, nowhere at all, and even though it was the same weather, the same air and the same threat of rain, the Island was different and I didn't have any way of figuring out where I was, and it occurred to me that I could call out, call to you, to anybody, and I shouted, I shouted a lot, and nobody came, nobody heard, and I kept on walking and this time it occurred to me that I could walk the other direction, toward the main door, you know, I was hoping with all my heart to find some statue, 'cause if I'd seen the guy throwing the discus, or the other guy fighting with his sons against the serpent, it would have been different because I would have known what part of the Island I was in, it was just at that moment I realized what good the statues are for, and the statues are there so you'll know where you're going, I didn't see the statues, they didn't appear, and not just that, but the plants were still the same weird ones, and I couldn't see palm trees or ceibas or yagrumas or royal spurges or Irene's rosebushes or anything, anything, just those weird plants, and I came to the conclusion that, since the Island is closed off on every side, if I walked in a straight line in any direction at all I'd have to run into a house, so I walked and walked in a straight line and I guess I must have been walking for hours because it started getting dark and my feet hurt and they started bleeding and I couldn't keep going and no houses appeared, no walls, and to make things worse my skin started burning and I got this rash and my skin got all red and I thought they were burning me at the stake like that saint Savona-I-don't-know-what-all that Miss Berta talks about, and I felt thirstier than I ever have, and hungrier, and at last, when I thought I was about to give it all up, I got to a place, not a place here, no, but a place where I had never been before.

A house, Sebastián, a castle, a palace, well what do I know, a really old building, you could tell it was about to fall down, with walls this wide, all chipped, unpainted, stained black and green, and taller than the walls are here, I swear, taller, and windows with iron bars, and there were plants growing out of all the cracks, ferns, hedge mustards, even a yagruma as thick as could be was sprouting from one of the cracks in the walls, and I didn't know how you got into that place, I walked all around it a couple of times and nothing, it didn't have a door, those walls were scary 'cause they were so tall and that's it, and even though it was night you could see it perfectly well, I've never seen a night like that, so clear I hadn't even lost my shadow, I still had my shadow just like it was noon, and I just kept walking and walking, about to faint I was so tired, calling my mamá sometimes, real low, I didn't want anybody to hear but my mamá, and around the house or the castle or the palace, you know, there was a forest that almost looked like the Island, a real forest forest, and who said once that forests have a soul, and that even if you clear a forest their souls always escape? who said that? was it you? it must have been you, nobody else thinks of those things, and then I got tired and sat down under a window, and I could hear somebody crying, sighs, sobs, and I thought it was me, my own crying was coming from somewhere else, from far off, from up high, from the window, I touched my cheeks, they were dry, I was tired, you know, and I didn't have the strength to cry, and I told myself you're in the schoolroom and you fell asleep at your desk and tomorrow, when Miss Berta opens up the room for classes, she'll wake you up, that's what I told myself, and I also told myself that probably my mamá would realize I hadn't come home to eat or go to bed and would start looking for me, and they'd have to come by the school and find me sleeping at my desk, and they'd wake me up and I'd tell them this nightmare, I'd tell them, Ay, what a dream I had, and we'd laugh about it, Sebastián, I was just fooling myself like a moron, I knew it wasn't a dream or a nightmare or anything, it all seemed as real as I do, and if it wasn't real, then I was as big a lie as all that was, 'cause I have dreamed before and I know when I'm dreaming and when I'm not, and I told myself calm down, boy, calm down, and I closed my eyes to try to think through how I'd gotten there because if a path goes one direction it also goes back, so there had to be some way to return, and I looked up high thinking about what your uncle Rolo once explained to us, remember? about how the stars, just like the statues, are good for when your path gets off track? I looked at the sky, there were stars out, so many and so bright that I didn't know which one could help me, the moon looked round and big and yellow, only it didn't do me any good either because when I stood up and walked to the right or the left, the moon moved with me, to the right, to the left, and the stars also moved from one side to the other, your uncle Rolo fooled us, you know, he fooled us, and I went back to circling the ruin, listening to the crying, the sobbing, the sighs, sometimes words, I even remember a phrase, I remember it because it called my attention, a man's voice said pretty loud, Dreaming in a sweet stupor was I, and I remember it real well because the word stupor sounded so nice to me, don't you think so? and I'm also sure I heard another man's voice, sadder, softer, that said, Were I to shout, who in the angelic hosts would hear me? it was so sad, Sebastián, so sad, and what do you know but on one of my trips around the building I find the door, and I don't know how I hadn't seen it before because I've never seen such a big door, it was enormous, with huge nails, wide open, and I walked on into the living room, I say living room because I don't know what else to call that place where I walked into, roomy, ceiling out of sight up there somewhere, and furniture, so much furniture you couldn't imagine, old furniture tumbled all over, lamps, books, clothes, old clothes, paintings of landscapes, of serious people who looked at me sternly and made me feel so sad, even sadder than I felt about being lost, and there were boxes, broken mirrors, especially one that was broken in a bunch of places and I looked at myself in it and, now you're going to be surprised: I didn't see myself, I met a man there who was smiling and bowed in the weirdest way, I've never seen anybody in my life bow like that, and he was wearing a costume, he had the strangest clothes on, and smiling, winking one eye, the guy was pretty ugly, you know? and his voice didn't come out of him, it came out of the whole house, or from up in the ceiling, and he said, Welcome, and I don't know what I answered back, I think I didn't, didn't answer, I just looked at him with startled eyes, and I imagine my eyes must have looked startled: he told me, Don't be scared, and he raised a hand in the air, a hand in which he was holding a black hat, like a magician's hat or like we've seen in old movies, and he asked me what my name was and I said, Tingo, at first I was planning to lie, planning to tell him your name or Vido's, but at the last minute my mouth betrayed me and I said Tingo, and I saw that the guy got serious and pensive, and he was looking at me like I was the ghost and not him, and he asked me, I bet you can't guess what he asked me, he got right up next to me and I could see his ugly face this close to mine, and I even smelled his vinegar breath, and he asked me, Aren't you Sebastián? and me, how was I going to start lying? I shook my head, No, sir, I'm not Sebastián, Well then, the guy answered with that voice that didn't come from him but from the whole house, then go tell that boy we're waiting for him, and he showed me the hat, just like magicians do at the circus, he showed me the hat like he was showing off something that was way too expensive, he put it on, and by God, Sebastián, you've got to believe me, at the same moment that guy who was so strangely dressed and so ugly put on his hat, he disappeared, yes, he wasn't standing in front of me anymore and I looked for him but there was nothing, he put on the hat and disappeared, and I was there just listening to his voice, or to the echo, repeating less and less clearly, Tell Sebastián we're waiting for him, and I threw myself on the ground and cried and cried till my eyes hurt, and when I opened them, I find myself with you, and I see I'm in the Island, and I realize I'm full of shit, it was just a dream.

Tonight is Christmas Eve,
to the woods we go, little brother,
to cut the Christmas tree,
because the night is still.
The three Kings and the shepherds
are following a star . . .

That's what Tingo sings all over the Island on December 24 in the afternoon. And Sebastián, who hears him, runs out to find Tingo and help him cut the tree when he sees the Wounded Boy writing again in his notebook. What are you writing? Notes. What for?

for deciding that tonight won't be Christmas Eve,
that we won't go to the woods,
little brother,

to cut down any tree even if the night
is still, for deciding there won't be any
kings or shepherds,
that the stars will go out
for deciding that the trees won't be lit
on Christmas,
and they won't set up the Nativity scene
for deciding that tonight there won't be
any big family spreads
with white linen tablecloths,
embroidered,
or any sets of fine china
or any of the silverware you usually see
on this one night a year
for deciding we won't cook congrí
or yuca, we won't make a salad of tomatoes
with rings of onion,
we won't roast suckling pigs in our patio pits,
that we won't bring turron from Jijona (my favorite)
or from Alicante (which is also very nice),
that there won't be cold beers
or red wine (in this sun-scorched land you have to
serve it chilled),
there won't be any more walnuts
or hazelnuts,
much less dates,
they've never been grown here and they never will be,
and that there won't be buñuelos or cheese with
guava jam (a dessert that would horrify the French)
for deciding that children won't sing
carols
while adults make obscene jokes
for deciding that no one will feel overcome with
religious emotion,
since, even though Christmas on the Island
has always been a pagan fiesta,

there are those who go out to see the moon,
the clouds, the night,
and think they can see messages in them,
occult messages from immortal,
all-embracing powers
for deciding that the characters
moving in this Island should not remember
that tonight
is the eve of the birth of the Son of God,
according to the conventions
of the Western calendar

Why do you want us to forget something that makes us happy?

So you'll get used to forgetting it, don't take it badly, I'm trying to be merciful, run along now, I need peace and quiet, let me write, we'll have time to talk later.

They say that on Christmas Eve someone saw the Barefoot Countess in the Fair of the Century. They say they saw her on the carousel horses, that they saw her going into the house of mirrors, in the labyrinth with no minotaur at its center (there never is a minotaur at the end of any labyrinth), just a mechanical old woman that was laughing all the time. They say she got her picture taken where, by just sticking her head above a cardboard painting, she came out with the body of a courtesan of the Sun King, of a Tyrolese peasant woman, of one of Velázquez's Meninas, of Orville Wright in his biplane. They say she fished for sausages and frying pans in the Wishing Well, and that she washed her face in the Fountain of Eternal Youth. They say she drank beer in Don Ramon's Tavern and sang while she drank songs of Manuel Corona and Sindo Garay. They say she saw an Errol Flynn movie three times, and that she went into Mayra the Cardreader's place and it was she (the Countess) who predicted the future. They say that that night they heard (they hadn't heard it in a long time) Cirilo's sorrowful flute. They say that, later, much later, someone saw her accompanied by a sailor, that they were walking arm in arm, passing by the Diana, like when you're leaving This Side to go into The Beyond. They say they were going along reciting a poem by René López, his most famous, the one that begins

> Ye ships that pass by in the night
> across the azure epidermis of the seas . . .

They say that the Countess looked happy as could be, that she laughed and tossed, as an offering, her ácana cane in the form of a serpent to Consuelo's Elegguá. They say the sailor kissed her forehead when they reached the little door that separates This Side from The Beyond. They say the Countess turned around and shouted, This is not an Island but a tree-filled monstrosity, and they say that she laughed, and how she laughed. And they say a lot of other things, of course, because telling stories costs nothing and people are capable of telling anything so long as it makes the others cry or get upset.

(Since it has been decided to abolish Christmas Eve, let's skip that day, turn the calendar and write: it is the morning of December 25.)

It is the morning of December 25. The deafening crash surprises Helena at the moment she is fixing breakfast for Sebastián. It is a deafening crash that sounds as if the whole Island had collapsed. She runs out into the Island and understands: nothing has happened, it was just one of the many tricks this damn place plays.

It is the morning of December 25. The deafening crash doesn't surprise Helena. She goes out into the morning, skirts the gallery, takes off down the little stone path that passes near the Venus de Milo, keeps skirting the fountain with the Boy and the Goose and continues toward Consuelo's house down the other little path that opens up between the Diana and the Discus Thrower. Before she even arrives, she observes the final timbers falling, the final pillars, and the immense column of dust that is rising from the ruins of what once was Consuelo's house.

No one knows what could have caused the collapse. Perhaps between the stronger winds and the heat of the sun, some crack in the roof may have opened wider than it should have, and the roof may have started to cave in together with the sand, and the rubble from it may have fallen down so fast that the force of the roof (when it caved in) may have made the columns (themselves already cracked) incapable of sustaining the weight, and they would have come down. When the columns give way, all that's left to do is to wait for the din; in a matter of minutes the house, which has had its history, will cease to be a house and become a useless mound of rocks.

Consuelo's ancient house may be an unusable rockpile now, but I want you to know that the house did have its history, in it lived a thin girl, not very tall, with large eyes, mouth, and nose, who danced all the time, yes, she danced to the strains of Delibes, Adam, Tchaikovsky, Minkus, danced and danced, morning, noon, and night she never stopped dancing, and she danced so much she made it to New York by dancing and became the first ballerina of a dance company over there, and got to be one of the greatest ballerinas of the century, yes sir, she did a *Giselle* like nobody else and that's something nobody can deny, and this is also where Julio Antonio the Handsome lived, they called him that for a good reason since I don't think there's ever been a nicer looking man in all the Island, and I'm not just talking about this Island, I'm talking about the whole Island (of Cuba), this is where Julio Antonio the Handsome lived before he went to Mexico with a woman who was also very pretty, she was a photographer, to meet his death (God doesn't allow, they say, men as good-looking as he was to remain on earth, He wants them all as angels up there with Him), and this is where a very nice little black woman lived who danced rumba in the Torres Brothers Circus, and that little black woman would spend all day crying over who knows what tragedies in her life and that's why they called her the Sad Rumbera, though she was a very good person, yes sir, and this is also where a scientist named Arsenio lived, who wanted to shield off the sun, put a roof over the Island, install gigantic refrigeration machines, import snow, so that while living in Cuba we could live in Iceland, and it goes without saying that the projects that the scientist named Arsenio had were never carried out, and this is where a certain Valdés (the husband of Espera Morales) lived, the one they called The Communist, who was always reading Lenin and of whom, for that same reason, everyone was rightly terrified, and the little old ladies would cross themselves when they saw him passing by, and the women would shut their doors and windows, and the men would interrupt their pool games when they saw him appear, and the children would start throwing rocks at him, and The Communist would just say, The time will come for my revenge, and this is also where Captain Caspio lived, a sailor who knew more about sailing than anyone else and who never dared to go out in a ship, since he had the theory that the horizon wasn't an imaginary line but a wall, and that ships crashed into it, and this is where a painter named Ponce lived, and a poet named Regino, and Lorenzo the pianist, and two acrobat brothers, and a priest named Carlos Manuel (like the father of our country), and another writer, Reinaldo, and Maité, the one with the little rabbit, and several well-known murderers whose names I won't mention (I don't like to bring bad luck), and of course this is where Consuelo lived, who spoke with the Virgin, and that alone is enough to make us cry until the end of time over the destruction of this history-filled house.

It has even been said that, before she lived in the Island, Consuelo the Mulatta lived in a little wooden house that rose by the mouth of the Almendares River, facing the tower of La Chorrera, near the mysterious Loynaz family mansion (the same one Dulce María would describe in an unusual novel). Consuelo, who was very young, lived happily with her mother, who was black and old, a former slave of the Simoni family. Having been a slave, Consuelo's mamá was a bit of a witch and a wisewoman. The mother never wished to speak about the daughter's father, so little was known about Consuelo's father, except that he must have been white: the mother's blackness had disappeared from Consuelo's skin. Being the daughter of a white man, Consuelo didn't lack for craftiness; racial mixing makes one suppose that, along with beauty, Consuelo possessed the indispensable attributes (craftiness, clairvoyance, and wisdom) of the perfect Cuban woman. They lived from embroidering. The honorable families (that is, the ones with money) in Havana would bring them nightgowns, bridal trousseaus, linen sheets, and white dresses. They say that in those years Consuelo wasn't yet aware of her divination abilities. On one of those days Consuelo told her mother, Every time I take my eyes off the embroidering I see fishes, lots of fishes. Her mother opened wide her blue-haloed eyes, worn out from suffering and embroidery, and asked, In dreams, you mean? No, I never dream, Mamá, you know that, I see fishes when I'm awake, right here next to me, next to you, when I take my eyes off my work, when I'm not looking at the thread or the cloth, that's when, Mamá, I see fishes. Her mother dropped the embroidering ring, stood up, went out into the radiant morning, looked far off, into the horizon where ships were sailing. When she sat down again she said, There's danger. Her daughter looked at her, not understanding. There's danger, a storm's brewing. Consuelo still didn't understand. Her mother got impatient, The fishes, child, the fishes! This conversation would have taken place around eleven in the morning. By three the waves were breaking over the reef and landing practically in the patio of the house. Half an hour later the sea had begun to rise visibly and it reached the stairs of La Chorrera and the sea mingled with the river, and with tremendous effort Consuelo managed to get her mother up on top of the table, and then she climbed onto another table when the sea entered the house and set about tearing it from its tired foundations, and the mother said, Don't worry about me, I'm a daughter of Yemayá, thanks to her my time has come, worry about yourself, you still have many things to do, and frightened, I told her, You can't abandon me, Mamá, you can't leave me alone, and she didn't reply, how could she reply, poor woman, when the sea was carrying off the house and we saw it going away (the house, I mean), entering the river, going away, that little house we had lived in for twelve lovely years, swept off by the sea like a little ship without a captain, defenseless, my little house (a poor house, true, but mine), swept away by the waves. The tables didn't withstand the waves, either. First the mother went out, as if on a raft, not happy about it but not afraid. When the mother realized the time had come to leave she shouted to Consuelo, Trees, child, lots of trees, and don't forget the Virgin! This time the daughter still didn't understand her message. It was Consuelo's fate to watch her mother swept out to sea, until she was no more than a little dot, nothing, in the midst of that immensity. The water began to carry off her own table, except it was her luck that it smashed against the walls of the tower, and a courteous policeman (sometimes they exist) saved her from a sea that was set on destroying Havana (it wouldn't be the first time — much less the last — that the sea tried to destroy the city). Two weeks later, the sea retreated without completely fulfilling its labor (not completing its labor to its final consequences was precisely its labor). The sea's retreat left unimaginable amounts of debris in Havana, algae, marine fossils, dead fish, remains of submerged galleons and drowned men. It was at that baneful time that Consuelo became conscious of the fact that she had been left homeless. I don't know if everybody knows all that phrase implies, *left homeless.* There's no dilemma that can compare. There's no hopelessness that can compare. There's no terror that can compare. It's that when a house is swept off by the sea, you don't just lose the roof that protects you from the elements, from the rain, from the coldness of the moon, you don't just lose the place where dreams, great ideas, and petty deeds are safe from the (stern) gaze of others, of the ones who look for you and study you to find out where in your body you hide your weaknesses, where you store up what shouldn't be visible, it's that you don't just lose what protects you and warms you, the place that allows you to be the most you of all the yous you can be, it's that a house isn't just a place for shelter and for modesty, a house is also the depository of your dreams, where you kept the candy boxes after the candy was gone, stuffed full of letters and photographs, that picture of the magazine model you wanted to look like, the place where you shared chimeras and ghosts, the place where you washed clothes (which is a manner of purification), and where you prepared food (which is a manner of communion), and where you bathed (which is a manner of becoming like the Lord), and where you slept (which is a manner of approaching the mysteries), a house is also the place for defecation (which is the manner of becoming skilled at returning to the earth what belongs to it), and the place of love (which is the manner for everyone to experience the joy of being expelled from Eden), and the place where you have the illusion that something in the universe belongs to you, where alone Pascal ceased to be terrified by the infinite expanses, since it is also the place you have built to your own scale, where you don't feel like a miserable speck on an infinite plain of space and time, it's putting limits on the Universe and saying categorically, This is my place, and it's good because it's my place. That's how Consuelo explained to her relatives the sensation of having lost the house. She explained it like that, grandiloquently, because she was a grandiloquent, sentimental woman, and also because it's necessary to put on record here that, being a character, she had the same defects as her author (which is why she had to mention Pascal, an author Consuelo hadn't met even in her dreams). It was, however, very explicit, so that her relatives would realize that being left homeless might be the most terrible thing that could happen to anyone. They didn't give her shelter, however. They claimed not to have enough space, they bemoaned not being able to help her (do we always need an excuse, a way of refusing that doesn't make us see how ignoble we are?). Consuelo began living with the beggars in the Plaza Vieja. There, in the arcades, in the galleries of palaces that had seen better times, she found a temporary roof to live under, to keep her from getting soaked in the rain or catching sick from the damp cold of dawn. Faced with her relatives' rejection, she decided to seek an interview with an old client who would perhaps be disposed to help her, the most honorable Miss Silvina Bota, social columnist for an important daily, who doubtless knew *all the spheres of power* (as she liked to repeat) and who belonged to a Ladies' Association for Neighborly Welfare. A bit old, a bit fat, Miss Bota nonetheless had the air of a little girl who didn't know what to do with her great age. She wore a sailor suit and a pageboy haircut. Her eyes were as sweet as her deliberate speech, full of learned words, Anglicisms, Gallicisms, archaisms. Consuelo was especially fascinated by her little hands (covered with jewelry), that pair of defenseless doves that flew about her words. She received Consuelo in her elegant office, her aged girlish face more gracious than ever. Consuelo repeated her monologue (which we will not transcribe again here) and felt she was being listened to attentively. Miss Bota had the ability to bite her nails without mussing her Avon *rouge.* No sooner had the embroideress finished her mournful discourse than Miss Bota asked in her soprano voice, And you say you are living in the arcades in the Plaza Vieja? Consuelo nodded, fervently. Miss Bota rose from her handsome Spanish Renaissance chair, and blurted, But you have a roof, those ancient and luxurious palaces were built for eternity, what are you complaining about? don't be so ambitious, Consuelo, when it rains you don't get wet, why should you want more than that? On another of those days, the beggars decided to demonstrate in front of the

Presidential Palace, they called it the March of the Homeless. Consuelo was the organizer. Since the demonstration was cruelly repressed, she had to flee, and thought that Marianao would be a good place to hide. And thanks to that act of fleeing (who can boast of knowing God's designs?) she met La Niña Ibáñez, who was a little old lady who had suffered a thousand misfortunes and perhaps for that reason always looked vivacious, her blue eyes twinkling, ready with a smile. La Niña Ibáñez, who had brought her storekeeper husband to ruin by giving away groceries to people without money, put her up for several days, gave her money and food, introduced her to Godfather with the aim that he would employ her, and introduced her, with different intentions, to Lico Grande. Lico Grande (a huge man, seven feet tall, so black he looked Mandingo) devoted himself with equal luck to watchmaking and gardening. He believed that God manifested himself in every thing in Creation, from the most insignificant ant to Miss Bota, and he liked to exclaim at times without rhyme or reason, I've realized that everything wants to keep on being what it is. Because of that, because God was a man, a mountain, a river, or a tree, Lico Grande devoted himself to planting the oddest variety of trees in the Island, which already belonged to Godfather. The latter (being a Galician, he couldn't resist the sight of a mulatta) hired Consuelo. Lico Grande and Consuelo were married. There are those who say it was during the First U.S. Intervention, there are those who say it was when Tiburón was president. The date doesn't matter: the Island remained the same no matter who was president (which is why you can't say time elapses there). What's certain is that in those years (to use a measure of time we can all understand) Consuelo knew about her powers and had the full use of them. So, for example, days before she met Lico Grande, wherever she looked she saw forests. On another occasion she started seeing crowns full of light. One night, next to a ceiba, the Virgin of La Caridad del Cobre appeared to her. It was nothing out of the ordinary, she explained, not according to what we mortals would call out of the ordinary, and yet it was out of the ordinary in a way that she could not (or would not) explain. There was something about her, she used to say, that looked realer than reality itself, a lightless radiance, a bodiless body, a mouthless smile, a voiceless conversation. As a result of the vision,

Consuelo walked around crying inconsolably for days and days. We've come to think that the Virgin made revelations about the fate of the Island. We never found out what she said.

A collapse. On Christmas morning. Each one of the characters we have seen appear and disappear like shadows in the Island is surprised, in their own way, by the deafening crash. Each one runs to where they think the catastrophe has occurred, and it is remarkable to note here that no two of them head in the same direction. Later, when they have figured out that it was Consuelo's old house that fell down, they will try to discover the meaning of the collapse. Though perhaps, just as in life, events should not necessarily have a meaning in literature, either.

Mercedes, could it be true that there was ever a palm grove here, a Virgin of La Caridad del Cobre, a house that they say was Consuelo's? Irene might be watering the flowers in the garden, or she might be sitting in one of the rocking chairs in the gallery, holding that stuffed falcon (the reader is free to choose). Mercedes might be approaching her to cut a bunch of roses to place in the Virgin's empty vase, or she might have just approached, clutching the skull of Hylas. Faced with the unexpected question, she might stand there not knowing what to answer, preferring to watch the tops of the trees of the Island. You've stopped to think, Irene might continue, how few things we know with certainty; and Mercedes (since she was copied from human beings, she could, after all, get very cruel if she wanted) might have been about to say, Just because you don't have any memory doesn't mean the rest of us have lost ours. Although (like human beings, Mercedes could also get condescending) she might have remained silent. They might stay there alone for a good part of the afternoon, speaking of completely non-trivial subjects, such as the best way to season black beans or the latest styles in Paris, or again Helena might approach them with a worried air.

And not one of them ever found out that the Barefoot Countess lived in Consuelo's old house. Nor will they find out. It won't occur to anyone that this rubble ought to be picked up. If there's nothing to search for there, what reason would they have for this to occur to them? For years, the Countess had been entering at midnight and lying down on the floor, on top of blankets she had been given, which she kept clean. You could imagine the immense pleasure the Countess felt at bedtime, just by seeing how the mocking smile on her face was replaced by a smile of well-being, of serenity. On that night of December 24 when there was no Christmas Eve, she lay down as she always did, by lamplight, accompanied by that little volume of Petrarch, *On the Solitary Life,* of which she never had time to read even one page. She fell asleep immediately. And had a few vague dreams, until from the midst of these imprecise dreams there arose with utter clarity the image of Doña Juana. And it wasn't Doña Juana as a ninety-year-old, sleeping at all hours with a rosary between her hands, but an exquisitely beautiful young woman everyone knew as Tita. And in this dream Doña Juana invited her to a party. And the Countess, who also looked young and lovely in her dreams, asked, What are we going to celebrate in this party? And Doña Juana, that is, Tita looked at her with smiling incredulity and replied, Are you crazy? we're going to celebrate the fact that the war is over, that we've triumphed over Spain, that the North Americans have left, that the Cuban flag is being raised over the Castle of El Morro, that we're becoming a Republic, at last, a sovereign Republic. And the Countess felt so elated she hugged Tita. And the two of them danced together to the strains of Perucho Figueredo's National Anthem. And the Barefoot Countess stayed like this, dreaming all night of the party that Tita threw, that party where they celebrated the emergence of a Republic called Cuba.

Sandokán is gone. He has written a beautiful letter to Uncle, where he says, among other things: Dear Rolo, the Island is getting too small for me, it's so hard to walk and walk for days just to meet a shore that brings you to a stop in front of a blue sea that is as monotonous as it is expansive as it is impossible. Dear Rolo, when these lines are in your hands I will be far away, I will have set sail in a ship that will travel to China, Korea, Japan, the Philippines, New Zealand, the South Seas, like Arthur Gordon Pym. I doubt I will return. I doubt you will see me again. I am fed up with living on a little dot. On the map of the world, any island is after all just a dot. I have always dreamed of living in the world, and the world is a succession of dots, a line. Do not doubt, however, that no matter where I go I will bring your memory with me, given that you were (and still are) the handsomest liaison ever to befall me in my life. Don't forget me. Be happy to see me set free.

Sandokán is gone. He hasn't written any letter to Uncle. They say he died at midnight, from a swift slash of the knife, in a fight provoked by a certain whore at a bar on the beach, the bar right next to the one where El Chori plays, the bar's called, I'm not sure, Tears of Gold, I think.

Sandokán is gone. He hasn't written any letter to Uncle since Sandokán doesn't even know how to write. He seduced (not a hard thing to do for a man of his attributes) a millionaire woman from Turin or Madrid (they don't know and it doesn't matter whether the millionaire woman comes from one city or the other). She's a millionaire. There's nothing blameworthy if a millionaire woman (or if not a millionaire, at least a woman with a solid bank account) should go to the Caribbean to find herself a man who can make her forget she's a millionaire, and can let her feel loved and can entertain her friends by dancing guaguancó or by singing a country song or simply by telling dirty Caribbean jokes. Nor does it seem blameworthy if a poor man from the Caribbean should use flattery (and other things of greater value) to beguile a millionaire ready to let herself be beguiled, who makes him forget he's a poor man from the Caribbean. You give what you've got to give. Isn't the world we call modern ruled by the strict law of the market? Haven't we arrived, after a long, bumpy road, at the primitive formula of *give me mine and I'll give you yours*?

Sandokán is gone and Uncle Rolo has been left in the grips of despair. He doesn't know whether he has gone as a sailor, as a corpse, or as a gigolo. Nor does he need to know. He has gone. Any one of the three paths leads to the same loneliness. Uncle loved him as we always love someone who shows us a world that isn't our own; that is, he needed him. Uncle has closed Eleusis, and has left word that he doesn't want to be bothered.

In her own way, Melissa believes she is a saint. It might be necessary to come to an agreement on what constitutes saintliness. If the important thing is the way in which man learns to purify himself to approach

God, Melissa qualifies categorically, with the slight detail that Melissa doesn't believe in God and is certain that evil is more just than good. For her, man can reach purification more swiftly through evil than through good and goodness. Good doesn't teach; wickedness does. Happiness doesn't make man wiser; misfortune does. Suffering is healthier then, than enjoyment. She insists: The only entertaining part of the *Divine Comedy* is the "Inferno." No one knows who Melissa's mother is, or her father, or her brothers, or her boyfriend, or her friends. No one knows anything about her, except that she awaits the time when evil will take over the earth. When hunger, disease, war will arrive. She dreams of an almighty State in which, she says in absolute sincerity, everything you can do is forbidden, and what isn't forbidden cannot be done, an endless frightening state where man doesn't matter, all that matters are ideas, and where man constantly suffers everyday misfortunes, which because they are everyday cease to seem like misfortunes and become tragedy, we have to find a way for man to save himself, man has gone down the wrong path, he doesn't know what he wants, he can't know it, it is necessary to save him, a State that will be a stern father and give orders and commands, and whose orders and commands are indisputable, that's what man (who still hasn't passed his infancy) needs, a State that turns man into the enemy of man, a State with ubiquitous eyes, with hundreds of armed hands ready to slaughter, to destroy, a State that encloses man within the four walls of his poverty and makes him go hungry and thirsty and leaves him sleepless, makes him feel his life is worthless, that all that matters is how this State can put his life to use, that turns each person's life into a file, into the number on that file, pleasure and satisfaction have to be eliminated, pain is the only way to learn, and it has to be put to use rationally, consciously. In her own way, Melissa believes she is a saint, the sacred prophetess of a cult yet to arrive. She climbs up to the terrace roof, naked, observes the Island with scorn, and with scorn she observes her companions. She awaits. She is sure that a future day (not very far off) will witness the Dawn of a New Era.

Fortunato, Lucio is drunk. You should find him sleeping at one of the tables in the outdoor cafes on Prado, call a taxi and take him to the Island. Fortunato, you should come in with Lucio, trying not to wake the others, trying to keep Irene from noticing the state her son is in. Luckily, Irene has fallen asleep in the living room rocking chair and you can come in as silently as possible, without waking her. Take him to his room, take off his clothes, put him in bed. You don't dare give him a shower, you'd make too much noise and all your earlier precautions would become pointless. Fortunato, look at him: Lucio looks so beautiful, half asleep, languid, naked on his bed. Sit down at the foot of the bed and contemplate his chest, his pubis, his thighs, his legs, his feet (especially the feet). Call him, Lucio! and caress the soles of his feet, the heel, the ankle. Kiss the heel, Fortunato, kiss the ankle so that Lucio will open his eyes. Now raise your head, look at him. He's calling you, Fortunato, in a quiet voice, and you say, What do you want? He, of course, doesn't answer, what could he answer? and turns facedown. Fortunato, there you have Lucio's powerful shoulders, his even more powerful buttocks, there you have the body that has aroused so many fantasies in you. Almost without your intending it, your hand goes to his back and initiates a faint caress, beginning at the neck, continuing along the whole spinal column down to that magical place where the buttocks begin. Feel, Fortunato, in the tips of your fingers, the reaction of Lucio's skin, how it wakes up and waits for fresh caresses. Get bold, go up to the buttocks, you'll see how the buttocks also wake up, also tighten. Lucio sighs. Get off the bed, take off your clothes, Fortunato, look at your friend, at Lucio, at your desire. You want to get closer and you don't want to get closer, and I understand you, since what you want is to prolong the moment, or rather, to freeze it, you'd also like it for reality not to defraud you, for the moment to reach the same level of enchantment as your fantasies. Fortunato, you can't help going over, your body demands it of you, and no matter how the fantasies gnaw at you, here you have Lucio's body, his real body, waiting for you, what else can you do? Start by kissing his feet. Smell them, kiss them. Move up little by little, without rushing, up his legs, to the thighs. Stop at the thighs before moving on to the buttocks. He has to need for your mouth to reach his buttocks, so the wise thing is for you to take your time, to wait, the wisdom of pleasure is in the waiting, remember that, it's in promising caresses that never quite come. Now you can start moving slowly toward the buttocks. Look at them, they're hardening to receive you. Kiss them, bite them softly, twirl, move your tongue across them, move your tongue rapidly so that Lucio will feel that rapid movement as a tormenting caress. Go round and round the buttocks until he gives up and opens his legs, to help you find what you're looking for. Then go, move in quickly, there at last you have that round darkness, the perfect darkness that is, which you've dreamed of for so long. Stop to look at it. I don't know if it will give you any satisfaction to know that no one has ever gotten as far as you before. Surely it will, you must like the idea: there's nothing so satisfying as the role of discoverer. So bring your tongue to the center of his desire, to make his desire unbearable. His desire, and yours, of course, because this sweet softness will endow you with a strength you've never known before. Follow the line of every fold with your tongue. Search out the round line. Follow it. Outline its roundness. Then, let your tongue enter with as much hardness as you can muster, as if you wanted to search with your tongue the bowels of Lucio. Look, he's biting his pillow. Look how he's moving. You're making him feel something he's never dreamed of (ever). Come out from time to time (to make him more desperate), pretend you're not going back in, kiss his back, his buttocks, return when he least expects it, vary the speed of your tongue as much as you can. Likewise, sometimes use your fingertips instead of your tongue. Don't forget you should be caressing his thighs and calves: as in war (and what else is love?), success consists in always attacking, never letting up. Fortunato, stop now: as in war, success consists in letting up when the enemy least expects it, to disconcert him, to attack again. Softly now, stretch out on top of him. Torture his neck with your mouth, while the beast of your virility, more beastlike than ever, fuller of veins and blood, more desperate, searches for just the right spot to jam in and disappear. Slip your hands under his arms and squeeze his shoulders tight. Then join with him. Finally, at last, he can't stand it any more and only wants for you to enter; that mixture (pleasing pain, painful pleasure) is just what he needs. If you see him cry, don't be afraid, ask him in your sweetest voice, in the voice that best contradicts the aggressiveness of the beast of your virility, Does it hurt? because (if he is honorable) Lucio will reply, For the first time in my life I'm happy, Fortunato.

Casta Diva reaches the rabbit cages very early, right after dawn. She has dreamed that Tingo and Tatina were turning into rabbits and that she went out and saw the Island invaded by rabbits. As was to be expected, she woke up shaken and ran to the cages where Homer Linesman opened up without looking at her, pronouncing an opinion about life that she didn't understand. And now she arrives at the cage where Chacho and Primavera live together, and she is unable to keep from retching. The foul smell escaping from the cages makes her think of a cadaver slowly rotting under the elements. Chacho, she calls, and the only response is a slight movement in the cages, a strumming of rabbits' feet. Can I feed them some grass? she asks Homer, but he's already melted into the morning grey. Casta picks up some of the grass piled there in a rusty pail. She opens the door to the cage of Chacho and Primavera. The rotting smell is stronger now and she has to make an effort not to vomit. She leans over a little. Inside, within the darkness of the cage, there is a frightened movement and silence. Casta Diva discovers the whiteness of Primavera, her red eyes observe her meekly. Next to her, she thinks she spies Chacho, but it can't be Chacho, that little undefinable thing that also looks at her with great terrified eyes. Chacho, she calls, and it must take her last drop of courage to enter the cage. Primavera doesn't even move when Casta enters. Chacho, however, lets out a screech and almost disappears under the white fur of the rabbit, which only moves her nose. Chacho, I brought you food, and she throws the grass down at the feet of the rabbit, which doesn't move. Casta Diva sings in her worn-out soprano, *Full of hope you search for the path that your dreams have promised for your worries, you know the fight is long and that it's cruel . . .* Chacho moves away from Primavera and lifts his little arms, covers his ears, screeches. Casta continues singing, *But you fight until you bleed for the faith that makes you stubborn . . .* The hair disappears from Chacho's little head, his eyes sink in until they are two purple shadows, as does his mouth, his head shrinks until you can't see the shadows that his eyes and mouth have become, his torso, his legs contract, just as the screech contracts, leaving an echo that also dissipates, his little head joins together with his feet to become an infinitesimal thing that slips into all that dried grass, all that shit.

Today I saw that the stars had started to go out, they say that when the stars start to go out, it's that the world is coming to an end, I don't get that, but since they say it I repeat it, the world's coming to an end as soon as next year comes, you know, next year the Island's going to fall to pieces, they say, I know that 'cause of the stars, because they started to go out, and because the ants lost their way back to their caves, that's something they also say, and the birds got lost, they couldn't get back to their nests, and Professor Kingston died, they found him with his eyes open, lying in bed like he was counting the rafters in the ceiling, and the Barefoot Countess hasn't come by here again, Uncle Rolo is sad, Irene doesn't even know her own name, my mamá stopped talking, my papá turned into a rabbit and disappeared into the shit in the rabbit cages, they say, and I don't get it, you know, that's why they call me Tingo-I-Don't-Get-It, because I never can get it, and I had to be the character in this book that doesn't get anything, and the only thing I get is that nobody gets it here, the others steal the cheese and I take the fall, and look how much I ask and nobody answers, it's 'cause there aren't any answers, you know, and if it's true that when the stars go out the world is coming to an end, then the world's going to end at any moment, I saw them (the stars, I mean), I saw them with my own two eyes, just like that, like they were going out one by one, until the sky was just a dark mass you couldn't call a sky anymore, and how's the world supposed to come to an end? is it going to be an explosion, a volcano, a hurricane, an earthquake? where's it all going to end for us? I bet I'll go with the explosion and end up in a better place than this, I really don't get it, with all the places you could get born in, why I had to end up in this Island, where you walk and walk and no matter which way you walk you're going to the sea, the sea's everywhere, why I had to end up in this heat, and have to feel like crying so much, and that's exactly what Helena says, I saw Helena crying, looks like she saw the stars going out too, and the ants and the birds wandering around lost, and she knows the Island's going to fall, and she knows more than I do, she seems to get it, she was saying she had a dream about a red king who was tying us to the trees so we could suffer the sun's punishments, a red king who cut off our heads so we could live better, 'cause according to that king a head just gets in a man's way, Helena says that that's what all the kings are like, red, green, or black, whatever color they are, and I don't know anything about that, they call me Tingo-I-Don't-Get-It for the simple reason that I don't get it, and the only thing I do get is that nobody gets it around here, and besides, there's nothing to get anyway, you know, the best you can do here is to shut your trap while you're watching the stars go out, a few more each time, two, three, four stars less every night, until there aren't any left and then the Island will blow up like God meant it to blow up, as for that, God's the one who knows how it ought to blow up, and the truth is, the more I think of it, I'd rather blow up with the Island, I mean what if it's true that there's nothing outside of the Island, what if the world doesn't exist, and it's a good thing that the raft Sebastián and Vido and I made wasn't worth anything, I'd rather have a bad Island I know than a good continent I don't know (and I bet the continent's a lie).

They constructed the raft out of logs stolen from the charcoal maker. They tied each log on with ropes and vines. For a mast they used a stick for knocking down lemons and for a sail, a linen sheet that Vido swiped from Miss Berta's drawer. Sebastián got hold of a compass and a book called *The Captain's Journal of Christopher Columbus.* Tingo brought bottles of water, a few pieces of bread and a can of condensed milk. They hid the raft behind the sea rocks, tied it with a rope to the surviving lumber of an old dock and met to make plans in the ruins of Barreto's (that tropical Gilles de Rais). Sebastián said categorically, We have to flee, there's no help for it, I have it on good authority that this land is starting to get sick, the stars are already going out, and a lightning bolt destroyed the red sandalwood tree of Ceylon, there's no birds in the trees, and Consuelo's house collapsed. He took out a great map of the world and spread it over the ground. The only way to flee is by sea, living on an Island means that sooner or later you have to face the sea. If we go up north, Vido said pointing to the map, we'll run into Key West, if we head northwest we might end up somewhere in Mexico, but if we head northeast we'd get to the Canary Islands, or even better all the way to Andalusia, except both northwest and northeast mean going over enormous expanses of ocean, the shortest, straightest, and surest route is north, Key West, from there we could go overland to New York, and in New York we could take a real ship to Europe, so I propose north. Sebastián seconded him. Tingo shrugged. They left that very night as soon as it was dark, so that the sun wouldn't harm them during their passage. Because, besides, as they say, the sun gives sailors hallucinations, makes them see islands where there's nothing but sea. And I wonder, Sebastián pointed out, raising a hand, couldn't this Island we live on be one of Don Christopher's hallucinations, couldn't we be an illusion for sailors who've lost their way? I have no doubt that we're just a mirage, that none of us actually exists and that we're trying to flee from a place that isn't real either. And as it was difficult to refute any of Sebastián's reasoning, there was silence. I think, Vido reasoned after a while, that even if we don't exist, we believe we do, and the belief is good enough to make us exist somehow, and I propose besides to keep on believing it so I can believe we're fleeing and believe we're finally arriving in Europe.

I'm going with you, says Mercedes, I'm tired of waiting, of spending my whole life waiting, waiting, waiting, it's so awful to wait! waiting for life to change, for life to stop being this monotony of getting up, going to City Hall, and coming back to go to bed so I can get up again the next day, go back to City Hall, and keep on going in a circle that never ends, I'm sick of walking along the same paths, through the same palm groves, by the same sea, the same houses, the same heat, always, always heat, autumn, winter, spring, heat! I'm sick of light, of my eyes always burning from the light, of being nobody on account of the light, I'd rather have been born in a land where time exists, where clocks had hands and the hands moved forward, listen to me, we don't live in an Island but on a sailing ship stuck in a dead calm, I should have left before, I should have followed my uncle Leandro, who fled to India, flee, flee, the only thing this Island proposes, flee, that's the magic word, the word that turns your life upside down just by mentioning it, as if in Brussels, in Rome, in Prague people didn't get bored the same way they do here, I guess they do, they must get bored, in some other way, but just as bored, that's why I've always thought the surest bet would be to live within the pages of a novel, God, what I wouldn't give to be a character in a novel! it's the only way to have a truly intense life, full of vicissitudes, an imaginary life, I dreamed of being the great character of a great book, I dreamed of being Nana as Venus in the Théâtre des Variétés, and that the theater would be full to see me, and going out almost naked and not caring if the timbre of my voice was like a cat's or if I moved clumsily about the stage, my natural grace would be so intense the public would have to applaud me wildly, yes, I'd be Nana awakening everyone's admiration even though I'd have Nana's tragic ending, or perhaps I'd be a governess, go to a house in London, find two diabolical children, two children who can see something I'm incapable of seeing, two children who make me undertake a battle against the forces of evil, God, what I wouldn't give to be a character in a novel! Alicia, for example, Alicia pursuing Arturo Cova through the labyrinths of the Colombian jungle, or the picaresque Moll Flanders, who was a whore at the age of twelve and for twelve years was a thief, and married her own brother, and became rich and died repentant, and who, tell me, who wouldn't like to have been for just a few hours Mathilde La Mole? Mathilde, generous Mathilde, carrying Julian's head, burying his head in a sumptuous ceremony, who wouldn't like to be Anna, the passionate Karenina? God, what I wouldn't give to be a character in a novel! anything would be better than the arid reality of every day in this Island, so wait for me, I'm going to flee too, I'm also going to hurl myself into the sea on that raft, now I understand my mother and comprehend that life is anything but this, boys, I want to be free, free, free even to end the days of my life tragically, rotten like Nana but free, yes, free, and you can only get that by escaping, confronting the horizon on a raft . . .

There's a problem. Turns out neither the boys, nor you, Mercedes, have taken into account the designs of the Island. Tonight a devilish gust of wind will rise up, and when they get to the sea rocks where they hid the raft, they'll find the cable broken, the raft drifting off, far from the beach, a little dot floating away (their hope is lost with it) to the horizon, Miss Berta's sheet unfurled to the wind.

The eyes of the Sacred Heart are living and watching her. It's no use trying to avoid them by getting lost in the pages of *Figures from the Lord's Passion.* She can't concentrate. The eyes fascinate her, they follow her everywhere and fascinate her. She has attempted various chores, apart from reading: darning, cleaning the ornaments on the shelf, looking for a good paragraph from Azorín for her Spanish class, preparing the pictures of Lake Leman for geography. Nothing. The eyes are staring at her, and if she turns her back on them, there go the eyes to bury themselves like two picks in her back. God, stop watching me! Miss Berta doesn't know what to do. She goes into the bedroom several times. Doña Juana is sleeping her gentle, perfect sleep, the rhythm of her breathing is steady; her hands, folded over her linen nightgown, hold the rosary as if she meant, with this posture, to anticipate death's surprise. Above the bed, the bronze cross that had belonged to Francisco Vicente Aguilera. Miss Berta regrets that classes have ended for the end-of-the-year vacations; the classes at least can distract her, she can forget the eyes, Doña Juana, and Psalm 23 that she can't stop repeating. She likes to find herself facing the boys, talking about all the things they don't know, so she can escape, so she . . . She goes to the window. Night is falling. The Island is disappearing, it is a mere impression. The verses of Psalm 23 return obsessively to her,

> The Lord is my shepherd,
> I shall not want.
> He maketh me to lie down in green pastures,
> He leadeth me beside the still waters

God, stop spying on me! Miss Berta, looking out the window, watches the Island as if she wanted to discover something miraculous in it. The Island is a dark thing that melts away under the arriving night and, when dawn comes, will it again become the same Island as ever, damper and more luxuriant perhaps, but the same as ever? And Miss Berta is just about to say, Miracles are just a con game to swindle simple minds, she's about to repeat, mockingly, the verses of the psalm, she feels ready to start blaspheming now, when beneath the avocado tree, two paces from the gallery, back turned to her, she sees a man with an umbrella. An old man. He sticks out because of his unsteady way of taking shelter beneath the umbrella and beneath the avocado tree, and his back is stooped, and you can just see, under his hat, how white his hair is. Who is it? What's he doing taking shelter beneath an umbrella and an avocado tree, when it isn't raining? He raises the lapels of his jacket. Must be feeling cold. Miss Berta strains to see him better, though night is a foggy glass in front of the foggy windowpane. There's one detail, one simple detail that startles her. And it's a particular that is probably of no importance, though there's no doubt that sometimes it is precisely the particulars that have the greatest importance. The old man dressed up in a black suit and hat, nevertheless is wearing worker's leggings and spurs that shine in spite of the foggy windowpane. Miss Berta goes out into the gallery.

— Good evening, sir, are you lost? how can I help you?

The old man turns halfway around, with difficulty, as if all his bones ached, and asks in a weak voice:

— I would like to have a glass of water, Miss.

— Come, come in here.

Berta takes him by the arm and leads him to her house thinking, If he's not a hundred years old he's not far from it, what does he need those spurs for? When they enter, the old man takes off his hat, sighing with relief.

— Please have a seat, instead of water would you prefer some cold linden tea?

— No, thank you, I'd like a little water, my throat is dry.

Berta notices that he drinks uncertainly, his hand trembling, getting his black suit wet. By the light of the lamp, she notes that not one more wrinkle could fit on his face, that his forehead almost disappears behind his eyebrows, that his eyebrows almost cover his eyes, that he has a large nose above a lipless mouth, that he has no neck.

— What is your name, old fellow?

He, however, does not reply. He is sitting with his eyes closed after finishing the water, as if he wished to retain forever the memory of the moment when the water refreshed his throat.

— Would you like some more? I can also make you a spot of coffee.

Without opening his eyes, the old man raises one of his trembling hands as if with that gesture he meant to demonstrate assent.

— Yes, I'd like some coffee, and at the same time I'd like to thank you, Berta, for all you are doing for me.

— Where do you know me from?

Berta prepares the coffee and brings it to him in the cup for visitors. He doesn't drink it right away.

— I know everyone, He says.

— Who are You?

The old man brings a hand to His chest and bows. When He moves His feet, you can hear, too loudly, the metal of the spurs. He opens His eyes and raises them to Berta, who feels a mixture of jubilation and terror.

— You! — she shouts.

— Well, He pleads, don't make such a fuss about it.

— Why have You been watching me all this time, what do You want from me?

— From you? nothing, I don't want anything from anybody, I'm tired, almost dead tired, I'm hungry and thirsty, and I'm sorry to disappoint you but I'm not the one who's been watching you, I don't watch, I don't have time to watch, I'm too disillusioned, too sad about the way things are going.

— So aren't You the creator of all that has existed, exists, and will exist?

— If you're going to start getting ingenuous about it . . .

— What did You come for?

— Ah, see, now that's a good question.

His eyes light up vaguely.

— What did I come for?

He pauses to smell the coffee, then adds:

— I came to warn you.

Berta stands up and can barely contain her anger.

— Warn me, about what?

— Flee!

— Why, why should I have to flee? why are You choosing me, out of all the people You could possibly choose, to give this recommendation?

— I haven't chosen you, Berta, in one way or another I've recommended the same thing to everyone, I can't appear to all the rest because not everyone is ready to receive me, but to you I can, I can tell you, so you'll feel relieved, that in dreams, through human presences or absences, through letters, books, disappearances, stars going out, deaths, or any other signal (I have an infinite number of ways to send messages, as you'll understand), I have shouted to each and every one, Flee!

— So why do we have to flee?

— Because I lost.

— What did You lose?

— The Island, Berta, the Island, you don't have your thinking cap on today.

— Maybe I'm denser than ever, but what are You telling me You mean by saying *I lost the Island*?

The old man sticks a finger in the coffee, looking even sadder than before.

— It means just that, that I lost it, on a bet.

— With whom?

The old man sighs again.

— No foolish questions, please, even a small child knows whom I always make bets with.

Berta walks from one side to the other, not knowing what to do or where to go, then turns toward Him with a threatening look.

— It's very easy to start playing with whomever, lose something that means so much to other people, and then give advice like that, like a bad father, Flee! Like fleeing's the only solution.

He looks at her like a child caught with His hand in the cookie jar, like someone asking, What do you want me to do? and instead explains:

— Fleeing isn't the best solution, I know, but it's the best one for getting your hopes up, a man flees a catastrophe and doesn't realize that the catastrophe follows him, instead he keeps the foolish belief that he's safe.

— This means that when You advise us to flee, You're actually offering us false hopes?

— Berta, I believe I have made a mistake by showing myself to you.

— You're a swine!

With an impatient knock on the arm of the chair, He laments:

— Woman, you love to moralize, it's time for me to go.

— What do I do with my mother? — Berta asks desperately.

— Doña Juana? She's happy sleeping, she'll be the one who comes out of all this the best, leave her, let her sleep.

And saying this, He finally drinks the coffee, picks up His hat, and stands up.

The ceiling of Berta's living room silently opens, without angels, without trumpets, without a great to-do, while He ascends with a swiftness and smoothness she wasn't ready for.

The only proof Berta has of the visit is the umbrella left by the side of the rocking chair.

And the truth is that on this morning of December 31, Uncle Rolo is telling everyone who wants to hear it that he saw how at dawn the Apollo Belvedere started losing its cape, its cape turning to dust, and how it lost the fig leaf that until today had covered its private parts, and how it lost its hair and its classic profile, and its base, and it all dissolved, and he says he saw how the Apollo Belvedere all ended up as a pile of dust. And everything Uncle is saying must be true: the Apollo isn't there. And Lucio affirms that the same thing happened to the Laocoön, that he saw it at the moment it turned to dust, the first thing that was consumed was the serpent, and there was a moment when that man and his two sons looked very odd, suffering over nothing, since nothing was attacking them, until later they too fell apart into a noisy pile of rocks. And everything Lucio affirms must also be true: the Laocoön isn't there, either. Nor are the Hermes of Praxiteles, nor the bust of Greta Garbo, nor the Venus de Milo, nor the Diana, nor the Discus Thrower, nor the Elegguá, nor the Victory of Samothrace that you used to see at the entrance. And as for the bust of Martí, it's as if it never existed. Nor can the crotons or the roses that were planted around it be found anywhere. The fountain is still there, but you can't see the Boy with the Goose in it, nor can you find the stagnant greenish water that had accumulated there through years of downpours. Also vanished are the stone paths, thanks to which it had been possible to venture in among all those trees without fear of the disaster of disappearing, without fear of the ghosts of the Island. The statues and the paths were like the Virgin, a means of feeling we were protected by a superior and eternal order, something sure in the midst of contingency, something that would outlive us; what's beyond argument is that, for all that man seems to regret that things outlive him, it turns out (being an inexplicable, paradoxical creature) he's happy at the same time that this is how things are, so that he can sing to these things (whether it's Niagara Falls or his own city) and leave some evidence of his time on earth, and also so that he can look with his ephemeral eyes at what has eternal value and feel that he has touched some bit of eternity, that he has caught some bit of it.

And it turns out that today is December 31, and according to human habits, we should suppose that the characters in this tale will celebrate the arrival of the New Year.

It is highly probable that a bit before nightfall, one could see the Wounded Boy leave Irene's house with his notebook, cross the Island, reach the courtyard, go out through the great door that opens onto Linea Street. Perhaps one could see him stop for a second in front of Eleusis, the bookstore, cross paths with a sailor, and continue toward the train station. Although it is also highly probably that he could be seen heading toward The Beyond, toward the carpenter's shop where they found him one night in late October. What is certain (or at least as certain as these things can ever be) is that when tonight, December 31, finally arrives, the Wounded Boy won't be in the Island.

The lights are on in the galleries. For all the good that does. If today weren't today, Merengue would have taken a rocking chair out to the gallery as night began to fall so he could smoke his H-Upmann and talk. Right away Chavito would have come out with his collapsible canvas stool and his smile, and he would have sat down facing his father, because there's no denying Chavito used to enjoy pumping Merengue for information, asking him about other times, which always, in memory, seem more fortunate. Mercedes would arrive with Marta, the two of them bathed and dressed to the nines, their necks and breasts immaculate with Myrurgia talcum; sighing, Mercedes saying that she comes there to forget for a few hours about that damned City Hall. Casta Diva would arrive, with her hibiscus-print apron and her air of a diva, exclaiming, Don't tempt me, don't tempt me because I have so much to do. And San Martín would have followed her, pretending to be upset, exclaiming with false anger, This woman! You just can't keep her in the house. Irene would come too with her palm leaf fan, talking about her family in Bauta. If it were a night like those of not long ago, Miss Berta would appear, looking like a doctor of pedagogy. And Uncle Rolo would also be sighted, reciting poems of Julián del Casal. And Helena would arrive, holding the flashlight and the keys to the iron gate, always watching over the Island. And the conversation would begin. And for the least excuse, guffaws would break out.

But today isn't any old day. Many things have happened and many more are still to come. Today is December 31, a special year's end, and it makes no difference at all that the lights are on in the gallery.

December 31? so what are you trying to tell me? I'm telling you we ought to celebrate it. And what do I have to celebrate, when you can see: I don't even remember my own name, when my memory's been erased and I don't even know who I am, when I'm here and it's like I'm nowhere. Irene paces the house without knowing where she's going, and then stops in the middle of the living room. Miss Berta consoles her, Come on, you'll see, it's a bout of amnesia, you'll recover your memory, you'll soon be the same Irene as ever. And she leads her toward the gallery, towards the Island at nightfall. Casta Diva is there, waiting for them, sitting on the ground, carrying Tatina, saying, Today I looked at myself in the mirror and didn't see me, God knows where my image has wandered off to, but it sure isn't with me, not in front of me like I'd like it to be. And at that instant, as if Casta Diva's words had given the order, a magnificent soprano voice emerges from among the trees,

E strano! E strano! In core
Scolpiti ho quegli accenti!

Saria per me sventura un serio amore?
Che risolvi, o turbata anima mia . . .

And Casta Diva is left stupefied, as if she were lost in some place only she knew about. It is highly probable that Cirilo's flute is also heard now, although the truth is that we can't be sure about this. At times shots are fired, police car sirens are heard, and who dares to say that they really are shots and police sirens? Mercedes comes with Marta by the arm. They look serious and sit down without even saying good evening. Merengue brings a tray of pastries, which he deposits, also in silence, on a little table Helena sets out. Helena and Uncle Rolo alike have just brought out more rocking chairs so that everyone can sit comfortably. Please, make yourselves comfortable because when the bell rings twelve, however the new year catches us, that's how we'll spend it. Nobody laughs at Uncle's joke. Where are the boys? The boys are over by the courtyard, Miss Berta says, serving lemonade in their glasses.

And there is no party, just an expectant waiting. Waiting for it to be twelve midnight and for Miss Berta's clock to ring twelve at last. And waiting for something else: they don't know what it could be.

And although they cannot know it, they are waiting for a young sailor to appear and for someone to shout Fire! (It should be noted: between the Fire and the word that designates it there exists an abyss of bewilderment; fire is one of the few things in this world that are more impressive than their names.) For a few endless seconds, the characters, who in one way or another are awaiting the arrival of a new year, will stand fascinated by the flames that will appear over by Miss Berta's and that will spread with unheard-of swiftness to the rest of the Island, consuming trees and houses, destroying all they encounter in their path without the slightest hesitation. Bright, vigorous, golden, the flames will grow higher and higher, swifter and swifter, more and more beautiful, and will cast colors into the night that will range from red to purple and will turn white up high. And they will not only grow higher, they will also advance in every direction, will take over the Island, take over the night, with the sureness and indifference that beauty always possesses. The characters' efforts will be to no avail. Their shouts and desperation will be to no avail. In short order the Island will become a devastated world, a world that can only be found in this book.

Because it turns out that she is face up, as always, hands crossed over her breast, holding the rosary (with soil from the Holy Land, blessed by Pius XII), in the position that is the best means of avoiding death's surprise. Doña Juana sleeps peacefully, with the serenity of those who were born to be eternal. And has a lovely dream. You have to recognize it: sooner or later the bonanza will come. After ninety years of a luckless life, Doña Juana has lain down to sleep happy dreams. What Miss Berta wouldn't give to read this page! What she wouldn't give to know why it is that her mother prefers sleep to waking! But Miss Berta is a character in this book; that is, she is condemned to remain within it and to appear only when she is invoked. And she doesn't appear now, cannot appear now. Doña Juana's bedroom, closed up against the December chill (it's a figure of speech), is lit only by the candle in the candlestick, white and Solomonic, before the image of La Caridad del Cobre. No one in the Island will ever know that Doña Juana is dreaming of Vienna. Not the Vienna of woods and waltzes, of course, for she has never in her life been there, but the ranch of her cousin, the poetess Nieves Xenes, in the little village of Quivicán. It is a dream that is set many years ago, when they first raised the flag over the Castle of El Morro, and Don Tomás first sat, looking like an honored and less than brilliant professor, in the seat of the president. Doña Juana was not a doña back then, much less Juana. Doña Juana would have been much too stern a name for that young woman, for that delicate and agile body, for the carefree woman who climbs trees in search of mandarin oranges, bathes in the river, and plays the dances of Saumell on the piano, or sings Pepe Sánchez, or goes straight to the hive because honey is a blessing for the skin and throat. They called her Tita. And her skin is a handsome dark color, her hair is jet black, her eyes intelligent and sparkling, her mouth always glowing. This description is perhaps a bit too obliging, but that's how Doña Juana looks in her dream and there's nothing you can do but tell things the way they are. It's a morning of celebrations in Vienna. A country party. The trees are decorated with silk bows and crepe paper flowers. Seven pits have been dug in the ground and seven cooks are roasting seven handsome pigs. In the kitchen, pots of rice and beans cook slowly. The yuca will be cooked later so that it's ready at lunch time. On a stage, a brass band is performing the first danzón, *Las Alturas de Simpson.* Sitting in the great wicker easy chair, dressed in black, you can see Luisa Pérez de Zambrana, the poetess. Next to her, dressed in white, the philosopher Varona. Both converse with Nieves, with Aurelia Castillo, with a young and gorgeous mulatto by the name of Poveda, and even with the one and only Esteban Borrero, who somehow overcame his habits to attend the party. Over there goes the dreaded Fray Candil in the company of his wife Piedad Zenea. A few young people are dancing. Others are lying on the grass, contemplating the sky, they say, which is a blue that Tita has just christened "turn of the century." The young children play around the pond, swing in hammocks, sled down the hills on palm bark, sing

> Dress up, little girl, dress up,
> here comes your sailor,
> in his pretty Navy suit
> he looks like a coachman . . .

They serve rum with coconut juice. Along with tamarind drinks, soursop shakes, lemonades, and sugarcane juice served nice and cold. They pass around pastry trays with *panecitos de gloria* and *buñuelos.* From his bedroom balcony, Uncle Chodo, who's been drunk for days, delivers a speech that no one can understand and that gives rise to laughter. Valentín the black jumps and shouts with boundless cheer, and everyone watches him and laughs and you'd even say they felt like jumping too, and Benjamina, who was going back and forth with a basket of plums, begins jumping, and even La Nene jumps up, tossing colored confetti into the air. Father Gaztelu passes by, sprinkling holy water, humming along with the danzón and reciting poems. From Havana has come a very serious, very old photographer with a camera on a tripod, to immortalize the moment. This more or less is Doña Juana's dream, and in it she is not yet Doña Juana but Tita, and she is sitting before the mirror, with her best friends helping her to dress, because she has a surprise for all the guests, and it is that Tita has thought of dressing up as the Republic, and has ordered a long dress made for her with great blue and white fringes, and a flame-red Phrygian cap, with the lone star. And the truth is that Doña Juana looks gorgeous as Tita dressed up as the Republic in her happy dream. And when they consider the moment right, and hear the band strike up another danzón by Faílde, and Uncle Chodo tires of his harangue, Tita goes out onto the terrace, descends the stairs leading to the garden, and appears there, radiant, among the guests, and there is a tremendous silence, even the brass band falls silent to watch Tita walk by dressed as the Republic. And in her dream Doña Juana is enchanted to see how Tita manages to enchant all those present with this simple costume. Even Luisa Pérez, the poetess, and Varona, the philosopher, stand up, surprised, reverent. Father Gaztelu sprinkles her with holy water and comes close to whisper to her, May God bless you, child. And it is the priest's gesture that gives the order for someone to yell, Hooray for free Cuba! and the brass band picks up the danzón again, and the party is a party once more. Tita, however, does not stop. In her dream, Doña Juana sees her keep walking contentedly down the palm tree avenue, skirting the pond, the boundary fences, the corrals, the sugarcane field, satisfied with her dress, singing out loud

> In Cuba, lovely isle of burning sun
> beneath its blue sky, beloved dark-skinned beauty,
> You are the queen of every flower . . .

and night begins to fall, and Tita keeps on walking through the fields dressed as the Republic, beneath the darkness of night, so dark you can't even see your own hands, and Tita keeps going, and Tita needs light to be able to venture through fields that have disappeared in shadow. Still dreaming, Doña Juana lifts a hand and searches for the candlestick with the white and Solomonic candle before the little print of La Caridad del Cobre. She holds up the candle to light Tita's way, but the candle falls onto her white linen nightgown. In reality, Doña Juana is burning. In her dream, Tita can see that everything is illuminated, that the fields are aflame as if day were beginning to dawn.

Epilogue

Life Everlasting

What be not writ we shall not affirm.

— Gonzalo de Berceo

It must be said that Flaubert was incorrect: no real good comes of it if a writer, in his work, imitates the way that God is present, but invisible, in His Creation. To begin with, God isn't even invisible. We see him every day, in the most unlikely forms: as a street sweeper, employee, child, lover, clown, enemy, writer (good or bad), fruit, cat, tree, flower . . . and if we don't see him as a statesman, it's because that's the devil's job. So if we insist that God isn't around, if we're unlucky enough not to believe He reveals Himself in every part of Creation (except for chiefs of state, of course), isn't His absence one of the main causes of despair? So why should writers imitate precisely the worst of God's attributes, invisibility? I'll take the liberty of making a confession: I'm the only one who can put out the fire; I'm the only one responsible for it. My characters wait for the firemen, their hopes dashed, and they pray, perhaps because they still expect a miracle, not knowing it all depends on me, not knowing that the miracle isn't God's to grant but mine, that in this case (and this case alone) we're basically one and the same person. I'd just have to tear up a few pages, and the Island would return to normal. If I made Doña Juana not wake up, not stretch out her hand, not knock over the candle, they'd reach the new year nice and happy. Perhaps I'll be moved by what I myself have to lose, be moved by the things of mine that will turn to dust in this fire; all the memories, all the happiness, the only place where I could ever be happy, so much so that I've come to think that my actual life, my real life, was the life I led on the Island, and that the rest of it, everything I lived after that, has been nothing but poor variations, pretexts for recalling my past, finding the best way to retell it, sometimes well, other times not so well. So you can conclude that my life really lasted only eleven years. Perhaps I'm not the only one this has happened to, perhaps every man is conceded a short span of life, a vigorous center of a few years around which the years that come before and the years that come after must revolve. This falls within the field of speculation. In any case, the one who's most hurt by the fire is me. And what pains me is that I'm the one who caused it. Well, of course, it was Doña Juana who stuck out her hand and knocked over the candle that set the blaze. That is, however, the superficial side of things. Why was that precisely what happened? I was shuffling, as anyone could tell, a limited number of possibilities. I could have forgotten about her. I could have had her wake up, resplendent in her ninetieth year, pick up the candle and walk out into the Island; the characters would have been surprised, Miss Berta would have cried . . . but instead, it occurred to me to start a fire. So there you have it, the Island's burning. The characters (I was in the courtyard) abandoned the gallery and entered the Island, fleeing, shouting, not knowing what to do, who to call, and that was on top of being unaware of the confusion the rest of the country was going through at that exact moment, since it's time to reveal that at that exact moment the President of the Republic, Fulgencio Batista, was fleeing by plane to the Dominican Republic with his family and his money, and the Columbia military base (two or three blocks from the Island) was left powerless, and the Rebels, with their long impetuous beards, were taking charge of the situation. And although I have tried to keep my characters on the sidelines of political life, obeying (too closely) Stendhal's famous stricture to the effect that *politics produces the same effect in literature as firing a pistol does in a concert,* the truth is that firing the pistol would seem inevitable to me now, even if we were listening to the Divine Maria Callas singing a Saint-Saëns aria. At bottom, there must be some relation between the flight of el Señor Presidente, the triumph of the Rebels, and the fact that Doña Juana sticks out her hand, bumps the candle, and causes the fire that put an end to the first eleven years of my life, which according to the opinion expressed above, is as much as to say my entire life.

It is true that the philosopher's stone
cannot be found.
But it is good to search for it.

— Fontenelle

Whatever the relation between these events may be, in the final inscrutable instance, in the final pointless instance, given that it cannot erase the main event (in this case, for me, THE FIRE, though History has ignored this fire and instead has put so much emphasis on the flight of the President and the triumph of the Rebels), the fact is that the blazes flared up over there, *chez* Miss Berta, for whole seconds that called into question the measurability of time. We stood fascinated before the blazes, which grew higher and higher, more and more beautiful, spreading with a swiftness that corresponded to our degree of fascination. I have the impression (I can't be sure) that Merengue was the first to react, to yell Fire! (as I've already noted, there's an abyss of bewilderment between Fire and the word that designates it, Fire is one of the few things in this world that are more impressive than their names), and to run to get water. Though, of course, by this time a few buckets of water did little or no good. Irene also ran to get the hose she used to use to water her garden. Nonetheless, the water only seemed to feed the vigorous flames, casting colors into the night that turned white up high, looking like stars that left the earth to try to fix themselves in the sky. At some point Morales the parrot, apparently as dazed as we were, was seen flying into the flames. It was the first (and last) time Melissa cried. And then came something truly astounding: after the parrot, many other birds began flying out of the trees, seagulls, canaries, parakeets, ducks, cardinals, mockingbirds, bluebirds, swallows, hummingbirds, and more, cheerfully circling the fire only to hurl themselves into it with an intense beating of wings. A long line of rats, jutías, and possums also abandoned their burrows to enter the flames. Uncle Rolo shouted like he was out of his mind. With Vido's help, Merengue continued hurling tireless and fruitless buckets of water while arguing with Saint Lazarus, Fuck it, you leprous old fag, why'd you forget us? Holding Tatina, Casta Diva cried. Practically naked, armed with a sledgehammer, Lucio looked like a character from a Greek tragedy (although the bit about the sledgehammer is somewhat reminiscent of what many, many years ago, millennia ago, was called socialist realism) struggling against adversity, a kind of Perseus ready to put a stop to the Medusa; I don't know if he realized (we didn't realize it either) how useless the blows of his sledge-hammer were: they knocked down walls that were going to be fuel for the flames, one way or the other. Mercedes walked up and down asking questions that no one understood, and returned to embrace Marta, who, with her closed eyes, illuminated by the flames, appeared the priestess of some ancient cult. Tingo had hidden himself beneath the red sandalwood tree of Ceylon, and was crying and not getting it (always, not getting it). Miss Berta said despairingly, The seven angels are holding the seven trumpets, He has opened the seventh seal, this is the fire of the golden censer, the fire of the altar, falling upon the earth . . . Seeing her kingdom in danger, my mother gave desperate orders. Professor Kingston appeared next to the bust of Greta Garbo, silent, a bit sad, accompanied by the sailor with long curly hair, large dark eyes (the same one — I realize now, after all this time — who Luis Cernuda met, the same one we have met in every port in the world; it's time to come to the conclusion that only one sailor exists, and every time we bump into a sailor it's The Sailor, Cernuda's sailor — some time later, I read this idea in *Querelle de Brest,* with no mention of Cernuda). I am aware that Professor Kingston is already dead, that he disappeared poetically in the Island pages ago and the logic of the structure indicates that he shouldn't be here, but what am I going to do if he appears, if I see him, if I almost hear him recite *The land of ice, and of fearful sounds where no living thing was to be seen,* and note that he is leaning on the sailor's shoulder (it's also time to state that a sailor appears so that you can lean on his shoulder, and even cry on it, since among other things a sailor appears for consolation). Likewise, though no one could tell where it was coming from, though she couldn't be seen, we heard of the Barefoot Countess's laugh and her voice, I told you, I told you and you didn't listen to me, I told you that you'd be wiped out, that you were destined for destruction. And I've already written that the flames not only grew higher, but progressed in every direction, taking over the Island and the night with the sureness, mercilessness, and indifference that sublime things possess. I should admit that my eyes too were filled with tears, though for a different reason. I didn't care less about any losses; I would have cared little enough even if I had known (and I didn't know at the time) that my life was coming to an end in that fire, enchanted as I was by the manifold radiance of the flames, by their voluptuous and ever-changing movement, which, while destroying all that was transitory, established a lasting beauty. You should remember that in borderline situations, when what's most important seems to be at stake, your mind gets distracted and focuses on details and rationalizations that have nothing to do with the finality of what befalls you. So, faced with the destruction of my house (the destruction of any house is the destruction of a hope, of a life, and even of a world), faced with so definitive a fact for me and for mine, I started thinking about the sacred side of that fire, about the reasons why the ancients had categorized fire as divine, and I came to imagine how happy the gods would be with the offering that was made to them on that passage from 1958 to 1959, and I was so ingenuous as to believe it would be exorcism enough, that the coming years would be replete with peace and good fortune. Underneath all this rhetoric I'm trying to say: I felt content. I would even have liked to lecture those around me, to tell them, Don't get discouraged, this fire is just the beginning of a New Era, a literally fabulous era when we'll be the Happy Elect, a Fire is the door that closes so that thousands of doors may open, the sign of a Wonderful New Life. Luckily I said nothing (since then I have been wise enough to repress my urges to lecture, as if I already had an obscure awareness of the falsity of any lecture, because lectures, like chiefs of state, are things of the Devil). I said nothing, and

> It is always dangerous to write
> from the point of view of "I."
>
> — Anthony Trollope

I ran out of there. I lost myself among the trees. I passed by where the Venus de Milo used to be seen, toward where the Laocoön once stood. I entered Uncle Rolo's house, which was open. No one, not even my mother, noticed my flight. Sandokán would never again sleep off a drunk in that bed. Dark, the library received me without offense. I didn't turn on the light. I didn't need it and didn't want to call attention. The catastrophe had done nothing to alter the calm of this untouched bit of earth. At most you could hear a whispering like that the wind produces in the bamboo. Not disturbing at all if you didn't know that a few short meters away a conflagration of colossal proportions was taking place. Like an experienced Theseus (who even takes the liberty of disdaining Ariadne's thread), I ran without seeing, but seeing in another way, to the very center of the bookstore where the carpet hid an unevenness in the floor. There was the wooden door. I opened it and, after closing it again above me, rapidly descended the stairs. At last I had reached a world of absolute calm. The fire was just a memory. It took me a long time to descend it, so I imagined it was an immense tunnel. At times I thought I saw a patch of light farther down; when I reached the place where I presumed the possible light had come from, I found the same darkness, and another luminosity even farther off. I also had the impression I was hearing voices. I suppose I did hear them, except that at some point I noticed that my own thoughts were acquiring real sonority independent of my will. My thoughts could be heard, they echoed in the tunnel, so that I thought it well to recite to myself the verses of that book I had stolen the afternoon when my mother had sent me to look for Uncle, and immediately I could hear them, incomprehensible, but of a beauty that made them crystal clear:

I pine for the regions
where halcyons fly
over the sea . . .

And it was like in those tales of the *Thousand and One Nights* where the magic words open doors that seemed closed forever, or allow the djinn to appear and resolve any problem and load us down with treasures. A chorus of voices answered me, reciting phrases, some known, others unknown, and the long tunnel lit up and I saw that it was actually no tunnel at all but a beautiful place of birches and cypresses and poplars and springs and calm brooks (for all that one tries to avoid clichés . . .) and a special light, an almost false light that could be that of dusk or of sunrise, a Fragonard or Corot landscape, with splendid flowers sweetening the breeze that carried, to top it off, the strains of a lute. The reader needs no warning to realize that this passage is a sham and a mystification. I must acknowledge at least three reasons for having written it. First, I always wanted to reach such a place, the kind of Cythera to which we all more or less aspire, with greater or lesser passion; I imagine that in my case the pretentious atmosphere of the place of my dreams was due to the landscape paintings my grandmother had in her house, which had their almost identical duplicates in every house we visited in those years in Havana; *impossible landscapes,* Lorca would call them, forthrightly idyllic, even more idyllic than the one I've just described, landscapes in which you could see damsels (in my memory I recall no damsels) strumming lutes. The second reason for lying so flagrantly was that when I sat down to write, my mind was blocked by the shameless whiteness, utterly unhidden and fairly infuriating, of the virgin page, to which there can be only one reply: write, write down the first thing you think of. (The virgin page has to be set right, filled with signs, any old signs: it will take charge of transforming the possible lie into revelation.) The third reason is the one I find most convincing: if all literature is a sham, what difference does it make if I pile one fairy tale on top of another? If in the end the reader knows he's being lied to, why pretend I'm not lying? The fact is, of course, that there are lies and there are lies. There's the lie of Victorien Sardou and the lie of Honoré de Balzac; there's the lie of Pearl S. Buck and that of William Faulkner. Too thorny a subject, I'd rather pass it over as quickly as possible. In the final analysis each had as much right to lie as the others. And while I'm abusing this digression, what happened to the eleven-year-old adolescent I used to be, after he went down the stairs of the infinitely dark tunnel and found himself in the midst of that bucolic scene? It should be made clear here that there was nothing madrigalesque about this landscape. It was a marabú grove. Wilderness. The indecisive hour preceding night had apparently arrived. My legs and arms were bleeding from the marabú branches. I heard no music, no voice, nothing, and the only possible smell was that of my own fear. When I finally managed to get out of the wilderness, I found myself in a desert region, a rocky place devoid of trees, over which a starless, moonless night was settling. In the distance, as in the tales that Helena (my mother) used to read me at bedtime, I guessed at a dubious little light. I ran toward it, if not with joy at least with a fair amount of resolve. I found a large house, in ruins. I found, besides, the inconvenience of a fairly wide, overflowing, and turbid river between the house and myself. Sitting on the bank of the river, I meditated for a long time on which path to follow. The river looked too dangerous to swim across. Furthermore, it goes without saying that I had never seen such a powerful river. The only river I knew was the ditch that passed behind the Island, crossing by the carpentry shop, where Vido bathed naked. Much less did I think of building a raft, given that there wasn't a single log there to make it from. I thought: Probably if I rest and wait for dawn, in the double light of a refreshed mind and the sun I'll be able to find a way to cross the river. I was about to lie down on the rocks, when I saw a little old man next to me. I don't know how he could get so close without my noticing. The fact is, there he was. Tiny, practically bald, dull little mouse eyes behind glasses with no lenses, several years of white beard, dirty tattered clothing. He stretched out his hand to me. Do you have a coin? I don't have any money, I replied. That's bad, that's bad, money's the force that moves the Earth, the Final Reason, the Logos, the *Causa Eficiens,* if you don't have any money it's because you're a spendthrift, no doubt. I couldn't respond. I merely watched the house and its promising little light. The old man came very close. I smelt a whiff of his empty stomach. Do you want to go to the house? Logically, I nodded. Yes, everyone does: few can, I've been trying to go for years and here you see me. The old man took out his false teeth and stood there looking at them for some time, with his brow furrowed like Hamlet in the scene where he finds the skull of poor Yorick. There's a ferryman, he said at last. Interested, I asked, When does the ferryman come? Between Christmas and Midsummer hardly ever, never, don't expect him. Have you seen him? I've spent years on this bank and I've only been able to see him a couple of times. And why haven't you used him then? He put his false teeth back in, chewed a few times, perhaps to check their efficacy, and showed me one of his dull mouse eyes so that I'd see it was made of glass. Going to that house'll *cost you an eye,* he explained, shrugging. Since you're missing an eye, must mean you already paid. Pretending he hadn't heard, the old man took a bag of coins from I don't know where and started counting them. Then he moved the bag up and down to make the coins jingle. Listen, the music of the spheres — Mozart, my foot! He looked at me in astonishment, turned scarlet red, and put the bag back where he had found it; that is, in some place I couldn't see. Calmer, he put an arm around my shoulders, I'm going to tell you a story. And just at that moment of supreme danger, at the edge of the abyss at the tender age of eleven, from the blackness, from the fog, from the nothingness, a ferry appeared, or rather the shade of a ferry, with a human shade, or nearly human, who shouted my name in a stentorian voice, Sebastián, Sebastián, and held out a human hand, or nearly human, to which I held tight. In his turn the old man held tight to me, weeping, whining, I want to go, I want to go. The ferryman, or the shade of the ferryman, pushed him so brusquely the little man went flying through the air. May the devil be with you, the ferryman shouted in an even more stentorian voice. The sensation I felt then was that of finding myself in a ferry and at the same time not finding myself in a ferry, of crossing a river and at the same time not crossing it, of being led by a ferryman who was next to me and was not. Partly to be polite but mainly to give the indispensable touch of reality to that illusory situation, I thanked the ferryman and told him he had acted with true bravery. I can't say that he looked at me or smiled because I could see nothing in that ghostly face; I can't say he touched me because, though he did, my body felt nothing. Now I do feel a deep tiredness and,

> Whether the work be horrible or glorious, terrible or divine, there is little to choose between. Only to accept it peacefully.
>
> — Charlotte Brontë

looking out the window (this window, here, the *real* window, the window of my house) I realize: it's a beautiful day, one of those days, so rare in Havana, when the excessive light doesn't erase everything, quite the contrary, and when the sky is a uniform blue, and a breeze is blowing (a breeze is blowing!) and you feel like going to the sea, taking a stroll along the empty coast, or strolling in the countryside, beneath a palm grove, next to a murmuring creek, above the hammock hanging from mango trees, watching peasant lads (young ones) pass by wearing hats, freshly washed clothes, leggings, guitars, guitars, singing happily, singing happily, yes, why not? singing happily. Outside the world is alive, ay! it rejoices. So what am I doing in here trying to write a page that maybe no one will read? Why don't I get dressed instead and go outside into the sunlight and converse and laugh with everyone else? I lie down in bed, my body aching, repeat the questions out loud. What's important is letting the arrow fly, not hitting the target, I tell myself. The phrase, obviously, is Lezama Lima's. I think of him, of that immense, fat, obese writer, closed up inside his house at 162 Trocadero, in the very heart of the most pestilent, horrible, and loudmouthed city on the planet, unable to travel farther than from the living room to the dining room, leaning on María Luisa (even while he was still alive, she had already become the perfect widow), hearing his neighbors' pricks and balls as music, trapped among dusty books, damp walls, suffocating, sunken into the rocking chair, writing on a scrap of paper, writing stubbornly, with the surefooted pace of a mule in the abyss. I think of Virgilio Piñera, erased from the dictionaries, from the anthologies, from critical essays, in his apartment at the corner of 27th and N, with that syrupy smell of gas and coffee grounds, up since four in the morning, pounding out, pounding out on his typewriter the verses of his last work for the theater, *A Pick or a Shovel?,* in verse and prose (unfinished), getting up constantly to sip a spoonful of condensed milk, or to listen to the Appassionata Sonata a thousand times (in music, it's Beethoven or no one), and to read in French, out loud, a page from the *Intimate Diary* of the brothers Goncourt, from the letters of Madame de Sevigné, from Casanova's *Memoires,* and Proust (again Proust, tirelessly Proust, for breakfast, lunch, and dinner, Proust). Now I recall, one night he exclaimed, once and for all (he knew it was once and for all), There might be all the distance in the world between Marcel Proust and myself, but the two of us are equal in the passion with which we sit down to write. So, does that mean that life was made for everyone else? Well, you don't have to get tragic about it, poor me! Things are what they are. Yes, because what's written *is also* life. No, it's more, much more, it's the triumph of order over chaos, of structure over formlessness, the *fiat lux,* the magic wand that transforms something with no feet, head, or sense into a universe, the additional, indispensable sine qua non. Sine qua what? Nothing, I'm not going to keep repeating clichés. What is the purpose of writing a novel? Silence. Impenetrable. Vast. Religious. Magnificent. Eloquent. Understandably, there's nothing for it but to return to the desk, to the shameless page dazzling me, to the ink, to the broken-tipped pen. I don't know how I leaped ashore. In the same way that I saw myself suddenly traveling in a shade of a boat across a tempestuous river, accompanied by the nearly human shade of the ferryman, so, with the same unreality, I saw myself on the opposite bank, in an even more inhospitable landscape if possible than that on the other side, but with the hope of the house that, a few steps away there, promised shelter, a little corner to sleep in (if I wished for anything it was sleep; if anything is unbearable it's prolonged wakefulness). I walked along, tripping over the rocky ground. I thought there were several luminous figures accompanying me, though much as I turned around to look I detected nothing, not even the river, much less the ferryman and his ferry. To be honest I should say: there was nothing behind me. I would like for this sentence to be understood in its strictest sense: nothing! Nothing at all. I know the word *nothing* is pretty hard to understand: I'm asking for a little effort: Nothing! Which meant, among other prodigious things, that my only alternative was to keep moving forward. So I concentrated on the house and on my own desire to get there. Two or three yards from the narrow, low door, I detected a well-dressed gentleman, in black tie or something of the sort, with a half-English, half-North American face, in other words a hieratical face, and a candlestick in his right hand: the promising little light I had seen in the distance! He gestured for me to stop. He articulated what I interpreted as a magic phrase, which sounded more or less like *The Portrait of a Lady* or perhaps *Princess Cassamassima,* I'm not sure. The door opened. Here is Sebastián, the Englishman announced, even more hieratical than his face. From the interior of the house a strange voice was heard, amplified by the echo, which ordered in super-Cuban Spanish, OK, Mister James, let him in. And I found myself in a gloomy living room, at the other end of which, sitting in a rocking chair, rocking, illuminated by light that entered diagonally through a window that wasn't there, or that came through the canopy ceiling of climbing vines that wasn't there either (the same light as in the paintings by Vermeer of Delft), was a man with a sad and bored and skeptical face, mocking greenish eyes, wrinkled brow, raven's nose, as described by Mr. Poe, thick lips predisposed to forming a disapproving frown. He received me without a smile, with an At last you're here, welcome, feel at home, I promise you a more wonderful journey than Nils Holgersson's through Sweden. Although I think I must have dreamed this last part, my eyelids were heavy, and exhaustion had gotten the better of me.

> I must make this work good at all costs, or
> at least as good as I *can* make it.
>
> — Dostoyevsky

When I woke up (if I did wake up), how surprised I was to find myself back in the Island. The Island without fire and without destruction. The gentleman with the mocking greenish eyes and the Edgar Allan Poe nose, who had received me and promised me a wonderful journey, smoked with calm and class, looking at me with no expression. Are you all right? he asked in his singular voice, making a languid gesture with his cigarette hand. Do you know who I am? A brief pause to suck on the cigarette, expel the smoke toward heaven as if invoking the deity, toss the cigarette with a listless gesture into the undergrowth, open wide his eyes, which shone more mockingly, smile, display of course his nicotine-stained teeth, sigh twice, three times, four times, touch his chest, on the side of his heart, with a beautiful, white, adolescent hand. You are authorized to call me Scheherazade. It seemed the light was becoming intimate. Surprisingly, the man became young again, turned, to my astonishment, into the Wounded Boy with his handsome Honthorst face, and from there he went on to become a woman, a beautiful woman. As the cruel sultan is eternal, she exclaimed in a powerful and even more mysterious voice, Scheherazade has found herself obliged to use countless pseudonyms throughout countless centuries. She turned toward me, eyebrows raised, the lovely hand on her breast covered with shining rings. Your primitivism (you're so young) will not conceal from you the fact that Scheherazade was (she is, I am, I will be) a brilliant woman, who decided (I decided, I decide, I will decide) to tell story after story after story to save her life, she realized (I realize, I will realize) the lifesaving possibilities that words have (and will always have), she had the insight that storytelling was (is, will keep on being) the only way (the only way!) to gain eternity, and she continued (I will continue, whether they like it or not) talking for a thousand and one nights, a thousand and one nights! and more, a whole lifetime so to speak, and as your primitivism won't conceal, she saved herself! Scheherazade saved herself! She was standing up in the midst of Irene's flowers, illuminated, dressed in a green peplos, lovelier and lovelier, looking at me with equally green eyes, captivating eyes that shone as brightly as the rings and bracelets. And in one second she turned again into the man with the Mr. Poe face. He began caressing his left palm with his right hand. He furrowed his brow before continuing: Then, with time, over the centuries, like a famous character of Mrs. Woolf, Scheherazade has changed bodies, sexes, names, has been known as Herman Broch, Alberto Moravia, Truman Capote, Azorín, Chordelos de Laclos, Alice B. Toklas (pardon me, I meant to say Miss Stein), Jean Genet, Vargas Llosa, Cervantes, José Soler Puig, Mlle. Yourcenar, Chaucer, Tibor Déry, Nélida Piñón, Laurence Sterne, Miss Austen, Leo Tolstoy, Carlos (Loveira, Fuentes, Montenegro, Victoria, Baudelaire, and Dickens — though the last two should rather be Charles), Enrique Labrador Ruiz, Clarín, Homer, E. M. Forster, Ryunosuke Akutawaga, Albert Camus, Tomás de Carrasquilla, Katherine Anne Porter, Bioy Casares, Mongo Beti, Thomas Mann, José Saramago, Cirilo Villaverde, Henry Fielding and *tutti quantti,* and if I don't mention them all it's because of that bit about *ars longa, vita brevis,* as you'll understand, life wouldn't be long enough for us, and I, your utterly unhumble servant, am no more than one of the prodigious incarnations of that superior woman, which is why I say: I authorize you to call me by my occult and real name, Scheherazade, though if you prefer you may also use Master, which is more natural, faster, familiar, and in the end means the same thing. The

Master allowed another long and sacred silence to grow. More and more intimate, the light concentrated on him as it came down obliquely through the ceiling formed by branches. I felt that I had disappeared. At least so I believed. Only he existed. Each of his gestures took on special meaning. He took out various pieces of paper from the pocket of his faded shirt, unfolded them, brought them up to his eyes. I heard him read:

> The task of the poet and the novelist is to display the vileness to be found beneath great things, and the greatness to be found beneath vile things.
>
> — Thomas Hardy

I heard him read, unemphatically but emphatically, his accent tired yet at the same time extraordinarily vivid: *The damnable circumstance of water on every side obliges me to sit up on the coffee table. If it weren't for thinking that water surrounds me like a cancer, I could sleep like a log. While the boys were shedding their clothes to go swimming, a dozen people were dying in a room from compression* . . . And it was the power of entering the Island for almost the first time, of feeling the sea's compression, the sense of confinement that any island causes, the possibility of recognizing it, revealing its mysteries, being present when day arrives, the light that makes colors invisible and erases them, the mist of light, *an entire nation can die of light as it can die of plague,* the authority of the sun, which insists upon the hammock and turns upward the useless palms of your hands, and seeing that there are no tigers passing by, allowing merely the shadows of their descriptions to alter, for a moment, the light's dominion, being present then at the mystery of night in the Antilles, the power of its aroma (made of so many fruits, so many aromas), because *the aroma of the pineapple can stop a bird,* and the sweet aroma of a mango, in the river, flowing, of course, allows you to attain revelation, and confessing the keys of a disbelieving mysticism, seeing how a rooster is sacrificed to make another's body come close to yours, make another's body yield, showing how two or more bodies get their pleasure in a banana grove, with the help of the

Heavenly Muse (how could you live without such satisfaction in this Island), while the dagger pierces the soursop, like any heart, and discovering not only the delight, the magical spell of love in the open, under the gloriously (terrifyingly) clear sky, white with stars, but also that other enchantment, the dance (it comes to the same thing), and wishing to live, to die, in this jubilant nothingness, where things don't exist, where they can't be defined or categorized or reported, where all you can do is feel, the paradise where reason is abolished, yes, *howling in the sea, devouring fruits, sacrificing animals, always farther down, until you get to know the weight of your island, the weight of an island in the love of a nation*. Consecrated, the words (which were not, as the reader might guess, the same ones I have just written) had the effect of making me intangible. Silence returned me, grievously, to materiality. I knew, on the other hand, that not any old word would have such power, that not any old word *was (it couldn't become)* The Word. So that I remained sunk in my silence like an infernal being who is conceded, as a greater punishment, the briefest possibility of contemplating Paradise.

"DANGER: Circumstance in which there exists a possibility, a threat, or a chance that some misfortune or adversity may occur.

— María Moliner

The Master called me over with a gesture and began to walk. Standing up, I followed his wary steps, I went behind him into the trees, the trees of the extensive, intense garden, and we reached its outermost edge, where a tall iron gate, old, rusty, elegant, excessively ornate, marked its boundaries with the world. The Master pointed to overwhelming darkness on the other side. Do you know what there is beyond here? he asked. I shook my head no, though I was thinking, No, Master, how should I know what's out there, when I don't even know where I am, I don't even know who I am. He joined his hands, raised them as if he were about to intone a prayer. He said nothing. When he separated his hands, a dove flew out from between them. I say *dove* to put a known name to that handsome white bird, which, escaping his hands, flew around our heads before crossing the gate and passing joyfully to the other side of the Island. A detonation sounded. The dove, the bird, stopped in midair, wings spread (image of bewilderment), and fell toward I don't know where, toward I don't know what bottomless pit. An imposing silence. The Master turned toward me. Understand? Do you know, at last, what's on the other side? Danger, extreme danger, it means we're surrounded, we're bordering on danger. Please remember, I was practically a child, so my question should be understood in all its innocence: Isn't there anything we can do? The Master received it with a condescending smile. Danger also has its attractions, he said, some dangers are delicious, there's a lot you can do against danger, and he kept walking into more intricate parts of the Island. Master, I'm afraid, very afraid, of the word *danger.* Afraid?

What does it matter to me that I'm making up this story?

—Jean Genet

As the well-advised reader will be able to deduce, I must abandon the tale, for a couple of minutes at any rate, to have a cup of coffee, go out onto the terrace, watch life passing by, or at least what we take to be life, life, because . . .

I'M AFRAID!

(afraid of what, come on, be brave, go ahead and say it)

NO!

. . . I need to regather my strength, breathe deeply, see that today is just another day (no day is just another day!), try pointlessly to forget the fear, the danger. Meanwhile, the Master and I are going deeper into the Island, the spectacle of the street is terrifying: it's been more than a week since the garbage trucks came by, bags of garbage are piling higher and higher on the corners, along with them the number of flies climbs as well, and the useless breeze blowing by smells foul. Threatening and fierce as a beast, the sun takes over the street. A crowd of men and women on bicycles, sweaty, whining, sad, tired, bored, fills the bright street, which is also fierce and also menacing. Others sit down on the sidewalks to wait, expressionless, for what, they don't know, there's nothing to wait for, they're not even sitting there to kill time, there is no time, time doesn't exist, time isn't a kid playing dice, there aren't any kids, there aren't any dice, on this street, in this city, time is a whirlwind of dust with two dates, birth and death. Speaking of kids, here comes one, he points a toy rifle at me, Bam, I killed you! And indeed he does kill me. Yes, dead. For the fifth, eighth, tenth time, they've just killed me. Dead of terror (the worst way to die), I close the door. And now, dead, what do I do? Keep going, Master, keep going with you through the garden (now the garden of this book), meaning: it was a transitory garden, which has been fixed by the word, the only means to eternity, yes, Master, keep going with you to discover where it is we're getting to. Yes, accompany me for now, he ordered, he looked sarcastically at me and continued, As for death, no need for worry, or at least no need for self-pity (I despise people who think themselves unlucky), I am a ghost

> What is a ghost? Stephen said with tingling energy. One who has faded into impalpability through death, through absence, through change of manners.
>
> —James Joyce

and I don't go around making a fuss about it, besides, we all are or have been ghosts, we all suffer or have suffered in this life (and I underscore *this,* because, as for the other . . .), you don't have any exclusive rights to suffering, it's characterized all Cuban literature, as you know. (Do you really think that being born here is an unmentionable party?) Follow me, you'll see, I promised you a wonderful journey and I have to — we have to! — keep the promise, let's keep on making our way through all these trees, you'll start to lose your sense of place, you won't feel like you're in a garden or anywhere, night is turning into a palpable event, a wall that you can touch just by holding out your hands, hold them, hold out your hands, touch the night, don't be afraid, remember that these opportunities only come once, now push on the little door, bend down to get through, don't let the bump on the head distract your consciousness, you need to keep it sharp, here we are, here's the candlestick, will it be enough light? yes, it's always enough light, even if this unfortunately isn't the Age of Enlightenment, rather quite the contrary. We had arrived in an immense place, full of shades. Being conscious of how deeply the question of truth is pondered in literature, I would like to swear to the reader that I am being truthful, that I am narrating the exact impression that everything I experienced then had on me, that I am striving for realism (yes, realism) insofar as possible, I'm not exaggerating, nor has it occurred to me for one second to distort the events I lived through, which today, thanks to the resplendence of words, I can relive more intensely. Everything I narrate here is autobiographical. No coincidence with actual persons or events is fortuitous. Shades, shades. Incorporeal. Not even forms, they were traces that drifted past, immaterial. That wandered. That moved like some sort of protozoans. He lifted the candlestick. One of those shades turned into an austere man in a very stern black suit, sitting at a table, on a Viennese chair, facing a glass of water and an open notebook whose pages were handwritten in tiny, crowded letters, there you have him, the prince of Lampedusa, poor man, even in death he thinks no one wants to publish his book, even in death he is unaware his novel has been translated into every language, he doesn't know (he cannot know; probably he doesn't care to know, either) that he is a genius, he tried to bring the poor light he held in his hands even closer, the shade returned to impalpability at the very moment another began to take bodily shape, now I could see a man with a beard, an emaciated face, delirious eyes, lying in bed, I didn't touch his sweating forehead, I knew it was burning hot, he uttered the name of a woman that I couldn't understand, Scheherazade called him, José Asunción! and the man lifted his head slightly, he seemed to smile, he looked at us, took a pistol from under the blanket with one hand, and with ceremonious movements aimed the barrel of the pistol at his chest, at his nightshirt on which he had drawn a heart, of course I shouted, or wanted to shout, No, don't do it! (as if he had read my thoughts, the Master motioned to keep me from shouting) there was a shot, I seemed to see his heart fly violently from his chest, of course there is no way to confirm this, it may be my morbid, my diabolical, my malevolent, my twisted imagination, and the shade became a shade once more, and he, the Master, once more raised the candlestick, a young man with dark eyes and a gaze that must at some point have been frightened (at this point it no longer was, it was instead the serene gaze of someone who had understood everything in a flash of discovery); they were bringing the young man before a firing squad, *I know my profile will be peaceful* (it was Scheherazade's voice), and the sound of the shot made him fall, and he, Federico, fell with his great serene eyes that had already attained revelation, he stood up heroically, the Master moved the candlestick aside, You shouldn't want, he said, to see any more knowing gazes for now, then another shade, given bodily form by the light, approached, came toward me, an old man, an old man? perhaps older than he looked, and is he unbalanced? who is this unbalanced, babbling, sniveling, hunchbacked, nearly naked, urine-smelling beggar who can't manage with his own soul, do you know him? don't you know him? take a good look, I'm going to bring the light closer, his name is also Federico, or the equivalent of Federico in his native tongue, Nietzsche, you ought to know him, his mind ranged so far . . . no, I'm wrong, it isn't him, it's Oscar Wilde, imprisoned for alleged immorality, and now, pay attention, you are facing Gérard de Nerval, he's about to hang himself with his belt in the Vieille Lanterne, singing, *Don't wait for me this afternoon, for night will be black and white* . . . (it was Scheherazade's voice), no, no, it isn't him either, it's Attila Jozsef throwing himself beneath the wheels of a moving train, and you should know: the man over there who's observing how the tiniest flower opens up, and who sits meditating, meditating, meditating, with a sorrowing face because the flower, so tiny a flower, opening up, awakens thoughts in him that are too profound and that torture him, that man is Wordsworth, and if you see him hanging from a cord in a hotel room it's Esenin, and if he runs away now it isn't Wordsworth or Esenin but Rousseau, Jean Jacques, the solitary traveler, he ended up in his final years as paranoid as Strindberg, it's him, Strindberg, writing *A Madman's Manifesto* in Paris, and if you see him transform into a woman you have Alfonsina who decided to end it in the depths of the sea, Virginia decided to end it in the depths of the river, Hart Crane also opted for the sea (ah! *La mer, la mer toujours recomencée . . .*), or this one, look, blond and dark, handsome, Dylan Thomas drinking eighteen whiskeys in a row to take him from sober madness to drunken madness and from there to death, and speaking of drunken madness look over there, Ricardo Reis, Alvaro de Campos, that multiple man, it's more convenient to call him Fernando Pessoa, and speaking of madness, you can see Hölderlin appear there next to the Neckar, and if you see him cutting open his belly, it's Mishima, and if you see him sightless, it's Homer, Milton, Borges, all at once, and if what he's doing is opening his veins, call out Petronius! and you'll see the elegant eyes of the arbiter of elegance, and that one shrinking up and wasting away in prison, call him Miguel Hernández! remind him, *So much suffering just to die* (the unmistakable tone of Scheherazade's voice), and that nun who my light is turning visible in her cell is Sor Juana Inés de la Cruz, and if it's a tall, pretty man who also shoots himself (did you hear the shot?), it must be Mayakovsky, Bulgakov, Cesare Pavese, Bruno Schulz, who didn't kill himself but was sent back to the street of crocodiles, that is, murdered one terrifying afternoon by a magnificent SS officer, as handsome as souls possessed by the devil usually are, and now my light gives us the beheading of Thomas More, and now my light gives us Don Miguel de Unamuno, living poorly (or dying poorly) with his tragic sense of life, and Camus, who already knows (though he doesn't understand it: it's absurd) that he has had his fatal accident, and now my light gives us Alejandra Pizarnik, and José María Arguedas, and the poor woman watching out the window is Emily of Amherst, and if you can see in the distance the two shades making love and attacking each other (it comes to the same thing, don't you think?), loving and shooting, shooting and loving, Rimbaud and Verlaine, and now my light gives us Isidore Ducasse, Comte de Lautréamont, and the ingenuous young boy who's already thinking of writing novels, the young boy *(I weep for Adonais — he is dead!)* who has been struck with thousands of arrows and for whom thousands of arrows more are waiting all along his path, that ghostly boy, dead, living, and dead, is you, Sebastián, and if I reveal it to you it is because

Life should not be a novel that is imposed on us,
but rather a novel that we invent.

— Novalis

it is my duty, as Master, as writer, as a man with a high sense of morality, no, understand, I have no choice, I can't tell lies, at most I can tell a lie that leads to truth, because I, you, he, we who write, are, like Cocteau, liars who always reveal the truth, and now, that's all, that's enough for today, I'll put out the candle and we'll leave Hades. He put out the candle, we left Hades. By magic, we were once more in the garden . . .

And time passed. Yes,

. . . TIME PASSED.

Having reached this point, I cannot but acknowledge it: the novelist must choose, select (lovely word: selection) a limited number of details from among the enormous abundance that life offers, for the simple reason that, as Maupassant said (he wasn't as crazy as we've been made to believe), *Telling it all would be impossible, because you would need a volume a day to enumerate the multiple incidents that fill our lives.* Long ago, novelists abandoned the pretense of writing it all, as Rétif de La Bretonne would have wished, or those gloomy demiurges named Balzac and Tolstoy. Humbler now, the miserable novelist must resort to whatever artifices he has at hand to keep the reader from noticing his impotence to say it all: syncopes, accelerations, summaries, brusque leaps. Time has become such a constant worry among novelists that it has gone from being one more theme, or the background of a production, to being, at times, the hero of the story, as in *Tristram Shandy,* or to being The Theme, as shown by Mann, Woolf, and the greatest of them all, Proust. As the reader will recognize, there are three possible times: the time of the adventure, the time of writing, and the time of reading. The time of the adventure . . . God, no! With the number of things still left to narrate, with the number of sorry, contemptible, nasty, pusillanimous, relapsed, solemn, insidious, pale, sepulchral, boring, tremendously ingenuous, and slightly, discretely wicked men and women (guardians of the cemetery, Sartre called them) who cannot do (don't even know how to do) anything but dedicate themselves to literary criticism, what will I accomplish by wasting time with a digression on time. So the best thing will be to return to the astounding instant when I was able to write in complete innocence

and time passed.

Of course, many nights had gone by with Scheherazade in that garden. In so-called reality (in the equivocal, the indecipherable, the ambiguous reality whose true name should be *fantasy*), he and I were alone. Now I should restrict myself, however, to the unequivocal, powerful fantasy whose true name should be *reality.* Each night Scheherazade made a different character appear. Thus, he made my mother appear, and Irene, and Lucio, and Uncle Rolo, and Professor Kingston, and Merengue . . . and he was retelling the story of each one in his own way, as he would have liked to tell it. Look at them! he ordered me one night. At who? Who else, at them. And all the characters of the Island reappeared, sitting on the rocking chairs in the gallery one cool and luminous October afternoon, drinking coffee, conversing . . . Do you know who they are? I looked at the Master full of surprise, the only way to look in cases like this. Yes, Master, I know, I responded timidly. He replied: Don't start in on the banality of explaining that it's Marta, Casta Diva, Chavito, Mercedes . . . anybody could know those details, that's completely unimportant, I'm talking about something else. I looked at them again, saw again that they continued to have exactly the same expression of happiness on a lazy afternoon. Scheherazade, the Master, had stood up, he couldn't contain his anxiety, and he took short walks, always accompanied by the light that came down diagonally from the ceiling. And at this instant I must admit that I was the one who was astounded, when I discovered that he had once more become the Wounded Boy and that he was holding in his hands nothing less than that notebook he had sat down in Irene's rocking chair to write in. Where did you get that notebook from, Master? I hate foolish questions, he responded, and then, casting a furious gaze at me with eyes that were not greenish but red, he said, Observe them well, why are they here, what have they come to do? *(compassionate gaze, sigh),* and now, pay attention, you're going to have a sign, I'm going to write in the book while you watch them. The characters began to change the color of their hair, their eyes, their noses changed, their mouths, hands, bodies, clothing, expressions, and postures, they were different, and not just different, but there were others, others besides them, changing, and they responded to so many names, René, Sofía, Foción, Alma, Felipe, Bárbara, Esteban, Ramón, Estrella, Gregorio, Maité, Pascasio, Oppiano, Luz Marina . . . They switched around so much, in such a short time, that I am unable now to give precise testimony of the changes. There was even a moment when they turned into exact replicas of myself. I saw myself multiplied, repeated five, six, seven times as if reality had been covered with mirrors. I raised my right hand and several hands raised. I was astonished and they were astonished. I sang and they sang. I laughed and they laughed. I cried and they cried. Do you know what's happening? the Master shouted in a voice of exultation characteristic of one who reveals to another the key to a great discovery, they are characters! — . . . ?

> Nor do I paint portraits. It isn't my style. *I invent.* The public, which doesn't know what inventing consists in, tries to find the originals everywhere.
>
> — George Sand

Do you mean they don't exist? The things you think of! quite the contrary, child, they exist more than we do *(brief pause, another sigh, compassionate gaze, inexplicable background music, another sigh, many sighs),* in some ways, of course, they're like us, there are ways in which we resemble each other, given that they've been made through a strange alchemy, Sebastián, with all their flesh and blood, with all their bones and arteries, with muscles and nerves, with their worries, joys, and uncertainties, their nostalgias and impieties, their greatnesses and miseries, they partake, as we do, of God and the devil, and of every mystery; but no, in the end, they aren't, we aren't, like you: we have the glow of eternity! Scheherazade cast me a profound, ironic, complicitous gaze, and ran circles around me with surprising agility. In one of these laps he lost his cheap clothes and appeared dressed in cape, cane, and top hat. I myself, who am I? Your character! if we're going to be honest, I'm being constructed from your entrails, and also from the entrails of that great writer, Virgilio Piñera, whom you loved so much and to whom you owed so much and will owe so much forever, the writer cursed and blessed with you (ah, you should have found a way to join with him!), and I'm also being constructed from many other entrails, of course, a character is made from the bodies and souls of so many cadavers one ransacks along the way. He continued spinning, moving the cane, taking off, putting on the hat, fluttering the cape. The other characters lost their bodily forms. They became outlines, turned transparent, disappeared. Not only them. As the Master went by, reality fell apart like the battered set of a play at the end of the season. Scheherazade and I, alone. The rest, gone. Just like a few pages back, *nothing at all.* Absolutely nothing, dear reader. Again I write: I know the word *nothing* is pretty hard to understand. Again I write: I would like for this sentence to be understood in its strictest sense: nothing! On this occasion that I am retelling I found myself alone with Scheherazade in the midst of the nothingness. On this occasion I didn't even have a path before me. She/he handed me the notebook and exclaimed between laughs, The world is without form: it must be given one, Sebastián, the world is a deep sea covered with darkness, your spirit and mine (which come to the same thing) are moving over the waters, don't you think it's necessary to make light?

I opened the book.

I wrote

light

and these five letters, so innocent in appearance, made the nothingness fill up with a magnificent, golden glow, and I saw that there is a world of difference between nothingness in the dark and nothingness in the light (day and night in the midst of nothingness). And

Scheherazade, who had gained an expression of blessedness when the light came, asked in her/his finest voice, Don't you think, Sebastián, that there should exist a firmament to separate the waters?

I wrote, of course,

firmament

and a firmament separated the nothingness, and instantly became the heavens, which, as if by magic, turned blue. And without being asked to do so by anyone

I wrote

earth

and our bodies ceased to levitate, our feet stood at last on something firm,

as you may imagine I continued
writing words, words, words,
words, words, words,
words, words,
words

wind
water
mountains
houses
rivers
trees

and with each word, something was added to reality. The world was shaped and set in order as I wished or desired. The Wounded Boy and I strolled through that invented world feeling a joy we could not contain. I know, or think I know, we got to a lake. We must have sat down on its shore (lakes are there so we can sit on their shores). In a gesture heavy with intent, he ordered, Bend down, look at yourself in the blue waters, which being newly created, and since we are the only humans, are not yet polluted. There, reflected in the waters, I didn't see myself, I saw him, saw the Wounded Boy whom Tingo and I had found on that night at the end of October, in the carpentry shop of Vido's deceased father. And the image in the waters, unsteady and rather ephemeral, allowed me to understand, in a flash of insight, what he had been doing with the notebook, and more important, it allowed me to understand who I was. Master, I said, I want to tell the story of my childhood, the story of the Island where I was born, in Marianao, on the outskirts of Havana, next to the Columbia military base, to narrate the story of the people who accompanied me and made me wretched or happy, to return to the final months of 1958 when we were drawing near, without knowing it, to a such a decisive change in our lives, to a hurricane that would open doors and windows, and destroy roofs, and throw down walls, we were unaware then of the power of History in the life of the common man, Master, we were unaware that we were the pieces on a chessboard in an incomprehensible game, we couldn't see that the flight of the tyrant and his family to the Dominican Republic, the entrance into Havana of the victorious Rebels (whom we took to be sent by the Lord) would transform our lives as much as if we had died on the night of December 31, 1958, to be born on the first of January 1959, with our names, bodies, and souls completely transfigured (although this, I know, will have no space in the novel: it will have to be narrated in other books). The Master, it seems, was not listening. He sat there smiling, motionless. His eyes acquired a special resplendence. He became young again. An intense, blinding radiance began to issue from his body. Only then did he react. Write, don't waste time, write! he shouted while spinning away, and I noted, as you will now note, distinguished and possible readers (by the confident gesture that accompanied the exclamation, the gleam in the greenish eyes, and the smile, as confident as the gesture), that he (or she) was properly conscious of the importance the phrase needed to be given. She (or he) continued spinning and ended up dissolving into smoke, into sparkling dust that rose on high and then fell upon the earth in the form of a generous rain. I understood, I understand: there was and there is only one path. Once more, then, I open the notebook. I write: So many stories have been told and are still told about the Island that if you decide to believe them all you'll end up going crazy . . .

> It is not the victory that I wanted, rather it is the struggle.
>
> — Strindberg

and there, next to the mango, mamey, and soursop trees, grow poplars, willows, cypresses, and even the splendid red sandalwood tree of Ceylon, tangled vegetation blooms, ferns and flowers, statues arise, the Discus Thrower, the Diana, the Hermes, the Venus de Milo, the bust of Greta Garbo, the Laocoön and his sons, the Apollo Belvedere next to the wooden screen in the courtyard, the fountain in the center displays the little boy with the goose in his arms, there are the houses, the great iron gate opening onto Linea Street, This Side separating itself from The Beyond. I return to a night at the end of October. Before me, Mercedes with her loneliness, Marta with her dreams, Lucio and his confusion, Uncle Rolo in his bookstore, Miss Berta who taught us classes while dreaming of God, Tingo crying over his ignorance, Merengue cleaning his pastry cart while thinking about his missing Chavito, Casta Diva and Chacho, Helena, Vido, Melissa, the Barefoot Countess, Professor Kingston, Doña Juana sleeping . . . I can see them: they are waiting. They are ready, I know, to come to life and repeat, transformed, the brief but vigorous period between one afternoon at the end of October (rain is threatening, they sense an unknown presence in the Island) and that historic date of December 31, 1958, when the devastating fire took place. They enliven. As I write, they enliven. Their eyes come to life, their voices resound. Footsteps, whispers are heard. Doors, windows open and close. Night falls. Day dawns. Frogs croak. An owl flies. A breeze rustles the tops of the trees. The intense smell of the pines and casuarinas awakens. The earth, too, has a special smell, as if it were raining. It is the kingdom, my kingdom, returned to life. The Island of my childhood before my eyes again. And the people who inhabited it. Their states of mind, their victories and failures, their destinies will depend on me, on this notebook. It's time to write: I write. For now, I occupy the place of God.

And now that the one doing the creating is me, of course things will not be, have not been, as they once were. I correct things. I choose. I recompose. I walk through the room, stick my head out the window onto the street where life becomes a hallucination. I, too, am a hallucination. I don't kid myself. I have no material value. When I step into the street, no one notices me. I don't exist. Then, who am I when I'm not in front of the dazzling paper? To feel that I'm alive, I return to my writing. I return irremediably to the paper. Words are enough. Allied, conspiring, powerful words. Is it not perhaps just and even necessary that in the beginning there was the Word, that the complexity of the world began with the simplicity of a word?

Havana, 1996

Translator's Notes

page

4, 9 *the fat years* Cuba's sugar boom during World War I, under the presidency of General Mario G. Menocal (1912–1920).

4, 9 *Treaty of Paris* signed December 10, 1898, to end the Spanish-American War.

9, 29 *vague pains in his muscles . . .* Quoting from Julián del Casal's poem, *"Tardes de lluvia"* ("Rainy Afternoons").

10 *The land of ice . . .* From Samuel Taylor Coleridge, *The Rime of the Ancient Mariner.*

29 *José María Heredia* Here Rolo is thinking of a number of Cuban poets and artists who died young. Heredia (1803–1839) is generally considered the first important Cuban poet; he died in exile in Mexico. Juana Borrero (1877–1896), Carlos Pío Urbach (1872–1897), and René López (1882–1909) were young Modernist poets, as was Julián del Casal (1863–1893), "the greatest of all." Arístides Fernández (1904–1934) was an artist.

39 *Salgari and the days of the pirates* Referring to Emilio Salgari (1862–1911), Italian adventure novelist whose books were popular in Cuba; one of them, *Sandokan,* provides the nickname for a character here.

59 *the Martí memorial* In every school in Cuba there is a memorial dedicated to poet and Independence leader José Martí (1853–1895), who died in the opening months of the final Cuban War of Independence.

61 *the death of Pius XII* On October 9, 1958.

64 *Lord, I'm coming . . .* The line is from the poem "Martirio de San Sebastián" by Eugenio Florit (born 1903).

77 *Francisco Vicente Aguilera* An important figure in the unsuccessful 1868–1878 war for Cuban independence, as are most of those associated with Doña Juana (who would have been born in 1868).

84 *that same month, the German cruiser the* Königsberg *went down, an earthquake completely destroyed the Italian city of Avezzano* January 1915.

111 *Epiphany gifts* January 6, *Día de Reyes* (Day of the Kings, known as Epiphany in English), is the traditional "Christmas" gift-giving time in many Catholic countries.

124 *El Chino Zayas* Alfredo Zayas, president of Cuba, 1920–1924.

138 *the day they hoisted the flag* May 20, 1902, marking the end of the U.S. occupation and the inauguration of the Republic of Cuba.

157 *The first stammering poet, Zequeira* Manuel de Zequeira y Arango (1764–1846) went insane in 1821. Heredia (see above) wrote of Niagara Falls during his New York exile, "Why do I not see / around your immense cavern / the palm trees, ay! the delicious palms . . ." Plácido, pseudonym of Gabriel de la Concepción Valdés (1809–1844), was shot in the aftermath of an unsuccessful uprising against Spanish rule. The same fate met Juan Clemente Zenea (1832–1871; referred to below as "the hapless author of *Fidelia*") during the unsuccessful first phase of the Cuban War of Independence (1868–1878). José Jacinto Milanés (1814–1863) fell into a prolonged depression in 1843, and insanity by 1852. El Cucalambé, pseudonym of Juan Cristóbal Nápoles Fajardo, was born in 1829 and "disappeared without a trace" in 1862. Luisa Pérez de Zambrana (1835–1922; referred to below as "the ghoulish poetess of *Returning to the Woods*") survived her husband and their five children to write some of her most moving verse. Casal: see above.

160 *the Little War of August* The brutally suppressed Afro-Cuban uprising of 1912, provoked by the outlawing of the principal Afro-Cuban political party, the *Partido Independiente de Color.*

160 *When the War of Independence broke out in Cuba* In October 1868; this phase of the war ended with the signing of the Pact of Zanjón in early 1878.

175 *Hatuey beer* The most popular Cuban beer, named after a legendary Taino chief who died resisting the Spanish conquest of Cuba.

187 *Cernuda* Spanish poet Luis Cernuda (1902–1963); one of his best-known poems is *"El Joven Marinero"* ("The Young Sailor"), 1935.

204 Honorable Women *Las Honradas,* a novel of social attitudes and the "question of free love," by Cuban writer Miguel de Carrión (1875–1929).

208 *the first two presidents of the Republic in arms* In the temporarily liberated eastern parts of Cuba, during the 1868–1878 War of Independence.

272 *the First U.S. Intervention* 1898–1902.

292 *Doña Juana is dreaming* Her dream takes place on May 20, 1902, when Tomás Estrada Palma was inaugurated as the first elected president of the Republic of Cuba. Unlike Miss Berta, who remembers the political and military figures associated with her mother, Doña Juana's dream is crowded with poets: Nieves Xenes (1859–1915), Luisa Pérez de Zambrana (1835–1922), poet and philosopher Enrique José Varona (1849–1933), Aurelia Castillo de González (1842–1920), José Manuel Poveda (1888–1926), Esteban Borrero Echevarría (1849–1906).

302 *I pine for the regions . . .* From Julián del Casal's poem "Nostalgias."

314 *José Asunción* Colombian poet José Asunción Silva (1865–1896).